THE
JANSON
EQUATION

The Paul Janson Novels

The Janson Directive
The Janson Command (by Paul Garrison)
The Janson Option (by Paul Garrison)

The Jason Bourne Novels

The Bourne Identity
The Bourne Supremacy
The Bourne Ultimatum
The Bourne Legacy
(by Eric Van Lustbader)
The Bourne Betrayal
(by Eric Van Lustbader)
The Bourne Sanction
(by Eric Van Lustbader)
The Bourne Deception
(by Eric Van Lustbader)

The Bourne Objective
(by Eric Van Lustbader)
The Bourne Dominion
(by Eric Van Lustbader)
The Bourne Imperative
(by Eric Van Lustbader)
The Bourne Retribution
(by Eric Van Lustbader)
The Bourne Ascendancy
(by Eric Van Lustbader)

The Covert-One Novels

The Hades Factor (by Gayle Lynds)
The Cassandra Compact
(by Philip Shelby)
The Paris Option (by Gayle Lynds)
The Altman Code (by Gayle Lynds)
The Lazarus Vendetta
(by Patrick Larkin)
The Moscow Vector (by Patrick Larkin)

The Arctic Event (by James Cobb)
The Ares Decision (by Kyle Mills)
The Janus Reprisal
(by Jamie Freveletti)
The Utopia Experiment
(by Kyle Mills)
The Geneva Strategy
(by Jamie Freveletti)

Also by Robert Ludlum

The Scarlatti Inheritance
The Matlock Paper
Trevayne
The Cry of the Halidon
The Rhinemann Exchange
The Road to Gandolfo
The Gemini Contenders
The Chancellor Manuscript
The Holcroft Covenant
The Matarese Circle
The Parsifal Mosaic
The Aquitaine Progression

The Icarus Agenda
The Osterman Weekend
The Road to Omaha
The Scorpio Illusion
The Apocalypse Watch
The Matarese Countdown
The Prometheus Deception
The Sigma Protocol
The Tristan Betrayal
The Ambler Warning
The Bancroft Strategy

Also by Douglas Corleone

One Man's Paradise
Night on Fire
Last Lawyer Standing

Good As Gone
Payoff

ROBERT LUDLUM'S™

THE JANSON EQUATION

DOUGLAS CORLEONE

GRAND CENTRAL
PUBLISHING

NEW YORK   BOSTON

Grand Central Publishing
Hachette Book Group
1290 Avenue of the Americas
New York, NY 10104

www.HachetteBookGroup.com

Printed in the United States of America

RRD-C

First Edition: June 2015
10 9 8 7 6 5 4 3 2 1

Grand Central Publishing is a division of Hachette Book Group, Inc.
The Grand Central Publishing name and logo is a trademark of Hachette Book Group, Inc.

The Hachette Speakers Bureau provides a wide range of authors for speaking events. To find out more, go to www.hachettespeakersbureau.com or call (866) 376-6591.

The publisher is not responsible for websites (or their content) that are not owned by the publisher.

Library of Congress Cataloging-in-Publication Data
Corleone, Douglas.
  Robert Ludlum's The Janson equation / Douglas Corleone. — First edition.
    pages ; cm. — (Janson series)
  ISBN 978-1-4555-7767-5 (hardcover) — ISBN 978-1-4555-8960-9 (large print hardcover) — ISBN 978-1-4789-7960-9 (audiobook) — ISBN 978-1-4789-7959-3 (audio download) — ISBN 978-1-4555-7768-2 (ebook) 1. Political corruption—United States—Fiction. 2. Political fiction. I. Title.
  PS3603.O763R63 2015
  813'.6—dc23
                                                    2014049887

For Jack

THE
JANSON
EQUATION

If you look at satellite photographs of the Far East by night, you'll see a large splotch curiously lacking in light. This area of darkness is the Democratic People's Republic of Korea.

—Barbara Demick,
Nothing to Envy: Ordinary Lives in North Korea (2009)

Officers wanted for hazardous journey. Small wages. Bitter cold. Long months of complete darkness. Constant danger. Safe return doubtful. Honor and recognition in case of success.

—Ernest Shackleton,
recruitment notice
for Shackleton's 1914
Antarctica expedition

PROLOGUE

Dongchang Road, Pudong New District
Shanghai, People's Republic of China

From the lobby of the boutique hotel across the street, Paul Janson surreptitiously watched three uniformed guards standing as still as statues just behind the main gate of the compound—not just guards, but *soldiers* from the People's Liberation Army, protecting what Janson now knew to be a government complex housing the PLA's Unit 61398, the bureau responsible for China's systematic cyber-espionage and data-theft campaign against hundreds of private and state organizations spanning two dozen major industries across the globe, with a cost to the victims of hundreds of billions of dollars.

The center building of the compound, which served as Unit 61398's HQ, stood twelve stories in height and contained over 130,000 square feet in space, enough to house offices for roughly two thousand people. Over the past six months, however, Janson had narrowed his interest to a single individual, a twenty-eight-year-old male who used the online persona Silent Lynx.

Lynx, like the wildcat common to northern and western parts of China, especially the Tibetan Plateau.

The pedestrian portion of the thick iron gate opened and the man Janson knew as Silent Lynx stepped past it, nodding back to one of the guards as he moved toward the second in a row of bicycle racks stationed just outside the compound. Lynx fished around the inside pocket of his jacket and plucked out a small key to open the lock on his bicycle, then walked the bike away from the compound before lifting his right leg over the frame and straddling it. As he slowly pedaled away, Janson exited through the hotel's revolving door and waded into the sea of pedestrians.

After six months in Shanghai, Janson longed for solitude. The bustling, modern Chinese city of seventeen million people, home to some of the world's tallest and most architecturally breathtaking skyscrapers, never failed to inspire awe in him, yet the constant traffic and its accompanying sounds—the honks of horns, the growling of engines, the squeal of brakes—actually made him nostalgic for past jobs on the Dark Continent.

As he strode along the pavement beneath the low gray sky, Janson remained hyper-alert, even as his thoughts repeatedly threatened to drift to his forthcoming holiday with Jessie on the Hawaiian island of Maui. His eyes flashed like a narrow beam of light on nearly every face that passed him. He searched for familiarity, for incongruity, for a gaze that turned too quickly from his own appraising glance.

Janson himself blended as well as anyone. With black dye he'd removed the salt from his salt-and-pepper hair and allowed it to grow to a length he hadn't worn in decades. His wide Caucasian eyes were masked by a pair of Ray-Ban Wayfarers, his usual pink hue muted with makeup. Incredibly, even in China the American rarely earned a second look.

From his periphery he watched Lynx turn down Qixia Road toward the construction site. The hacker pedaled at a faster pace than was usual for him, and Janson silently willed him to slow down before someone took notice.

Meanwhile, Janson turned north on Dongtai Road in the direction of Lujiazui Park, suddenly wishing he had asked his associate Jessica Kincaid to remain in Shanghai until the mission was finished. Right now she'd be watching him through the scope of her sniper's rifle from one of the observation decks in the Shanghai World Financial Center, whispering in his earpiece when she noticed something or someone out of place. But, no, Janson would have to do without his eye in the sky today. Jessie had done her job and deserved the extra time she'd spend in Hawaii.

It was Jessie, after all, who'd afforded Janson the opportunity to make contact with Lynx several weeks ago. Following months of surveillance both online and off, Janson had decided that the money-hungry, ego-obsessed Silent Lynx was ripe for recruitment. But how to get to him?

Ultimately, it was Jessica Kincaid's charms that had opened the door. After tracking Lynx to a swanky Shanghai nightclub called Muse, Janson had Jessie make the approach. Following a few drinks and some not-so-subtle flirtation, she led him outside, toward the western bank of the Huangpu River, where Janson was waiting to pitch the twenty-eight-year-old hacker the deal of a lifetime. In exchange for specific intelligence concerning the operations of his cyber-espionage unit, Janson would provide Lynx with a new identity and enough currency to escape China and the People's Liberation Army once and for all.

Today the parties would finally make the trade via two separate yet simultaneous dead drops, and Janson would leave Shanghai with hard evidence that the People's Republic of China was responsible for stealing trade secrets around the world.

* * *

ONE OF UNIT 61398's VICTIMS was the Edgerton-Gertz Corporation, an American biotech giant that had lost billions of dollars in trade secrets to cybertheft every year for the past six years. Edgerton-Gertz was Janson's client and the reason he was now in Shanghai. CEO Jeremy Beck had been referred to Janson's private security consulting firm CatsPaw Associates by someone in the upper echelon of the US State Department—Janson's employer during the years he worked as a covert operative. Though his time in Consular Operations was falling ever further behind him, Janson's memories of working as a government-sanctioned killer refused to fade. Which was why he'd started the Phoenix Foundation, his valiant attempt to save individual covert government operators whose lives were wrecked—their psyches shattered—by their covert government service.

Glancing at the second hand on his watch, Janson surmised that Lynx was approaching the empty construction site, future home of another neck-craning high-rise to add to Shanghai's already über-impressive cityscape. There, just out of sight of the suit-and-tied swarms on the street, the Chinese hacker would find a marked brick-and-mortar concealment stuffed with the currency and identification he'd need to escape the People's Republic for good. Unbeknownst to Lynx, tucked into the rear cover of his new South Korean passport was an ultrathin GPS device that would allow Janson to track his recruit should Janson be betrayed.

Janson turned left onto Century Avenue, one of Shanghai's many tourist hot spots, rich with four-star hotels, restaurants, bars, and museums. As he fell in line with the mob passing Lujiazui Park, Janson felt a familiar sensation, his field instincts suddenly tingling. Was he being watched? And if so, by whom? The silver-haired Chinese woman seated alone on the park bench? The Northern European tourist with razor-sharp features, piercing blue eyes, and longish blond locks who was about to pass within ten feet of him? That young Middle Eastern couple sipping tea at the outdoor café?

Or am I imagining things?

Was that taxi at Janson's seven o'clock moving slower than the rest of the traffic? And that Shanghai cop riding the Segway, had Janson seen him standing outside his hotel earlier in the day?

Before he had time to decide Janson shot a look across the street and spotted the mouth of the alley at the coordinates he'd been sent just before he left the hotel.

Slipping his hands into his pockets, Janson picked up his pace and crossed with the tide at the next intersection. Keeping his head low, he continued to scan the slow-moving traffic and the faces of the pedestrians who passed him. When he reached the far corner he lifted his eyes to the countless windows on the opposite side of the street. Within any of them there could well be a sniper with his scope trained on the alley or even on Janson himself. Scanning each window for a fraction of a second, Janson searched for a glare, for the subtle movement of curtains, for the muzzle of a rifle protruding through a sliced screen.

Ducking into the designated alley, Janson maintained his swift pace. The passage was long and narrow and smelled of sesame oil. Up ahead an older man in a filthy white apron stepped out of a rear screen door with two bloated black trash bags in each hand and a lit cigarette dangling loosely between his lips. He stole a fleeting glance at Janson, then turned and hurled the bags into an open royal-blue dumpster, snuffing out his cigarette against the graffitied brown-brick wall before swinging open the screen door and returning inside.

Counting his steps, Janson dug into his pants pocket and shoveled out an old BlackBerry with no battery. As he gazed down at the dead screen resting on his palm he suddenly fumbled the device, "inadvertently" kicking it toward the brown-brick wall as it hit the pavement. Lowering himself onto his haunches to retrieve it, Janson smirked at the unique concealment method that Silent Lynx had chosen: a gutted and freeze-dried rat that resembled roadkill.

Fitting, to say the least.

Quickly Janson lifted the rat and gently tore open the Velcro strip along its stomach. He dug his fingers inside and closed them around a tiny black flash drive before resealing the Velcro and setting the rat back in its place. He picked up the useless BlackBerry, stuffed everything inside his front pants pocket, and continued up the alley, which opened onto a small unnamed road behind Jinmao Tower.

He turned left, then left again, placing him back on Dongtai Road, where he rejoined the hustle and bustle heading toward Century Avenue.

As he reached the corner of Dongtai and Century, a teeth-rattling report sounded from a few blocks away, startling him. Some of the pedestrians spun their heads in the direction of the noise; others dismissed the bang as a car backfiring. All continued walking without pause.

Janson, of course, knew the sound, had felt it in his stomach. It was the sound of a .38, and after a moment it fired again—from the direction of the empty construction site where Janson had made his dead drop.

Turning left onto Century Avenue, Janson did his best to lose himself in the throng, his heart suddenly racing, his breathing unusually heavy. Silently, he mouthed his longtime mantra—*clear like water, cool like ice*—and carefully considered his next action. Lynx had undoubtedly been made—and murdered—which meant that Janson couldn't return to his hotel.

Time to move to Plan B.

Which meant hailing a taxi and immediately heading to Pudong International Airport.

As he pushed toward the taxi stand on Century Avenue, Janson glanced at his watch and imagined himself squarely in the scope of a PLA sniper's rifle. If the sniper was merely waiting to get off a clean shot, Janson knew he'd be dead in a matter of seconds.

Sweat dripped from his hairline; his stomach tightened.

Clear like water, cool like ice.

Moments later he'd managed to control his breathing. But for the first time in the six months he had been in the city, Janson felt dizzyingly unsure whether he'd make it out of Shanghai alive.

Ducking into a taxi, Janson shouted his destination in Chinese. Then thought better of it. Keeping his head low while trying not to make it look too obvious, he instructed the driver to make a right on Zhangyang, followed by a sharp left onto Fushan Road.

Moving along streets on which Janson knew traffic would be thinning out, the driver made the peculiar turns and zig and zags without comment.

After fifteen minutes of directing the driver through a complex maze around Shanghai's cityscape, while surreptitiously watching the rearview mirror for a tail, Janson finally felt comfortable enough that they weren't being followed.

In Chinese he thanked the driver for his cooperation. He pushed himself up on the cracked vinyl backseat and asked the driver to take him to his final destination.

Although his pulse slowed, Janson wouldn't feel entirely safe until takeoff.

PART I

The Senator's Son

ONE

Ten minutes after the Embraer Legacy 650 touched down at Hickam Field on the island of Oahu, Paul Janson stepped onto the warm tarmac and was immediately greeted by Lawrence Hammond, the senator's chief of staff.

"Thank you for coming," Hammond said.

As the men shook hands, Janson breathed deeply of the fresh tropical air and savored the gentle touch of the Hawaiian sun on his face. After six months under Shanghai's polluted sky, smog as thick as tissue paper had become Janson's new normal. Only now, as he inhaled freely, did he fully realize the extent to which he'd spent the past half year breathing poison.

Behind his Wayfarers, Janson closed his eyes for a moment and listened. Although Hickam buzzed with the typical sounds of an operational airfield, Janson instantly relished the relative tranquility. Vividly, he imagined the coastal white-sand beaches and azure-blue waters awaiting him and Jessie just beyond the confines of the US Air Force base.

Hammond, a tall man with slicked-back hair the color of straw, directed Janson to an idling olive-green jeep driven by a private first class who couldn't possibly have been old enough to legally drink. As Janson belted himself into the passenger seat, Hammond leaned forward and said, "Air Force One landed on this runway not too long ago."

"Is that right?" Janson said as the jeep pulled away from the jet.

Hammond mistook Janson's politeness for genuine interest. "This past Christmas as a matter of fact. The First Family vacations on the windward side of the island, in the small beach town of Kailua."

The three remained silent for the rest of the ten-minute drive. Janson's original plan upon leaving Shanghai had been to land at nearby Honolulu International, where he'd meet Jessie and be driven to Waikiki for an evening of dinner and drinks and a steamy night at the iconic Pink Palace before boarding a puddle-jumper to Maui the next day. But a phone call Janson received thirty thousand miles above the Pacific changed all that.

Janson had been resting in his cabin, on the verge of sleep, when his lone flight attendant, Kayla, buzzed him over the intercom and announced that he had a call from the mainland.

"It's a US senator," Kayla said. "I thought you might want to take it."

"Which senator?" Janson said groggily. He knew only a handful personally and liked even fewer.

"Senator James Wyckoff," she said. "Of North Carolina."

Wyckoff was neither one of the handful Janson knew personally nor one of the few he liked. But before Janson could ask her to take a callback number, Kayla told him that Wyckoff had been referred by his current client, Jeremy Beck, CEO of Edgerton-Gertz.

Grudgingly, Janson decided to take the call.

* * *

As the jeep pulled into the parking lot of a small administrative building, Janson turned to Hammond and said, "The senator beat me here?"

The flight from Shanghai was just over nine hours and Janson had already been in the air two hours when Wyckoff phoned. From DC, even under the best conditions, it was nearly a ten-hour flight to Honolulu, and Janson was fairly sure there was snow and ice on the ground in Washington this time of year.

"The senator actually called you from California," Hammond said. "He'd been holding a fund-raiser at Exchange in downtown Los Angeles when he received the news about his son."

Janson didn't say anything else. He stepped out of the jeep and followed Hammond and the private first class to the building. The baby-faced PFC used a key to open the door then stepped aside as Janson and Hammond entered. The dissonant rumble of an ancient air conditioner emanated from overhead vents, and the sun's natural light was instantly replaced by the harsh glow of buzzing fluorescent bulbs.

Hammond ushered Janson down a bleak hallway of scuffed linoleum into a spacious yet utilitarian office in the rear of the building, then quietly excused himself, saying, "Senator Wyckoff will be right with you."

Two minutes later a toilet flushed and the senator himself stepped out of a back room with his hand already extended.

"Paul Janson, I presume."

"A pleasure, Senator."

Janson removed his Wayfarers and took the proffered seat in front of the room's lone streaked and dented metal desk, while Senator Wyckoff situated himself on the opposite side, crossing his right leg over his left before taking a deep breath and launching into the facts.

"As I said over the phone, Mr. Janson, the details of my son's disappearance are still sketchy. What we do know is that Gregory's girlfriend of three years, a beautiful young lady named Lynell Yi, was found murdered in the *hanok* she and Gregory were staying at in central Seoul yesterday morning. She'd evidently been strangled."

The senator appeared roughly fifty years old, well-groomed and dressed in an expensive tailored suit, but the bags under his eyes told the story of someone who'd lived through hell over the past twenty-four hours.

"The Seoul Metropolitan Police," Wyckoff continued, "have named Gregory their primary suspect in Lynell's death, which, if you knew my son, you'd know is preposterous. But of course my wife and I are concerned. Gregory's just a teenager. We don't know whether he's been kidnapped or is on the run because he's frightened. Being falsely accused of murder in a foreign country must be terrifying. Even though South Korea is our ally, it'll take time to get things sorted out through the proper channels." The senator leaned forward, planting his elbows on the desk. "I'd like for you to travel to Seoul and find him. That's our first priority. Second, and nearly as important, I'd like you to conduct an independent investigation into Lynell's murder. Now may be our only opportunity. I'm a former trial lawyer, and I can tell you from experience that evidence disappears fast. Witnesses vanish. Memories become fuzzy. If we don't clear Gregory's name in the next ninety-six hours, we may never be able to do so."

Janson held up his hand. "Let me stop you right there, Senator. I sympathize with you, I do. I'm very sorry that your family is going through this. And I hope that your son turns up unharmed sooner rather than later. I'm sure you're right. I'm sure he's being wrongly accused, and I'm sincerely hopeful that you can prove it and bring him home to grieve for his girlfriend. *But* I'm afraid that I can't help you with this. I'm not a private investigator."

"I'm not suggesting you are. But this is no ordinary investigation."

"Please, Senator, let me continue. I'm here as a courtesy to my client Jeremy Beck. But as I attempted to tell you over the phone, this simply isn't something I can take on." Janson reached into his jacket pocket and unfolded a piece of paper. "While I was in the air, I took the liberty of contacting a few old friends, and I have the names and telephone numbers of a handful of top-notch private investigators in Seoul. They know the city inside and out, and they can obtain information directly from the police without having to navigate through miles of red tape. According to my contacts, these men and women are the best investigators in all South Korea."

Wyckoff accepted the piece of paper and set it down on the desk without looking at it. He narrowed his eyes, confirming Janson's initial impression that the senator wasn't a man who was told no very often. And that he seldom accepted the word for an answer.

"Mr. Janson, do you have children?"

As Wyckoff said it there was a firm knock on the door. The senator pushed himself out of his chair and trudged toward the sound.

Meanwhile, Janson frowned. He didn't like to be asked personal questions. Not by clients and not by prospective clients. Certainly not after he'd already declined the job. And this was no innocuous question. It was a subject that burned Janson deep in his stomach. No, he did not have children. He did not have a family—only the memory of one. Only the stabbing recollection of a pregnant wife and the dashed dreams of their unborn child, their future obliterated by a terrorist's bomb. They'd perished years ago yet it still felt like yesterday.

From behind, Janson heard Hammond's sonorous voice followed by a far softer one and the unmistakable sound of a woman's sobs.

"Mr. Janson," the senator said, "I'd like you to meet my wife, Alicia. Gregory's mother."

Janson stood and turned toward the couple as Hammond stepped out, closing the door gently behind him.

Alicia Wyckoff stood before Janson visibly trembling, her eyes wet with mascara tears. She appeared to be a few years younger than her husband, but her handling of the present crisis threatened to catch her up to him in no time flat.

"Thank you so much for coming," she said, ignoring Janson's hand and instead gripping him in an awkward hug. He felt the warmth of her tears through his shirt, her long nails burrowing into his upper back.

If Janson were slightly more cynical, he'd have thought her entry had been meticulously timed in advance.

Wyckoff brushed some papers aside and sat on the front edge of the desk. "I know your professional history," he said to Janson. "As soon as Jeremy gave me your name I contacted State and obtained a complete dossier. While a good many parts of the document were redacted, what I *was* able to read was very impressive. You are uniquely qualified for this job, Mr. Janson." He paused for effect. "Please, don't turn us away."

"Turn us away?" Alicia Wyckoff interjected. "What are you talking about?" She turned to Janson. "Are you seriously considering refusing to help us?"

Janson remained standing. "As I told your husband a few moments ago I'm simply not the person you need."

"But you *are*." She spun toward her husband. "Haven't you *told* him?"

Wyckoff shook his head.

"Told me what?"

Janson couldn't imagine a scenario that might possibly change his mind. He'd just left Asia behind. He needed some downtime. Jessica needed some downtime. In the past couple of years they'd taken on one mission after another, almost without pause. Following two successive missions off the coast of Africa, Janson and Kincaid had promised themselves a break. But when Jeremy Beck called about the incessant cyber-espionage campaign being perpetrated by the Chinese government, Janson became intrigued. This was what his post–Cons Ops life was all about: changing the world, one mission at a time.

Wyckoff pushed off the desk and sighed deeply, as though he'd been hoping he wouldn't have to divulge what he was about to. At least not until *after* Janson had accepted the case.

"We don't think Lynell's murder was a crime of passion or a random killing," Wyckoff said. "And we don't think the Seoul Metropolitan Police came to suspect our son by themselves; we think they were deliberately led there."

Janson watched the senator's eyes and said, "By who?"

Wyckoff pursed his lips. He looked as though he were about to sign a deal for his soul. Or something of even greater importance to a successful US politician. "What I say next stays between us, Mr. Janson."

"Of course."

The senator placed his hands on his hips and exhaled. "We think Gregory was framed by your former employer."

Janson hesitated. "I'm not sure I understand."

"The victim, Lynell Yi, my son's girlfriend, is—*was*, I should say—a Korean-English translator. She'd been working on sensitive talks in the Korean Demilitarized Zone. Talks between the North and the South and other interested parties, namely the United States and China. We think she overheard something she shouldn't have. We think she shared it with our son, and that they were both subsequently targeted by someone in the US government. Or to be more specific, someone in the US State Department."

"And you think this murder was carried out by Consular Operations?" Janson said.

Wyckoff bowed his head. "The murder and the subsequent frame—all of it is just too neat. Our son is not stupid. If he *were* somehow involved in Lynell's murder—an utter impossibility in and of itself—he would not have left behind a glaring trail of evidence pointing directly at him."

"In a crime of passion," Janson said, "by definition, the killer isn't thinking or acting rationally. His intellect would have little to do with what occurred during or immediately after the event."

"Granted," Wyckoff said. "But according to the information released by the Seoul police, this killer would have had plenty of time to clean up after himself."

"Or time to get a running head start," Janson countered.

Wyckoff ignored him. "Lynell's body wasn't found until morning. She was discovered by a maid. There wasn't even a 'Do Not Disturb' sign on the door. Whoever killed Lynell *wanted* her body to be found quickly. *Wanted* it to look like a crime of passion."

Janson said nothing. He knew Wyckoff's alternative theory was based solely on a parent's wishful thinking. But what else could a father do under the circumstances? What would Janson himself be doing if the accused were *his* teenage son?

"Tell me, Paul," Wyckoff said, dispensing with the formalities, "do you *honestly* believe that powers within the US government aren't capable of something like this?"

Janson could say no such thing. He *knew* what his government was capable of. He'd carried out operations not so different from the one Wyckoff was describing. And he would be spending the rest of his life atoning for them.

"Before I became a US senator," Wyckoff continued, "I was a Charlotte trial lawyer. I specialized in mass torts. Made my fortune suing pharmaceutical companies for manufacturing and selling dangerous drugs that had been preapproved by the FDA. I made tens of millions of dollars, and I would be willing to part with all of it if you would agree to take this case. Name your fee, Paul, and it's yours."

For something as involved as this, Janson could easily ask for seven or eight million dollars. And it would all go to the Phoenix Foundation. A payday this size could help dozens of former covert government operators take their lives back.

Janson had to admit he liked the idea of looking closely at his former employer.

And if by some stretch of the imagination the US State Department was indeed involved in framing the son of a prominent US senator for murder, the government's ultimate objective would likely have widespread repercussions for the entire region, if not the world.

"I have one condition," Janson finally said.

"Name it."

"If I find your son and uncover the truth, you'll have to promise to accept it, regardless of what that truth is. Even if it ultimately leads to your son's conviction for murder."

Wyckoff glanced at his wife, who bowed her head. He turned back to Janson and said, "You have our word."

TWO

S top apologizing," Kincaid said during the ascent. "You made the right decision."

Janson knew Jessie was right, yet something about the mission kept tugging at his thoughts. The more he contemplated the next several days, the less confident he felt that he and Kincaid would merely be searching for a nineteen-year-old kid in a city of ten million and conducting an independent investigation into his girlfriend's death.

Before Kincaid arrived at Hickam Field and they'd boarded the Embraer, Janson phoned Morton, his "computer security consultant" in northern New Jersey. Twenty minutes later Morton forwarded a complete and up-to-the-minute copy of the Seoul Metropolitan Police Department's electronic investigative file on Lynell Yi's murder.

According to the file, a sixty-three-year-old maid named Sung Won Yun had discovered the girl's body in a room at the Sophia

Guesthouse, central Seoul's oldest and most traditional hanok. A preliminary visual inspection by the coroner indicated that the manner of death was homicide. The mechanism of death appeared to be asphyxiation, the cause of death manual strangulation, a form of violence often perpetrated by a man against a woman because of the required disparity in physical strength between the victim and the assailant.

The coroner estimated the time of death to be between midnight and four o'clock on the morning the corpse was discovered. This was consistent with police interviews of two fellow guests who claimed to have heard voices—a young man's and a young woman's—raised in anger shortly after midnight that morning. Although neither of these earwitnesses could identify what exactly was being said, both agreed that the heated discussion had been held in English rather than Korean. Given these accounts, police theorized that Gregory Wyckoff killed his girlfriend, Lynell Yi, in the heat of passion. No specific motive was given.

The owners of the hanok, who confirmed that Gregory Wyckoff and Lynell Yi had checked into their establishment the previous day, turned over to police color copies of the couple's US passports, and the part-time clerk who had handled the check-in easily picked Gregory Wyckoff out of a photo array.

Latent prints had been lifted at the scene and were pending examination and comparison. Partial fingerprints found on the victim's neck were removed from the corpse using a process known as cyano-fuming, so that the powdering and lifting could be conducted later at the lab.

No other suspects or persons of interests were named, and there was no mention in the entire file of the sensitive work being conducted by Lynell Yi at the time of her death.

Once the Embraer reached its maximum cruising altitude, the

executive jet leveled off and Jessica Kincaid stepped into the center of the cabin and stretched while Janson looked on, wishing they
were sipping mai tais at Duke's Barefoot Bar in Waikiki.

"So, who do we know in Seoul?" she said.

Janson reluctantly pushed from his mind the image of Jessie
in her appealing red two-piece on the powdery sands of Waikiki
Beach and opened his laptop. In addition to the many contacts
he'd made during his career with Cons Ops, over the past few
years Janson had developed a vast network of Phoenix "graduates,"
former covert government operatives who had benefited from the
foundation's efforts. Some had been afforded completely new
lives—new identities, new homes, lucrative careers in academia
or public service, even in the private sector. Others had been afforded sufficient capital to fund their own ventures. Just about all
had achieved a substantial amount of success.

Now when Janson needed *their* help, he didn't hesitate to call
upon them to take advantage of their various positions and skills.
Most were extremely grateful for the opportunity to repay their
debt to Janson; others took some convincing.

*"What Phoenix grants, Phoenix retrieves to pass on to the next
guy,"* he'd tell them. *"That's the way it works. That's the way it is."*

In the end, all complied. Janson, of course, never mistook the
former operatives for his own personal army. He used them only
on CatsPaw missions such as this, where millions were at stake for
the Phoenix Foundation.

Janson paused on the first name he came across. He hadn't
needed his computer to know that Jina Jeon was at the top of his
list. But he didn't want it to appear to Jessie that he'd picked Jina's
name out of thin air, as though it were always resting at the tip of
his tongue.

Jina Jeon was both a contact from his time in Consular Operations *and* a Phoenix graduate. She'd also been Paul Janson's lover long before Janson had ever met Jessica Kincaid.

Janson scrolled down to the next name on his list.

"Nam Sei-hoon," he said. "He's with South Korea's National Intelligence Service."

"And you trust him completely?" Kincaid said.

"Nam Sei-hoon is one of my oldest and closest friends. I met him while I was with SEAL Team Four."

It never escaped Janson that leaving the University of Michigan to enlist in the navy was the decision that had placed him on the path to becoming a skilled killer. Shortly after enlistment Janson had shown a genuine gift for combat, and in the navy such talents rarely go unnoticed. At the time he joined his team at their headquarters in Little Creek, Virginia, Paul Janson had been the youngest person ever to receive SEAL training—a distinction that no longer held much meaning for him. Following his first tour in Afghanistan, Janson was awarded the Navy Cross, the Department of the Navy's second-highest decoration for valor. Then came tour after tour after tour, with no breaks, until he was finally captured in an Afghan village just outside Kabul. He was held by the Taliban in a six-by-four-foot cage for eighteen months. He was starved. Tortured. Nearly killed after each of his first two escape attempts. His third attempt at escape was successful. By the time he was found, Janson weighed only eighty-three pounds; he was a shell of the man he'd been. He seldom spoke of the events that followed his recovery. When pressed, all he would allow was that he attended Cambridge University for graduate studies on a government fellowship, and was thereafter recruited to a black ops team under the control of the US State Department.

"Any Phoenix grads in South Korea?" Kincaid asked.

Janson nodded without looking up. "Jina Jeon. Though I'd like to avoid using her if we can."

Kincaid paused midstretch. "Why's that?"

Sure, one of the reasons Janson didn't want to contact Jina Jeon was their past romantic relationship. But that wasn't the primary reason. Like all Phoenix beneficiaries, Jina Jeon possessed a telephone fitted with an encryption chip that would give Janson a direct line to her, and she knew that the powers behind the Phoenix Foundation could call on her for help at any time. What Jina Jeon didn't know—and what Janson didn't *want* her to know— was that *he* was behind the foundation.

There was another reason too. And that was the reason Janson finally offered to Kincaid.

"She has difficulty playing by the rules," he said.

All Phoenix graduates were required to play by a set of rules when they provided their assistance. Specifically, three rules, known as the Janson Rules.

No torture.

No civilian casualties.

No killing anyone who doesn't try to kill us.

For any former covert intelligence operative, following these rules was easier said than done. But Janson suspected that Jina Jeon, in particular, would have difficulty playing nice. Not because she wasn't a good person, but because of what Consular Operations had made her.

Which wasn't very different from what Consular Operations had made Janson himself.

"*You were the Machine,*" Cons Ops director Derek Collins had told Janson during one of his many exit interviews. "*You were the guy with the slab of granite where your heart's supposed to be.*"

It was true. Janson had been a machine, taking orders from

his superiors without question, committing crimes in service of his country, killing again and again and again. Then one morning he'd woken in a cold sweat and began ruminating on the dozens of people he'd executed. Some victims, of course, had had it coming to them. Others hadn't, and those were the killings that suddenly sickened him.

"You tell me you're sickened by the killing," Collins had said to him. *"I'm going to tell you what you'll discover one day for yourself: that's the only way you'll ever feel alive."*

Janson refused to believe him. He could heal, he knew. He could be saved. First, Janson had to admit to himself that he'd been a frozen-hearted assassin. Once he was able to admit that, he vowed to atone for his transgressions. He couldn't alter the past, couldn't change what he'd done. But he *could* change what he was.

* * *

HOURS LATER, AS KINCAID SLEPT, Paul Janson continued poring through the thousands of online articles that made mention of Senator James Wyckoff of North Carolina. He'd started by combining the senator's name with keywords such as "Seoul" and "Pyongyang" and "Beijing," then branched out by identifying the words most likely associated with the current talks between North and South Korea. Recurring issues among the four parties involved in the talks included North Korea's nuclear program; the sanctions put in place against North Korea's hermit regime for its human rights abuses and its defiance in the face of international law; and of course the possible (albeit improbable) negotiation of an actual peace treaty to replace the Korean Armistice Agreement that ended the Korean War six decades ago.

Wyckoff's votes on Korean issues seemed to ebb and flow with popular opinion. No surprise there, since Wyckoff was expected to seek his party's nomination for president of the United States during the next primary season. He'd voted multiple times for sanctions against the North but certainly wasn't a hard-liner. In fact, it was difficult to discern where he stood on the most vital Korean issues. He was a smart politician. With his votes, he was giving himself room to maneuver to the right or the left depending on which way the wind happened to be blowing in an election year. The way things stood now, the American people saw the rogue regime in Pyongyang as a definite foe, but they had no appetite for military action following the long and costly wars in Iraq and Afghanistan. Supporting harsh sanctions against the North continued to be the most prudent stance, politically speaking.

Janson figured he could all but rule out the possibility that Gregory Wyckoff was framed for murder in Seoul because of his father's political positions on Korea.

What continued to nag Janson, however, was the question of why Gregory Wyckoff and Lynell Yi were staying at a hanok in central Seoul when Gregory Wyckoff was renting an apartment just across the Han River. When he'd asked the senator and his wife, they'd dismissed the paid stay at the traditional Korean house as irrelevant.

"The low-rent apartments in Seoul can be gloomy," the senator suggested, "especially in winter. I saw pictures of Gregory's flat. From the outside it looked like the DC projects. The interior was clean, maybe even quaint, but nothing spectacular. Three or four rooms separated by sliding doors, a kitchen–dining room combination. If they couldn't travel far because of Lynell's work, it would have made perfect sense for them to stay a night or two in a traditional hanok."

Janson disagreed, though his opinion was actually favorable to the senator's theory of his son's innocence. If Lynell Yi had indeed overheard something during the sensitive North-South talks in the demilitarized zone and then passed it on to her boyfriend, it was possible that both she and Gregory were frightened enough to abandon Gregory's apartment until things cooled off. Or at least until the couple decided what to do with the information.

The question then would be *What had Lynell Yi overheard?*

"Something to drink, Mr. Janson?"

The words were spoken in a slow, sensual voice and Janson nearly turned to remind Kayla to call him Paul. But he caught himself. Instead he grinned and said, "I admit I'm a bit foggy, Jessie. But I'm not *that* foggy."

Kincaid gracefully lowered herself into the deep leather seat next to Janson. Clearly she was still in character. The real Jessica Kincaid didn't do much gracefully—unless you counted taking out a human target with a .50-caliber M82 from 1,600 meters.

Janson looked into her pale-green eyes. "Don't tell me you're jealous of Kayla now."

Kincaid scrunched up her features and rolled her eyes. "*Jealous?* Sorry, Charlie, but I don't *get* jealous."

Definitely jealous, Janson thought. The more Jessie's *get* sounded like *git*, the more anxious he knew she was. Tension drew out her Southern drawl, her Appalachian backcountry twang.

"You know," Janson said, gently brushing her smooth face with the back of his fingers, "you're beautiful when you're jealous."

Her eyes widened and her cheeks flushed, the way they had just before they first made love in a sparsely decorated hotel room in the Hungarian town of Sarospatak soon after they met.

"*I see the way you look at me,*" she'd said that evening.

"*I don't know what you mean,*" he'd lied.

Complicating things, then as now, was Janson's reluctance to place Jessica Kincaid in harm's way. He knew more clearly than anyone that Jessie could handle herself better than most soldiers on the planet. Yet the thought of losing her to violence was never very far from his mind.

She'd recognized that fear in him from the very first and never once hesitated to call him on it. Jessie had insisted on taking risks—putting her life on the line—in nearly every mission since. And Janson often felt helpless to stop her.

"So," he said, "were you able to get some sleep?"

"Some," she said. "But I'm wired. Those eight days in Waikiki really rejuvenated me. Tropical vacations do that; you should try one sometime."

He smiled and dropped his chin to his chest.

"Now who's jealous?" she said, leaning over to deliver a tender kiss on his lips.

As with every kiss, he relished it. If life had taught him anything about love, it was that any single kiss—even the most routine, the most perfunctory—could be the last.

A few minutes later Janson closed his laptop. "I've made a strategic decision," he said. "Since we have two distinct tasks and not a hell of a lot of time to accomplish them, when we get to Seoul, we're going to split up."

"You think that's a good idea if Cons Ops is involved in this? They already tried to kill you once."

Janson smirked. "*You* already tried to kill me once. But do I hold it against you?"

"Sure seems that way, considering how often you bring it up."

Janson rested his hand on her knee and gave it a tender squeeze. "Anyway," he said, "the odds of Cons Ops being involved in this are astronomical. Senator Wyckoff based his assertions purely on paranoia. Unless he knows something he's not telling us, there's not a single fact implicating State. We don't know *who* Lynell Yi overheard, or *what* she overheard—*if* she overheard anything at all. Even if she *was* killed by one of the parties to the talks, it's more likely to be China or North Korea—or even South Korea—than it is to be the United States. Remember, whoever did this didn't place just anyone in the frame; they placed the son of a sitting US senator. That's *assuming* Gregory Wyckoff is innocent to begin with. And that's a fairly large—and probably false—assumption."

"All right," Kincaid said, after taking it all in. "So we split up. Who does what?"

"I'm going to start by searching Seoul for the senator's son. By the time we arrive the kid will already have a roughly forty-eight-hour head start. But given the geography, chances are he won't make it out of South Korea."

"So then, why the hurry?"

"Because if Gregory Wyckoff's going to have any chance at all of beating these charges, we're going to need to find him before the police do."

Kincaid nodded. "So while you're searching for the kid . . ."

"You're going to start the independent investigation into Lynell Yi's murder. The first thing you'll need to do in order for you to gain any ground with the locals is obtain some cooperation. So you're going to pay a visit to a man named Owen Young."

"Owen Young?" Kincaid said. "His name sounds familiar."

"It should. He's the US ambassador to South Korea."

THREE

Embassy of the United States
Jongno-gu, Seoul, South Korea

Jessica Kincaid wasn't happy. As far as she was concerned Janson was sending her directly into the lion's den without so much as a whip.

Her taxi pulled to the curb across from the massive embassy compound. She reached forward to pay the driver in South Korean won then opened the rear door and braced herself against the hard afternoon wind.

Toto, I've a feeling we're not in Honolulu anymore.

Kincaid stuffed her hands into the pockets of her long black overcoat as the orange Hyundai Sonata pulled back into traffic. Turning a full 360 degrees, she took in her surroundings. Kincaid always delighted in discovering new cities, particularly those, like

Seoul, that wrestled with striking the proper balance between tradition and modernity.

Head down against the bitter chill, she marched to the end of the block, wishing she were back in the warmth of Incheon International, which also happened to be the most dazzling airport she'd ever been in. Although she didn't have time to enjoy the amenities, she'd seen signs directing passengers to a casino and a spa, a theater with live performances, a cultural museum, even a Zen garden. There were ice-skating rinks and designer shops and world-class restaurants to be explored. For Kincaid, a lengthy layover at Incheon International would have served as a perfectly acceptable substitute for a luxury Hawaiian vacation in and of itself.

When she reached the intersection she stopped and surveyed the imposing US embassy. Unlike the architectural masterpiece that served as Seoul's futuristic air hub, the embassy possessed the doomed look of a maximum-security prison. In a city crowded with modern skyscrapers, the embassy stood alone, like a schoolyard brute that no one else wanted anything to do with.

As she moved closer to the monstrosity, the hordes of South Korean officers stationed behind the embassy's tall, spiked fences came into sharper focus. Several of the uniformed guards were gathered around a civilian vehicle that had just entered the compound. The Caucasian driver stood off to the side, arms folded across his broad chest, as the guards opened the trunk and the hood, inspecting every last detail. Kincaid suddenly wondered if she'd be subject to a strip search. Hell, from the looks of things, she worried that security protocols for former State employees might also require a cavity search—especially for disgruntled snipers like herself.

She glanced longingly over her shoulder at the countless galleries and performing arts centers, stole a cursory look at the lone snowcapped mountain in the distance. Kincaid was about to step foot on US soil, yet she felt as though she was sneaking behind enemy lines.

An odd feeling given that Jessica Kincaid rightly considered herself a lifelong American patriot.

When she finally reached the outer entrance she produced her US passport. "I have an appointment with Ambassador Young."

The guard's head-to-toe leer was almost as invasive as a strip search would have been.

Nearly an hour later she was seated outside the ambassador's office door, having been relieved of her smartphone and all other electronic devices. Her overcoat hung on a coatrack against the wall opposite her. As she waited, she crossed her legs and kept her head down. There was nothing particularly intimidating about being inside a US embassy, except that it was the turf of her former employer. Not just the US government but the US State Department.

Just a few years ago, Jessica Kincaid had been a member of Consular Operations, the State Department's clandestine intelligence unit. She'd served not only as a field agent but as a crucial component of Cons Ops's elite Sniper Lambda Team. In fact, she was the best they'd had. Kincaid was the crème de la crème, which was why *she* had been sent to Regent's Park in London to carry out the beyond-salvage order on Paul Janson. Because of her extraordinary skills (and because she'd chosen Janson as the subject of an extensive paper she'd been required to write during training), she had personally been given the directive to terminate Paul Janson.

Terminate with extreme prejudice.

Of course, she didn't know it then but she'd been lied to. Janson wasn't the enemy; he hadn't deserved to die. Once she finally realized that, she couldn't help but wonder how many other men and women she had executed were innocent. How many others had been betrayed by their own government? How many had children, loving husbands or wives?

Given their respective histories with Cons Ops, Kincaid didn't understand why Janson had sent her to the embassy immediately upon arriving in Seoul. How could he, of all people, trust anyone in the US State Department?

But then, Paul Janson was the smartest man she'd ever known. Even if he wasn't entirely forthcoming about them, he'd certainly had his reasons. And it wasn't her place to question his orders, regardless of how intimate their relationship was when they weren't in the field.

Still, a shiver ran down her spine just sitting in what she considered to be hostile territory. As far as she was concerned, Cons Ops and State were the enemy, and they always would be, regardless of any lingering ties Paul Janson might share with them.

* * *

TWENTY MINUTES LATER a well-dressed young man with close-cropped blond hair finally stepped out of the office and announced, "The ambassador will see you now."

Kincaid rose and steeled herself for what she expected to be a confrontation.

Ambassador Owen Young was standing stiffly in front of his desk, arms at his sides, when Kincaid entered his office. The Korean American statesman thanked his chief aide with a barely perceptible nod, then took Kincaid's hand in his and offered her a seat and a superficial smile.

During the flight, Janson had briefed Kincaid on Korean etiquette. Although he had grown up in San Francisco and attended the University of Pennsylvania and Cornell Law School, Owen Young had been born in Seoul and served at the US embassy— first as chief of political military affairs then as ambassador—for the past eleven years. Like most Koreans, he'd be eyeing Kincaid's body language, watching for demonstrations of knowledge of (and respect for) Korean culture.

"Thank you for agreeing to see me, Ambassador," she said with a slight bow before taking her seat.

"Of course," he said. "Who of us can turn down a request made by the legendary Paul Janson?"

Kincaid wasn't exactly sure how she was meant to take the ambassador's statement, but she wasn't about to ask.

"So," the ambassador said from behind his desk, "I understand you are in Seoul on behalf of Senator Wyckoff. I, of course, am aware of his son's situation and greatly concerned. But, as I told Mr. Janson, any assistance I might be able to provide is extremely limited. I may be able to seek the most perfunctory of professional courtesies, but I'm afraid the investigation itself will have to play out with the metropolitan police, and the legal process will move forward in accordance with its normal routine. Once Mr. Wyckoff is apprehended, he will be afforded a fair trial, rest assured. I, however, have no influence with law enforcement or with the South Korean courts."

The ambassador's speech was every bit as rigid as his posture. Kincaid had read Young's online bio on the plane and wondered how he could have been effective as an assistant US attorney in Washington, DC. Maybe he'd been more dynamic in his youth, but these days he'd no doubt lull his juries to sleep.

"I'm sure both the senator and Mr. Janson perfectly understand your professional limitations under these circumstances, Ambassador. What they're more interested in is whether you would be able to tell us anything about Lynell Yi that might aid in our investigation."

Young, whose shiny black hair was streaked with silver, leaned back in his chair and looked up toward the ceiling as though searching for something to say. The corners of his lips finally turned down in a frown. "I am afraid there is not much I can tell you about Ms. Yi. I knew her for only a brief period of time."

Kincaid maintained her poker face. Janson had explained to her that Koreans often preferred to hedge their response to a question rather than providing a blunt no. This cultural etiquette was apparently a defense mechanism, designed to save face.

"You may learn more from what the ambassador doesn't say than from what he does," Janson had cautioned her.

"From my understanding," Kincaid replied, "Ms. Yi worked here as a translator for the past six or seven months."

"I would have to see her personnel records," he said. "I don't believe she was with us quite that long."

Kincaid didn't attempt to mask her incredulity. "She was hired specifically for the four-party talks, wasn't she?"

The ambassador gave no response.

"The negotiations being held in the demilitarized zone," she prodded.

"Yes, I know which talks you are referring to. I simply fail to see the connection. Ms. Yi was the unfortunate victim of a domestic dispute, from what I have been told. All the evidence I've read about in the news points to her being murdered in a fit of rage."

Kincaid tilted her head to the side and took a different tack in an attempt to keep the ambassador off balance. "Was Lynell Yi an effective translator, Ambassador?"

Young shrugged. "As effective as any translator I've worked with, I suppose."

"Did she discuss her personal life at all?"

The ambassador shook his head. "She was a quiet girl. I never discussed anything with her aside from her translations."

"These are the translations that were made during the ongoing talks in the demilitarized zone," Kincaid said.

"Yes, of course."

"Who are the parties to these talks?"

"The North and the South, of course. Us, by which I mean the United States; we're South Korea's chief ally. And the Chinese. But surely you already know that; it's public knowledge, Ms. Kincaid."

"Sure," she said, "but I'm still unclear about what is being discussed during these talks."

"Well," he said with a condescending grin, "that information is classified, I am afraid. I can no more discuss it with you than I can with a reporter from CNN or the BBC."

"But you *can* shed some light, can't you, on what exactly Ms. Yi herself was working on when she was killed?"

"Surely, you understand that that would be improper, Ms. Kincaid."

"Haven't you spoken to the Seoul Metropolitan Police?"

"I spoke briefly with a detective. He told me that Ms. Yi had been the victim of a homicide. We discussed nothing else of substance."

"The detective wasn't curious about the victim's work?"

A slight smile appeared on the ambassador's lips. "No, of course not. I suspect he had no reason to be. Guests at the Sophia Guesthouse, where Ms. Yi was murdered, overheard an argument between her and her boyfriend just prior to the murder. From what I understand, most of the evidence speaks for itself. The fact that

Mr. Wyckoff has run, I believe, is further evidence of . . ." He trailed off, searching for the proper words, then finally continued. " . . . of what, unfortunately, transpired that evening."

"Speaking of overhearing," Kincaid began, "during the four-party talks, do you think it at all possible that Ms. Yi overheard something she shouldn't have?"

Young spoke without hesitation. "I would think not, though I am not sure what relevance you believe your question might have." He folded his hands atop his desk. "I sincerely hope that you and Mr. Janson have not been giving Senator Wyckoff false hope by inventing wild conspiracy theories. The senator and his wife are going through quite enough right now, I am sure."

"I'm only following up on the senator's suggestions," she said with a smile of her own. "Part of our job is to rule out alternative theories of the murder."

"I see," he said as he moved to rise from his seat. "Well, I wish you and Mr. Janson luck with your investigation. And, please, send Senator Wyckoff and his wife my deepest sympathies."

Kincaid didn't move. "Just a couple more questions, Ambassador, if it's not too much trouble."

Young sighed heavily but returned to his seat. "I do have another appointment this afternoon. So, please, proceed. But your brevity will be much appreciated."

"These talks you are involved in, can we assume they cover many of the same issues that were discussed during the previous six-party talks, the negotiations that also involved the Russian Federation and Japan?"

"The Korean issues are well-known around the world, Ms. Kincaid."

"So, North Korea's nuclear program? Trade normalization? The lifting of sanctions?"

"I believe all of those issues would sound familiar to anyone who reads *Chosun Ilbo* or the *New York Times*."

Kincaid recognized the finality in the ambassador's answer. "One last question, Ambassador." She rushed her words to prevent him from declining. "Was anyone in this embassy close to Ms. Yi? Anyone who might know her a little better than you did?"

Young's eyes darted to the doorway, where he'd acknowledged his chief aide just minutes earlier. "No one that I know of," the ambassador said. "She was an introvert, from all accounts."

"Did she have any direct contact with the other parties? Contact that may have excluded the US envoy?"

Young finally stood. "None that I am aware of," he said curtly. "Now, if you will excuse me, Ms. Kincaid, I really must prepare for my next appointment." He punched a button on his intercom.

The young man who had led Kincaid into Young's office replied, "Yes, Ambassador."

"Jonathan, please show Ms. Kincaid to the exit. Our meeting has come to an end."

FOUR

Fifteen minutes after Jessica Kincaid left the US embassy, Ambassador Owen Young gathered his briefcase, slipped into his hunter-green overcoat and black fedora, and called downstairs to have his car warmed and ready. Young's life had taken a decidedly difficult turn since he and the rest of the world learned the extent to which the National Security Agency was spying on its enemies and allies, even its own citizens. Given the broad scope of NSA targets, it seemed unlikely that the telephones inside the embassy in Seoul weren't tapped. So Young had stopped using them for everything but the most innocuous of tasks. From his office, he called his dry cleaner, his wife's interior decorator, and made appointments for haircuts and oil changes and dental checkups. He used his personal cell phone only to call his home or office. For everything else, he used telephones only he knew about.

One such telephone was a landline at a twenty-first-floor apartment he rented under a false name in the Gangnam district.

Gangnam was a word the entire industrialized world was now familiar with, thanks to the South Korean pop artist who called himself Psy. The word actually meant "south of the river," which was where Gangnam-gu was located—south of the Han.

As he waited in traffic on the bridge the ambassador considered what he would tell Edward Clarke, the current director of the State Department's Consular Operations. There was no question in his mind that matters had just become even more complicated. Young experienced a twinge of anxiety over how Clarke would react.

But then, the appearance of Paul Janson and Jessica Kincaid in Seoul wasn't *his* fault; what did *he* have to worry about? It was Clarke who would have to explain himself.

A few minutes later Young was cruising through the ritzy residential area he hoped to one day call his permanent home. By the end of this year, if everything remained on track with Clarke and the others, he would be able to. He'd already planted the seed with his wife, Mi-ho, and their three children. The only part of the plan that wasn't yet thought out was precisely what he'd tell his wife about the source of his financial windfall. A number of ideas were already rolling around in his head. In the end, it didn't matter so much. He'd probably resign his post as ambassador and tell his wife and children that he was taking an early retirement from public service because of a business deal that was too good to pass up. His wife didn't ask too many questions, after all; it was part of what endeared her to him.

This cozy apartment in Gangnam, for instance, had initially been rented for someone else, someone the ambassador enjoyed spending time with—a Canadian diplomat who had since moved on to another area of the globe. His wife had never questioned his need for the place, which he'd told her was an investment property he intended to rent out. Something he'd never quite gotten around to. But as he often joked with his chief aide, Jonathan: *What my wife doesn't know can't hurt me.*

In the lobby the ambassador nodded to the doorman, who returned the gesture with a respectful bow, then he headed straight for the elevator. He stepped out on the twenty-first floor and walked to the end of the hallway, now feeling slightly nostalgic for Severn, his former Canadian mistress. He wondered if she would consider a trip to Seoul in the not-too-distant future. With the money he'd have by the end of the year, he would even offer to pay her way. How could any enthusiastic traveler such as Severn turn down a first-class ticket on Korean Air and a week's stay in this stunning apartment overlooking the Han River?

Inside the apartment he shed his overcoat and set his fedora on the small but elegant dining room table. Then he picked up the phone. Although no one but Severn knew he kept this apartment, he had his line checked regularly for bugs. The last time was just a few days ago, so he felt secure as he dialed Clarke's number. Clarke's phone would be clean; the director was not a man who took chances with his privacy.

"Records Department. Winston speaking."

Young smiled. "Just the man I was looking for."

Their code was taken from George Orwell's *1984*, which turned out to have even more relevance now than the day they first adopted it. NSA had indeed become Big Brother on steroids, at least in the ambassador's opinion.

"It would seem that Diophantus is in jeopardy," Young said into the receiver.

"How so?"

"Have you not been apprised of the senator's new hires?"

Clarke sighed. "I just heard from Honolulu. Believe me, Paul Janson doesn't know anything. Wyckoff sent him on a fishing expedition; he thinks the senator's paranoid. Janson only took the assignment for the payday."

"He came all the way to Seoul just to confirm the kid's guilt? I find that hard to believe."

"He's collecting an eight-million-dollar fee, Ambassador. Janson's going to look for the senator's boy. We just have to be sure to find the kid before he does."

"I just met Janson's associate at the embassy. She doesn't seem to think she's on a fishing expedition. She seems suspicious. She repeatedly asked about the four-party talks and the translator's role in them."

"Of course Jessica Kincaid's suspicious. Since the day she left Cons Ops, she's been seeing conspiracies everywhere. It's only natural for a former intelligence agent. But Janson's got a level head; he'll rein her in. The fact that he sent Kincaid to you in the first place tells us he trusts State completely."

"Even after Mobius?"

Owen Young had only been let in on the Mobius Program well after the fact. But ever since he learned of the breadth and sophistication of the operation, he'd been in awe of the possibilities of clandestine operations. If the invisible hand of Consular Operations could create (and for years control) a visionary billionaire like Peter Novak to carry out their global agenda, then they could accomplish just about anything. It was why he had trusted that Diophantus would be an unmitigated success. This incident with the translator and the senator's son was the first error he'd seen made. But it was a significant one. And it had to be corrected without delay.

"Ambassador, we've worked with Janson since then. He got what he wanted: the Mobius Program was shut down. And we've been keeping tabs on him ever since. As far as Janson's concerned, Mobius was an isolated incident."

"We are in agreement, Director, that the stakes involved in Diophantus are even greater." He paused for a breath. "I believe we should err on the side of caution."

"As we have been, Ambassador."

"I do not need to remind you that the only reason we are having this conversation in the first place is because your man allowed the kid to escape."

Edward Clarke hesitated. "You want me to eighty-six Janson, is that what you're saying? Because my predecessor attempted just that in order to salvage Mobius. That directive very nearly blew him and everyone else involved out of the water."

Young considered this. "You say that Janson is just fishing, that it is the woman who is suspicious, correct? In that case, you need not eliminate Janson."

"You want me to take out Kincaid." Clarke's words didn't take the form of a question. "If I set my people on Kincaid, that's the one certain way we can expect to involve Paul Janson. There's more going on between him and Kincaid than just a working relationship, Ambassador."

"Then I anticipate he will be too distraught to continue the job for the senator."

Clarke smirked. "You don't understand. If Kincaid is taken out, Paul Janson will find out who's behind it even if it kills him."

"Perhaps it *will* kill him. You have faith in your current asset, do you not?"

The director exhaled audibly. "Ambassador, you're asking me to kick a fucking hornet's nest. You do realize that, don't you?"

"I'm not asking you to kick it, Director. I'm asking you to dispose of it. There is a significant difference."

* * *

EXASPERATED, EDWARD CLARKE slammed down the receiver. The sensation felt strangely unfamiliar. He'd slammed down plenty of phones in his time, but he hadn't had the pleasure in maybe ten or fifteen years. Technology had gotten in the way. Hanging up on someone no longer gave you the same satisfaction as marching out of a room and slamming the door behind you. Hell, it probably wouldn't be long before slammable doors were taken away too, replaced by those sliding contraptions on *Star Trek*.

Clarke stood from behind his desk and paced the length of his office in silence. He'd spent his entire adult life in the shadows of power, first at Langley then with Consular Operations. He'd taken plenty of shit over the span of his career, but none of it had become public and none of it had been personal. As deputy director of Consular Operations he'd taken the most, but he also had the opportunity to witness firsthand the incredible reach of genuine power. His predecessor, Director Derek Collins, had altered the course of history on several fronts, and to this day no one outside the Beltway even knew his name. He'd never had a website or even a Wikipedia page. Everything he did, every masterful stroke he took in his years as director of Cons Ops, had been performed behind a virtually impenetrable curtain. *That* was true power.

Now that power belonged to Edward Clarke. And like his predecessor, he wasn't afraid to wield it.

Unfortunately, even the most powerful men in the most powerful nation on earth had to rely on other human beings. In this case, Clarke had to rely on several. The ambassador was turning out to be more of a pain in the ass than he ever expected. Clarke was all but certain that it was because Owen Young had a much different, a much *lesser*, motivation. All the US ambassador to Seoul was interested in was the money.

Edward Clarke's motivation, on the other hand, was noble and pure. He was doing what he was doing for the good of the country. Like Collins before him, Clarke had vision. He saw threats others refused to see, acted on dangers others chose to completely ignore. Maintaining the status quo in Asia would be a monumental mistake for the United States of America. Most US politicians were too busy banking their votes and lining their pockets to see past the next election cycle. Clarke, however, suffered no such nearsightedness. If those who dwelled aboveground in Washington insisted on sitting on their hands while the world moved in a direction contrary to American interests, it was up to those who lived in the shadows to take swift and powerful action.

Clarke stopped pacing and lifted the receiver from his desk. The current trouble had started with a simple leak, but Clarke had moved without hesitation to contain it. It was a simple task, yet somehow his most reliable asset in Asia had fucked it up, royally. The Wyckoff kid should have been buried with the translator, but now they couldn't even locate him. The Seoul Metropolitan Police were having no more luck than Clarke's people. If they could at least get the kid into custody, Clarke would have options.

First of all, regardless of what his girlfriend might have told him (and it was possible she'd told him nothing), no one would believe a word the kid said. He was a nineteen-year-old stoner accused of murder. If Gregory Wyckoff had been promptly apprehended, Clarke could have simply let the South Korean criminal justice system run its course. Now, however, he had to play his hand much more cautiously. He continued to hope for an immediate arrest— after all, someone could get to the kid as easily *inside* prison as out—but he needed to take additional steps.

Unfortunately, the ambassador was right when he asserted that the senator from North Carolina had thrown a monkey wrench into the works. He'd hired the one man who knew precisely how Consular Operations worked. That move turned this entire contingency into a footrace. Arrest or no arrest, they *had* to get to the kid before Paul Janson did. And Clarke was sure they could. But the ambassador, understandably, didn't want to take that chance. The only way to be 100 percent positive that Janson and his partner, Jessica Kincaid, didn't find the kid before they did was to take them out of the picture. So Edward Clarke was now forced to issue the same directive his predecessor once had.

After several rings a voice finally answered. "This is Ping."

"Our asset in Seoul has a new directive."

"I see."

"The kid is still a go, but there are two individuals in Seoul who need to be tended to first."

"Understood."

"You may be familiar with them. They're both former Cons Ops."

"Their names in the order you'd like this task accomplished?"

Clarke sighed heavily but didn't hesitate. "Jessica Kincaid," he said. "And Paul Elie Janson."

FIVE

War Memorial of Korea
Itaewon, Yongsan-gu, Seoul

One of the most powerful men in South Korea stood just four feet eleven inches.

As he entered the second-floor exhibit, Paul Janson spotted Nam Sei-hoon standing with his hands clasped behind his back, gazing wistfully into a massive display case housing life-size wax figures depicting a particularly brutal battle from the Korean War. The small man shifted his eyes up and to the left as he caught a glimpse of Janson's approach in the reflective glass. As Janson sidled up beside him, Nam Sei-hoon said softly without looking at him, "I never tire of this place, Paul."

Janson bowed his head and remained silent as his old friend cleared his throat and ran a finger beneath his left eye to catch a falling tear. As far as Janson knew, the three-floor museum was the largest of its kind, a marvel of modern architecture that housed centuries of national memories, capturing both the jubilance and the misery associated with war, the latter of which Janson himself knew all too well.

The Korean War exhibit in which they stood was one of eight main exhibits on the grounds. Two of the pieces Janson observed outside had already stuck in his mind like a pushpin. One, the *Statue of Brothers*, which portrayed a South Korean officer embracing his younger brother, a North Korean soldier. The other, the *Peace Clock Tower*, a sculpture consisting of two clocks, the first reflecting the current time, the second memorializing the date of the invasion from the North. The second clock was to be replaced when the two Koreas were one again. Both pieces represented the South's passionate desire for Korean reunification.

"I am grateful that you contacted me," Nam said, finally turning his weathered face to Janson.

Nam Sei-hoon suffered from a rare genetic disorder known as Fairbanks disease, which had stunted his growth around the time he reached puberty. Janson knew of only two other people with the disease, the actor Danny DeVito and former Clinton labor secretary Robert Reich. But while both DeVito and Reich handled their condition with comic self-deprecation, Nam Sei-hoon took the opposite approach. Despite his meteoric rise to power within South Korea's National Intelligence Service, Nam remained ultra-sensitive about his height and was notorious for destroying the reputation and career of any man or woman who dared make light of his diminutive stature.

"I appreciate your seeing me on such short notice," Janson said, immediately regretting his phrasing. He bit down hard on his lip and quickly turned to the business at hand. "I'm trying to locate someone who may be on the run in the city. As the eyes and ears of Seoul, I thought you might be able to help."

Nam spoke slowly and deliberately. "I assume you are referring to the senator's son, the murder suspect who has thus far managed to elude police?"

"That's right," Janson said quietly. "I was hired by the boy's father to find him."

Nam Sei-hoon raised an eyebrow. "An exfiltration?"

Although there was no hint of accusation in Nam's voice, Janson quickly shook his head. "No, I have no intention of aiding in an escape. Senator Wyckoff believes his son is innocent."

"Innocent men do not flee."

"They do when they're frightened teenagers."

Nam Sei-hoon, whose once dark crown had matured into a blinding white, turned back toward the display case, leaving Janson to stare down at his profile.

"So you too believe this boy is innocent?" Nam said.

Janson detected an unexpected reticence in Nam's voice; his expression remained inscrutable. "I'm reserving judgment until I have all the facts. Including the kid's side of the story. When I find him, I'm going to encourage the boy to turn himself in to police. I trust the South Korean criminal justice system to decide his guilt or innocence."

"That's quite noble of you." When Nam next turned his body to face his old friend, his features had softened considerably. "Of course, I would offer you my assistance either way," he added, smiling. "Our friendship is such that the parameters of your mission are irrelevant to me, Paul."

Janson felt a wave of relief wash over him. In the past he'd often relied on Nam Sei-hoon's numerous contacts in the global intelligence community to obtain information and grease the wheels that needed greasing. Janson would have been confounded had his longtime friend denied him assistance now that Janson came to him personally. Such an unexpected setback would have been devastating to his search. Especially since Janson's own contacts on the Korean peninsula were limited—and the clock continued ticking.

Janson treasured Nam Sei-hoon's friendship partly because of how unlikely it was. Years ago Nam had singled him out during joint US-ROK live-fire training exercises. By then Janson was already part of the most elite platoon within SEAL Team Four, so Nam had measured him against not only the best, but the best of the best. Of all the US Navy SEALs whom Nam had observed over the years, he had chosen only Paul Janson to join him for dinner at his home in Seoul. Little did Janson know at the time that the dinner would become the first of many the two men shared.

Because of his position in the National Intelligence Service, Nam Sei-hoon traveled the world, liaising with his counterparts on every continent. Whenever Nam was about to leave the Korean peninsula, Janson received a call. If he happened to be within a couple thousand miles of one of the cities Nam was visiting, Nam would insist they get together for a meal. And it was at those meals that their friendship flourished.

Despite the difference in their ages and stations, Nam had always treated Janson like an equal. When they engaged in worldly discussions, Nam listened to Janson in a way that made Janson feel as if they were the last two men on earth. For Janson, a man who had never been close with his father, it was a remarkable experience that imbued him with an extraordinary level of confidence. And that confidence later provided Janson the fortitude to make some of his most crucial decisions, including his decision to leave Consular Operations in pursuit of a more virtuous life.

Glancing furtively over his shoulder to identify potential eavesdroppers, Nam said, "So, how can I help you, Paul?"

"Senator Wyckoff informs me that his son spends an inordinate amount of time in cyberspace. I was hoping we might be able to track him down that way."

"Quite possibly," Nam said. "Is the boy a professional?"

"'He knows his way around a computer' is how the senator phrased it. From my conversation with them, I don't think Senator and Mrs. Wyckoff are very close to their son. And I'm fairly certain they have no clue what he's been up to these past few years."

"A shame," Nam said. "But in these times, not as uncommon as we would like to believe."

"The police seized the kid's computers—one desktop and one laptop. As far as I know they haven't yet extracted any information, so I thought that might be a good place for us to start."

Nam seemed to consider this. "I am sure I can gain access to the boy's computers," he said, "*if* I declare it a matter of national security. Of course, since I head the Department of North Korean Affairs, it would be helpful if you possessed information linking either the senator or his son to the Kim regime, no matter how tenuous the connection."

In his head Janson ran rapidly through the senator's votes on North Korean sanctions. He knew there was nothing there, and if there was, Nam Sei-hoon and the National Intelligence Service would already know about it. Like any good spy, Nam was fishing. Which was particularly understandable under the circumstances. The South lived under a constant threat from the North, and the situation had recently worsened considerably. Kim Jong-il's death and his son Kim Jong-un's impromptu rise to power had made an unpredictable situation even more uncertain and extremely volatile.

Janson finally shook his head. "So far I've found nothing to suggest that the Wyckoff family has any ties to Pyongyang, political or otherwise."

"Very well," Nam said. "Then we will merely have to invent a narrative."

*　*　*

"TELL ME WHY I shouldn't hang up."

"CatsPaw. What have you got for me?"

Janson tucked his chin into the upturned collar of his overcoat as he waited for Morton's response. His exposed ears were frozen, his eyes tearing from the cold, hard wind. As he moved briskly along the sidewalk, he flashed on the tarmac at Hickam Field on Oahu, on the gentle caress of the Hawaiian sun on his cheeks. Just then it was hard to believe that Honolulu and Seoul were on the same planet, let alone in the same hemisphere.

Morton said, "A reverse dox can be every bit as complicated and time-consuming as a straight dox, ya know. And the name you fed me, he's no script kiddie."

Janson's brows dipped in frustration. "Speak English, Morton."

"Hold on. I'm on the New Jersey Turnpike and it's backed up worse than *I* was during month two of my OxyContin addiction."

Janson continued walking. He loathed speaking to Morton. He usually delegated the job to Jessie or someone else at CatsPaw, but today he had no choice but to call the hacker himself. As much as he detested hearing about Morton's traffic and constipation issues, he needed the information he'd requested earlier from the plane, and he needed it fast. The longer it took to find Gregory Wyckoff, the worse it would be for the kid. And the senator didn't seem like a guy who was keen on excuses.

"Did you find him or not?" Janson finally demanded.

"Easy, easy. Of course I found him. I was just trying to explain that it wasn't a cakewalk. Doxing someone who's good with a keyboard and wants to remain anonymous is a tough task. But if I have enough information about his online activity I can usually find him within an hour. Reverse doxes, on the other hand, can be a real bitch."

"But you found Gregory Wyckoff's handle in cyberspace," Janson pushed.

"I found him, sure. But he'd buried himself well, which is what I was trying to tell you. Your guy's no script kiddie—he knows his shit."

Janson said nothing as he passed the Seoul Central Mosque. If only he'd used his Muslim legend to meet with Nam Sei-hoon; then he could duck into the warm mosque and mutter a few prayers while his face thawed.

"All right," Janson said. "I don't have much time. Tell me what you learned about the kid's online life."

"He goes by the screen name Draco-underscore-Malfoy-nine-five."

"What the hell's a Draco Malfoy?"

"He's a student at Hogwarts School of Witchcraft and Wizardry."

"*English*, Morton."

"This *is* English, man. He's a character in *Harry Potter*. Draco Malfoy's a bad seed, lives in the Slytherin dorm. Voldemort commands him to kill Dumbledore, but he doesn't have the balls to go through with it. In the end I think Draco switches sides and becomes Harry's friend."

"Thanks for the *Harry Potter* history lesson. But right now I don't give a damn about fictional characters. Tell me about Gregory Wyckoff. What have you learned?"

"Well, I actually think his screen name is telling. This kid's nineteen. He's been active online using various identities since he was twelve. Started out as a black hat."

"A black hat?"

"In tech lingo it's someone who uses their knowledge of software programming to do mischief."

"What kind of mischief are we talking about?"

"Well, in Gregory's case, minor shit. At least to start with. He defaced a few websites, trolled some forums. But within a couple of years he'd moved up to DDoS'ing—knocking sites offline by swamping them with junk traffic—and stealing databases of personal information, which he then sold to various crooks and thieves in Eastern Europe, mainly Ukraine."

"What's he been up to recently?"

"That's the thing. Roughly three years ago he seems to have turned a corner. Maybe he got pinched, maybe he grew a conscience, I don't know."

"We know he didn't get pinched," Janson said. "The kid doesn't have a criminal record. Nothing on his juvenile sheet either."

"If he got pinched, there wouldn't be a rap sheet if he cooperated and went to work for the feds. Happens all the time these days. No more honor among thieves, ya know."

"So he started ratting out other hackers?"

"Not necessarily. But at that point his online career takes an odd turn. He starts working with Anon and other groups who claim to be hacktivists."

"By Anon, you mean *Anonymous*? The organization that attacked the Church of Scientology?"

"Right. Scientology, PayPal, MasterCard, Visa, Sony, and a whole bunch of other sites, including some Middle Eastern governments during the Arab Spring. But they're not really an organization. Anonymous is more like an online subculture."

"Great job, Morton. Now, how is all this going to help me find the kid in Seoul?"

Nam Sei-hoon had parted company with the promise to contact Janson when the NIS spy gained access to the computers being held as evidence by the Seoul Metropolitan Police. If history was any indicator, Janson expected to hear from Nam before nightfall, but he couldn't count on it. And if Gregory Wyckoff was half as savvy with computers as Morton was telling him, there was a good chance the kid had wiped his hard drives before going on the lam. It was also possible that the computers the police seized were never used in Wyckoff's covert activities. For all anyone knew, Wyckoff's personal computer could still be in the kid's possession.

"Hey," Morton said, "I've never been to Seoul. Hell, I've never even been to Philadelphia, which is practically in my backyard. If it weren't for the annual Black Hat convention in Vegas, I'd never leave Jersey at all."

"What are you saying, Morton?"

"I can track your man online, but I can't find him for you in real life. That's going to be up to you."

"Fine," Janson said, "then let me ask you this: If you were in a foreign country accused of murder, regardless of your guilt or innocence, where would *you* hide out?"

"I guess I'd try to find my peeps."

"Your peeps?"

"My people, ya know. Fellow hackers. From what I've seen of this guy online, you're not going to find him at some aboveground Internet café, casually logging on to his AOL account with his Capital One Visa. You're going to have to go underground. If I were him I'd use my network of fellow cyber-enthusiasts to hide my ass until the heat died down."

"Now we're getting somewhere, Morton. Next question: If everyone online is anonymous, how do you know which city anyone lives in?"

"You don't, necessarily. But if you're in some kind of serious shit in a foreign country, you can ask for help in an online forum. If someone who reads your post is in the area, he can send you a direct message and offer to help without exposing too much about himself publicly."

"There's no other way to find out which hackers live where?"

"Well, even if someone hides his IP address, you can usually figure out where he's from by what he talks about and when he's online, time zone–wise. You can also collect hints from his views on politics and shit, but that takes time. Also keep in mind that the best hackers are also skilled social engineers—and the best of the best are masters of deception."

"So how do we go about finding one of these hackers in South Korea?"

"Well, you, my friend, are in luck."

"Am I? Why's that?"

"Because I just happen to chat regularly with one of the baddest cyber-motherfuckers in all of Asia. And I just happen to know for a fact that he resides in Seoul."

"Great. How do I find him?"

"I can't pinpoint him on a map, ya know. But I can give you his screen name and you can try to locate him yourself. Just don't let on how you got the lead. And be extremely careful. From what I've heard, this guy will chew you up and spit you out as soon as look at you. He's got the reputation of a natural-born killer."

"What's the screen name, Morton?"

"L-zero-R-D-underscore-W-one-C-K-three-D."

Janson fixed on the letters and numbers in his head:

L0rd_W1ck3d

"Lord Wicked?"

"Lord-motherfucking-Wicked, my friend."

SIX

Dosan Park
Sinsa-dong, Gangnam-gu, Seoul

As the brutal cold burrowed deep into her bones, Jessica Kincaid couldn't shake the feeling that she was being followed. She lowered her head against the gusting wind and stole another glance over her left shoulder but saw no one.

You're being paranoid. You're the one doing the following.

Across the way, Ambassador Young's chief aide entered an upscale Korean restaurant named Jung Sikdang. Kincaid cursed under her breath. She couldn't very well walk into the restaurant; Jonathan would recognize her right away. And she sure as hell didn't want to wait around outside in the bitter cold for an hour while Jonathan enjoyed his evening meal. *Damn.* She'd been so sure he was heading straight to his apartment, where Kincaid could knock on the door and, hopefully, corner him alone. But no. An hour of surveillance, wasted.

After leaving the US embassy, Kincaid had headed north to the Sophia Guesthouse in Sogyeok-dong. It was her first time visiting a traditional hanok and she was instantly charmed. Fewer than a dozen rooms surrounded a spartan courtyard with a simple garden and young trees that stood completely bare in solidarity with the season.

Rather than poke around uninvited she went straight to the proprietors, a husband and wife of indistinguishable age. Both spoke fluent English. Although wary at first, they gradually opened up to Kincaid once she agreed to join them for afternoon tea.

Seated on low, comfortable cushions, Kincaid asked the couple whether they had ever seen Lynell Yi or Gregory Wyckoff before their recent visit. Neither of them had. Nor had they personally overheard the loud argument that was alleged to have taken place the night of the murder. The guests who *had* overheard the argument—a young Korean couple from Busan—had already checked out. Kincaid had seen their home addresses listed in the police file Janson had obtained on the plane, so she moved on.

After tea, Kincaid asked if she might have a look around, and the couple readily acquiesced. As they walked through the courtyard toward the room where Lynell Yi's body was found, the husband launched into a semicomposed rant about the disappearance of the hanok in South Korean culture. The one-story homes crafted entirely of wood, he said, were victims of the South's "obsession with modernization." As he pointed out the craftsmanship of the clay-tiled roof, he noticed Kincaid's chattering teeth and explained that the rooms were well insulated with mud and straw, and heated by a system called *ondol* that lay beneath the floor.

The wife took a key from her pocket and opened the door to

number 9, the room in which Wyckoff and Yi had stayed. It was located in the newer section of the hanok. Kincaid was surprised to find that the two-day-old crime scene was already immaculate. There was no yellow police tape, no blood or footprints or any other evidence to be seen. According to the husband, a team had rushed in and cleaned the place up and down the moment the police indicated they were finished. Kincaid made a mental note to check whether this was normal procedure in the Republic of Korea.

The room itself was cozy, about half the size of a one-car garage. But it was also elegant in an understated way. There were no beds or chairs, just traditional mats, a pair of locked trunks, and a small color television set you probably couldn't purchase in stores anymore. She'd seen the room in evidence photos, but the pictures didn't do the place justice.

Kincaid walked to the window, which was made of a thin translucent paper that allowed in natural light. She placed her hand on one of the speckled walls and thought that if she gave it a solid punch, her fist would land in the next room. So much for proving that fellow guests couldn't possibly have overheard an argument between the victim and the accused. But what truly puzzled her was that the police noted no signs of a struggle, except for a fallen lamp. Given the size of the room, that seemed all but impossible, especially considering the fact that Lynell Yi had apparently been the victim of manual strangulation.

"Tourists from the West still love to stay in hanok," the husband said, collapsing her thoughts. "They do not come to Seoul to stay in a high-rise they can see in New York City or London."

Kincaid nodded. She understood his passion, and unlike Janson, she could certainly understand why the young lovers might have slipped away from their modern apartment nearby to experience an amorous night in a traditional Korean home. Maybe she was just more romantic than Paul—or maybe Paul had previously been inside a hanok and had been reminded of the six-by-four-foot cage he'd been kept in during the eighteen months he spent as a prisoner of the Taliban in Afghanistan. That would certainly be reason enough for him to dismiss the hanok as a desirable place to stay. Either way, Kincaid didn't think Janson's theory that the young couple had been on the run held much water.

* * *

FOLLOWING HER VISIT to the Sophia Guesthouse, Kincaid waited in line for a dish of spicy chili beef then headed south back to the US embassy. By then it was nearing five o'clock Korean time, and she was hoping to catch Jonathan exiting the embassy after calling it a day. Jonathan was probably in his mid- to late twenties, not a teenager but certainly closer to Lynell Yi in age than most people employed at the embassy. And the ambassador's glance toward the doorway, when Kincaid asked if there was anyone in the office who knew Lynell Yi well, made her suspect that Jonathan might hold some of the answers to questions she had about Yi's job, maybe even her relationship with Gregory Wyckoff.

Jonathan exited the embassy at a quarter after five and walked to the subway station at Chongyak. There he took the 1 line, and Kincaid hopped into the subway car trailing his. He got off just two stops later and boarded the 3. On the 3 train, he seemed to settle in for a lengthy ride. And lengthy it was; he didn't step off the train again until they were south of the Han River in Gangnam-gu.

Kincaid continued to watch the restaurant. As she held her arms across her chest against the cold, she experienced that feeling again. That odd sensation that while she was watching Jonathan, she too was being watched. But by whom?

She searched the faces of the few people on the street braving the freezing weather. She eyed a group of teenagers huddled at the far corner of the park. She counted four males and two females, all probably under the age of eighteen. An unlikely bunch of spies, to say the least.

To her left, she spotted a vagrant hunched over on a park bench.

A vagrant? In these temperatures? How could he possibly survive the night?

The sun was dipping low behind the mountain; dark was falling fast. If she didn't identify her stalker soon, it would be all but impossible. She reached into her pocket for her phone to call Janson but then thought better of it. She'd already informed him that she'd followed Jonathan to the restaurant. She could handle this on her own.

She turned away from the restaurant, retreating into the park. The group of teens paid her no attention. The vagrant didn't stir. Two males were walking fast straight toward her, but as they approached she noted they were holding hands, exposing their fingers to the cold. In this weather, that was true love.

A minute later she moved past the couple, deeper into the park. She stole another look over her shoulder. Had any of the people she'd seen earlier followed her? None that she could tell. But she felt a pair of eyes on her nevertheless.

Kincaid quickened her pace as her pulse sped up and her head filled with images of men in fedoras and dark trench coats, with handguns hanging at their sides.

In the center of the park she spun around and spotted movement in a copse of trees. An animal? No. Unless a grizzly bear had escaped from the Seoul Zoo, this creature was too large to be anything but a human being.

She continued moving forward as though she'd seen nothing.

But she heard a rustle and was suddenly sure that whoever was following her knew he'd been made. Which meant that he was probably a professional.

With no one else in sight and the cover of dusk protecting him, her attacker finally made his move and launched himself out of the shadows.

Kincaid didn't hesitate, didn't bother looking back, just took off in a sprint across the park in the direction of the river. Over the shrieking gusts of wind she heard her pursuer make contact with bushes and low tree branches as he cut a parallel course north toward the Han, attempting to overtake her.

But Kincaid was fast. Fastest of her class at Quantico, where her professional life began. In the time since she'd left Virginia to join the FBI's National Security Division, she'd put on a few years but not a single extra pound. And her world hadn't paused since she'd been stolen away by the State Department after catching the eyes of some spooks from Consular Operations.

It was times like this when brimming with confidence counted, and that was a trait she'd had in spades all the way back to her childhood in Red Creek, Kentucky. She'd taken that confidence with her when she boarded a Greyhound bus, leaving her daddy behind for the first time in her life. And over the years that confidence had been refined, first by the bureau, then by Cons Ops, and most recently by Paul Janson.

She charged through a row of bushes and found herself back on a street. She paused a moment to catch her breath, which was billowing in large white puffs before her eyes. Through the mist she eyed a taxi, and her arm shot up almost instinctively.

The orange taxi slowed and pulled to the curb and Kincaid opened the door and dove into the backseat, shouting, "Go, go, *go*."

As the taxi peeled away Kincaid raised her head just in time to see a tall Korean man breaking through the bushes, stopping on a dime, then raising his arms with a gun in his hands. She watched him take aim and nervously waited for the sound of a gunshot, the shattering of window glass, the buzz of a bullet as it streaked by within inches of her face.

Mercifully, the assassin never fired.

SEVEN

Cheongwha Apartments
Itaewon, Yongsan-gu, Seoul

Full dark yet still no word from Nam Sei-hoon.
Fortunately, since the time he left Nam at the War Memorial, Janson had scored the aid of another old friend, this one going back to his days in Consular Operations.

Until roughly ninety minutes ago, Janson had assumed Grigori Berman was dead. Over the past couple of years all attempts to reach the bearlike Russian had failed. Given his longtime associations with the Russian *mafiya*, it would have served as no surprise for Janson to learn that Grigori Berman had met a violent end.

But that evidently wasn't the case.

"Dead?" Berman had said in his thick Russian accent. "No, no, Paulie! I am very much alive, comrade. I was just, let's say, on an extended vacation."

Janson didn't bother asking where Berman had been and Berman in turn didn't utter another word on the subject. Janson could think of myriad reasons why the big man might have needed to remain off the radar for a while.

"Hearing from you, Paulie, is like hearing from an old girlfriend. It warms my heart, yet I cannot help but wonder what it is you want from me."

Janson didn't need to remind Berman that the Russian was still in his debt. Back when Janson worked for Cons Ops, Grigori Berman, who'd been trained as a number cruncher in the former Soviet Union, had been in the business of laundering millions for his Russian mob associates by setting up shell corporations around the globe. When Consular Operations finally decided to drop the dragnet on the Russian syndicate Berman was working with, Paul Janson deliberately let the effusive accountant go. Despite the protests of his Cons Ops colleagues, Janson viewed the decision like a chess move. Grigori Berman may have been a manipulator, a liar, and a thief. But he was also talented, clever, and—unlike his co-conspirators—nonviolent. Placing him in a prison would have done neither Janson nor Cons Ops any good. Having a man like Berman in his debt, on the other hand, gave Janson the potential ammunition to outsmart and outmaneuver scores of other criminals who *were* violent—evil men who were irredeemable and who would inevitably do irreparable damage to society.

In hindsight, Janson's chess move was one of the most brilliant of his career. A few years ago when Janson was framed for the contract murder of billionaire philanthropist Peter Novak, it was Grigori Berman who discovered that the $16 million placed in Janson's offshore account as alleged payment for the hit actually originated from Novak's own foundation. Shortly after that discovery, Berman took a sniper's bullet in the chest—a bullet that had been meant for Paul Janson. Thankfully, the large Russian recovered. And not only was Berman not angry afterward, but he also risked everything to help Janson put the final nail in the coffin of the Mobius Program—by manipulating a crooked foreign banker and causing the then *president of the United States of America*, Charles W. Berquist Jr., to receive and accept an illegal $1.5 million personal contribution, which Janson then used as leverage.

Now that Janson thought about it, maybe Grigori Berman's debt *had* been paid.

Well, Berman doesn't need to know that.

"So, what can I do for you, Paulie?"

"I'm trying to track down a hacker in Seoul. Goes by the screen name Lord Wicked." Janson spelled out the queer combination of letters and numbers.

"Ah, *Lord Wicked*," Berman said.

"You've heard of him."

"Everyone in the cybersecurity industry has heard of him. He's a living legend."

"Can you help me locate him?"

"Ordinarily, I would say *nyet*. A man of his prowess, he undoubtedly reroutes his servers to countries all over the world. But since you know which city he is in, I should be able to dox him within the hour."

"Dox him?"

"Unearth his personal details," Berman said. "His real name, his home address, his telephone number. Maybe even his mother's maiden name."

"Skip the mother's maiden name," Janson said. "Get me the rest as quickly as you can."

* * *

FIFTY-SIX MINUTES LATER Grigori Berman called Janson back with the details.

"His name is Jung Kang," Berman said. "Or Kang Jung, if you place the last name first as the Koreans do. He has two known addresses. One is in Itaewon, in the Yongsan district. The other address is in Gangnam—you know, like the song, Paulie? *'Heeeyyy, sexy lady! Oppa Gangnam style...'*"

"I've heard the song, Grigori. How about giving me the addresses?"

Twenty minutes later a young woman exited the main lobby of the Cheongwha Apartments, and Janson slipped in with a practiced pronunciation of the Korean term for "thank you" and a warm smile.

Since Janson was already in Itaewon when he spoke to Berman, it made sense for him to check out Kang Jung's Yongsan address and leave the Gangnam address for Kincaid, who'd last reported to him that she'd followed the ambassador's chief aide to an upscale restaurant across from Dosan Park. But when Janson called Kincaid to relay Kang Jung's Gangnam address he received no answer. Once ten minutes passed without a callback, he began to feel slightly on edge. But he was sure it was nothing. Maybe the ambassador's aide had dropped into the restaurant for a single drink then returned to the subway station for the remainder of his ride home. Kincaid would no doubt contact him when she popped back up on the surface.

Janson took the elevator to the eleventh floor. He was pessimistic about this being the right place. Itaewon was known as a Western town, a district popular among tourists and expats and US military personnel stationed in Korea. Because of its demographics and plethora of counterfeit goods, Itaewon had been likened to a Chinatown, only for North Americans and Western Europeans. Which made it an *unlikely* residence for a wealthy man with a clearly Korean name like Kang Jung.

The indistinctiveness of the apartment building made him further suspect that Kang Jung's true address was the one in Gang-nam. According to Morton and Berman, "Lord Wicked" was a king-pin who made millions of dollars selling "dumps"—stolen credit card and corresponding personal information—to hardened criminals from Vancouver to Estonia. Odds were he was living large. Or at least larger.

Janson stepped into the dim hallway, took a left, and rounded the corner. Outside apartment 1109, he paused and listened at the door, careful to stay clear of the peephole. He'd heed Morton's warning and be cautious, sure. But he wasn't there to take Kang Jung into custody; he was there to cut a deal for information. Kang Jung would have little reason to kill him.

Then again . . .

When he heard nothing but a television tuned to an old sitcom with a laugh track, Janson finally rapped on the door.

He stood off to the side and waited for the peephole to darken, but it never did. He listened for the sound of heavy footfalls but continued to hear nothing but the television. He was about to give the door another knock when it opened a crack and the tiny features of a little girl poked out.

"*Hashiljul ashinayo?*" Janson said. *Do you speak English?*

"*Chogum hajul arayo,*" the girl replied. *I speak a little.*

"Is your father home?"

"He may be."

"He *may* be? Would you mind checking for me?"

"I'm not allowed to use the phone. I'm grounded."

"The phone?"

"My father lives in Gangnam," she said. "I live here with my mother."

"I see," he said, deflating at the validation of his assumption that he was at the wrong address. "Is your mother home?"

"No, she's out."

"You're here all by yourself?" Janson said. "How old are you?"

"Thirteen."

"OK, I'm sorry to have bothered you."

Janson turned toward the elevator bank.

"Wait," the girl called. "What do you want with my father?"

Janson scrutinized her. "You seem to speak more than a *little* English."

"I'm fluent," she said. "Now, what do you want with my father?"

"It doesn't have anything to do with you. It's just business."

"What kind of business?"

"You're a curious young lady, aren't you?"

"Answer the question," she said.

"I want to pay your father for some information."

"What kind of information?"

"Adult information."

Janson turned to leave again.

"Computer information?" the girl called out to him.

Janson spun back to face her. "Maybe. What do you know about it?"

"My father doesn't work with computers."

"He doesn't? What does he do?"

"He's a chef."

"Is that so? What type of food?"

"Neo-Korean," she said. Then: "You look like you don't believe me."

"Let's just say I have information that contradicts what you're telling me."

"You don't even know my father's name, I'd bet."

Janson thought about it and decided to play along. "Your father is Kang Jung."

The corner of the girl's mouth lifted in a smirk. "You're wrong. You don't know what you're talking about. You're looking for the wrong person."

"Is your father's surname Kang?"

"Yes."

"Well, then, who's the right person? Who's Kang Jung? Your mother?"

The girl shook her head and then opened the door wider. "Why don't you come in?"

"That wouldn't be a good idea."

She rolled her eyes and motioned inside. "It would be if you're looking for Lord Wicked," she said.

EIGHT

Kincaid looked over her shoulder, scanning the mass of pulsating youths. Madonna's "Ray of Light" emanated from all sides of the ultramodern club as she searched for the man who'd been following her since Dosan Park.

Once she'd jumped into the taxi and realized that the gunman wasn't going to be able to get off a shot, she felt around in the pockets of her overcoat for her phone. But it was gone. She must have dropped it while sprinting through the park, trying to evade her pursuer. She leaned forward and asked her driver whether she could borrow his cell phone. He responded in Korean by telling her that he didn't speak any English, then closed the sliding partition that separated the front seat from the back.

After ten minutes of driving around Gangnam, she had the taxi pull over. She didn't want to travel too far, because she still hoped to make it back to the restaurant in time to catch Jonathan leaving.

Clearly, she hadn't traveled far enough. Because as she searched the streets for a public phone to call Janson, she caught sight of the tall Korean man who had aimed the gun at her.

When his eyes fell on her she had no choice but to begin running again.

He chased her up and down busy city streets, past narrow alleys, through the blinding cold. She attempted several evasive maneuvers she'd learned while in Cons Ops and a number of advanced tactics she'd been taught by Janson. But she simply couldn't lose the man with the gun. He was fit. He was trained. He was professional. And he seemed pretty damn determined to catch her and kill her.

Kincaid eventually ducked into a subway station in order to surround herself with people and catch a breath. When she realized the man had followed her into the station, she jumped into a subway car. She hopped off at the first stop only to spy him coming after her like a horror-movie monster when she finally surfaced again.

Following failed attempts to hide in a department store and disguise herself, she finally lost her tail using a complex sequence of buses, subways, and taxis.

She went almost an hour without seeing him.

Relieved, she was about to enter a Korean Starbucks to look for a public phone when her would-be assassin's visage materialized in the reflective window.

Again she ran. Hard and fast and for what felt like forever. When she finally realized she was tiring and that it was just a matter of time until the killer caught up with her, she decided to try to turn the tide. As Janson was constantly telling her:

"Turn the hunter into the hunted, the predator into the prey."

When she turned down what looked to be a quiet side road and spotted a massive glass-and-steel structure bleeding partygoers, she decided that was where she'd make her stand. She slipped the bouncer at the rope line a hundred dollars in American currency, checked her coat, and immediately lost herself in a horde of dancers.

As she searched over her shoulder, her body still pumping madly with adrenaline, she hoped like hell her pursuer had followed.

She wormed her way through the thick, sweaty crowds, watching for the killer while simultaneously trying to memorize the layout of the exotic four-level nightclub. Cher's "Life After Love" gave way to an unfamiliar Korean pop song before the deejay spun a remixed cut of "Lose Yourself." As the song ended, a catchy techno beat came over the speakers and the mood of the entire nightclub transformed at once. Energy levels rose to the roof; the dancing became faster and far more intense. The Vengaboys' "We Like to Party" blasted from the speakers.

Less than a minute into the song, Kincaid finally spotted her armed stalker.

Only he won't have a gun anymore, she thought. When patrons entered the T-Lound nightclub, they had to pass through a metal detector. She might not be able to outrun him. But Jessica Kincaid prayed that, by ducking into the popular dance club, she'd at least managed to level the playing field.

* * *

SIN BAE SLITHERED THROUGH the crowd looking for the woman. He'd had to strip and stash his Daewoo DP-51 before he entered the club. The disassembled handgun lay buried in a shallow grave in a small patch of earth between two concrete buildings just across the street. If all went well in the club he'd retrieve it and move on to Itaewon to terminate Paul Janson before renewing his search for the senator's son.

Eliminating Janson's partner, Jessica Kincaid, had proven far trickier than he expected. She was fleet-footed and equipped with more stamina than any woman he had ever known. Not only had Consular Operations and Janson trained her well, but she possessed some physical attributes that made her an even more difficult target. Her eyes, for instance; she had the sight of a hawk.

Although he was no longer advantaged with the element of sur-prise, Sin Bae decided he wouldn't need it. This was hardly his first job. It was, however, the first time he'd been given an order to as-sassinate a pair of former Cons Ops agents. He'd previously killed members of South Korea's National Intelligence Service, as well as clandestine officers from the United States' Central Intelligence Agency. But never an agent, former or otherwise, of Cons Ops.

Sin Bae was mildly curious as to how Paul Janson and Jessica Kincaid had come to draw the ire of Consular Operations. But he would never learn the reason and he could live with that. He had orders to carry out, instructions as urgent as they were clear. Once Janson and Kincaid were eliminated and the elusive Gregory Wyckoff was dead, he'd contact his handler Ping in Shanghai and await his next assignment.

He moved up the stairs to the second floor and spotted her almost instantly. Curiously, she had cozied up to a middle-aged Korean gentleman at the bar. A few moments later she guided the man toward the center of the dance floor.

Had she not seen Sin Bae enter the nightclub? Or did she think that because he had to pass through a metal detector she had nothing to fear? If that was the case, her overconfidence—and her severe underestimation of Sin Bae—would ultimately be her undoing.

Alternating colored lights made it difficult to see through the crowd to the dance floor. Disorienting, but not debilitating. He could still get the job done with no one the wiser. But he'd need to be smart about it. There were simply too many bodies on the dance floor. It would take time for him to get close to her, and he did not want to risk her spotting him as he made his approach.

So he stood back and watched. Waited. Was this beautiful young woman actually seducing a paunchy, balding stranger almost old enough to be her father? From the way she danced with him, it certainly seemed so. A waitress walked over to the couple carrying a tray of test tube shots and Jessica Kincaid quickly downed two of them. To calm her nerves, perhaps.

Good, he thought. That meant she indeed suspected that the threat had passed. Sin Bae might possess the element of surprise after all.

He considered his options. Perhaps he would kill her on the street as soon as she left the bar. Or perhaps he could do it right there in the club. If she no longer thought there was a threat, maybe she would head to the restrooms. With the right approach, Sin Bae could easily get to her in one of the ladies' room stalls.

He was amused by her behavior, though somewhat surprised that she'd succumbed to a false sense of security simply because the metal detector downstairs had removed the handgun from the equation. Little did she know that Sin Bae's true weapon of choice remained on his person.

As Sin Bae tugged on the arms of his suit jacket and shot out the cuffs, a drunk man—a European tourist, no less—suddenly knocked into him, spilling an amber liquid down the front of his jacket and shirt before dropping and shattering his glass on the floor. Sin Bae was tempted to take a shard of that glass and slit the man's throat from ear to ear. But then, that would jeopardize his objective. Instead, he allowed the man to move on with a hard glare that left no question as to whether the man should come anywhere near him again.

When his gaze returned to the dance floor, he surveyed the crowd for Kincaid. He spotted the older Korean man she had been dancing with, the one with the round bald spot on the top of his head, but he appeared to be alone. And every bit as perplexed as Sin Bae.

Impossible. He'd taken his eyes off the subject for merely a few seconds.

Sin Bae cursed inwardly, then started searching the faces of each young woman in the crowd. This Kincaid was wily. He knew from the time he'd spent tracking her that she could lose a professional pursuer as easily as most can tie a shoelace. And she didn't give up. Clearly, Miss Jessica Kincaid wasn't ready to die.

Movement suddenly drew Sin Bae's eyes toward the stairs leading back down to the first floor. He couldn't be sure but he thought he'd spotted the back of her head. He should know it by now, he mused; he'd been chasing after it all night.

He started toward the stairs, stoic and confident.

He *would* find her.

And he *would* kill her.

He *would* finish her, tonight.

NINE

Who the *hell* was able to dox me?"

From the couch, Janson stared at the girl across the modest living room, trying to keep his jaw from dropping.

"*You?*" he said. "*You're* Lord Wicked?"

The girl folded her arms across her flat chest. "Answer. My. Question."

"I can't tell you that. But rest assured, it took an entire team."

The girl picked up a remote control and muted the flat-screen television on the wall above her head.

"I'm sorry to hear that you can't reveal your sources," she said. "Because this is a quid pro quo. You came to me for information? Well, I'm not going to tell you a damn thing unless you tell me who doxed me."

Janson rose from the couch. "Look, I don't care what you do for a . . . living. I just need help, and you may be the only person in all of Seoul who can provide it."

"Then tell me *who* doxed me."

"That issue is closed, young lady." He caught himself pointing a stern finger in her direction and quickly withdrew it. "Look, this isn't a game. I won't leave here until you tell me what I need to know."

"What are you going to do?" she said. "Torture a thirteen-year-old girl?"

Janson maintained his calm. "I don't torture *anyone*."

"No?" she said, her demeanor suddenly lightening. "Not even if you're paid well? Because I will give you *good* money if you bring me the heads of everyone who was involved in doxing me."

Christ. The girl looked completely serious. Janson wondered why she'd given up her identity to him without much persuasion if she was so hell-bent on keeping it secret.

He turned to the door. "This was a bad idea after all. I'm going to go pay your father a visit in Gangnam."

"*No,*" she shouted. "Don't go see my dad. Just tell me what you want to know. And hurry, because my mother will be home within the hour."

So that was it. Her father was her Achilles' heel. That was why she'd given in when he'd been standing in the hallway.

"All right," he said. "I'm trying to locate a hacker who is somewhere in Seoul. I already have people watching his credit cards and his cell phone, but he's not using either. So the only way I might find him in time is if I know more about him, and the guy I'm looking for supposedly lived most of his life online."

"Find him *in time*?" she said. "What does that mean?"

Janson had wanted to avoid mentioning the police, but the clock was ticking. And if he was to give this girl—this "Lord

Wicked"—the best chance of helping him locate Gregory Wyckoff, he'd need to be entirely honest with her.

"Have you heard about the murder at the Sophia Guesthouse? It happened less than seventy-two hours ago."

"Of course," she said. "It's been all over the news. I've followed every update online."

Janson frowned. "You don't get out much, do you, kid?"

The girl shook her head. "There's nothing out there for me," she said softly.

Her words briefly froze him. He considered asking her about her business, where she was stashing her cash. Was she sure she was safe? But he had more pressing matters at the moment.

"The suspect's name is Gregory Wyckoff," he said, "and he's nineteen years old. He's the son of a sitting US senator, and he's on the run. He may be innocent, and the senator's hired me to find him and try to get to the bottom of what happened the other night."

The girl nodded. "You want me to reverse dox him? That will take time."

"I've already had someone reverse dox him."

"The same guy who doxed *me*?"

Janson ignored the question. "His online identity is Draco-underscore-Malfoy-ninety-five."

He hoped for a flash of recognition, but her expression didn't change.

"OK, I'll help you," she said.

"Thank you."

"But you'll have to leave me with a way to contact you, because this will take a little while and if you're still here when my mother gets home, she'll call the police and have you arrested."

"I understand."

As Janson wrote down his number, he thought again about

Jessie, who still hadn't returned his call. Because time was of the essence (and because he doubted their involvement), he'd decided to go at State and Cons Ops head-on. By sending Kincaid straight to the US embassy, he was essentially shaking the tree to see whether anything fell out. He'd assumed that if Cons Ops *was* involved, they'd telegraph their moves and he'd see them coming from a mile away. Now he worried he may have made a lethal mistake—a mistake for which he knew he could never forgive himself.

"Here," he said, handing the girl his number. "How long do you anticipate this taking?"

"I'll have something for you within half an hour."

Janson turned to exit the apartment.

"I've only let my guard down *once* in the past twelve months," she said to his back. "To some guy I've been chatting with. He told me he lived in the UK, but I traced him back to the States."

Janson looked back at her. "And?"

"Tell me something. This douchebag who doxed me, does he happen to live in New Jersey and drive a beat-up old Honda?"

TEN

Kincaid started down the stairs, weaving through the line of scantily clad women with martinis and highballs in their hands. She didn't look back to determine whether her pursuer had followed; she could already *feel* his eyes on her, as surely as she'd felt them while standing across from the restaurant in the freezing cold in Dosan Park.

Gridlock on the landing between floors one and two required her to throw a few sharp elbows, which earned her a barrage of sharp words and dirty looks—but didn't slow her down.

When she reached the bottom of the stairs she recalled the layout of the first floor and headed left toward the room where she'd checked her coat. As she moved through the crowd she felt for the reassuring outline of the handgun in her waistband.

On the second floor Kincaid had done what most of the single ladies in the club were doing—she'd looked for a man. At first she merely thought a guy would help her to blend in, allow her time to spot the killer before he spotted her, giving her an advantage, maybe allowing her the time to get behind him. Then she noticed something that sparked a much better idea. She went to the bar and squeezed between two men, a younger one flirting theatrically with a young woman, and an older one who looked as though he'd already given up for the night and was now determined to get sloshed.

She had spotted the older man from across the room, selected him because of the bulge beneath the left breast of his suit jacket. When she reached the bar she pressed her right side against his left to confirm what she'd thought she saw.

"*Choésong hamnida*," she said, apologizing to the man for nudging him to the side and causing him to tip over his drink. She knew she'd slaughtered the Korean phrase, but hoped the floor-shaking music had drowned out all but its essence. She grabbed a rag off the bar and helped him clean up the spill.

"It is fine," the man said in English, his speech clearly slurred. "You are American, yes?"

She smiled as she turned to face him. "Yes, yes, I am. Did my awful pronunciation give me away?"

"I *love* America," he said cheerfully, ignoring her question. Though it was possible he hadn't even heard her over the music. "I *love* the New York City. Is that where you are from?"

Kincaid kept an eye out for her stalker. "Not quite," she said. "I'm from a small town in the heartland. It's called Red Creek, Kentucky."

"Ah, Kentucky!" he cried. "I *love* Kentucky bourbon *and* Kentucky Fried Chicken. Can I buy for you?"

She leaned into him, hoping she didn't reek of sweat. "You want to buy me a bucket of Kentucky Fried Chicken?"

The man threw his head back as though she'd just dropped the funniest line he'd ever heard. Then his head came forward and butted the top of hers just as he started to speak.

"Terribly sorry," he shouted. "So, so sorry." When he saw that she was uninjured, he returned to his initial train of thought. "I meant, can I buy you a Kentucky bourbon? Wild Turkey, maybe? Or Jim Beam? Perhaps Old Grandfather?"

"Old Grand-*Dad*," she said, correcting him.

"Very well!" He reached over the bar and shouted in the direction of the bartender. "Two shots of the Old Grand-Dad!"

Kincaid's eyes caught sight of her pursuer climbing to the top of the stairs.

"Do you want to dance?" she said.

"Dance? Yes, sure." He searched for the bartender. "Let me just get our drinks."

"He can *bring* them to us. I really, really want to get out there with you." She turned to the bartender. "Will you serve us the drinks out on the dance floor?"

"Of course," the bartender said in near-perfect English, with a near-perfect smile. "I will have someone bring them to you." He looked at the older gentleman in the suit. "Have fun, you crazy kids."

When they reached the dance floor, Kincaid immediately got into the rhythm of the K-pop as her partner looked on, slack-jawed. She spun around and slowly backed her rear end into him, moving it methodically against his midsection.

He reached around her body and clasped his hands in front of her stomach. When he did, she quickly spun around to face him, leaving their lips only inches apart. She ran her hands up the sides of his legs, up his rib cage, and felt for the holster beneath his jacket.

There it is.

As she nuzzled his neck, she slipped her hands inside his jacket and ran her fingers up his torso. He threw his head back, his eyes rolling upward in ecstasy.

She shot a look across the dance floor and saw her pursuer standing near the top of the staircase with his arms folded across his broad chest, watching her.

A young woman in a short skirt carrying a tray of neon test tubes tapped her on the left shoulder.

"Two shots of Old Grand-Dad," the young woman said.

Kincaid took one of the test tubes and threw it back. Her dance partner waved a hand in front of his face, declining his own. "No, thank you. But please, put both drinks on my tab," he slurred.

Kincaid winked and grabbed the second shot and put it to her lips. Her dance partner's eyes widened to show her he was impressed.

"They're small," she said as she pulled him close to her again. She let him smell the bourbon on her breath then planted a sensual kiss on his cheek as her hands once more traveled inside his jacket.

As she moved up toward the holster, she considered how he might have gotten inside the club with a gun. Probably he was a cop, though she knew from Janson that most cops in Seoul didn't carry firearms. Which meant that her dance partner was most likely a specialist armed officer with the Seoul Metropolitan Police. Either undercover or off duty. Given his slurred speech and the pungent scent of scotch coming off him, she assumed it was the latter.

From the corner of her eye, she watched a drunk young European man collide with the killer, spilling a drink down the front of his jacket and shirt. A perfect diversion.

She seized the opportunity.

* * *

BECAUSE PATRONS WERE NEITHER entering nor exiting the club in droves at that hour, the coat-check girl had abandoned her station in the enormous coatroom. But Kincaid couldn't know how long it would be until she returned, so she had to hurry. Concealing herself between two racks of overcoats, she breathed heavily and examined the weapon in her hands.

A 9mm Daewoo.

She ejected the magazine and counted thirteen rounds. Popped the magazine back in place and pulled the slide, chambering a round. She switched the safety off and cocked the hammer. Sneaked a look between the coats.

He has to have seen me.

A tingle of anxiety rushed up her spinal cord and she shivered. Just before she'd reached the coatroom she slowed just enough to catch a glimpse of him in her periphery. She hesitated a few seconds to afford him enough time to spot his prey.

He knows where I am. Why isn't he here yet?

Did he think it was too much of a risk to kill her inside the club? Was he waiting for her to make her exit before resuming the chase? Well, Kincaid wasn't going to give him the satisfaction. She could sit here all night. She'd wait for the coat-check girl to return to her post then try to get her attention without startling her. She'd ask her if she could borrow her cell phone and she'd call Janson, fill him in on her situation.

After a few minutes her haunches began to tire. She shifted to one knee but kept the handgun held out in front of her. She'd have to be cautious with all these people around.

No civilian casualties.

If he'd had to stash his gun, would she still be able to prove he'd been trying to kill her once police arrived on the scene?

Maybe she should aim for the leg. Then again, maybe she

wouldn't have to fire at all. Maybe she could pull the gun on him and lead him somewhere private. Ask him who he was working for. If he wouldn't talk, she could smack him in the teeth with the butt of her gun.

No torture.

She'd play things by ear. But first he had to come after her. First he had to show his stone-cold face. He'd have to confront her.

She shifted onto her haunches again, waiting.

Where are you, you son of a bitch?

ELEVEN

S in Bae watched the woman duck into the coatroom on the first floor of the T-Lound nightclub. He'd spent time in this building back when he was conducting surveillance on a target from the National Intelligence Service. His subject had been a young man from Jeollabuk-do, Korea's agricultural heartland, who was naturally enthralled with Seoul's party circuit. Sin Bae spent more time following him in bars and dance clubs than he had spying on him at his home and office combined. Many of the young man's meetings took place right here in T-Lound. Meetings with a supposed dissident from the North.

Once Sin Bae had collected enough evidence of the young man's betrayal, he expected his Cons Ops handler Ping to turn the photos and videos over to the South's National Intelligence Service. Instead Ping issued Sin Bae new orders handed down directly from Washington. He was to kill the young traitor. Catch him alone at his Seoul apartment and place a single bullet in the back of his skull. For all-too-personal reasons, Sin Bae was happy to do it.

He waded through the sea of teens and twenty-somethings drinking and tripping and rolling, trying to dance the drugs out of their systems. Keeping one eye on the coatroom, he moved toward the restrooms. Down that corridor, past the restrooms was a private room occupied by the club's manager, whom Sin Bae had passed on the stairs just minutes earlier. The office, which contained a small hidden door that opened onto the rear of the coatroom, would be empty. So as he slipped down the hallway, he dug into his pocket for his lock pick. Once he reached the door it took Sin Bae only seconds to gain access.

In the plush private office, Sin Bae flashed on the night he'd terminated the young man from the National Intelligence Service. It had been one of the few jobs over the years of his secret employment with Consular Operations that actually afforded Sin Bae pleasure. Killing was one thing. Executing a young man selling secrets to the North Korean regime in Pyongyang was quite another.

Sin Bae once lived in Pyongyang. As a young boy, he'd attended the city's schools, played ball on its streets, and pledged allegiance to the Communist Party. Although he came from a family of modest means, Sin Bae enjoyed his early childhood. But that childhood ended abruptly on a brisk September evening when his family's humble apartment in the city capital was visited by several agents from Kim Il-sung's security force.

He'd been seven when it happened. When his mother and father and sister and grandparents were forcefully taken from their home and tossed in a political prison camp called Yodok, based on allegations that Sin Bae's uncle had criticized and conspired against the party.

Sin Bae didn't truly understand what was happening. While he nearly hyperventilated from fear, his mother told him they were going on an adventure.

Sin Bae curled his fingers around the door handle and slowly twisted it in his hand. When he peered inside, the racks upon racks of heavy coats reminded him of Yodok winters.

When he and his family finally arrived at Yodok, Sin Bae's mother could lie to him no more. The camp was surrounded on every side by steep mountains and treacherous rivers and other natural obstacles, by barbed wire and watchtowers and uniformed men with large guns. The people already living at the camp appeared skinny and filthy; many of them seemed sickly and close to death. They wore rags and ate insects off the ground.

The night his family arrived and were thrown in their hut, Sin Bae held his younger sister Su-ra in his arms, rocking her gently as she cried herself to sleep.

Now as Sin Bae lightly stepped foot through the door leading to the rear of the coatroom, he pushed Yodok from his mind.

Jessica Kincaid sat on her haunches holding a handgun in front of her. He took another light step and was only a few feet behind her. He could sense her breathing heavily.

With his right hand he reached across his body and gripped his left cuff link.

He took another step forward then lifted his arms above Kincaid's head.

In a single fluid movement he extracted the garrote from his cuff link and wrapped the wire tight around her throat again.

He counted the seconds in Korean.

Il . . . i . . . sam . . . sa . . . o . . .

When he reached *shibo*, former Cons Ops agent Jessica Kincaid would be dead.

TWELVE

All Jessica Kincaid glimpsed was a sliver of his shadow. Instantly she shot backward off her haunches as the wire closed around her throat. Pushing her body back against his, she raised the Daewoo with both hands and attempted to aim the barrel of the gun over her shoulder. But with her breathing cut off she felt herself fading, sinking rapidly into a lethal panic.

Her finger hesitated over the trigger, just long enough to allow the assassin to knock the gun from her hand. But as his arm shot up to parry the Daewoo, the garrote mercifully loosened against Kincaid's throat, permitting her to manage a breath. When the gun hit the floor, her attacker immediately kicked it with all his strength. It spun in circles as it skidded, stopping several racks away, out of sight.

Kincaid reached back and clawed at his face. Felt her fingernails dig into his flesh. But the garrote continued to cut into her throat.

She had six, maybe eight seconds before she lost consciousness.

Within twelve she'd suffer irreparable brain damage.

After fifteen there would be no coming back.

With her breathing cut off she couldn't make a sound. Not that it would have helped her over the earsplitting music in the dance club. The coatroom was slightly quieter than the bar, but even in here a scream couldn't carry ten feet.

If she was going to survive, Kincaid would have to fight off the killer herself.

She leaned her chin forward and tried to throw her head back to break the killer's nose but couldn't gain the necessary momentum with the wire wrapped around her throat. All she had were her legs.

Although her legs were exhausted from the earlier chase, she felt her adrenaline pumping and her muscles tense. She bent at the knees and attempted a sudden thrust.

Her legs shot backward as her assassin fumbled for his footing. She thrust again and felt the killer's back slam into the wall. The wire loosened once more.

This was her last chance.

She threw her right hand forward then plunged her elbow backward into his abdomen. Behind her, the assassin seemed to momentarily lose his breath, so she grabbed hold of his right arm and attempted to fling his body over her shoulder.

He was too heavy, too strong.

You're not gonna die in a stinking coatroom, Kincaid!

But in the time it took her to attempt the throw, her attacker had regained his position and tightened the garrote around her throat again.

Kincaid flailed her arms helplessly. A white frame surrounded her vision on all sides and she suddenly felt as though she were drowning. She imagined herself struggling in the ocean, about to be pounded by a thirty-foot wave off Oahu's North Shore, with Paul Janson nowhere in sight.

Two seconds passed, then four.

When she reached six, she felt herself dropping into a deep, painful sleep from which she knew she would never wake up.

*   *   *

ON THE SECOND FLOOR of the T-Lound nightclub, Park Kwan spun around one last time, searching for the girl. But she seemed to have vanished into the ether. Deeply disappointed, he attempted a step back toward the bar and stumbled, catching himself on another man's shoulder.

The man shot him a look that made Park glad he was carrying his gun.

Oh hell, he thought. I'd probably better get home anyway.

He had work in the morning and was in for a battle. Already his head pounded; nausea had crept into his stomach.

His last few drinks suddenly shot like a geyser into his esophagus but he quickly managed to swallow them down.

Not here. Please, not here.

That would be the scene that finally ended his career.

At the bar he hailed the bartender and requested his check.

"No luck with the woman?" the bartender said in Korean as he swiped Park's credit card.

Park smiled. "So she *was* real after all. I thought I might have hallucinated the entire evening."

"No, she was quite real. And she was *hot*."

"And now," Park lamented, "she's gone."

The bartender nodded and set Park's tab down with a pen.

As he signed the receipt, Park wondered what had possessed the young woman to dance with him. Surely she hadn't put on that show for the price of two drinks of Kentucky bourbon.

Shit.

Gasping, he quickly checked his back pocket for his wallet.

It's gone.

When he looked up to inform the bartender that he'd been pickpocketed he realized he'd set his wallet down on the bar in order to retrieve his credit card. A lightning bolt of relief traveled through his body.

Then a thought.

Slowly, he reached inside his suit jacket.

"You OK?" the bartender said as he picked up the signed receipt. "You look as though you've seen a ghost."

Just my early retirement, Park thought.

But no, that wasn't all. Someone could get hurt.

"The girl," Park shouted, "did you see where she went? She took something from me."

The bartender pointed to the stairs. "I think I saw her heading back down to the first floor. She looked as though she was in a hurry. Do you want me to alert the bouncers at the front door?"

"No need," Park said. "I'll take care of this."

He snatched his credit card off the bar, stuck it into his wallet, and headed off. He couldn't allow anyone to know what had happened, not even the bouncers. If word got out that he'd brought his gun into a nightclub and had it stolen from him, he'd not only be out of a job, he'd be disgraced.

He snaked through the crowd down the stairs, his head rapidly clearing as the reality of his situation sank in.

On the first level he surveyed the dance floor and thought, It will be impossible to find her in here. But then, would she really steal a police officer's gun only to run downstairs and continue dancing? She'd have to be insane. She'd know that Park would realize his weapon was missing before too long. He was drunk, not catatonic.

She must have bolted outside.

He darted toward the front entrance then remembered the frigid temperatures and doubled back for his overcoat.

When he reached the coatroom, the girl who had taken his coat and given him his ticket was nowhere to be found.

So much for getting out of here in a hurry.

He gazed into the coatroom; there had to be at a least a few hundred coats and jackets. He glanced at his ticket and spotted a number. Surely each rack would be marked.

He stole one last glimpse over his shoulder to see whether the coat-check girl was returning, then opened the short gate and stepped inside.

He checked the ticket again—"92-E."

As he passed through the first aisle he felt confident he would find his coat. Then he would find the woman who had stolen his gun. He couldn't arrest her, of course. He'd be humiliated. But he could certainly threaten arrest, and interrogate her to find out why she'd done it. The reason, that was all he wanted from her now. Well, that and his service weapon.

His eyes suddenly caught on something, a small piece of black steel on the floor not ten feet away.

My gun!

He scrambled toward it, filled with new hope. He picked it up off the floor and examined the gun in his hands.

Wonderful, he thought. I shall live to work another day.

* * *

KINCAID THOUGHT SHE WAS seeing things. The garrote had cut off the oxygen to her brain. Her life was flashing before her eyes in reverse.

But, sweet Jesus, shouldn't it be moving a bit faster?

And why did it begin with the man she'd danced with upstairs? She had only a couple of seconds of consciousness left. Couldn't her mind just hit the highlights?

Wait, that is *the guy I danced with upstairs.*

She wondered whether she had the strength for one last move to try to get his attention.

She braced her body against her killer's as warm blood dripped down the collar of her shirt. She again kicked her feet, only this time out instead of down, barely reaching the nearest rack of coats.

The front tip of her foot knocked into one of the sleeves, causing it to sway.

She watched the man she'd been dancing with for a reaction.

After a moment that felt like forever, he twisted his neck and shot a wild look in her direction.

He'd sensed the movement and was trying to figure out precisely where it had come from.

Kincaid narrowed her eyes and concentrated on him. She looked down at his hands and felt a rush of excitement when she saw that he'd found the gun.

The drunken man finally turned his entire body toward Kincaid and her assassin. He spotted them. Froze for just an instant as he analyzed the situation then lifted his weapon and trained it on them.

Shit, he's not going to be able to get off a clean shot.

But the wire around her throat suddenly loosened and she knew that the killer had seen the man too.

Maybe just enough of a diversion.

She seized the opportunity, throwing her head forward then slingshotting it back into her killer's face.

This time her skull connected with his nose.

The garrote fell from around her throat.

She stole a deep breath then spun, throwing an elbow to the right side of the assassin's face. More blood shot from his nose.

With a well-placed kick, she swept his legs out from under him and he fell to the ground like a stone. But before she could pounce on top of him to pummel him, he popped back up to his feet and took off in a dash.

Kincaid started after him but only made it a few steps before she staggered into the wall, light-headed and short of breath.

She was alive and ready to go on the offensive. But reality dictated that she needed some time to recover from the attack.

For the time being, the bastard who'd tried to kill her would have to wait.

THIRTEEN

Seoul Station
Donja-dong, Yongsan-gu, Seoul

Paul Janson stepped outside the French bistro Café des Arts and proceeded into the dense flow of pedestrian traffic inside one of Seoul's primary rail stations. For the fifth time in as many minutes he checked his phone, but Kincaid still hadn't called.

Where the hell are you, Jessie?

He was also waiting for a callback from the thirteen-year-old prodigy Kang Jung, aka Lord Wicked, with information on the online user Draco_Malfoy95, aka Gregory Wyckoff. But either the precocious teen was taking her sweet time, or Wyckoff was every bit as good at burying himself in the depths of cyberspace as Morton and Berman had suggested, if not better. Janson assumed the latter.

Particularly since his lengthy captivity in Kabul, Janson considered himself a man of extraordinary patience. But all of his virtues tended to fly out the window where Jessica Kincaid's safety was involved.

Jessie. Every couple had its origin story—its cute little anecdote about how boy met girl, how girl played hard to get, how boy ultimately won girl's affections—and Janson and Kincaid's was as riveting as any.

They'd met in London. On a bright, clear afternoon in Regent's Park. Janson had been dodging a sniper's bullets when he finally realized his situation was becoming more precarious with every second he spent running. And he refused to die cowering behind a gazebo. He had to act, fast.

Turn the hunter into the hunted, the predator into the prey.

After surveying the park and locating then stealthily approaching the position of the sniper's nest, Janson silently hoisted himself up the trunk of the tree, reached for the metal rigging supporting the sniper's perch, and yanked hard, sending both the hunter and the hunted tumbling to the earth.

Following a significant struggle, Janson finally gained the superior position, only to hear the killer hiss, "*Get your stinking hands off me.*"

Only *your* sounded a hell of a lot more like *yer.*

When Janson finally looked into his would-be killer's face, he saw not the stone-hard visage of a former colleague as he'd expected, but the high cheekbones and piercing green eyes of a youthful American beauty.

Their relationship immediately following that first encounter was rocky to say the least. But as the truth became clearer, Kincaid turned from sworn enemy to friend. Then from friend to protégée, and from protégée to partner. Somewhere along that time line they became lovers and were lovers still, but for reasons they both understood too well, they would never be together in the most conventional sense of the word.

Waiting for his smartphone to buzz in his overcoat pocket as he strolled through the atrium of Seoul Station was no longer an option. He needed to take aggressive steps to locate Kincaid, and fast.

He reached into his pocket and closed his fingers around his phone just as it began to vibrate. He glanced at the screen, hoping to find Kincaid's number flashing before his eyes. But the call was coming from a Korean mobile number he didn't recognize. He lifted the phone to his ear, leaving no time to speculate.

Before Kincaid voiced her second word, he said, "Where the *hell* have you been?"

"I went dancing."

She sounded as though she'd contracted a nasty case of laryngitis in the hours since Janson last saw her. His ire instantly morphed back into concern; he knew something was wrong, and that it wasn't something as simple as a dead battery in her phone.

"Are you all right?" he said. "Where are you? I'll come and get you."

"Easy, cowboy. I'm fine. But it's become abundantly clear that someone doesn't want us nosing around in Lynell Yi's murder investigation."

"What happened?"

As Kincaid took him through the evening's events, beginning with her escape through Dosan Park, Janson moved quickly through the station, his eyes scanning every storefront and corridor for a discordant face or furtive movement.

Once she'd finished debriefing him, Janson attempted to set up a rendezvous in order to regroup and restrategize, but Kincaid wouldn't hear of it.

"We have even more ground to cover than before," she said, "because now we've got another question that needs to be answered. Whoever came after me has got to be Lynell Yi's killer. So while you're searching for Gregory Wyckoff, I have to go looking for the assassin. And after I find him and find out who he's working for, I'm going to dance on top of his corpse."

"You're *not* going to look for him, Jessie. At least not *alone*. I'll—"

"I'm *not* alone," she said. "I've made a friend."

Momentarily taken aback, he said, "What do you mean you've made a friend? Who? The guy you swiped the gun from?"

"His name's Park Kwan, and he saved my life, Paul."

"You just got finished telling me he was fall-down *drunk*."

"He's sitting at a table fifty feet away drinking coffee right now. He's sobering up."

Janson sighed. "Where *are* you, Jessie?"

"We're at a café in Gangnam. I'm calling you from Park Kwan's cell phone, so be sure to store the number. And don't worry; he's a cop."

Cops worried Janson every bit as much as everyone else, if not more.

"Is he involved in the metropolitan police investigation?" he said.

"No, all he knows about Yi's murder is what he's heard on the news and what I've told him."

As Janson approached one of Seoul Station's omnipresent mobile phone charging terminals, someone caught his eye. Actually, some*thing* caught his eye: a vintage pair of Matsuda eyeglasses. The Japanese designer frames were rare; he'd last seen them on a college student during a weekend jaunt with Kincaid to Newport, Rhode Island. He recalled commenting on them, complimenting the kid then telling Kincaid that he knew a man who would wear nothing else. In fact, he'd told her, that man would fly all the way to Tokyo in search of a new pair every time he needed to update his prescription lenses. From afar the glasses resembled John Lennon's iconic eyewear, but up close you could tell these frames were actually handcrafted pewter. Matsuda had stopped making them in the late nineties, and they were becoming more and more difficult to find.

But it wasn't just the glasses that grabbed Janson's attention; it was how the polished pewter shimmered against the backdrop of the owner's mocha face, how the glasses brought out the man's eyes, which were the color of dark chocolate.

Janson continued past the mobile phone charging station as though he hadn't recognized Vik Pawar. The Mumbai assassin, Janson knew, had been stationed in Pakistan in the spring of 2011, and was actually on standby to take out the man believed to be Osama bin Laden, when and if the president gave the order. Of course, certain voices in the White House argued that such a measure would be a revolting waste of political capital. Those voices ultimately prevailed, and SEAL Team Six raided the Abbottabad compound in a high-risk, high-reward mission dubbed Operation Neptune instead. But Pawar was *that* good— so good he'd been trusted by the commander in chief to take down the world's most wanted man following a grueling ten-year search.

Last Janson heard, Vik Pawar had been working inside Sri Lanka.

Like a light switch, a thought suddenly clicked in Janson's mind. "The garrote that man had around your throat," he said urgently into the phone, "do you know whether it was attached to a white-gold cuff link?"

"Sorry," Kincaid said, "but while I was being strangled I didn't think to check. Tell you what, Paul, when I find the son of a bitch, I'll be sure to ask."

Janson ignored her flip remark. "While you worked for Cons Ops did you ever hear of a covert operative named Sin Bae?"

"No," she said. "Who's Sin Bae?"

Janson's voice fell to barely a whisper as he tried to piece together the puzzle in his head. "If my gut feeling's right, he's the man who just tried to kill you."

* * *

ONCE HE FINALLY GOT Kincaid to promise to remain in the café with the cop until he called her back, Janson punched in the private number for Nam Sei-hoon.

"I was just about to call you," Nam said as soon as he surfaced on the line.

"What were you able to learn?"

Nam lowered the volume on a television in the background. "That the metropolitan police are no fans of the National Intelligence Service, for one."

"Interagency animosity, huh? Your country's becoming more like the States every day."

Janson slowed as he passed a mirrored wall. If Pawar was tailing him, he was apparently giving Janson some room. Or it could be that Pawar was merely instructed to watch him. But then if Janson was right about the identity of Kincaid's would-be killer, Pawar might well have passed surveillance on to another agent, someone whom Janson didn't recognize from his previous life in Cons Ops. In which case, he was in danger. Because a Cons Ops agent was just as likely to terminate a subject in public as he was in private. Janson knew some operatives who actually got off on the practice:

a drop down a steep flight of concrete stairs made to look like an accident; a poisonous pinprick or blow dart that caused an instant myocardial infarction. Under certain circumstances, the more public the setting the better. Often a good crowd could even negate the natural disadvantage of closed-circuit television cameras.

With enough people around, a spacious atrium like the one at Seoul Station could feel as tight as a coffin, as it did now.

Janson felt his pulse race now as it had not long ago in Shanghai. Being taken out in public had long been one of his greatest fears. There were so few ways to defend against such an attack. And seldom was there room to run. Like now. Janson didn't see these throngs of people as witnesses who could thwart an attempt on his life but as the iron bars of a cage impeding his escape.

"I was finally able to gain access to the boy's computers," Nam Sei-hoon said in Janson's ear. "As you suggested might be the case, the hard drives have been wiped."

Janson cursed.

"Not so fast, Paul. Remember, I am not a man without resources. I've had one of my trusted allies in the cyber-intelligence unit take a look at these hard drives, and he was able to restore some of the information that had been erased."

"Anything useful?"

"Not to a novice like myself. But my ally in the cyber-intel unit was able to identify one of the individuals whom Gregory Wyckoff communicated with online via an IRC."

"An IRC?"

"An Internet Relay Chat. I'm told they're used for real-time text conversations. Communication is by invitation only, and the IRC the Wyckoff kid used offers a generous amount of anonymity. But it just so happens that one of the individuals the kid chatted with is being watched vigorously by my friend in the cyber-intel unit."

"Why might that be?"

"This individual is the leader—or alleged leader—of a left-leaning political hacktivist community here in South Korea."

"Like the Anonymous organization in the West?"

"Very much like them. Here, they're known as the Hivemind. The collective has been a thorn in the side of our present political leadership. Over the past two years, they defaced the president's official website and disseminated private emails stolen from government servers. Now they are believed to be working on an elaborate plan to rig our next elections."

"Who is this leader the kid chatted with?" Janson said anxiously. "What's his name and where can I find him?"

"Paul, this is a delicate matter. If you approach this individual for information, you must be careful not to alert him to our ongoing investigation. You cannot reveal how you obtained his identity or location. You must go in with a solid cover story that will stand up to close scrutiny."

"Discretion's my specialty," Janson assured him. "After I leave him, he'll know even *less* than he did before I got there." He glanced at his watch. "But listen, Gregory Wyckoff is running out of time here. What's this hacker's name?"

"He goes by the username Cy. Cy spelled as it is in the word *cyber*."

Nam gave Janson the hacker's real name and address.

"Got it. Thanks, old friend."

"Let me know if you need anything else, Paul."

Janson surreptitiously glanced over his shoulder, scanning again for Pawar or another familiar face.

"As a matter of fact," Janson said into the phone, "I have one more favor to ask of you."

FOURTEEN

At the taxi stand outside the station, Janson slipped into the rear of the orange Hyundai and informed the driver of his destination. As the taxi pulled out of the station's parking lot, Janson's eyes remained glued to the rearview. He identified three distinct pairs of headlights. One of the vehicles trailing them was a taxi similar to the one Janson was in; another was a shuttle bus. The last and most suspicious appeared to be a dark Samsung SM5. The driver appeared to be young and female; the passenger seat was empty.

Janson's taxi traveled north past City Hall then made a right onto Jongno 1GA and gained speed until it passed Tower Records. In the rearview Janson could still make out a pair of headlights belonging to a dark SM5. But since he'd momentarily lost sight of the vehicle, he couldn't be sure it was the same one that had followed his taxi out of the parking lot.

Nighttime traffic on 1GA slowed the taxi to a speed below ten miles per hour. In the rearview the dark SM5 remained three or four cars back, even when a lane conveniently opened up on the left. Janson could no longer tell whether the driver was male or female, but he continued to observe only one head.

Janson's eyes ping-ponged between the speedometer and rearview as his taxi passed a number of familiar fast-food restaurants then slowed to a speed below five miles per hour as it turned right onto a minor road called Sup'Yodaragil. As the driver made the turn, Janson gripped the door handle and waited until he could no longer see the SM5's headlights in the rearview, then he opened the rear passenger door, tucked his left shoulder, and tumbled out of the moving vehicle. He rolled beneath a parked Kia Sorento and watched as the dark SM5 made the right turn after the taxi.

From his vantage point under the Kia, Janson recognized the driver as the young female who'd followed his taxi out of the station. He waited sixty seconds then popped back out from under the Kia and walked briskly back toward the main road, crossing a McDonald's parking lot.

Though he didn't raise his arm, another orange Hyundai entered the lot and rolled to a stop directly in front of him. Janson quickly opened the rear passenger-side door and jumped inside.

Inside the taxi, Janson said nothing. The driver already knew his destination.

* * *

NIKA VLASIC ANNOUNCED the taxi's position as she completed the right onto Sup'Yodaragil. She waited a moment in silence. When she heard no response, she touched the Bluetooth device in her right ear to make certain she hadn't lost it when she swung her head around to make sure she could pull off the freeway without getting T-boned by a carful of drunk teenagers peeling out of the McDonald's drive-through.

Finally, Clarke spoke, his voice brimming with incredulousness. "He's heading *south* again?"

"Affirmative," Nika said. "And it's a back road. I'm going to need someone to pick him up before the next turn."

She checked herself in the mirror, proud that she could finally speak American English with barely a whisper of her Croatian accent.

"Max will have him at the next intersection," Clarke said in a huff. "You're about to pass Paik Hospital. Make the next left onto Mareunnaegil."

"Copy," she said, instinctively tugging on the leather sleeve of her jacket to hide the bracelet tattooed around her right wrist.

"Nika, you know these roads. Any idea where the fuck he's headed?"

"Negative. There's a major artery a little farther south, but he could've taken it straight from the rail station."

"Shit. You still have a visual?"

She narrowed her eyes and focused on the rear window of the taxi. "Affirmative. Subject is in the rear, behind the passenger seat."

A rare flutter caught in her stomach. During her Cons Ops training Nika had often heard anecdotes involving the operative known as the Machine. Now she was a few car-lengths behind him, and depending on how the rest of the evening went, she might have the opportunity to meet him, maybe to seduce him. She might even be given the directive to kill him, which would instantly transform Nika Vlasic into a legend in her own right.

She grinned at the thought. Who in her village would have guessed that Nika Vlasic, the jade-eyed, raven-haired girl with a faceful of freckles—the product of a rape in the name of Serbian ethnic cleansing—would have risen from the ashes of the Croats' war for independence and been handed an opportunity to live the American dream?

In her rearview mirror, she watched Max Kolovos pull up behind her in a silver Kia Morning. She brought the SM5 to a stop at the following intersection and made the left turn past Paik Hospital. She checked to make certain the Bluetooth in her ear was off, then switched on the radio to await further instructions.

* * *

JANSON'S SECOND TAXI slowed as it approached the campus of Sungkyunkwan University. SKKU, a private research university in the northern section of central Seoul, was widely considered one of the world's top institutions for higher learning. So it didn't surprise Janson when he was told that the university's main campus was where he'd find the hacker known worldwide as Cy.

"Thank you," Janson said into his phone.

"You are very welcome," replied Nam Sei-hoon. "My agent tells me that the taxi is still being followed but by a different vehicle. A silver late-model Kia Morning."

"Great. I've only seen a couple hundred of those since I arrived in Seoul."

"It's a very popular vehicle," Nam conceded. "I will advise you when—and at this point *if*—they discover they are following an imposter."

Janson smiled. Rolling out of the backseat of a moving car during a slow right turn was an old-school ruse he hadn't used in years, and he might never have the opportunity again. "Please pass along my thanks to your man. I know folding yourself like a pretzel and hiding on the floor in the rear of a Hyundai is no picnic. But he was the consummate professional. Even I barely knew he was there."

Nam chuckled. "I would have done the deed myself, Paul. But my head would not have been visible in the backseat once I popped up to take your place. Your pursuers would have thought you magically vanished. Maybe not so startling given your reputation."

"Well, at least you would have been more comfortable."

"You're quite certain you have no tail on you now?"

"Free as a bird," Janson said, checking the rearview. "Thanks again."

The taxi pulled to a stop at the curb. Janson thanked Nam's driver and stepped out of the vehicle into the cruel cold. He turned up the collar of his overcoat and pressed his chin to his chest, wondering if he shouldn't have had the driver take him right up to the building where he and Cy had agreed to meet. But then the fewer people who knew Janson's precise location, the better. People could be bought. Could be tortured or otherwise manipulated. Even the most loyal of agents could be turned.

FIFTEEN

E dward Clarke sat quiet and still in his dark office, studying Google Earth's detailed map of Seoul.

Where the hell is he going?

According to Max Kolovos, Janson's taxi had just circled the newly constructed Dongdaemun Design Plaza, which meant that despite Clarke's best efforts Janson had probably already made his tail and was sending Clarke's assets on a wild goose chase around Seoul.

A private line on Clarke's phone glowed red and he lifted the receiver. "Where are we with Kincaid's phone?" he said, no longer trying to mask his annoyance.

"We were able to recapture the signal," Hong said.

Finally. Clarke ran a rough hand through his brittle, thinning hair but somehow managed to hold his tongue. At least for the moment.

"But you're not going to like the result," Hong added.

"What do you mean?"

"The signal is still coming from Dosan Park."

"She returned to the *park*?"

"Negative, sir. I have two men there and there's no sign of her. We believe she may have dropped her phone earlier when your asset first gave chase. It appears to be the only explanation."

"Un-*fucking*-believable," Clarke said.

The ambassador's people had gone through the trouble—and, moreover, taken the risk—of placing a remote GPS device in Kincaid's cell phone while she was at the embassy, and they *still* couldn't track her across a single city.

"Are they at least looking for the phone?" Clarke said. "Maybe Janson sent something to her that might help us."

"Um, negative, sir."

"Well, why the hell *not*?"

"Sir, it is pitch black in Dosan Park. Do you really want my men scouring the grounds with flashlights?"

Sarcastic prick.

Clarke hung up the phone. He considered contacting Ping again but then thought better of it. He'd been receiving bad news from Shanghai all night. If Sin Bae had located Gregory Wyckoff, Clarke would have received a call.

Shit. This night was going all to hell. Worst of all, with Clarke on the opposite side of the globe, there was damn near nothing he could do about any of it.

* * *

Nika Vlasic intercepted the orange Hyundai as it turned south onto Dasanno. "Got him," she said.

She watched the silver Kia Morning break out of the right lane and bust an illegal U-turn like a drunk who'd just spotted a DUI checkpoint up ahead.

Idiot, she thought. If Janson hadn't made his tail yet, surely that move would give them away. Janson wasn't stupid, after all. On the contrary, by all accounts he was rather brilliant.

She pressed the button on her Bluetooth. "I have Jan—" *Shit.* She quickly corrected herself. "I have Trotter. Any instructions?"

Nika thought it was ridiculous to be using a code name for Janson, but Clarke had insisted upon it, as usual. *"You never know who's listening,"* he'd said.

"Yeah," Clarke said. "When the taxi stops, I want you to make contact."

A surge of excitement pulsed through Nika's veins. Even under the thick black leather she could feel the gooseflesh forming from her wrists up to her shoulders.

She instinctively yanked her sleeve down to cover her tattoo bracelet. She wasn't ashamed of the tattoo, of course, though she often had to hide it when she was conducting surveillance. Anything that made you stick out was a crippling disadvantage in covert work. But she *was* admittedly embarrassed by the scar the bracelet was disguising. She thought it made her appear weak and stupid, like a defenseless child. She'd received the tattoo when she was sixteen years old, but she'd been tugging at her sleeve in order to cover her scar since she was twelve. Ever since she'd attempted to end her hard life.

"What shall I do once I make contact?" she said.

"For the time being, just keep him busy."

"Acknowledged," she said with a mischievous grin.

Little did Edward Clarke know, she'd been hoping he'd say that.

* * *

Twenty minutes later Clarke lifted the receiver to his ear.

"It wasn't him." Nika sounded like a child who'd been sent to the principal's office; her voice betrayed the accent she'd shed long ago.

Clarke immediately simmered, felt his anger rising like lava, traveling north up his neck into his ears. In the dim light of his office, he could feel his lobes glowing red.

He drew a deep breath and controlled his voice. "How the hell did that happen?"

"I don't know. Jan—" She cursed under her breath. "*Trotter* stepped into that taxi at Seoul Station and I never once lost sight of him. So you'll have to ask Max."

"So who the hell got *out* of the taxi and where?"

"The taxi pulled into a lot near the plaza and dropped the man near a bar. I thought the situation was perfect. I parked and followed the man inside. He actually held the door for me."

"Who *was* it?"

"I've no idea. It was a Korean man. Younger than Trotter but about his size."

With his free hand Clarke rubbed at the knot forming in the back of his neck. If neither Nika nor Max had fucked up, then Janson had fooled them. And if he fooled them, he didn't do it on his own. At least two men had helped him, the driver and the imposter. And if Janson sneaked out of the taxi while it was out of sight, he probably wasn't traveling on foot. Which meant there would be a second vehicle with a second driver, a third individual overall.

Who the hell is helping him?

Clarke hung up the phone. His primary objective now was to learn the identity of Janson's accomplices. Then shut them down.

SIXTEEN

P aul Janson ducked into the inky darkness of the dormitory basement with his hands in the air, as instructed. He'd stuffed his phone into his pocket and pressed a Bluetooth device into his ear.

In his ear the synthesized voice said, "Lose the overcoat."

Janson sighed. "Are you kidding me? It's colder in here than it is outside."

"Remove the overcoat," the synthesized voice said. "I will not ask you again."

Janson slipped out of the coat and held it out at his side. He couldn't see a thing, so he wasn't sure where to set it down.

"Drop it on the floor," the voice commanded.

"It's cashmere," Janson said through gritted teeth.

Janson briefly regretted allowing Kang Jung to set up the meeting. The precocious thirteen-year-old had called while he was en route to the university. His initial plan had been to take Cy by surprise. Thanks to Nam, Janson knew the hacker's real name, knew precisely where he lived on campus. But when Kang Jung called with little information on Gregory Wyckoff, aka Draco_Malfoy95, he impulsively asked her if she could introduce him to the head of Hivemind. Janson hoped that by allowing Cy to maintain his anonymity (at least in his own mind), the hacker would be more forthcoming with information.

Following several calls to Janson and presumably multiple IRC chats with Cy, Kang Jung finally told Janson that Cy would meet him for a price. Janson haggled. In the end, they agreed on $1,200.

Now Cy, unaware that Janson already *knew* his identity, was making him jump through these ridiculous hoops. But Janson didn't want to say anything, didn't want to scare the kid away. After all, as infamous as he might be online, the hacker was just a college student in real life.

Janson released his overcoat and it dropped to the floor. Two small hooded men, presumably fellow students, approached him from behind, performed a perfunctory pat-down and snatched his overcoat, then quickly retreated into the shadows.

The synthesized voice in Janson's ear said: "There is a metal chair twelve steps straight ahead. Walk to it and sit down."

Janson lowered his arms and moved forward, his footfalls echoing off concrete walls he couldn't see. After ten steps, he reached out in front of him and felt the metal back of a folding chair. He maneuvered around the chair and sat down.

"Can I have my overcoat back now?"

One of the small men emerged from the corner of the room and flung Janson's coat over his head like a blanket over a birdcage at naptime. When Janson removed the coat from his head, a large figure was sitting approximately ten feet away from him. The individual held a flashlight in his lap, the beam lighting his face, which was hidden behind a mask. A Guy Fawkes mask—the visage that had become ubiquitous since the emergence of online groups like Anonymous and international movements like Occupy Wall Street.

You've got to be kidding me, Janson thought.

Still, he had to admit that, combined with the voice synthesizer, the effect was creepy. The leader of Hivemind clearly had a flair for the dramatic.

"You have my money?" the mechanical voice said.

Janson reached into his pocket and slowly withdrew twelve one-hundred-dollar bills in US currency.

"You've come to me for information," Cy said as he counted the bills.

"That's right." Janson didn't want to spend any more time in this basement than he absolutely had to, so he came right to the point. "I'm looking for a young man who goes by the username Draco-underscore-Malfoy-nine-five. Lord Wicked advised me that you might be familiar with that name?"

Cy folded the bills and stuffed them into a shirt pocket. "I am."

"Can you tell me where to find him?"

"Why are you looking for him?"

Janson didn't hesitate. "I was hired by his father. The kid needs some help. He's in trouble with the law and we have reason to believe he's also in grave danger."

Janson stared at the grinning mask, waiting for a response.

"Draco is a member of the Hivemind," Cy finally said through the synthesizer. "The Hivemind takes care of its own."

Janson masked his frustration and nodded. "That's why I've come to you. I need to find Draco before the police do. Before *anyone* else does."

"I do not know where he is," Cy said. "I last chatted with him roughly ninety-six hours ago."

"Four days ago?" Janson said. "Do you recall the conversation? Did Draco say anything that might explain why people are after him?"

Cy said nothing. Janson wished he could observe the expression behind the mask.

"What's the purpose of the Hivemind?" Janson prodded. "What does the Hivemind do?"

Although both Nam Sei-hoon and Kang Jung had furnished him with this information, Janson hoped his questions would serve to lay a foundation and get Cy talking. Like a good trial lawyer, Janson prided himself on his ability to elicit knowledge that a witness wasn't eager to relay.

Sure enough, the hacker straightened in his chair and puffed out his considerable chest. Boldly, he declared: "We speak for those who cannot speak for themselves. We steal secrets from the powerful and disseminate them to the powerless. We make the opaque transparent. We bring light to darkness. Because we believe that people should not fear their leaders. Leaders should fear their people."

"Is that why Draco is in danger?" Janson said. "Did he steal secrets? Did he discover something he wasn't supposed to?"

"Four days ago," Cy said, "Draco contacted me through an IRC. It was a private channel, but Draco said that he could not take any chances with the information he'd unearthed. He asked to meet with me in person. He said it was urgent."

"And?"

"And he remained cryptic. All he said was that he turned up something big. In his words, something 'earth-shattering.'"

A glimmer of hope started to swell in Janson's chest. "Did you meet with him?"

"Despite my misgivings, we made an arrangement to meet the

next day," Cy said, "in a square, not far from here. Unfortunately, Draco never showed up."

The hope in Janson's chest instantly began to deflate. "He had to say *something*," Janson pressed. "Something that will help me find him. Something that will give me a clue about what he discovered or at least who it involved."

Cy sat perfectly still, the beam of light held steady on his mask. "We have never seen each other," he said finally. "So when I agreed to meet with him, I asked how I would know him. He said he would be wearing a light-blue baseball cap with the logo of the Tar Heels from the University of North Carolina."

"Anything else?"

"He told me to approach him slowly and sit down next to him on the bench. Then I was to provide him a code word."

"What code word?"

"The code word was Diophantus."

SEVENTEEN

Where are you?" Janson asked.

"We're still in Gangnam. We're going to return to Dosan Park to look for my phone."

"Don't bother, Jessie. If your phone wasn't compromised at the embassy, it is now."

"At the embassy? So you're sure it's—"

"It's them, Jess. You were right."

Janson could almost hear her smile over the phone. It didn't matter that both their lives were on the line, not to mention the fate of Gregory Wyckoff and undoubtedly others. Jessica Kincaid was right, and though she might not rub it in with words, she'd allow a few moments of unbroken silence to do it for her. Janson couldn't help but smile himself; it was one of the many things he loved about her.

"What did you find out?" she finally said.

"Hold on." Janson tried the door to a badly beaten black Daewoo, and it opened. He quickly ducked inside and slammed the door. He scanned the dorm parking lot but it was quiet. In this weather, students who weren't studying were drinking their asses off indoors, like civilized people.

He reached under the steering wheel, manipulated the wires, and started the engine. He backed out of the space and turned left out of the lot.

"Listen, Jessie," he said. "There's been a slight change in plans."

He told her what he knew. It wasn't much, but it was enough to allow him to determine their next move. The attack by Sin Bae and the presence of Vik Pawar had finally convinced Janson that Senator Wyckoff had been right from the start—Consular Operations *was* involved in the murder of Lynell Yi and the subsequent frame of Gregory Wyckoff. Now he and Kincaid needed to find out why.

"Once I left Cy at the university," Janson said into his Bluetooth, "I checked the nearby square where Cy and Gregory Wyckoff were supposed to meet. I searched the grounds, under the benches, even emptied the trash receptacles. And nothing."

"Then?" Kincaid said.

"As I was leaving the square I pulled out my BlackBerry and Googled the name Diophantus."

Cy had conceded that the name Diophantus meant nothing to him. He'd intended to look it up on the Internet once he left his IRC chat with Wyckoff but then he'd become sidetracked with another incoming instant message.

"Is that something you'd usually do?" Janson had asked. "Google a word or a name you weren't familiar with?"

"Sure," he'd said. "In our online forums, Draco constantly threw out esoteric terms I'd have to look up. He is a smart guy. Probably the smartest link in the Hivemind."

"At the square," Janson told Kincaid, "I scanned the Wikipedia page for Diophantus."

"Who was he?" she said.

"He was a mathematician in ancient Greece. Third century. People call him the father of algebra. His work evidently led to tremendous advances in mathematics and the study of Diophantine equations."

"Which means?"

Janson picked up on the impatience in Kincaid's voice.

"As far as I could tell, Jessie, it meant absolutely nothing. Diophantus looked to me like a seventeen-hundred-year-old dead end."

Janson turned onto a main road and continued. "If Gregory Wyckoff attempted to send Cy a message with the code word, Cy didn't get it. But then, Cy hadn't known the reference. So I thought maybe someone else might. I called Nam Sei-hoon. I figured if Nam didn't understand the reference, maybe his agent from the cyber-intelligence unit would."

"What did Nam say?"

"Nothing. My call went straight to voice mail. Nam was probably at home and sound asleep with his wife by the time I called. I left a brief message and returned to the university to find a vehicle."

The dorm parking lot had seemed like the ideal place to start. Earlier, Janson had noticed a number of old beaters that wouldn't present a challenge for him to break into and hot-wire.

As he searched the lot, he pressed his Bluetooth into his ear to call Kincaid. The wind was blowing viciously and he didn't think Jessie would be able to hear him if he used the handset.

As he scrolled through his contacts for Park Kwan's mobile number his eyes caught instead on Kang Jung's. The thirteen-year-old would no doubt be out cold, but he could leave her a message to call him back. It was another Hail Mary, but Janson figured that given enough shots in the dark he might eventually hit a target.

To his surprise, Kang Jung not only answered her phone but sounded alert.

"Sorry to call so late," Janson said. "Did I wake you?"

"Nope. I'm still studying."

"At this hour?"

"It's why man invented Adderall."

Janson felt a pang of pity as he had earlier at her apartment. For the moment he pushed it aside and said, "Does the name Diophantus mean anything to you?"

"Uh, the father of algebra and Diophantine geometry? Sure. I mean, I don't have posters of him on my walls or anything, but..."

The corner of Janson's mouth turned up in a half smile. "Who *do* you have posters of? Justin Bieber?"

"Please."

"Sorry."

Janson could hear her fingers gliding over a keyboard.

"So, what do you need to know about him?" she said.

"Gregory Wyckoff mentioned the name in an IRC chat," Janson said. "I was just wondering if it meant anything among cyber-enthusiasts like yourself."

"Hmm. Interesting," she said following a few moments of silence.

"What is?"

"I'm on his Wikipedia page."

"Yeah, that's where I went. Unfortunately, it wasn't very helpful."

She sighed. "No offense, but that's probably because you don't know what to look for."

"Are you implying that you do?"

"I do."

"And you found something?"

"I did."

"Care to share it?" Janson tried to keep the skepticism out of his voice.

"Did you happen to notice that the page was recently updated?"

"So?"

"So. It's not a hard-and-fast rule, but generally speaking there aren't many updates for guys who died seventeen centuries ago in Alexandrian Greece. Miley Cyrus, sure. Justin Bieber, absolutely. But as far as I can see, Diophantus isn't scheduling any new world tours or running around with Lil Za egging houses in Calabasas."

"Point taken." With Kang Jung still on the line, Janson returned to his browser and typed in the term "Diophantus." He clicked on the link to the mathematician's Wikipedia page. "Can you tell who updated the page?"

"Of course. I'm going into the page's history now."

He waited a moment. "Was it Gregory Wyckoff?"

"No, the username is just a series of letters and numbers that don't seem to mean anything. But that doesn't mean it wasn't Gregory who made the changes. It may be the changes themselves that are important."

"But anybody could view this page, right? So he couldn't have—"

"That's the *brilliance* of it," she said. "You can hide a message in plain sight."

Janson began scanning the text: the mathematician's biography and bibliography, his professional history and influence. Nothing appeared out of the ordinary, nothing seemed out of place.

"Looks like another dead end," he muttered.

"Not so fast. I think I found it. Let me just cut and paste this and..."

"And what?"

"I got it!"

"Got what?"

"Look at the introduction," she said. "Fourth sentence from the top."

Janson silently read the sentence:

Diophantus coined the term χψχονταχτψυνφινηοδπκ *to refer to an approximate equality.*

"That's the sentence that's been changed," she said. "Specifically, the term itself."

"The one in ancient Greek?"

"That's the thing though. It's *not* ancient Greek."

"Then what is it?"

"On first sight," she said, "it's gibberish, just a string of symbols. But when I cut and paste the term into a Word document and change the font, it becomes something else entirely. Something completely unrelated to Diophantus and mathematics."

"What's the message?" Janson said anxiously.

"I just texted it to you."

Janson exited his browser and opened his text message. It read: *cycontactyunjinhodprk*

In his ear, Kang Jung said, "It reads, 'Cy, contact Yun Jin-ho, DPRK.' DPRK is the—"

"The Democratic People's Republic of Korea."

"Right," she said. "The official name for our lovely neighbor to the north."

* * *

IN JANSON'S MIND, the consequences of Wyckoff's capture by police were now even greater. If they found the kid before Janson and Kincaid did, Wyckoff was as good as dead. Likewise, if Cons Ops found him. But Janson couldn't risk devoting the entire mission to looking for Gregory Wyckoff, because clearly there were larger stakes at play. Cy's admission that he'd received an urgent message from Wyckoff four days ago telling Cy that he'd discovered something—in Wyckoff's words, something *"earth-shattering"*—meant not only that the senator's son might indeed be innocent, but that he might hold information about powerful world players and events, which if they were allowed to unfold could reverberate across the region, if not the globe.

"You need to search for the kid," Janson said. "If you're certain you can trust him, use Park Kwan. But he can't inform anyone in his department. We don't know who else is in on this, and we can't afford to trust anyone."

"All right," Kincaid said. "What about you?"

"I'm going to follow the only lead Gregory Wyckoff left. I'm going to try to find out what it is the kid discovered. Because if Cons Ops gets their hands on him before we do, the kid is dead. And we can't allow his secret, whatever it is, to die with him. Because given everything we know—about him and about his passions—there may well be countless lives at stake."

"So where are you going now?"

"I'm going to visit an old friend."

"In Seoul?"

"Not in Seoul," Janson said. "I'm heading north, into the demilitarized zone."

PART II

"An Intelligence Black Hole"

EIGHTEEN

Daeseong-dong, aka Freedom Village
Demilitarized Zone (DMZ), South Korea

I need to cross into the North."

Janson's words froze Jina Jeon at her kitchen table. She said nothing, didn't so much as blink. Janson attempted to read her but as close as they'd once been, Jina Jeon was one woman whose head Paul Janson had never been able to enter. Even now he couldn't tell whether she was frozen in surprise or fear, or something else entirely. Jina Jeon remained as impenetrable as the border on which she lived.

Janson snapped his fingers in front of her eyes, hoping to make light of their conversation. "Janson to Jeon," he said. "You there?"

Finally, she shook her head. Jina Jeon was every bit as beautiful as the first time he'd ever seen her. Somehow she'd maintained every scintilla of youth, her skin smooth, her jet-black hair long and shiny.

"You're not *seriously* considering infiltrating the North, are you?" she said.

Janson leaned back in his chair in the modern kitchen. Gazed out the window onto the acres of farmland that made this contemporary home feel so anachronistic.

"After all these years," he said without the hint of a smile, "do you really need to ask me that?"

Although she didn't say anything, Janson knew from her expression that she did. And he understood. How could he not have anticipated her reaction? She'd changed her life in immeasurable ways; he *knew* that when he decided to come to her for help. Hell, he'd been the one responsible for those changes, even if she'd never know it herself. The Phoenix Foundation had remade her, from a cold-blooded covert agent to a warmhearted farmer living a peaceful existence with her mother in a quiet village. Albeit a village less than a mile from one of the most dangerous places on earth.

"Why?" she said. "Why in the world would you want to cross into the North?"

"I have to find someone," he said.

Once Kang Jung texted him with Gregory Wyckoff's message to Cy—*Contact Yun Jin-ho, DPRK*—Janson thought he'd need to start from scratch again.

"Christ," he'd said to the thirteen-year-old through his Bluetooth. "That's going to be impossible. Like finding a particular grain of sand on a seven-mile stretch of beach."

His thoughts fleetingly returned to Kincaid and her two-piece on the white sands of Waikiki.

"Not necessarily," the teenager said. "Think about it. The citizenry in the North aren't allowed to contact anyone outside their country. If they were to get caught, they'd spend the next decade of their life in a gulag—*and* they'd be condemning their family to the same fate."

"In other words, we can surmise that this Yun Jin-ho must have safe access to a telephone or a computer that can reach outside North Korea's borders."

"Exactly," Kang Jung said. "And the only people who have such access work directly for the regime in Pyongyang."

"Great," Janson said. "And Pyongyang only has a population of what? Three million?"

"More like three and a half. But I might be able to get you even closer. I can hack into the North's system."

"Isn't that dangerous?"

"I do it all the time," she said. "Let me try to find this guy for you. I'll call you back in one hour. Sooner if I get lucky."

Before he could thank her the line went dead in his ear.

"Who?" Jina Jeon said, rising from her chair and drifting over to the refrigerator. She opened the door and pulled out a bottle of Pulmuwon Spring water. Twisted the cap and put the mouth of the plastic bottle to her lips as though she was suddenly parched. "Who do you need to find in the North?"

"A man named Yun Jin-ho. He works at the palace in Py-ongyang."

Jina Jeon stared at him in disbelief. "You have no idea what you're asking. It's almost impossible to cross into the North. And even if you could, you'd never make it to the capital city, let alone the palace itself. Paul, it's a *suicide* mission."

"I have to try."

"Why? This Yun Jin-ho, what can he tell you? The people loyal to the regime would die before they gave you information. Especially those who work directly for that madman in the palace. Did you not hear? Kim Jong-un had his own uncle killed. The Great Successor ordered that his uncle—his own flesh and blood—be stripped naked and thrown into a cage to be eaten alive by a pack of ravenous dogs that had been intentionally starved for days!"

Janson smiled. "He had his uncle executed, yes, I'll give you that. But the Hong Kong paper that originally printed the story about the dogs is a rag. Even the US State Department, which is apt to believe anything, thinks that the part about Jang Song-thaek being eaten alive is dubious."

She shook her head wildly and sat across from him again. "You are splitting hairs. The manner of execution does not matter."

"I'm sure it mattered to Kim's uncle."

"This is not a time for jokes, Paul. You don't understand; the fact that we don't know the true story is at least partly the point I'm making. We know *nothing* about the palace. Pyongyang is an intelligence black hole."

Janson was sure he'd heard the expression used in reference to North Korea before. Possibly from Nam Sei-hoon himself. But more likely from the former director of Consular Operations, Derek Collins.

"Not quite a black hole," he said, debating how much to tell her.

After forty-five minutes Janson had received a callback from Kang Jung. She'd continued searching for intel on Yun Jin-ho. And she'd found some information from an unlikely source, namely the database of South Korea's National Intelligence Service.

Yun Jin-ho was actually an NIS asset being run by Nam Sei-hoon. But Janson couldn't risk asking Nam because he'd ultimately have to tell his old friend where he'd received the information. And he couldn't do that, or Kang Jung could wind up in a juvenile detention center, or worse.

Janson looked into Jina Jeon's eyes and decided he could trust her with the information, that it would never go any farther than this room. "Yun Jin-ho is a spy," he told her. "He's selling secrets to South Korea. I need to find him without exposing him to Pyongyang. *And* without alerting his handlers in Seoul."

Jina Jeon gazed deeply into Janson's eyes, as though she were looking directly into his soul. "Paul, you have to tell me everything. If I'm going to help you, you can't leave me in the dark. What are the stakes here? Because what you're about to attempt could have lethal consequences. I need to know that this is worth the risk before I offer my help."

"All right," Janson said, leaning forward, setting his elbows down on the table in front of him. "Here's what I know..."

* * *

"WE'LL NEED EQUIPMENT," Janson said as he and Jina Jeon labored north against the freezing wall of wind on the open field.

"Remember our friend Cal Auster?"

"The weapons dealer?"

Jina Jeon smiled mirthlessly. "None other."

"Last I heard he was working in Turkmenistan."

"Not anymore. He screwed over some radicalized Pakis and went into hiding."

"Where is he located now?"

"Not far from here, actually. Several miles south between my village and Seoul."

Janson lowered his head, hoping to hide how heavily the cold was affecting him, how he could feel it in the marrow of his bones. Jina Jeon, for the most part, appeared immune to the frigid temperatures, nearly as impervious to the arctic winds as she had initially been to Janson's arguments for crossing into the North. There was a time, Janson recalled, not so long ago, when mundane conditions such as inclement weather weren't an operational factor for him either. But that was clearly no longer the case, and to Janson this subtle detraction drilled into him the fact that he was no longer young, that his days of feeling invincible were long over, that his constitution—his health, his strength, his resilience to the elements—would only roll downhill from here.

He wasn't old, at least in terms of his numerical age. Sure, Jessie was much younger, and while sometimes (in private) she made *him* feel younger, more and more often her presence (in public) made him feel like a fossil. Although she didn't look it, Jina Jeon was much closer to Janson in age, and for the first time he wondered if his unwillingness to settle down with Kincaid stemmed from more than simply his petrifying fear that he would lose her to violence just as he'd lost his wife, Helene, and their unborn child.

Our child would have been how old now?

Janson winced. For a man who didn't believe in torture, he could certainly do a number on himself every so often. He couldn't help it. Even after all this time, the irony continued to eat at him. That Helene, a free spirit, a virtual pacifist, had been taken by violence instead of him. That *she*—someone sympathetic to the Kagama cause—was murdered by the KLF, a group that purported to fight for the freedom and safety of their people. But the Kagama Liberation Front were terrorists, nothing more, nothing less. It was often said that one man's terrorist was another man's freedom fighter, but that was bullshit as far as Janson was concerned. Sure, there was a fine line between the two, but a line nonetheless, a line any genuine soldier would recognize. Freedom fighters didn't target civilians, didn't torture, didn't kill those who weren't trying to kill them. Stepping over that line turned any soldier into a terrorist. Which was why he and everyone who worked with him were required to follow the rules, the Janson Rules, the rules that drew a clear and unambiguous line in the sand. The rules were what made Janson and his people soldiers rather than mindless killing machines.

Jina Jeon pointed toward the horizon. "We're coming up on the Bridge of No Return. You've probably seen it portrayed in movies. James Bond is swapped for another prisoner on the bridge in the beginning of *Die Another Day*."

"The name of the bridge sounds more than a little ominous."

"Actually, it earned the name at the end of the Korean War. At the time, the bridge was being used solely for prisoner exchanges. Many of the North Korean soldiers held captive by the States refused to return home. The Americans gave them a choice: remain in the South or cross back over into the North. If the prisoner chose to cross the bridge, he would never be permitted to return."

Janson had always been a student of history, and he knew more about Korea's sordid past than most. But this was his first sojourn into the demilitarized zone, more commonly known as the DMZ.

There was more than a little irony associated with the DMZ. For one, the border was anything *but* demilitarized. In fact, the DMZ was the most heavily militarized border in the world.

The DMZ was also widely considered the most *dangerous* border in the world. And for good cause. Officially, the North and the South remained at war. The Korean Armistice Agreement, signed in 1953 at the "end" of the Korean War, effectively concluded hostilities between the two sides by creating a mutual cease-fire. But the cease-fire was, by definition, temporary, designed to last only until a final peace settlement could be agreed upon. Of course, such a settlement had never been achieved. To this day, tensions between the governments of the North and the South not only persist but often rise to a level that places the countries—and their chief allies—on the brink of another full-scale war. During Janson's tenure with the Department of State, escalation frequently seemed inevitable. And nothing had transpired since that made him feel any differently about the issue today.

On the contrary, the death of Kim Jong-il and transition of power to Kim Jong-un introduced myriad unknown and potentially volatile components into the equation.

Janson stared into the distance, where a thick mist rose from the ground, blotting out the first signs of life he'd noticed since leaving Jina Jeon's village. The outline of a large bus was now all that remained visible.

Which made Janson briefly contemplate the second irony connected with the DMZ. The second irony was, in his mind, even more absurd. Despite the fact that the DMZ remained the world's most dangerous border, the area was also a wildly popular tourist attraction among visitors to South Korea.

The most celebrated spot among guests was the Joint Security Area, or JSA. Inside the JSA tourists could visit the truce village of Panmunjom. Nowhere else in South Korea could a common Joe get so close to North Korea (and North Korean soldiers) without getting himself riddled with bullets.

As if the driver had read his thoughts, the tour bus Janson was focused on roared to life, emitting a gray cloud of carbon monoxide that instantly blended with the fog.

"The Joint Security Area," Jina Jeon said, handing Janson a pair of field glasses, "is where the current talks are being held."

Through the small field glasses, Janson could just make out the main attraction of the Korean Demilitarized Zone, a scattering of short, stout buildings. Three South Korean soldiers stood perfectly still in the shadows of the structures, facing their North Korean counterparts, from a distance of maybe twenty or thirty yards. Both sides wore dark aviator glasses despite the incessant gray sky. All six men were armed. All twelve of their fists were tightly clenched as though hand-to-hand combat could break out at any given moment.

Janson removed the field glasses from his eyes. "I assume you didn't bring me here to suggest that I attempt a one-man assault on the Joint Security Area."

Jina Jeon shrugged. "You might as well, considering your overall odds of success. But, no, I brought you here to show you the tunnel."

NINETEEN

Uiam Lake
Chuncheon, Gangwon-do, South Korea

The cabin of Cal Auster's Weekender was cramped but at least it was warm. Janson sat next to Jina Jeon on one side of the long, narrow table while the owner sat cross-legged opposite them, deftly working his Samsung Galaxy with well-callused thumbs.

"I'll be just another minute or two," Auster assured them without looking up. He'd used the same words twice before, twenty-five minutes and fifteen minutes ago, respectively.

The hell with warmth, Janson thought, rising from the plush booth. I need some air. He excused himself and went topside, acknowledging Auster's captain/bodyguard, who sat soundlessly in the cockpit smoking a cigarette.

Janson stuffed his hands in his pockets and savored one of

nature's many panoramic masterpieces. The crisp air served to sharpen his view of the mountains in the distance. The limbs of the shoreline's trees, many of which barely clung to life this time of year, seemed to be reaching out over the lake as though to rescue a drowning soul. Only in nature, Janson thought, could so little look like so much.

Chuncheon, known as the City of Lakes, was the capital of Gangwon Province and a popular destination among East Asian tourists. Janson was sure the tranquility of the area appealed to the arms dealer's generous sense of irony. He was also certain that Cal Auster took refuge here only after mapping out several different routes of escape. He wondered for a moment whether any of those routes involved crossing into North Korea. Knowing what he knew of Cal Auster, the weapons dealer might already have a deal in place with Pyongyang, perhaps brokered by one of Auster's numerous contacts in Moscow.

When he returned to the cabin, Janson found Cal Auster on Jina Jeon's side of the table, he leaning in with whispers, she scooting away. Janson considered whether she might have pulled away from Auster because she'd heard Janson's footsteps. Surely her hearing was better than that of Auster, who'd spent all of his adult life demonstrating the capabilities of increasingly loud and powerful firearms.

"There he is," Auster rang out gregariously. He made no effort to stand but did tuck his smartphone into the breast pocket of his sports jacket. "Paul, Paul, Paul, how long's it been?"

"Not nearly long enough," Janson deadpanned.

Auster cackled and slapped at the table like a raucous drunk, though Janson knew the weapons dealer's primary vice came in the form of a powder. More than a few times Janson had heard Auster boast that he hadn't touched a drop of alcohol since he was a teenager. *"Why dim your senses when you can* enhance *them?"* he'd say. *"Why use rabbit ears when you can watch life hap-pen in* HD?"

"Have a seat, Paul," Auster boomed, pointing across from him. "Tell Uncle Cal what you need today. How can I make you happy?"

Janson sat, doubting his decision not to return to the Embraer 650 in Seoul in order to recover what he needed. But with Cons Ops keeping watch, he knew he couldn't have risked it. He reached into his pocket and produced a wrinkled index card, slid it across the table toward Auster's tapping fingers.

Cal Auster lifted the index card and held it at arm's length from his deep-green eyes.

Farsighted, of course, Janson thought. Spent most his life star-ing down distant targets. Now he's too vain to put on a pair of reading glasses.

As he went over the list, Cal Auster stroked his goatee, then ran his hand over his shaven head, brows lifted in theatrical disbe-lief. *"Wow,"* he said, "that's quite a Christmas list. Sure hope Santa hasn't seen you doing anything naughty in the past twelve months." He laughed at his own remark then slowly settled himself. "It's none of my business, of course, but are you planning on storming Taiwan? I've equipped sub-Saharan despots on the eve of war with less than this."

Janson sat expressionless. "Best to be prepared, I figure."

"Be prepared." Auster bared his teeth in a grin. "That's right, I'd almost forgotten. Paul Janson's a Boy Scout now. Or so I've heard."

A long silence followed, as Janson pondered how much Auster might have heard, whether the weapons dealer might know about the Phoenix Foundation.

"Whatever you've heard," Janson said, eager to fill the quiet,

"I'm sure it's half-true and ninety percent false. Can we get down to business now?"

Cal Auster set the index card facedown on the table. "Of course, of course, of course." He stared up at the low ceiling in thought. "How soon do you need this stuff?"

"How soon can you get it to me?"

"How much are you willing to pay above retail?" When Janson didn't reply, Auster added: "See, Paul, I'm like Amazon. I can offer you standard shipping for free. But that's going to take a while. If you want me to expedite..."

"I need it today."

Auster sighed dramatically, as though he were being put-upon by yet another unrealistic customer. "Ah, well, that would require our Super-Duper Special Priority price. Hell, even Amazon doesn't do *same day*."

"Sure, but Amazon's not using their drones yet."

Cal Auster's face went blank, his skin paling instantaneously. The fifty-one-year-old weapons dealer never did exhibit much of a poker face.

Janson shrugged while holding Auster's gaze. "You're not the only one who has his ear to the ground, Cal. I'm sure you know that." Janson reached across the table, lifted the index card. He plucked a pen from his pocket and wrote a percentage on the back of the card, then slid the card back across the table. "*That's* how much I'm willing to pay, Uncle Cal."

Auster glanced at the number and nodded languorously, as if he'd just stepped down from a lifelong high.

Janson studied Auster's eyes in order to gauge the threat. Would Auster suddenly fly off his meds and put a knife to Jina Jeon's throat? Janson didn't think so. In a way, Cal Auster was like the regime in Pyongyang. Belligerent, yes. Bat-shit crazy at times? No doubt. But in the end, both Auster and the leadership in North Korea proved themselves to be rational actors, hell-bent not on creating infinite chaos but on self-preservation.

After several tense minutes that passed like hours, Cal Auster finally conjured a smile and rattled off the terms of the sale like one of his cherished automatic weapons. "Give me four and a half hours. Cash up front—sorry, no CODs. I don't take personal checks and I don't accept American Express. And as any good pimp will tell you, Visa is not quite *everywhere* you want to be. Exchanges can be made within twenty-four hours but only for defective products and only for identical merchandise. Our return policy, which you'll find listed on my middle finger, is: fuck you. No exceptions." He pushed himself out of the booth. "So, Mr. Janson. May I assume you won't be needing a gift receipt?"

TWENTY

Edward Clarke, undersecretary of state and director of Consular Operations, looked around the table at the faces of his four colleagues and thought, This looks like a scene taken straight from Mobius: The Next Generation.

Actually, Clarke didn't mind making the comparison in his head; the Mobius program had been an unmitigated success for a long time before it became an unmitigated failure. And he didn't mind that many of the people involved in the Diophantus program had worked underneath the players connected with Mobius; indeed, he was one of them. What caused no end of apprehension, however, was the fact that he was facing the very same antagonist as his predecessor had.

But then, no one but a rogue Cons Ops agent with a severely

misguided sense of morality could have created a crisis of the kind they now faced. So the fact that Diophantus was now in jeopardy because of the actions of Paul Janson was no coincidence. No co-incidence at all. His past betrayal of Consular Operations was, in fact, the very reason Senator James Wyckoff of North Carolina had sought Janson's assistance in the first place.

Clarke made a mental note to contact Lawrence Hammond, the senator's chief of staff, immediately after the meeting to ask whether Wyckoff and his wife had received word of any further developments from Janson in South Korea. Hammond had last called Clarke from Honolulu to say there had been radio silence. Clarke found it odd that Janson wasn't keeping the senator in the loop—unless of course, there *had* been communications, and it was Larry Hammond who'd been taken out of the loop. After all, the distinguished gentleman from North Carolina trusted no one these days. Even the press was speculating about Senator Wyck-off's mental health in the wake of his son's disappearance. Another twenty-four-hour news cycle like the last one and the majority leader would no doubt ask Wyckoff to resign his seat for the sake of the party. Presidential primaries were around the corner and pol-itics *always* took precedence over loyalty.

Clarke took a sip of ice water then topped himself off from the crystal carafe. He sat at the head of the table. To his left were Douglas Albright, director of the Defense Intelligence Agency, and Sanford Hildreth, director of the National Security Agency.

On Clarke's right sat Ella Quon, deputy director of the CIA's National Clandestine Service, and her chief systems engineer, Eric Matsumura.

"Let me start," Clarke began, "by briefing you on the latest. We've pinpointed Paul Janson."

Albright of the DIA barely let Clarke finish his second sentence before cutting in. "Then I assume you won't be discussing Janson in the present tense during this meeting."

Clarke held up a hand. "Let's not start things this way, OK?"

"We shouldn't be *starting* anything at this point," Albright barked. "You should have waited and called us in at the end, once Janson was eliminated."

"Douglas, please—"

"Please, *my ass*." Albright pounded his fist against the mahogany. "I was sitting in this goddamn seat at this goddamn table in this goddamn room when your *predecessor* agreed to take Janson out. I don't need to remind anyone here about the outcome of Derek Collins's directive. If he'd succeeded we wouldn't be sitting here right now, and I wouldn't have suffered my first goddamn heart attack a few years ago. So don't 'please' me, Eddie. Tell me that Janson is history and that this crisis is over and done with."

Ella Quon spoke as if the previous interaction hadn't just taken place in front of her. "Where is he?" she said calmly.

Clarke turned to her, grateful for the interruption. "The DMZ," he said.

"The demilitarized zone? This sounds serious. Do we know why he's there?"

"Because he's a fucking golem," Albright cut in. "I've said it before and I'll say it again."

"What's a golem?" Quon inquired.

The NSA director, Sanford Hildreth, sighed deeply. "Ella, think: Victor Frankenstein's monster."

Albright smirked. "Derek Collins's monster is more like it."

"Look," Clarke said, trying to regain control of the room, "there's no question we've created some monsters in our day. Look at the *Jason Bourne* incident, for Christ's sake. But the fact of the matter is—like it or not—we *need* monsters. It'll be one of those very monsters who's going to clean up this mess for us tonight."

"*Your* mess," Albright shouted. "Let's not forget it was another of your monsters that created this mess to begin with. If Gregory Wyckoff had been elimin—"

"You want to talk about *messes*, Doug? Let's talk about messes." Clarke rose from his chair and leaned forward with palms pressed down on the table. "The DIA is *still* under investigation for things you've done at Guantanamo. Forcing detainees to watch gay pornography, draping them in the Israeli flag, humiliating them using female interrogators, *drugging* them like lab rats."

Albright cocked his head. "So now you're a bleeding heart, concerned with our treatment of terrorists. Let me tell you something, Eddie, enhanced interro—"

"I don't give a *fuck* about the terrorists, Doug, and you damn well know it. My point is that you got caught, that you turned *good policy* into an international debate that's irreparably damaged the moral standing of this country."

Quon shook her head. "Edward, there's really no need for this."

"No *need* for this? This coming from a company woman? While we're on the subject of messes, let's chat about the scorching heat *your* agency has come under. Spying on *Congress*? Not just on Congress but on the *Senate Intelligence Committee*? The very legislative body that's charged with overseeing and regulating *all of us*?"

Quietly, Sanford Hildreth said, "Let's get back to the matter at hand, shall we?"

"Sure, we *shall*," Clarke said to the NSA director. "But first, let's take a gander at NSA. You may well be sitting in the greatest mess in the *history of intelligence*. Just about every fucking American citizen thinks he's being listened in on, thanks to you. Little Sally's afraid to make a ten-minute call to Aunt Suzy about Uncle Harry's prostate cancer, *thanks to you*. And why? Because some pimple-faced *schmuck*—some goddamn twenty-nine-year-old *civilian*—skipped out of Honolulu and went straight to Hong Kong and Moscow with the entirety of our nation's secrets. Talk about *messes*. At least our operation is at risk from Paul Janson. He may well be a monster of our own creation, but he *is* a monster. Janson's a black ops superman. Your entire agency ate shit from a ninety-pound computer geek named Edward-fucking-Snowden."

Clarke gazed at his colleagues' forlorn faces, satisfied that he'd finally gotten that rant out of his system. Holding in your temper, as he had been doing for the past few days, wasn't healthy.

Now let Albright scoff all he wants. At least the dirty laundry at Cons Ops doesn't get aired in public.

Clarke sat, brushed some imaginary lint from his suit jacket. He needed sleep, that's what he needed. *Real* sleep, four or five hours of *continuous* sleep, *in a bed*. And he could use a decent meal. Not pub food. And certainly not takeout. He needed a home-cooked meal, the kind his *first* wife used to make. Hell, even his second wife could whip up a batch of spaghetti and meatballs. But this one, fuck. He was lucky if she could find the number to call and order a pizza delivery.

Who am I kidding? It's all a matter of trade-offs. And not just with women, with everything. Life's just one big series of trade-offs.

"All right," he said. "Now we can return to our *mutual* problem. From here on out, however, there will be no pointing fingers. I'm the one who took the bull by the horns to make Diophantus a reality—no one else—so if there happens to be a pile of bull*shit* in the pen, I'll clean it up. But until then, I don't want to hear about how badly it stinks. Are we understood?"

All four of them nodded, even Albright.

"Good," Clarke said. "Now I'll tell you what I know about Paul Janson and what I intend to do about him." He took a swallow of water. "As I was saying before, we've pinpointed his location to the DMZ. Specifically to Daeseong-dong, otherwise known as Freedom Village." He turned to Quon. "Ella, earlier you asked *why* he's there and insinuated that Janson's presence at the DMZ means that he knows exactly what we're doing. That's a reckless jump we needn't make just yet."

Quon frowned. "You're suggesting Janson's in the Korean Demilitarized Zone to sightsee?"

"I have a former operative living in Daeseong-dong. Her name is Jina Jeon. Janson knew her and knew her well. He may well be in the DMZ seeking her help."

"Then whatever information Janson *does* have at this point is spreading," Quon said. "As is our exposure."

"Not necessarily. When I say Janson knew her well, I mean it in the biblical sense. Forgive me, Ella, for my crudeness, but for all we know Janson may have headed to Daeseong-dong just to get his dick wet."

"I find that hard to believe."

"With all due respect, Ella, I don't expect you to understand. Because you don't *have* a dick."

"I won't dignify that with a response."

"One way or the other," Albright chirped in, "we don't know. So I think it's smart to assume the worst."

Clarke nodded. "I fully agree. Which is why no one who has had substantial contact with Paul Janson over the past forty-eight hours will be around after the next forty-eight."

Sanford Hildreth leaned forward. "And this is something we can be assured of?"

Clarke turned to the NSA director. "Sandy, I'm sure that regardless of who I decide to call first with the news, you and your agency will be the first to learn the outcome of tonight's operation."

Albright said, "What about Kincaid? And the Wyckoff kid?"

"Both as good as gone."

"Perhaps then," Quon said, "we should move on to the business of reunification." She turned to her chief systems engineer, who placed an open folder in front of her. "As designed, I've been briefing the White House about 'the situation' for the past several weeks."

Clarke nodded. "What's been the president's reaction?"

"Disbelief, at first. Followed by reluctant acceptance." She flipped a page in her folder but didn't look down. "The president is concerned about the potential costs of reunification. He wants the South to avoid escalation, no matter what political price the Blue House has to pay. The president prefers that the *next* administration deal with reunification rather than his."

Of course, Clarke thought. That's all US politicians are good for these days—kicking the can down the road.

Albright spoke up. "The White House understands that we're looking at a hard landing?"

The so-called hard landing referred to the chain of events that could potentially result from a *sudden*, rather than gradual, collapse of the North Korean regime, a scenario that could conceivably create an unprecedented humanitarian crisis in which the South and the United States would face massive rebellion and unrest, not to mention mass migration.

"I've pressed the possibility upon them," Quon said, "but I've had to be subtle. There are some smart people in the Oval Office these days. If someone suspected we were so much as trifling with the situation, let alone directing it, it would lead to an investigation."

"I assume we're all right with the legislative branch?" Albright said.

Quon came as close as she ever did to smiling. "Congress has its head up its own ass, as usual. They're far more concerned with whether they are being spied upon than they are about foreign intelligence." She turned to Clarke. "The scandal you mentioned is a blessing in disguise for Diophantus. The intelligence committee is preoccupied with what's going on in Langley, and we all know the current Congress can't walk and chew gum at the same time."

Clarke turned to Albright. "And the Defense Department?"

Albright smirked. "Most of the department is excited about the possibility of a hard landing. No one's happy with the slash in defense spending. Half of them would rather remain in Afghanistan and return to Iraq. Korean reunification will give them ammunition to call for new spending. Most of the department's champing at the bit."

Clarke looked to Sanford Hildreth. "Sandy?"

The NSA director shrugged. "Anything to move us away from the fucking surveillance debate will make us happy at NSA. Hell, we'd take another Cuban Missile Crisis just now if we could get our hands on one."

TWENTY-ONE

Janson figured he needed a solid four hours of sleep, so he set the alarm on his BlackBerry for 3 AM sharp. He placed the phone on the nightstand next to the utilitarian double bed in Jina Jeon's second-floor guest room and kicked off his shoes before lying down fully clothed and staring up at the dark ceiling in thought.

When the alarm woke him he'd gather his things and head north to the tunnel. The tunnel wasn't his first choice for crossing into the North, but Jina Jeon had assured him it was his best chance at success. Personally, Janson had preferred the idea of entering North Korea through Kaesong in North Hwanghae Province. The city of nearly two hundred thousand was the site of the Kaesong Industrial Complex, a joint North-South venture just north of the DMZ and one of only two locations in the DPRK accessible from the South. Built a decade ago, the eight-hundred-acre complex represented part of South Korea's experimental Sunshine Policy, a reaching out—in this case through economic exchange—to their neighbor in the hope of advancing reform and appeasing the irascible regime in the North.

Janson had hoped to find one of the thousand South Koreans employed at the Kaesong Industrial Complex and cut him a deal similar to the one he'd cut with Silent Lynx in Shanghai. He'd pay the employee a large enough sum of money that the man would never have to return to work, and could retire to a third, more desirable country. But Jina Jeon convinced Janson that the plan would never work; in addition to the one thousand South Koreans employed at the complex were nearly *fifty* thousand North Koreans, most of whom remained loyal to the Pyongyang regime. Besides, she'd said, security procedures at the industrial complex were no less stringent than those at a supermax prison in the United States.

In the darkness of the guest room, Janson closed his eyes and envisioned the tunnel. Thirty years ago a joint South Korean–US investigation team assigned to the DMZ tripped a North Korean booby trap, which killed one American and wounded several others. The incident led to the discovery of an infiltration tunnel running under the demilitarized zone. A year later a second infiltration tunnel was discovered. Confronted with the discoveries, North Korea initially denied building the tunnels. Following a close inspection, which revealed drill marks for dynamite clearly pointing toward the South, the DPRK insisted that the tunnels were dug for coal mining—despite the fact that none of the discovered tunnels contained any coal.

Officially, the South had discovered four such incursion tunnels. But as Jina Jeon explained, the actual number was closer to twenty.

"There are seventeen more that I know of," she'd said. "Their discoveries were never made known to the public. Partly because South Korea doesn't want to show their entire hand, and partly because the Blue House didn't want to antagonize the palace while the Sunshine Policy was in effect. Some people believe that there are another half dozen or so tunnels that have yet to be discovered."

"But if the North dug these tunnels and the South knows about them," Janson had argued, "surely they're guarded heavily on both sides."

"True," Jina Jeon had told him. "But the North are not aware of the tunnels dug by the *South*. Many were started, but only one such tunnel was ever completed. For years it has been used by South Korean fugitives attempting to flee the country."

"And you know its precise location?"

"I do," she'd said. "The tunnel is guarded by no one on either side. But be warned; it is short and narrow and absolute *hell* to pass through."

* * *

TWENTY MINUTES LATER Janson was dreaming of Kabul. Of walking alone along the rugged mountain terrain in the darkness. *Alone?* Where were his men? He'd lived this dream more times than he could count and his men had always been with him. Where were they now? Was this not a dream at all? Was he walking north across the expanse of the Korean Demilitarized Zone, heading for the incursion tunnel dug by the South?

Confusion as dense as an autumn fog enveloped him.

Janson wasn't in a dream at all; as far as he knew, he'd never even thought it was a dream. He heard the crackling of a small rock, tumbling down the hillside from his right. He spun and reached for his weapon, but the men were already upon him, circling him with raised Kalashnikov assault rifles—AK-47s from another era—shouting at him to get facedown on the ground, to spread his arms and legs like an eagle.

But the men weren't speaking Korean, they were speaking a language Janson knew too well.

Pashto?

As the men swarmed in on his prostrate figure he lifted his head as high as he could and saw the stone-cold, bearded faces of the Taliban.

Breathing rapidly, Janson shot up in the bed in Jina Jeon's guest room, drenched in a cold sweat.

As his breathing became even and his pulse slowed to near normal, he listened to the nothingness of the house. He was thirsty but didn't want to creep downstairs at the risk of waking Jina's mother. But, no, that wasn't right; when they'd returned from the meeting with Cal Auster in Chuncheon, Jina had informed him that she'd be taking her mother to Seoul for the night, for an early appointment with her mother's cardiologist the next morning. He was welcome to stay and rest before he left for the tunnel.

A creak downstairs made him recall the crackling of the lone rock rolling down the hillside.

The sound shouldn't have been there. Not in his nightmare, where he was alone. And not now, while he was alone in the house.

Maybe Jina Jeon had dropped her mother off at her hotel in Seoul and returned home?

By the time he finished the thought, Janson was already out of the bed and in his shoes, searching the room for items that could be turned into improvised weapons.

Unfortunately the room was spartan. He'd left his equipment—even his go-bag—in the barn out of respect for Jina's mother. Now he wished he'd held on to his go-bag. Jina's mother would never have known what was in it.

But then, it was *Jina's* suggestion—no, her *request*—that he leave all weapons outside the house.

Something in his chest sank like a stone, but he quickly pushed it aside and readied himself for whatever was to come.

First he considered escape routes. The ground below the window in his room would be covered. As would all easily identifiable points of ingress and egress. And if Jina Jeon had indeed betrayed him, the intruders would know the layout of the entire house.

They'd know precisely which room he was in.

Which he could make work to his advantage.

Janson opened the door an inch or so, sneaked a look out into the hall, and listened. As far as he could tell, whoever had entered the house had not yet made it up to the second floor.

Perhaps Janson had yelled when he was startled awake? If so, he'd inadvertently bought himself some time.

He eyed the door across the hallway—Jina's bedroom? Yes, he remembered Jina saying that her mother slept in the lone bedroom on the first floor so that she didn't have to deal with the stairs.

Janson darted across the hall without making a sound. Jina Jeon's bedroom looked nothing like the guest room. All the furniture was made of strong, dark wood, expensive but nothing frilly. The bedding was black, as were the curtains that covered the wide windows. Nothing particularly feminine. Arranged in the Japanese tradition of feng shui, if he wasn't mistaken.

As he searched for makeshift weapons, he heard the creak of one of the lower stairs leading up to the second floor. No time; the intruder was on his way.

Probably intruders, plural. If Cons Ops was coming for him, they'd come heavy and they'd come prepared.

They knew what Janson was capable of. Sources inside Cons Ops told him that operatives and officials alike still referred to him as the Machine.

Janson stood next to the door frame with his back pressed against the wall. He'd closed the door to the guest room but left Jina Jeon's door ajar, not just in the hope of duping the intruder but so that he could see and hear what was happening on the rest of the floor.

Light footfalls in the mouth of the hallway caused the hair on his arms to stand up straight as nails. But with the fear came the adrenaline. His head instantly cleared. He relaxed his fingers even as the rest of the muscles in his body tensed.

He flashed on Cal Auster saying: *"Be prepared."* Saw the monstrous grin on his face. *"That's right. Paul Janson's a Boy Scout now. Or so I've heard."*

Could it have been Auster who set him up? Could it even be Auster's man who'd come to eliminate him, maybe the captain/bodyguard back on Auster's boat? Auster had felt threatened when Janson mentioned the drones. Could he have felt threatened enough to kill Janson?

What was the arms dealer whispering in Jina's ear when Janson stepped back into the cabin after taking some fresh air upstairs?

Would Cal Auster have come himself?

No, Janson thought. Not in a million years.

Someone's on the other side of this wall. He could sense a presence. Almost smell the predator's scent like highly attuned prey.

He lowered his center of gravity.

Turn the hunter into the hunted.

The muzzle of a Beretta came into view. Sent into the bedroom as though it were a scout.

What it was, was a mistake.

Janson waited until he could see the pale finger held against the trigger, then he reached out and gripped the barrel of the weapon. First he thrust the gun up and away, so that it wasn't pointed at him. Then he twisted the barrel with every bit of strength he had in his right hand. Twisted it brutally, until he heard the gunman's finger break—*snap* like a decrepit piece of wood—inside the Beretta's trigger guard.

With his left hand he chopped at the gunman's throat, silencing the yelp of pain resulting from the broken finger before it reached the killer's lips. He followed with a powerful palm to the nose, pushing up and inward toward the brain.

Blood from the gunman's shattered nose spurted onto Jina Jeon's immaculate hardwood floor.

Janson yanked the assassin into the room and thrust him up against the wall Janson had been leaning against twenty seconds earlier. He pressed his left forearm hard against the gunman's throat.

"How many?" Janson breathed.

"Fuck you," the gunman croaked.

In the inky blackness of Jina Jeon's bedroom, Janson recognized the voice before he recognized the face. His eyes widened in disbelief. Widened in anger. Worst of all, widened in betrayal.

He knew this man, not just from Consular Operations.

But from the Phoenix Foundation.

Phoenix had been infiltrated.

"You went back to them," Janson spat. But even as he said it, he knew it wasn't true, just wishful thinking. The man he was looking at wasn't merely an ungrateful or unsuccessful Phoenix graduate. Janson's initial presumption had been correct; his had been an outright betrayal. "No, you didn't, did you, you son of a bitch? You had never left them."

Janson brimmed with fury. So many questions, so much to sort through, so many lies. But now wasn't the time.

Janson leaned into Heath Manningham's face. "I will break you into so many pieces, Clarke will think I shoved a pipe bomb down your throat. Now come clean—how many inside, how many out?"

The young Londoner attempted a smile as crimson leaked out from between his teeth. "You think it will matter?" he said with the slightest of British accents. "You think you'll walk away from this house alive?"

"Are you *really* ready to die for those bastards?" Janson hissed.

"Weren't you?" Trembling, Manningham met Janson's gaze. "God knows you were willing to *kill* for them. It's the life we chose, isn't it? You know better than anyone, Machine, you can't just walk away."

"I *did* walk away," Janson growled. "And I thought I'd helped you do the same."

"Walked away, did you?" Manningham said, managing to steady his voice. "You're still trying to sell that heap of shit to yourself, are you? Tell me. How many have you done since you 'walked away'?"

"I have *rules*."

"Right, the rules. *Kill only those who try to kill us.* Guess I qualify then, don't I, mate? Why don't you feed me the bullet sitting in that chamber and drop the bloody curtain on this charade?"

TWENTY-TWO

Kang Jung was just about to log off her computer. It was late and even Lord Wicked needed her beauty sleep (*ha!*) from time to time. As she backed up her systems to an anonymous server in Estonia, she heard the landline ring in her mother's bedroom. It was unusual for her mother to receive a call so late (she didn't receive many calls at all), so Kang Jung went to her wall, placed her water glass against her ear, and listened.

Her mother sounded upset, but Kang Jung couldn't make out what she was saying.

Almost immediately after she last heard her mother speak, Jung's door flew open. She dropped her glass to the floor and it shattered to pieces as she turned to find her mother standing slumped over in the door frame. Her mother's eyes appeared red and puffy, but they didn't so much as twitch toward the fallen water glass.

"I have to go out," her mother said in Korean. "I am afraid it is your grandfather."

"Grandfather?"

"He is at the hospital. He was apparently having chest pains. Luckily, his neighbor found him and called an ambulance."

Kang Jung felt her features crumple with worry. Grandfather was one of the few people in this world whom she adored. She'd feared something like this ever since his wife died of complications from a stroke nine months ago. Kang Jung was not nearly as fond of the woman who had replaced her grandmother six years earlier, but she knew Grandfather had loved the woman and was suffering greatly over her loss. Suffering, perhaps, more over the loss of his second wife than he had over his first.

"I want to come with you to see Grandfather," she heard herself saying. It wasn't true, however; Kang Jung didn't deal well with death. She accepted it as a fact of life, but she didn't dare watch people suffer. She didn't go to hospitals, she didn't attend funerals or memorial services, no matter how much she cared for the person who died. She wanted to remember her few loved ones as they were: healthy and alive.

Maybe it was selfish to avoid hospitals. But as far as funerals and memorial services went, who but the survivors (most of whom she *didn't* care about) would know?

"You stay here," her mother said. "It is a school night. You need to sleep. Keep your phone near your bed and leave your ringer on. If things look bad, I will call you, and you can take a taxi to the hospital. I will leave money on the kitchen table."

She almost refused the money, but then remembered: Her personal wealth wasn't something she could ever explain. To anyone, really, and certainly not her mother.

"Thank you, Mother" was all she could manage.

Then her door closed and her mother was gone.

It wasn't until after her mother left that she found it strange that a neighbor would have discovered Grandfather. Like her, Grandfather kept largely to himself. He often told her he had no friends in his apartment building, and he wanted none. Had he really stepped out into his hallway and called for help instead of dialing for the ambulance himself?

Maybe people behaved differently at death's door. She thought not.

She left her room and stepped into her mother's. She picked up the landline to see the name of the neighbor who had just called. Oddly, the listing was restricted. No name. No telephone number. And certainly no address.

She thought of phoning Paul Janson.

He would think I am just another silly kid with an unruly imagination.

She admired the American too much to allow him to think such a thing.

* * *

JANSON DIDN'T KNOW whether he had an additional two or three minutes, so he decided to forgo the air choke and applied a blood choke instead. He spun Heath Manningham around and took him to the floor while hooking the bend of his right arm around Manningham's neck. He clasped his hands together and exerted intense pressure with his biceps and forearms on both sides of Manningham's carotid artery, cutting off oxygen-rich blood to the brain. In eleven seconds the double-dealing Phoenix graduate was out cold. Janson checked the spy's pulse then rose and exited Jina Jeon's bedroom.

With Manningham's .45 Beretta in hand, Janson quickly cleared the guest room and headed downstairs. Although Manningham wouldn't talk, Janson was sure there would be more agents outside. He stayed clear of all windows, since his would-be assassins could well be snipers. He couldn't rule out their taking over one of the neighboring houses or barns as a staging area. If Jina Jeon was involved—even more of a likelihood now that he knew about Manningham—setting up snipers' nests around the house would have been easy as cake.

Jina Jeon.

It butchered him to learn he'd been betrayed by Heath Manningham, but if he was to discover he'd been double-crossed by Jina Jeon, it might be more than he could take. Her treachery could well spell the end of the Phoenix Foundation.

Janson couldn't lie to himself, couldn't pretend that it might be for the best; he was too invested in Phoenix and too proud of what he'd accomplished. He didn't believe in "signs" or a god that worked in mysterious ways. At least in Manningham's case—and who knew how many others?—he'd failed extraordinarily, by any measure. He and his team did their due diligence on Manningham, yet Edward Clarke and Consular Operations had outsmarted him. Janson would never again underestimate State, and he would never again question whether Cons Ops was an adversary or an ally. He only hoped it wasn't too late, for him, or for Kincaid.

She was right all along. He grinned despite the grave situation. *If we both survive this, I'm never going to hear the end of it.*

With the fingers on his left hand he cautiously parted the blinds in the living room. The Jeon farm had a good deal of property, but several neighboring houses and barns remained within sniper range. Ducking low, he crossed under the large bay window and entered the kitchen.

Dare he?

Go big or go home, he thought as he scanned the room in which he'd eaten dinner with Jina Jeon and her mother just hours earlier.

After eyeing a block of cutlery, he opened several drawers and cabinets, as quickly and as quietly as he could. In one of the drawers he found a pristine set of silverware, in another a number of towels, hand and dish, and a couple of washcloths. He was surprised to find a bread box, less surprised to find it stocked with bread. In the cabinets, the usual things: dishes, glasses, canned and dry goods, and spices galore. Nothing called out to him as a viable alternative to his original idea.

In the end, there was no debate to be had.

He would do what had to be done.

* * *

ALL INTELLIGENT PEOPLE are lonely, Kang Jung told herself as she sat on her bed. We live in our heads.

As she surveyed her room in the faint light, locking briefly on her iMac, her MacBook Air, her iPad and her iPad Mini, her iPod and her iPhone, the irony wasn't lost on her: she was so *connected* that she was *disconnected*. Kang Jung had hardly any life at all; Lord Wicked was world renowned.

As a criminal, she thought sadly.

Oh, how to escape this wasteful melancholy? She was worried for Grandfather; that was all. When you loved so few, you loved those few so deeply.

She trudged into the kitchen in her oversize pajamas. The linoleum was cold, almost cold enough to make her run back to her bedroom to fetch her slippers. But she'd be in and out. All she wanted was something to drink.

Opening the refrigerator door, she started at a light rap on the front door.

Janson?

No. Janson didn't know that her mother had left; he'd have texted her, not just dropped in unannounced. Besides, he was in the DMZ, preparing to cross the border into North Korea. He wasn't in Seoul making social calls.

The phone call her mother received earlier continued to nibble around the edges of her thoughts. Something about the call wasn't right. Grandfather wouldn't have stumbled into the hallway seeking help if he was having chest pains. Even if it was an emergency Grandfather was still Grandfather, as obstinate and self-reliant as ever. Despite his age, he'd retained all of his mental faculties. If he'd been experiencing chest pains, he would have picked up the phone and called for an ambulance himself.

Another rap at the front door, this one more insistent.

She eyed the ottoman in the living room. She could drag it in front of the door and peek through the peephole.

But what if whoever is standing on the other side has a gun?

A moment later it didn't matter. The man or woman on the other side of the door had stopped waiting for her to answer and started working the lock with a key or some other device. She had only seconds to think.

Nowhere to run to. Nowhere to hide.

She was trapped like a rat in a cage. And whoever stood on the other side of the door would not be standing there for long.

The dead bolt was unlocked.

The doorknob began to turn.

TWENTY-THREE

Seconds before the explosion lit the night sky over Freedom Village, Janson pitched Heath Manningham's unconscious form from the window of Jina Jeon's second-floor guest room. He then hastened across the hall, lowered his head, and sprinted toward the mattress propped up against the window. He struck the mattress—and grabbed hold of its sides—just as he heard the pop of the exploding .45. As the bullet ignited the gas he'd leaked from the stove, he rode the mattress spread-eagled in a free fall until it struck the hard ground.

When it did, Janson felt as though he'd just been smacked in the chest with a baseball bat. Every last breath of air had been knocked out of him. He waited a moment before attempting a deep breath, hoping he hadn't broken a rib and punctured a lung. Once he'd convinced himself that wasn't the case, he rolled off the mattress, scrambled to his feet, and in a dash headed straight for the barn.

His entire plan was a gamble. He'd rolled the dice counting on the razor-slim possibility that Jina Jeon hadn't betrayed him. If she had, he'd likely be running into an ambush as he made for his go-bag. Even if Manningham's plunge and the subsequent explosion had created enough of a diversion to lure the agents away from the barn, he still intended to move forward with the plan that Jina Jeon herself had devised. Janson would snatch his go-bag and race north for the tunnel. If his means of crossing into the North had been given up by Jina Jeon, he was a dead man—even if he somehow managed to escape this initial attempt on his life.

He entered the barn cautiously, found no one. The purchases he'd made from Cal Auster in Chuncheon appeared intact. The lion's share would have to remain behind; he could only carry so much. He ran the zipper across the go-bag to make sure he wasn't strapping a bomb to his back; then he closed the bag and raced out of the barn, away from Jina Jeon's property, into total darkness, heading north.

*   *   *

KANG JUNG RETREATED to her bedroom, her sanctuary. Lord Wicked's lair. She scanned her possessions for something she could use to defend herself against the intruder.

Damn, why do they have to make electronics so small these days?

She might have had a chance with one of those bulky computer towers that housed her first hard drive, but what the hell could she do with a MacBook Air—impress her attacker with its advanced video-editing features?

No, she thought. But I *can* create a live feed at a private web address and send the link to Janson.

It probably wouldn't prevent the intruder from killing her. But at least then the tall, dark, and handsome American could avenge her death.

She slammed her bedroom door, turned the lock, and pushed her small armoire in front of the door. It wouldn't stop the intruder, but it would hopefully buy her time.

* * *

As HE SCURRIED NORTH toward the tunnel, Paul Janson felt a light vibration against his outer thigh. He didn't want to stop, didn't want to sacrifice his momentum or his adrenaline. But it could be Kincaid. She could be in trouble, and Janson couldn't risk ignoring the call.

He stopped dead in his tracks, dropped to the ground, and removed the BlackBerry from his pocket. It wasn't a call at all. It was a text message, from Kang Jung. There were no words, just an odd link consisting of nine numbers and ending with .kr—the two letters appended to all South Korean domains.

Don't click it, he thought, hearing Morton's voice in his head. Don't click anything, ever. One fucking click on an unknown— or worse yet, disguised—link, and you can inadvertently end the world as we know it.

Janson pictured Kang Jung's inexpressive face, heard her soft voice saying, "There's nothing out there for me."

Could someone have gotten to her? Christ, she'd been the one who set up his meeting with Cy via an Internet Relay Chat. Janson had involved her in this. He alone was responsible for her safety.

Don't do it, Morton shrieked in his head. Don't fucking do it.

Janson clicked on the link in Kang Jung's text.

And found what appeared to be a live feed from a young girl's bedroom, though not your typical young girl's bedroom. Stuffed animals and eerily lifelike dolls rested among a small fortune's worth of state-of-the-art technology. In fact, were it not for the plush toys and figurines, what Janson saw could well have been a feed from an underground Apple store.

On the walls were posters: Albert Einstein sticking his tongue out. Carl Sagan staring off into the cosmos. Neil deGrasse Tyson eating a Yodel.

That answers my earlier question.

There was no doubt in his mind that this was Kang Jung's bedroom back in the Cheongwha Apartments in Itaewon.

Janson fought off a wave of panic. Once he'd established that he was looking at Kang Jung's bedroom, his first thought was that she'd been kidnapped.

From the BlackBerry's tiny speaker he could hear the rattling of a doorknob. At first he saw no door in the frame, then realized that a white wooden armoire was pressed against the door, concealing it, and a pang of fear clutched at his chest again. He punched up the volume and watched the scene unfold, helpless to do anything from thirty-five miles away in the demilitarized zone.

* * *

KANG JUNG STARTED at the first pound on the door. Taking a deep breath for strength, she leaned over and peered into the eye of the MacBook's webcam.

"I know you can't get here in time," she said, attempting to maintain a courageous calm but failing phenomenally. "And that's OK." She flinched at another strike on the other side of her door. She turned and noticed that the armoire had shifted. She spun and spoke to the camera, annoyed because everything that came into her head sounded so damn melodramatic. "I ask of you only one thing," she finally went with. "If I am killed tonight, *avenge me*."

She opened her desk drawer and withdrew an antique letter opener she'd bought at a flea market. The seller had told her it was used by an American general during the Korean War. She'd known the seller was full of shit but she'd bought it anyway, because the seller had been a sixteen-year-old boy and he'd been cute, even if he had been a complete dullard.

Kang Jung held the letter opener out like a sword, then turned it in her hand so that the blade was pointing down. It reminded her of the deranged man dressed like his mother in the shower scene from *Psycho*.

The sound of a female voice emanating from the other side of the door surprised her. The woman spoke with an Eastern European accent.

"Jung," the voice said, "I just want to talk to you for a moment, honey. There's a very bad man on the loose—a killer—and we know you've been communicating with him. I just need to ask you a few questions and then I'll leave, I promise. I'm not here to hurt you, dear."

Kang Jung gripped the letter opener and wondered if the female was the only one out there. If so, maybe Kang Jung could take her. The girls in school used to mess with her. Until two summers ago when she learned tae kwon do and returned to school and kicked some major mean-girl ass. She grinned. This woman on the other side of the door clearly didn't know who she was fucking with. Not Kang Jung, the socially insecure computer geek.

Here in her room surrounded by her computers—*you stepped onto my turf, bitch*—she transmogrified into Lord Wicked.

* * *

JANSON, TOO, WAS SURPRISED to hear a female voice emanating from the opposite side of Jung's door. But it didn't diminish his fear. If anything, hearing that female voice amplified his alarm for the teenage girl who'd so selflessly assisted him. If his instincts were correct—and they usually were about things like this—on the other side of the door stood the woman who had followed his taxi from Seoul Station. And if so, her sweet voice was no more authentic than the gold Rolex watch a young man tried to sell him a few months ago in Shanghai. If this woman was working with Cons Ops, no matter what her background, she'd invariably be a heartless killer.

On his tiny screen, the armoire began to slide. Kang Jung stood just to the side of the camera, carrying what looked to be a small knife, but was more likely something as simple as a paperweight or letter opener.

What could Janson do? He quickly ran through his options. The police would never make it in time; even if they did, they would be walking into a slaughter. Most of the force wasn't even armed. Kincaid and her new friend Park Kwan remained in southern Seoul, searching for Gregory Wyckoff. Even if they could cross the Han River in time, as much as he'd like to tell himself differently, their mission to locate the senator's son was the more important one. Kang Jung's life was at stake, but so were the lives of countless others.

That left Nam Sei-hoon.

"*I was finally able to gain access to the boy's computers,*" Nam Sei-hoon had said. "*As you suggested might be the case, the hard drives have been wiped.*"

Janson had cursed.

"*Not so fast, Paul. Remember, I am not a man without resources. I've had one of my trusted allies in the cyber-intelligence unit take a look at these hard drives. He was able to identify one of the individuals whom Gregory Wyckoff communicated with online via an IRC... It just so happens that the kid he chatted with is being watched vigorously..."*

Cy, Janson thought. The National Intelligence Service was listening in on—or reading, as the case may be—Cy's Internet Relay Chats.

That's how they found Kang Jung—she'd arranged the meeting with Cy using an IRC.

On-screen, a young woman materialized. He couldn't be sure but Janson thought that she indeed looked like the woman in the dark SM5 who had followed his taxi out of Seoul Station.

Christ, Janson thought. It was neither Jina Jeon nor Cal Auster who had betrayed him. The treachery had come from one of Janson's oldest and closest friends.

Nam Sei-hoon.

TWENTY-FOUR

Nika Vlasic looked upon Kang Jung and saw a girl not much older than Nika was when she opened the vein in her right wrist. This girl looked nothing like she had. She was clean, she was dressed in fresh pajamas, she was surrounded by thousands of dollars of technology that would help her to learn and go to college and succeed in the world without killing, the little bitch.

This girl wasn't the product of ethnic cleansing. She wasn't violated when she was nine. She didn't become pregnant by rape at age twelve, wasn't forced by the man who'd raped her to undergo an abortion in a burned-out factory.

Nika grinned as she stared at the letter opener the girl held in her fist. Then she looked squarely into the girl's eyes and began to swell with anger at the resentment this child harbored for her.

What the fuck did I ever do to you, kid? I told you I only came here to talk.

Nika ignored the threat from the letter opener and advanced, though she wasn't going for Kang Jung as the girl probably thought. She went for the girl's mobile phone instead. Quickly she scrolled through the call log.

No calls in the past half hour. Good. Even though a couple of agents were posted downstairs to delay or divert the cops, Nika didn't want to deal with making a hasty escape from a high-rise apartment building.

The girl attempted to shuffle by her, but Nika snatched the collar of her pajamas and in one fluid movement tossed her onto the bed. As Nika drew near to her, the girl lashed out with the letter opener.

Swing and a miss.

Nika grabbed the girl's right wrist and twisted it until the letter opener clanged to the floor.

"Why so hostile?" Nika said evenly.

"What do you *want* from me?" the girl cried.

"Where is the American?"

"Which American?"

Nika smiled, glanced down at the girl's right wrist, which she continued to hold in her grip. Just as Nika suspected, this young girl had never attempted to kill herself. How nice that must be. She'd probably never been raped either. Probably she was still a virgin, the little bitch.

"If you want to live," Nika said calmly, "do not play games with me." She twisted the girl's wrist again. "Understand?"

The girl yelped but nodded. Tears spilled freely from her eyes.

"Now tell me," Nika said. "What is the American doing in the demilitarized zone?"

* * *

JANSON FROZE. If Kang Jung told her what she knew—about Dio-phantus and the Wikipedia entry and the South Korean spy Yun Jin-ho in Pyongyang—the operative would be left with no choice but to kill her. And if Kang Jung revealed what Janson was doing—crossing into the DPRK to locate the South Korean spy—his mission was over. Nam Sei-hoon would never allow Janson to get near Pyongyang. He'd start a war with the North if he had to.

Kang Jung's only chance was to remain silent.

On his screen Kang Jung spoke so softly he could barely hear her, even in the quiet of the pitch-black field.

"The American told me that the Hivemind sent him there. He went to see a hacker named Cy at the university. I don't know exactly who or what he was after, but Cy told him he'd find it in a secret Hivemind facility in the DMZ."

Amazing, Janson thought. Even better than keeping silent, Kang Jung had fed the operative a plausible lie.

Unless they've already gotten to Cy. Then the woman would know Jung was lying, and it would cost the girl her life.

"This facility," the woman said, pulling at her own jacket sleeve as she hovered over Kang Jung on the bed, "is that where Gregory Wyckoff is being hidden?"

Kang Jung shook her head slowly. "I swear to you, I don't know. The American gave me only the information I needed to help him connect with Cy and..."

"And *what*?"

"And help him locate the facility."

"And you did this?"

"Yes."

"*Where is it?*" the woman hissed.

"About forty kilometers north of Seoul. There's a castle that looks as though it belongs to a fairy princess."

The woman sneered. "You're fucking with me, kid." She gripped Kang Jung by the throat. "I assure you, fucking with me is *not* a good idea."

"No, I'm *not*," Kang Jung rasped. "I swear. You can look the castle up yourself on my computer. The facility's in the basement of the castle at Everland Resort."

"Everland Resort?" The woman loosened her grip.

Janson watched in amazement at the girl's brisk thinking in the face of peril, as Kang Jung drew a desperate breath and said, "It's a water park."

* * *

KANG JUNG SLOWLY sat up on the bed as the dangerous woman stepped over to use her laptop computer. The woman unwittingly stared directly into the camera.

Kang Jung suppressed a satisfied grin. *Now he knows your face, bitch.*

She wriggled her butt toward the right side of her bed, keeping her eyes locked on the woman. Technology had made everything smaller, too small to be made into weapons. But it had also transformed all her devices into wireless creatures. Creatures that once or twice a day needed to be charged. So as not to lose any, Kang Jung assiduously kept all the wires and adapters in one drawer. In her nightstand. On the right side of her bed.

The woman glanced over but said nothing. Kang Jung could see that she'd pulled Everland Resort up on the screen. The woman was staring at the fairy princess's castle.

"You're not making this shit up, are you, kid?"

"No," Kang Jung said. "Several of the Hivemind are teenagers who work at the park. That's how they gain access to the castle anytime they want."

The woman nodded as if to say, *Makes sense*. Her eyes remained glued to the monitor.

Kang Jung reached behind her and with a pinkie surreptitiously opened the tiny, soundless drawer. She reached her slender hand inside and pulled out the first wire she touched. It felt magnificently familiar, of course; it was the USB cord she used to connect her laptop to her printer when the Wi-Fi connection was down.

With her hands tucked behind her, she wound each end around one of her wrists to ascertain the size of the cord.

Briefly she wondered if she'd have entertained such a devious thought had the intrigue surrounding the American translator's murder not come directly to her door.

Well, it did come to my door, didn't it?

She glanced back at her nightstand. Unwound one end of the USB and snatched the TV remote control next to her lamp. She placed the remote in her lap on the bed and wound the USB around her wrist again, this time with both hands out in front of her.

She drew a deep breath.

Stabbed at the power button on the remote.

The television across the room blinked to life. On the screen, several scantily clad women danced vigorously to earsplitting K-pop.

The woman immediately spun toward the television.

When she did, Kang Jung launched herself from the bed. Swinging the USB cord around the woman's neck, Kang Jung clung to the woman's back for her life.

Beneath her the woman bucked like a mechanical bull, trying to throw her off. But Kang Jung only tightened the cord around her throat, wrapped her strong legs around the woman's waist, and rode her harder.

As the woman thrashed from one side of the room to the other, Kang Jung swung her head in the direction of the camera.

Madly determined—but still terribly frightened—at the top of her lungs, she bellowed five blissfully histrionic words: "If I die, *avenge me!*"

TWENTY-FIVE

Unidentified Tunnel
Demilitarized Zone (DMZ), South Korea

I've lived through worse.

That would be the best Paul Janson could say to Kincaid if he made it out of the tunnel alive. Even that would be a stretch. Hell, the smell alone was nearly enough to overwhelm him.

Since he'd returned to the United States following his eighteen-month captivity in Kabul, Janson had masked his feelings of claustrophobia. A master at disguising his fears, Janson found that hiding his panic in tight places was one of the most challenging obstacles in his everyday life. True, the Embraer 650 was convenient, maybe even necessary, for carrying out his work in connection with CatsPaw and thus the Phoenix Foundation. But the whole of it was that he couldn't board a commercial airliner for any substantial length of time even if he tried. First class was tolerable—for a time; after a few hours he'd break out in a chilled sweat and have to throw off his seat belt and pace up and down the aisles. Coach was almost a physical impossibility for even the briefest of flights; he could barely survive a jaunt from Dulles to LaGuardia these days.

As he crawled along the dirt, the ceiling appeared to be falling in on him. It wasn't a cave-in, he knew, but a symptom of his claustrophobia. He stopped, maneuvered himself as best he could to dip into his go-bag, and plucked out a canteen for a slug of water.

The Machine. He smirked; if only that were true, life would undoubtedly be much easier.

Some people, like Kincaid, wore their hearts on their sleeves. But Janson never had. Janson dealt with his emotions internally, no matter how brightly they burned. Perhaps that was why Janson had so much trouble achieving closure. The bombing that killed Helene and his unborn child in Caligo, the betrayal of his superior Alan Demarest in Afghanistan—these events haunted Janson with such a ferocity, it felt as though time had frozen. They were wounds he knew would never heal. Paul Janson was no Machine. He'd never been one. He simply lived in his head. Shielded himself from friends and lovers every bit as much as he shielded himself from his enemies. Because, as hard and cold as people thought he was, past pains simply ran too deep.

"There's nothing out there for me," Kang Jung had said. Even though he traveled the world and pushed himself into people's lives to atone for the sins in his past, Janson often felt the same way.

In the blackness, he smiled sadly. He could still hardly believe what he'd seen on his BlackBerry only an hour ago. When Kang Jung attacked the woman in her room, he was sure the fight would end with the teenager dead. Instead, Kang Jung effectively applied an air choke, though she probably didn't even know its proper name.

Using the USB cord, Kang Jung had executed the choke with rare precision. No doubt a result of her knowledge of anatomy rather than any specific training, she'd used the USB to cut off the air flowing to the woman's heart and lungs by closing off her windpipe. It took the girl a full three minutes, during which she was nearly thrown from the woman's back several times, but in the end, Kang Jung brought down her prey like a professional. Hooking her legs around the woman's waist and keeping her face out of clawing range had saved Kang Jung's life and nearly ended that of the assassin. In fact, Janson hadn't been sure the woman was still alive until Kang Jung, wiping sweat from her forehead, leaned over and checked the woman's pulse.

"Unconscious," she'd said into the camera to her audience of one. "But her heart's still beating. What do I do now?"

Janson had immediately called Kang Jung's cell phone. When she picked up, he told her that she'd need to get to safety because there were no doubt agents who would come upstairs after a certain amount of time.

"You can't use the door downstairs," Janson had told her, "because they'll find you. Do you have any neighbors with firearms?"

"I'm in *Seoul*, not Arlington, Texas."

"Well, do you have any neighbors who you can completely trust?"

"Not with my life," she'd said. "People can't be counted on for anything." She paused. "But wait. I *do* have the perfect hiding spot."

Janson didn't like the idea until he heard it in full, then he urged her to get there, and fast. "Bring your phone, but remove the battery, just in case they have a lock on you. Only put the battery back in the phone for sixty seconds so that you can check for a text message from either me or my partner, Kincaid, letting you know how we're going to get you out of there."

"All right," she'd said.

"And, Jung..." He paused. "You did one hell of a job. Thank you."

"Think nothing of it," she'd said and then she was gone.

Janson had called Kincaid on Park Kwan's phone and directed her to the apartment in which Kang Jung was hiding.

"How can she be absolutely certain it's empty?" Kincaid asked.

"Jung has hidden cameras placed all over the apartment. The images go straight to her iPad Mini, which she has with her."

"Cameras?" Kincaid said. "Why would she have hidden cameras stashed in her neighbor's apartment?"

"Because she's not just a hacker extraordinaire and world-renowned Internet villain. She's also a bit of a vigilante. She'd hacked this guy's computer and found kiddie porn. She thinks he might be an online predator, so she's keeping an eye on him. The guy went away on vacation with one of his buddies." He hesitated as he thought about the implications. "In Thailand."

"The capital of sex tourism," Kincaid said. "Wonderful."

"It's something that can be dealt with later. Right now, I need you to collect Kang Jung and get her somewhere safe."

* * *

IN THE TUNNEL Janson continued through the stench, stopping every so often to retch. In addition to feeling as though the walls were closing in on him, he'd encountered all sorts of underground creatures in the past few hours—rats, cockroaches, things he couldn't even name.

All this to get to the most inhospitable country on earth.

All this to, in all likelihood, get myself captured or killed.

Janson considered the latter preferable to the former. There was no way he could do time in a North Korean gulag. He'd spend his days and nights praying—begging—for death. Provoking his guards to the point where they would have no choice but to put a bullet in the back of his skull. He couldn't live through another period like the one he'd lived through in Kabul.

He steered his mind away from thoughts of gulags and thought instead of the history that created this hellish hole in the planet.

The demilitarized zone, a strip of land 160 miles long and 2.5 miles wide, slashed the Korean peninsula in half and served as a buffer between the North and the South. Lined on both sides with electrified fences, landmines, tank traps, and armies in full battle readiness, the DMZ was the most heavily fortified border the world had ever known. In short, it was a powder keg just waiting to explode.

Over the past sixty years, since the end of the three-year Korean War, there had been numerous incidents and incursions that could very well have erupted into another full-scale war. In the sixties skirmishes claimed the lives of nearly a thousand soldiers, the fatalities split almost evenly between the two sides. In the seventies it was discovered that the North Koreans were planning an invasion through a series of infiltration tunnels. The invasion, had the tunnels not been discovered, would have included tanks and tens of thousands of troops.

Peace talks had been consistently unsuccessful. The South demanded of the North reforms that would inevitably collapse the illusions constructed by the Kim regime in order to keep control of its people. The North, for their part, needed all kinds of assistance, and would gladly take, take, take, but give nothing in return. Even in the face of a terrible famine that took millions of lives, the North remained belligerent, continuing its quest for nuclear weapons. Missile tests moved forward even as economic sanctions led to complete isolation and near collapse. Meanwhile, the North took umbrage at US–South Korean joint military exercises and consistently attacked unpopulated areas south of the DMZ in a futile attempt to stop them.

The collapse of the North Korean regime seemed inevitable, even to its closest ally, China. Yet no one seemed to be doing much to prepare. Even South Korean politicians were reluctant to discuss reunification, relentlessly avoiding questions from the international media, wholly ignoring the issue during their campaigns, merely touching on the sacrifices that would have to be made if the Korean peninsula became whole again in their inauguration speeches.

The adrenaline from the attack at Freedom Village had finally subsided; exhaustion was setting in. At any moment now any one of his limbs could give out. Short of breath, he feared he'd run out of air. Anxiety gnawed at him from within.

Still, Janson pushed on.

Given the events of the past few days, he wasn't certain of much. Especially whom he could and couldn't trust. Yet his instincts convinced him of one thing: he could be sure that if he *did* die in this tunnel, he would be dying for a good and noble cause. That in itself was enough to drive Janson forward.

* * *

"WHAT THE HELL do you mean you don't know where he is?"

Edward Clarke couldn't believe what he was hearing. On the other end of the line Vik Pawar became silent, save for his heavy breathing.

"That *wasn't* a rhetorical question," Clarke shouted. He reminded himself he'd have to be cautious with Vik Pawar. Pawar was Clarke's representative in Korea. He was the only agent who knew the details of Diophantus, the only agent who could single-handedly make or break the operation.

"I told you what I know, sir. Once Manningham entered the home, we maintained radio silence as per our orders. I was positioned in a neighboring structure watching Trotter's window through the scope of my sniper rifle. After nearly fifteen minutes I saw movement at the window, but I couldn't make out who it was so I didn't have a clean shot. Next thing I know Manningham takes a header out the window."

"He jumped?"

"I don't know, sir. That was my first belief, because seconds later the house exploded. But the way Manningham fell, he must have been unconscious. It was just a two-story drop, but he landed as though he'd just jumped off the top of the Empire State Building."

"You think Trotter did him?"

"He was the only one in the house, sir."

Clarke nearly slammed the handset against his desk but held back, gritting his teeth in the kind of frustration that causes cancer. "What happened after the explosion? Where was Trotter? Are you certain he wasn't in the house?"

"I'm fairly sure he made it out, sir. A mattress was found on the ground on the east side of the house. It was in fair condition, which means it wasn't blown through the window from the force of the explosion. More likely Trotter used it to jump to safety moments before the house went up in flames."

Son of a bitch. Sandy's right, Janson is a fucking golem.

Clarke bit down on his thumbnail, a habit he'd abandoned years ago. "And we have no intelligence on where he's headed?"

"None whatsoever, sir."

Without another word, Edward Clarke clicked over to the line holding Max Kolovos. "Where were we?" he said.

"Sir, I had just told you that I found Nika in the girl's bedroom. It appeared that she had been strangled. I felt for a pulse and determined she was alive, so I removed her to an empty stairwell, where I performed CPR. She eventually came to, but she's still out of it."

"Is she with you?"

"No, she's with the agent supplied by the little man."

Nam Sei-hoon, the little prick. If he hadn't helped Janson lose his tail after Seoul Station, Janson would already be dead. But no, Nam had to "keep up appearances."

Now Nam Sei-hoon had led his agent to an apartment in Itaewon to get her ass kicked by a pint-size ninja with Mark Zuckerberg's computer skills.

"And the girl?" Clarke said. "You have no idea where she is?"

"We've combed the entire area, sir. There's no sign of her. It's as though she's a ghost."

A ghost. This is the kind of shit I have to deal with.

"Well, Max, I'll let you in on a little secret. She's not a fucking ghost, she's a little girl. Now *find* her."

"Yes, sir."

Clarke was about to hang up when he recalled something Max had told him before he'd taken the call from Vik Pawar. "Wait a minute. You mentioned something earlier. About the girl's laptop. You said it was powered on and there was a web address still in the browser?"

"That's right, sir. The page was for a place called Everland Resort. It's apparently a water park roughly forty klicks north of Seoul."

"North?"

"Yes, sir."

"That may be just the break we've been looking for. Keep searching for the girl. I'll contact the little man and see if Nika's come around. If so, maybe she can tell us why she was surfing the net, exploring water parks when she was supposed to be interrogating a goddamn grade schooler."

TWENTY-SIX

National Intelligence Service Headquarters
Naegok-dong, Seocho-gu, Seoul

Nam Sei-hoon arrived at his office before dawn, which wasn't entirely unusual. To his colleagues, he seemed to be in a dark mood, which wasn't entirely unusual either. From all outward appearances, in fact, there was nothing particularly unusual about Nam Sei-hoon this morning. Inside, however, he stood on the brink of fury like never before.

How could the Americans have been so stupid?

Even if no one else in Washington did, Edward Clarke knew the stakes of this operation. Yet over the past seventy-two hours, there had been one colossal mistake after another. First, the US envoy inadvertently allows the translator Lynell Yi to overhear a sensitive discussion concerning Diophantus. Once Clarke assured Nam that the translator would be taken care of, Nam had been ready to put the matter aside. But, no, it turns out that the translator's live-in boyfriend is not only the son of a sitting US senator but an activist whose primary mission is to capture and disseminate state secrets. Fine, Nam had thought then, it could still be cleaned up. But then the assassin Clarke sends manages to eliminate the translator but allows the boyfriend—the true danger in all of this—to escape. And Nam *still* had not received a plausible explanation for this. A Cons Ops agent who can't handle two adolescents in a tiny hanok? Nam wished he could know what transpired in that room, but he'd probably never be given the full story.

No matter, Clarke had pledged, the boy would be found and filleted before he could do any damage. But then the boy vanishes into the ether, and who but Paul Janson is called upon by the senator to locate his son. Still, Nam Sei-hoon had figured, because of his long relationship with Janson, he could maintain some control of the situation. And sure enough, Janson contacted Nam and arranged a face-to-face meeting immediately upon his arrival in Seoul.

All Clarke had to do was find the boy, and Janson's visit would have been for naught. In the meantime, of course, Nam had to keep up appearances. He couldn't simply refuse Janson's request for assistance, and he couldn't botch things to a degree that would give his participation away. Paul Janson was a brilliant spy; he'd know instantly if Nam Sei-hoon attempted to sabotage his mission right from the start.

Then Nam bore witness to another flurry of Clarke's missteps. A botched attempt on Janson's partner, the female sniper, Jessica Kincaid. And *still* Clarke's people couldn't find the boy. *What incompetency.* Yet on whom does Edward Clarke place the blame? Squarely on the shoulders of Nam Sei-hoon. And for what? For assisting Janson with a Cold War maneuver to escape his shadow.

When Janson requested this simple favor, what was Nam Sei-hoon expected to say? *Sorry, Paul, but I'm short-staffed; all my men have come down with the flu.* Preposterous.

But, no, Clarke had something more sinister in mind. Clarke thought Nam should have ordered one of his men to kill Janson. To put a bullet in him in the rear of one of the taxis. Even more pre-posterous. This chaos wasn't of Nam's creation; it belonged fully to the Americans. Why should Nam order the execution of his old friend, a man he'd broken bread with more times than he could count? If Clarke wanted Janson dead, let him do the deed himself, the coward.

Nam Sei-hoon had already been forced into a number of shameful undertakings. The one he regretted most was giving up the young girl Kang Jung. He'd made Clarke guarantee that no harm would come to her, but Clarke's word was good for nothing, even when it came to matters of life and death. From the begin-ning Nam had known that he could only trust Clarke insofar as their countries' interests coincided.

Nam sighed. At this point he knew Paul Janson—a man he of-ten thought of as a surrogate son—would have to die. And Nam would deeply regret the loss, to be sure. But the fact was, the future of the Korean peninsula was at stake. So, if Paul and a thirteen-year-old girl had to be sacrificed, so be it. Many, many more lives would be lost before all this was over. None, however, would die in vain. Nam would make damn sure of that.

He opened a secure line and dialed Edward Clarke in Wash-ington.

"Have you located Janson?" Nam said.

"Not yet. After the explosion, my people scoured Daeseong-dong. We're now watching our former operative Jina Jeon in the unlikely case that Janson makes contact."

"Unlikely case? You had said they were lovers?"

"Right. But Janson may believe that Jina Jeon betrayed him." Clarke told Nam about the mother's medical appointment in Seoul.

Good, Nam thought, with no small measure of relief. *Better Janson believe he's been betrayed by Jina Jeon than believe he's been betrayed by me.*

He shuddered to think of what Janson would do to him if he discovered Nam's treachery.

"What of the Korean girl in Itaewon?" Nam said.

Clarke hesitated. "We haven't found her either."

Again, Nam felt relieved.

As he waited for Clarke to continue, the director coughed loudly in his ear.

You are vile, Nam thought.

When Clarke spoke again, his voice was tired, resigned. "I'm afraid I have some more bad news. But first some good news. As you know, we recovered the girl's laptop computer."

"Go on," Nam prodded.

"The last page opened was a website for Everland Resort, a water—"

"I know the place."

"Right. Well, the female operative we sent in to extract information says the girl gave up the location of Gregory Wyckoff. She claims that a facility at the water park is being used as a headquarters for the Hivemind, and the Hivemind is hiding Wyckoff there."

"That may be the dumbest thing I ever heard."

"Well, I sent two of my peop—"

"Then bring them *back*. It's a waste of precious resources. It is simply not true. The girl lied to your operative. This thirteen-year-old not only defeated your agent in combat. She *outsmarted* her, too. And you as well, evidently."

Nam could hear Clarke breathing heavily, reining in his famous temper.

"Fine," Clarke finally said. "Anyway, the other bad news is that this young lady visited a Wikipedia page recently as well."

"So?"

"The Wikipedia entry was for Diophantus."

A full minute of silence passed.

Nam was the first to speak. "If Janson and his ... *researchers* ... are using Wikipedia to discover the meaning behind Diophantus, then they don't have any hard information. At least not yet."

"Unfortunately, that's not so."

"What do you mean?"

"Apparently, the Wyckoff kid is even cleverer than we thought. He left a message behind on the Wikipedia entry. Not in full view; it was hidden. But apparently the young girl figured it out."

Nam felt as though a spider were crawling up his esophagus. "What is this message, Clarke?"

"We don't really know what it means," he said. "But it reads, 'Contact Yun Jin-ho, DPRK.'"

The spider reached the back of Nam's tongue and he nearly gagged.

"Are you all right?"

Nam didn't respond. His spy Yun Jin-ho was in no way connected to Diophantus, at least in no way that Nam was aware of. But then, why had the boy sent such a message?

Nam stared at the phone on his desk. He was helpless to contact Yun Jin-ho; the spy wasn't scheduled to make another dead drop for ninety days.

Suddenly he was struck by a bolt of panic.

Is Yun Jin-ho still under my control?

"Does that name mean anything to you?" Clarke pressed.

"I will have to look into it and get back to you."

Nam was about to hang up the handset when he heard Clarke call out: "There's one more thing you need to know about."

More? Nam just wanted to get off this damn phone and clear his throat with a drink of ice water. "What is it, Clarke?"

"We discovered one last thing on the girl's computer."

"Let me guess," Nam said. "Is it a photo of you and me fishing on the Potomac in a boat named *Diophantus*?"

"It may as well be."

Nam suddenly felt light-headed.

"The girl sent a link to a live feed capturing what was happening in her bedroom when our agent entered and interrogated her. We presume the link was sent to Janson."

Nam thought about it. *Janson knows they discovered Kang Jung?* There was only one way that Cons Ops could have discovered that the girl was helping Janson—through Nam Sei-hoon himself, who received the information from his cyber-intelligence unit, which was monitoring Cy's Internet Relay Chats.

Something I boasted about to Janson.

Nam's light-headedness gave way to raw ire.

"*Find Janson,*" he yelled into the phone. "Find him *now*, Clarke. Find the Machine before he comes for *me!*"

TWENTY-SEVEN

Northern Side of the Demilitarized Zone
Democratic People's Republic of Korea (DPRK)

Janson emerged from the hole just before dawn, his arms and legs caked with mud, his face as black as the tunnel walls. Though he could barely see through the heavy fog, he was grateful just for the clean breaths he could take as he belly-crawled on his elbows through the dampened, overgrown grass. Rising slowly from his hands and knees, he discovered that every inch of his body ached. His head was as heavy as a truck; he needed sleep. But this was no place to rest. If he were seen, he'd be shot on sight or, worse, delivered to a labor camp from which he'd never be released. And here, deep in the DMZ, he couldn't rule out the risk of setting his head down on a landmine.

Rest would have to wait.

Though moving forward wouldn't be much safer. He could

stumble over a trip wire rigged with explosives. Enveloped in the opaque mist, Janson could walk directly into an electrified fence and not know it until his flesh started to sizzle. A copse of trees stood roughly a hundred yards away to his left; a bullet fired from a sniper's nest could rip through his throat at any moment.

Undoubtedly, he was in far more danger now than he had been immediately following the shots that killed Silent Lynx at the construction site in Shanghai.

Because now, without question, Janson was behind enemy lines.

He crept low. Moved as quickly as possible while keeping his eyes peeled for booby traps. The fog made that challenge exceedingly difficult, but he took some comfort in the fact that if he couldn't see a few feet in front of his face, North Korean soldiers couldn't spot him either. Especially from any significant distance. To snipers he'd be all but invisible. A ghost.

Surely not the only ghost plodding through the high grass of the Korean Demilitarized Zone, he thought.

Unfortunately, the fog also prevented Janson from seeing where he was going. And with frigid winds blowing in from Siberia, he had to navigate through threadlike slits instead of wide-open eyes. He only needed to walk a straight line, but even that was a test in this weather.

He gritted his teeth. His blackened face was already frozen; he'd have to take precautions against frostbite. Frostbite led to amputations, not only of fingers and toes but also of ears and noses. He tugged on his ski cap, tucked his face into his black North Face coat, and moved forward.

His destination was the Reunification Highway, otherwise known as the Pyongyang-Kaesong Motorway. The distance from the DMZ to the capital city was roughly 215 klicks, or 133 miles. Much too far to walk, of course; Janson needed a vehicle. Once he obtained one, then he'd begin worrying about the numerous check-points and tank traps along the multiple-lane highway. *Then*, he promised himself, not a moment before.

A sound in the distance caused Janson to drop flat on his stomach. He listened. The noise resembled the hum of an engine. Janson knew he wasn't yet close enough to the highway to hear its traffic. Which meant that the engine he heard undoubtedly belonged to a military vehicle on patrol.

He inched forward and continued to listen. The vehicle was moving east to west at no more than ten or fifteen miles per hour. Janson mused that its presence was as close as he'd ever come to describing something as a blessing in disguise.

He lifted his field glasses and spotted the vehicle just as it rolled to a stop. From Janson's vantage point, it appeared to be a jeep, military green and as old as the DMZ itself. He couldn't be sure but he thought he could make out at least two soldiers inside.

At least I'm not too close to a cluster of landmines, Janson thought. Unless even North Korean soldiers were occasionally caught by surprise. Certainly a possibility given what little he—or anyone else for that matter—knew about the country.

"Pyongyang is an intelligence black hole," Jina Jeon had told him.

Through his field glasses, Janson watched the soldiers exit the jeep on either side. Each of the men carried what appeared to be a Chinese-manufactured AK-47. The fact that he could make out the weapons meant the fog was beginning to lift. For better or worse, it meant that Janson would have to work even faster than he'd anticipated.

He reached for his go-bag. Silently, he assembled his M110.

He set himself then peered through the scope. Instantly he spotted one of the soldiers standing casually behind the jeep.

He quickly scanned the area for the second.

The second man was no longer visible.

Where did you go? Why the hell would you wander off?

Before he finished the thought Janson's instincts kicked in; he realized he'd been spotted. Maintaining a tight grip on his rifle, he rolled fast to his left just as thick patches of dirt and grass began kicking up all around him. The crackling of the AK-47 resonated in his chest.

Ignoring the universal pain in his body, Janson pushed himself to his feet and started running, stealing a look back to try to determine from which direction—*directions*, plural now—he was being fired upon.

In a serpentine pattern he crossed the stretch of open land heading south and slightly east toward the copse of trees. Following a few agonized seconds of internal debate, he'd decided that heading back toward the tunnel was suicide—*even if* his being spotted was just a stroke of poor luck and his point of ingress into the North hadn't been compromised.

That tunnel, Janson intuited, was far less likely to serve as his means of escape than as his grave.

As he ran, Janson had no hope of consciously avoiding booby traps. Each time his combat boots hit the ground he risked detonating a landmine. Every time he lifted a boot to move forward he gambled his life on there not being a trip wire set directly in his path.

The soldiers' shots were wild. A half dozen or so buzzed by within a few feet of him, but most of the bullets came nowhere close. Janson felt fortunate that the fog hadn't lifted altogether. The mist made him an elusive target.

Not quite a ghost anymore, he imagined as he ran, but still more difficult to trace than an ordinary man.

Once Janson had moved far enough away, the shots became fewer and farther between. He slowed as he considered dropping into the tall grass and spinning around, setting his rifle and waiting for one of the soldiers to step into his sights. But then he heard the engine of the jeep roar to life.

He took off again.

When he reached the tree line, Janson experienced a small measure of relief. Although he wasn't by any means safe, the trees would at least help slow the soldiers down, and hopefully help level the playing field.

As he checked his magazine Janson surveyed the area beyond the southern tree line. He was surprised to find just how close he was to the border. In the distance he could make out a tall metal fence topped with rings of barbed wire.

Shit. A shot from the soldier's assault rifle struck the bark of a tree just a few yards away. Janson immediately slipped out of his go-bag, dropped the M110, and collected his Beretta. He fired once through the fog in the general direction of the soldiers—then bolted for the electrified fence on the border.

The grass surrounding the fence was waist-high on both sides.

Janson fired several shots from staggered positions then dove for cover behind a thick tree stump roughly halfway between the fence and the forest.

Over the next several minutes the air above his head grew still and silent as the soldiers searched for their quarry.

Turn the hunter into the hunted, he thought, breathing heavily, the predator into the prey.

Strangely, the silence remained absolute. Janson stifled a cough in his throat. The dead air of the tunnel still lay at the bottom of his lungs like a fungus.

Come on. *Give me a sound, any sound,* so I know where you are.

Still nothing but silence save for his steadying breaths.

Patience, Janson thought. Patience.

In the cold, wet grass he waited.

TWENTY-EIGHT

Outside 322 Sowol-ro
Yongsan-gu, Seoul

From the street Sin Bae watched the American woman escort the girl into the opulent lobby of the Grand Hyatt Seoul. From his pocket he extracted his phone. He would need to contact Ping for information on the hotel. In the meantime, however, Sin Bae couldn't remain outside, exposed. So he headed for the pretentious apartment building looming across the roadway.

The girl's name, he'd been told, was Kang Jung. She was thirteen years old, as fresh-faced and beautiful as his sister Su-ra had been at that age. Su-ra, all those years ago. Sin Bae profoundly regretted what would have to be done to the girl.

And he couldn't help but accept the fact that her blood would be on his hands—in more ways than one.

Had he succeeded in eliminating Gregory Wyckoff when he did the interpreter at the Sophia Guesthouse, this child would never have become involved.

She should not be here, Sin Bae thought with a touch of sadness. This girl should be at her school.

Thinking of her, he flashed on the labor camp in which he'd been imprisoned as a child. At Yodok, Sin Bae and Su-ra had attended a school nothing like the one in which they'd studied in Pyongyang. At Yodok the teachers behaved viciously; fellow students fell out of their chairs from hunger. Some children went mad right before his eyes.

He often looked around the cramped classroom in terror. Dirt clung to every child's hair, and fleas covered their bodies. There was no soap and little water at Yodok. Everyone was weak. All but a few were missing teeth.

After a half day in school, under the constant threat of violence from armed guards, Sin Bae chopped wood, hauled logs, grew corn, and pulled weeds, while his sister Su-ra worked from afternoon till evening in a dilapidated sweatshop on the opposite end of the camp. Everyone at Yodok was forced to work, even the too old and the too young. For many, labor quietly became a death sentence.

But Sin Bae was strong. He could handle the work, he could handle the constant berating from teachers, even the occasional beating. He could handle the appalling conditions. What he could not handle was being separated all but one hour a day from his sister, Su-ra.

Sin Bae waited outside the apartment building for only a few minutes before a young man, exiting, held the door open for Sin Bae to come in from the cold. Inside, Sin Bae immediately took the stairwell up. When he reached the top floor, the eleventh, he peered through the narrow vertical window set in the dark-red steel door. It was just after 7 AM and many of the young professionals who inhabited the building were leaving for work. From the stairwell Sin Bae watched the hallway to see which flat on the south side of the building—the side facing the Grand Hyatt—would be vacated first.

Ten minutes later a young couple stepped out of their apartment and locked the door. Sin Bae waited until the elevator doors met then entered the hall. As he neared the couple's door the bark of a small dog caused him to hesitate. He did not wish to kill the dog. But he also knew he would not be able to concentrate if he had to listen to the canine scratching and yapping from behind a closed bedroom door.

He listened carefully. After several seconds he determined that the barking was emanating from the apartment on the opposite side of the hall. He continued on, removing the lock pick from his pocket.

Sin Bae stepped into apartment 11-E and locked the door, then headed straight for the picture window facing the hotel. He pushed aside the lavish curtain. Removed a small pair of binoculars from inside his jacket and focused on the sidewalk in front of the lobby.

As he watched the sidewalk, he made his call to Ping in Shanghai.

A few minutes later, when he spotted the back of the man's head, he thought he was imagining things. He looked again, focusing on the round bald spot at the top (what the Americans called "a silver dollar"), and watched as the man twisted his plump neck to inspect his surroundings. As implausible as it seemed, now there was no doubt. The middle-aged man was the same paunchy Korean whom Jessica Kincaid had danced with at the club the night before last. The man who had distracted Sin Bae from his mission, the man who'd allowed Kincaid to escape Sin Bae's grasp in the coatroom of the T-Lound nightclub.

This was the man truly responsible for the involvement of the teenage girl who reminded Sin Bae so much of his sister, Su-ra. The girl Sin Bae was now under orders to kill.

He closed his eyes. Something akin to anger rose in Sin Bae's chest as he set down the binoculars to contemplate his next steps.

* * *

THE RAP AT THE hotel room door startled Kincaid as she stepped out of the bathroom.

She promptly shook it off, realizing that it must be Park Kwan on the other side of the door. After peeking through the peephole, she undid the chain, unlocked the dead bolt, and opened the door. Park Kwan stepped past her with a smile on his face.

"I may have a lead on the boy," he said.

"What kind of lead?" she said. "How strong? How reliable?"

He grinned confidently. "As reliable as facial recognition software."

Kincaid's eyes widened in horror. "You didn't speak to anyone at your department, did you? I told you *specifically*—"

"No, no." Park Kwan lifted his palm in a defensive gesture that left Kincaid feeling guilty for pouncing on him. "This has nothing to do with the South Korean government at all. *This* is a private enterprise."

Kang Jung, who'd been sitting at the room's lone desk, leafing through the hotel's in-room dining menu, swiveled around to face them. "The International Finance Center *Mall*?" she exclaimed.

Park Kwan nodded in the girl's direction. "Precisely."

"But," Kang Jung said, abruptly rising from her chair, "the kiosks at the mall only estimate an individual's age and gender. The mall sees nearly two million shoppers every month, and most of them are probably around Gregory Wyckoff's age. How could that possibly help us?"

Park Kwan's grin broadened. "The software is somewhat more sophisticated than the mall's owners and the system's creators would have you believe." He turned to Kincaid. "See, South Korea's privacy laws prohibit companies from collecting personal information from customers without their consent. Legally, they cannot admit to recording and storing customers' images. But as a practical matter..."

"Big Brother is watching," Kang Jung said with a sour expression. "Those bastards. When I get to a computer I am immediately going to hack into their system and—"

"Wait, young lady," Park Kwan said, raising his palm again. "Let's not lose sight of what is important at this moment. We need to find the boy. More than privacy may be at stake here. Given what we already know, this entire city may be at risk."

Kincaid said, "Tell us what you've discovered."

Park Kwan cleared his throat and adopted a more serious, more professional tone. "Jung is right. The idea behind the mall's facial recognition software is to estimate a customer's age and gender in order to permit advertisers to tailor their interactive ads. But, as I mentioned, the software actually goes much further than that. It is a secret very few people know."

"How did you get so lucky?"

He blushed ever so slightly. "I have a lady friend who works at the conglomerate that makes the software. She knew I was looking to retire from the police department, so she offered to recommend me for a job in their security division." He sighed. "I passed the interview process, as well as the background check and drug tests.

But—and looking back, I suppose this shouldn't have surprised me—the company has prospective employees followed by in-house investigators to determine what their private lives are like before the final hire. Like any organization that hires employees who will handle sensitive material, this company wants to make certain that their candidates are not potential targets for blackmail. That they are not in the kind of debt that would motivate them to sell confidential information to competitors or the media.

"In my case," he continued solemnly, "they discovered that I drank, and they feared that my intoxication would lead me to divulge trade secrets." He cocked his head to one side then the other. "Which I suppose I am doing now as we speak." He shrugged his wide shoulders. "Well, the joke is on them because at the moment I am as sober as a stone."

"But if you were not hired..." Kang Jung began.

Park Kwan turned to her with a sheepish expression. "My lady friend—she, too, partakes in the spirits, if you will."

"All right," Kincaid said, anxious now for Park Kwan to get to the crux, "when did the software pick up Gregory Wyckoff at the mall?"

"The morning he went missing."

"*Jeez Louise*," Kincaid burst out. "That doesn't help us. He could be *anywhere* by now."

"*Please*, Louise," Park Kwan shot back, "wait until I am finished." He exhaled audibly then sucked in his gut and puffed out his chest. "It is not the fact that his face was captured that is important. It is what he was captured doing that is vital."

Kang Jung stepped forward, her voice quiet and contemplative. "He stole something, didn't he?"

"Correct, young lady," Park Kwan said. "He swiped a smartphone from the purse of a cashier at one of the mall's accessory kiosks. She thought she simply misplaced the phone and has not yet contacted the carrier. So I am having the signal triangulated. We should have news of his whereabouts—or at least the direction in which he is traveling—shortly."

"*And* a record of who he called," Kang Jung said, almost to herself. "Maybe even which websites he visited."

TWENTY-NINE

One soldier paced along the electrified fence; the other remained several hundred yards away with the jeep. A light snow had begun to fall. From behind the tree stump in the overgrown grass, Janson considered his Beretta but then thought better of it. He didn't want to risk exposing his position to the second gunman.

The soldier clenched his AK-47, alert and ready, as he trudged along the fence in Janson's direction.

Perched on his haunches like a tightly coiled spring, Janson took a deep breath and steeled himself. He intended to take the soldier down with a choke hold before they could be spotted by the gunman with the jeep. But just as Janson was about to launch himself, the soldier sensed his presence and spun toward him, aiming the assault rifle directly at Janson's head.

Janson didn't hesitate. Like a cornered king cobra, he sprang at the soldier anyway, clutching the barrel of the rifle and jerking it away from his face. The gun went off, three successive shots straight up into the blank sky, and Janson realized he had to act swiftly before the other soldier made his approach.

There wasn't time to execute a choke hold. Instead, driving his shoulder into the gunman's chest and grabbing the backs of his knees, Janson lifted the soldier up and flung his body backward, dumping him against the fence.

Instantly upon impact the soldier's upper body began to convulse.

Over the hiss and sputter of thousands of electric volts, the soldier shrieked—but there was nothing Janson could do to ease his suffering.

Covering his face against the sparks and the stench of charring flesh, Janson dropped to his knees and snatched the fallen AK-47.

As the current cut off and the soldier's corpse thumped against the hard ground, Janson swung the rifle in the direction of the jeep tearing toward him.

Janson restrained himself from firing.

He didn't want to blow his blessing in disguise to kingdom come.

Instead of running, he dropped into a crouch. A thinning fog still hung conveniently in the air like a threadbare bedsheet drying in the breeze. And stationary targets, though easier to hit, were more difficult to see. Particularly in the mist.

The jeep roared toward him, though not at full speed. The driver was exercising caution; he clearly didn't want to plow the military's jeep into the electrified fence.

Janson didn't want that either.

The jeep was traveling at roughly forty miles per hour. Not fast, but fast enough to make braking on the frozen earth a problem. A problem Janson meant to use to his advantage.

He popped up from his crouch so that the driver would see him through the fog and falling snow. Then Janson confused him.

From roughly a thousand yards away, Janson ran straight toward the oncoming jeep, the dead Korean's AK-47 swinging from his right arm.

The driver instinctively slowed, then caught his mistake and accelerated.

Janson knew he was playing a dangerous game of chicken but saw no other choice. He waited until the jeep was almost on him, then feinted left but broke hard to his right.

The driver bit and there was no time to correct course. The jeep fell into a skid and continued sliding sideways for several seconds before finally coming to a dead stop a few hundred yards from the fence.

Janson, who'd been racing after the vehicle from the moment it passed him, halted just as the jeep did. In one fluid motion he planted his left foot and raised the AK-47. With the selector locked in the lower semiautomatic position, he aimed through the sight into the driver's-side window and pulled the trigger.

Following one crisp and concise burst, the driver's body slumped forward against the steering column.

Janson released his breath in a puff of smoke, then lowered the rifle and hustled toward the vehicle—all the while mouthing a silent entreaty that he hadn't damaged the windshield too badly.

*   *   *

A LITTLE OVER AN HOUR later the body of the soldier was clear of the vehicle and the blood and bits of skull and brain were cleaned up as well as Janson was ever going to get them using the few tools he had at his disposal.

After a few minutes of rest, he changed into spare fatigues he'd found in the rear of the jeep and collected his weapons and go-bag. As far as Janson could tell, the soldiers hadn't been able to alert reinforcements. Of course, given the potential punishment for allowing an infiltrator to escape, it was possible they'd simply chosen not to sound the alarm. At least not until they had Janson dead or in custody.

The windshield of the jeep had suffered a minor crack, which had begun to spiderweb. No doubt it would get worse in the hours to come, forcing Janson to change vehicles.

But for now he could see the field in front of him well enough. He started the engine and backed away from the fence before swinging the jeep around so that it was facing north.

There were just 110 miles between him and the capital. And only a million-man standing army with a $6 billion annual budget to try to stop him.

With his right foot, Janson pressed down hard on the accelerator and moved forward through the thinning mist.

THIRTY

Reunification Highway
Kaesong, DPRK

The vehicle in which Janson was now traveling held at a steady fifty miles per hour. Although the speed was slower than he would have liked, he had to admit he felt bizarrely comfortable. The temperature inside his compartment was well below zero, but at least he was protected against the ruthless Siberian winds. His unrelenting claustrophobia, on the other hand, kept him on edge, made his entire body feel as though it were being stuck repeatedly by countless pins and needles. The stench was unpleasant but tolerable. Especially considering the fact that he was packed head to toe among thousands of cheap frozen seafood lunches and dinners destined for the Kaesong Industrial Complex.

Knowing he'd never make it past the first checkpoint, Janson had abandoned the jeep as soon as the Reunification Highway came into view. With his go-bag strapped to his back, he moved parallel to the road through the dense forest to the east, hoping to spot a vehicle in which he could hide. Problem was, traffic heading north along the six-lane Reunification Highway was light; *beyond* light—the road was very nearly deserted. So when he spotted the small white truck with the fresh-fish logo, he didn't hesitate to step onto the roadway to flag it down.

Seeing the KPA uniform, the driver, whose truck bore South Korean tags, pulled to the side of the road. By the time the driver noticed that the soldier wasn't Korean, his engine was turned off and his door was standing open. Janson helped the driver down from the cab and tried to reassure him that he was safe. In fact, he was about to receive the deal of a lifetime.

Even now, as the truck rumbled on toward the Kaesong Industrial Complex, Janson's greatest concern remained the driver. Simply standing outside his truck in the frigid winds, the man had been sweating. Janson noted too that the man's voice grew shakier with every sentence he uttered. It had been difficult enough to understand the driver's slaughtered English at the start of the conversation; by the end Janson was just nodding and flashing more Korean currency.

He's going to fold the moment he pulls up to the checkpoint, Janson thought.

But no. Since Janson and Kincaid had arrived in Seoul just two days ago, Janson had encountered innumerable surprises, from the brilliant thirteen-year-old girl who fought off a well-trained Cons Ops agent at least twice her age to being betrayed by one of his oldest and dearest friends.

The traitor's name hung in Janson's head like a bloated body at the end of a noose.

Nam Sei-hoon.

When the truck finally slowed, Janson tried to envision the KPA checkpoint they were no doubt approaching. From the freezer in the rear of the vehicle he willed the driver to remain calm and cool. After all, the driver had nearly as much at stake as Janson himself. He'd accepted a bribe to smuggle an American into the Kaesong Industrial Complex. Even if the man lied and said he had been threatened, there was no guarantee that the North Koreans would believe him. They wouldn't *want* to believe. Why arrest one when they could arrest two—an American *and* a South Korean? Surely the driver knew he'd be thrown into the same labor camp as Janson, at least until one or both could be executed.

The man had a wife and three school-aged children waiting for him back in South Korea. His family was the reason he'd risked his life and accepted the bribe in the first place. The poor guy had to commute more than a hundred miles every day into the bowels of North Korea, and for what? To earn 160 bucks a month, a fifth of the minimum wage in his home country of South Korea.

No, Janson felt confident that the driver would remain strong. He'd tell his lies and collect his money and return to the South, never to set foot in the North again.

Given the man's motivation, Janson felt certain of it.

Still, as the truck rolled to a sudden standstill, Janson gripped the Beretta tightly in his right hand, his finger hovering over the trigger.

Just in case.

* * *

SIN BAE STEPPED into the Grand Hyatt Seoul wearing a thick overcoat and a baseball cap pulled low over his eyes. Both items borrowed from the apartment he'd just vacated. He suffered no illusion that the coat and hat would provide a disguise, but he didn't want his face and form to be captured by the ubiquitous surveillance cameras monitored by the hotel. And of course, he didn't want to enable staff and other hotel guests to provide an accurate description of him to police once the job was done.

Moving quickly through the luxuriant, modern lobby, he surveyed the scene. The first trick would be finding out in which room the man, woman, and child were hiding. There were 601 rooms and suites in total according to his handler Ping, who had accessed the Hyatt's computer system from Shanghai. Unfortunately, Kincaid's name was not in the Hyatt's database. Evidently, the resourceful American woman had checked in using a false identity, undoubtedly one of many she kept at the ready.

Sin Bae now needed to access the closed-circuit television system. He might not learn exactly which room the trio had taken, but at a minimum he hoped to discover the floor on which they were placed. Since he had no intention of attempting to force his way inside Kincaid's room, that was the only information he truly needed. She and the man she was with were no doubt armed. Therefore, his strategy involved luring all three out of the room in order to strike.

Sin Bae took the stairwell to the second floor. According to the building's layout, which Ping had forwarded to him, that was where he would find the security office. Ping had also been able to purchase (or perhaps trade for) some intelligence. Specifically, he learned that no more than two officers occupied the security room at any time. Several other guards, sometimes dressed in plainclothes, patrolled the hallways and staffed the main lobby.

Sin Bae didn't need a photograph to recognize one such guard. The individual was obvious. A young Korean male, dressed in a dark-blue suit with a muted red tie, walked right past him in the second-floor hallway. Sin Bae turned and watched him punch the button to summon the down elevator.

Sin Bae returned to the stairwell and descended one flight to the lobby. Just as he entered, so did the guard he'd seen upstairs. Sin Bae looked on as the man stepped over to the front desk, stopping briefly to flirt with a young staffer. The guard leaned in as he spoke to the comely desk clerk, and even touched her arm in a familiar manner before heading outside and liberating a package of cigarettes from the inside pocket of his jacket.

When he exited, the guard acknowledged a pair of doormen then turned left. Surely hotel rules prohibited him from smoking directly outside the main entrance.

Sin Bae followed the man around the corner, keeping his eyes peeled for outdoor surveillance cameras. The man turned again at the rear of the mammoth hotel and moved toward a line of dumpsters, where he fished a silver lighter out of his right front pant pocket and thumbed the flint wheel. Slowly, he turned his back against the wind until he was facing the hotel.

Sin Bae scanned the area for bystanders. When he saw no one, he reached for his left cuff link and quickly advanced on his target.

*　*　*

WHEN THE DOOR to the freezer finally opened it was the driver's face Janson saw—and mercifully, he was alone. As Janson stepped down from the tailgate he noticed how calm the man now was, how unrushed and unafraid. A broad smile materialized on the man's face; clearly he was proud of his accomplishment and already thinking of the many ways in which his family's life was about to change for the better.

After the driver took his money and drove off, Janson gazed up at the tall buildings of the sprawling industrial park. The 800-acre complex housed more than 120 South Korean companies, which employed North Koreans at a rate of roughly $45 a month. Appalling, yet still a better opportunity than most for men and women in the North.

Not surprisingly, the light industrial park was forced to close its many doors when tensions inevitably rose between the hostile neighbors.

For Janson, Kaesong represented a real shot at making it to Pyongyang to locate Yun Jin-ho. When Jina Jeon's house was blown to pieces, so was his original plan to have Kang Jung help him pinpoint Yun Jin-ho's location via computer in the morning. When Kang Jung was subsequently attacked in her home, any pieces of the plan that might have remained intact were obliterated. Janson had thus entered North Korea blind. Although his path was still in no way clear, the first leg of the Reunification Highway had proven successful—and bolstered Janson's confidence.

Yet he was under no illusion. Even if he made it to the capital city and located Nam Sei-hoon's spy, he'd still face the uphill challenge of convincing Yun Jin-ho to trust him—not only a complete stranger but an *American*—and to cooperate. Surely it would be no easy task.

But first things first.

Clear like water, cool like ice.

One precious step at a time.

THIRTY-ONE

Kim Il-sung Square
Pyongyang, DPRK

Janson couldn't help but feel as if he'd just stepped onto a film set in Burbank, California. Though he had traveled the world, he'd never once set foot in a city quite like this.

Draped in freshly fallen snow, Pyongyang seemed to Janson like a well-preserved corpse: lovingly manicured; meticulously arranged; respectfully presented. Despite a population of over three million, however, the capital of North Korea gave the distinct impression of serving merely as a vessel, a shell, a foundation for a city utterly devoid of life.

The architecture was as old as the nation itself, erected atop the rubble of the Korean War. Yet there was not a speck of graffiti to be found. While poverty ran rampant in the rest of the country, not a single homeless person lurked in these city streets.

The sky was as white as the snow, and clean. Only one motor vehicle—the old, gray Pyeonghwa Pronto he'd hot-wired in Kaesong—could be seen from Janson's vantage point in Kim Il-sung Square, making it impossible to imagine a traffic jam.

The sidewalks were litterless. But lifeless as well.

The impressive structures, Janson thought sadly, were indeed set pieces, show-things for visitors who would never be permitted to view the hundreds of thousands, perhaps millions, of wrongly imprisoned and starving.

Janson broke away from the depressing (albeit scenic) vista to continue his hunt for Yun Jin-ho.

In Kaesong, Janson had realized that the industrial park represented his last opportunity to obtain some intelligence. Of course, his cellular phone had become useless the moment he entered the tunnel in the DMZ. And calls to South Korea from the North were barred—*except* calls emanating from the Kaesong Industrial Region, which housed the North's only South Korean companies.

So Janson had stealthily entered the buildings, looking for a landline.

The mission was less difficult than he imagined. Much of the complex was not currently in use. With Kim Jong-un as a landlord, Janson supposed, it shouldn't have come as a great shock.

Once he located a functional yet unoccupied office, Janson immediately tried dialing Park Kwan. When the call went straight to voice mail, he hung up and attempted Kang Jung. Both had their phones shut off, just as he'd feared. Good security on their part; bad luck for Janson. At least until he spotted an inconspicuous slip of paper posted on a cork bulletin board on the wall directly behind the desk.

The paper listed the area codes inside the People's Democratic Republic of Korea, nearly all of them within Pyongyang's city limits, since the capital was just about the only place in the country where telephones were permitted. Janson's first thought was to call the Swedish embassy, which provided Protective Power for US citizens in North Korea. Risky, but initially it seemed to be his only option.

Then his finger slid down the page to a spot where two international calling codes were enumerated. Although the countries were identified by Korean symbols, Janson recognized the codes. The first belonged to Russia, the second to China.

Janson's heart began to beat faster. Before entering the tunnel, he had tried reaching both Morton and Grigori Berman. Neither hacker had answered his phone. Janson now had at least one more shot at contacting Berman in Moscow.

He lifted the handset of the old phone and dialed the Russian's number from memory.

Grigori Berman picked up on the first ring. Ten minutes later, Janson had a Pyongyang address for Yun Jin-ho. An address that was unavailable even in Nam Sei-hoon's system at the National Intelligence Service in Seoul. Although Janson repeatedly asked, Berman refused to divulge his source. After a few halfhearted attempts, Janson decided not to press the issue.

"All right, forget it," he finally said just before hanging up. "Again, *spasibo.*"

"You are very much welcome, Paulie."

Janson would later regret not pushing harder.

* * *

WHEN JANSON FINALLY LOCATED the address, a few blocks north of Kim Il-sung Square, he decided his best bet was simply to ring the doorbell of Yun Jin-ho's apartment. But when he reached the top of the front concrete steps, the yellowed label next to apartment 5B didn't contain Yun's name.

Janson considered the possibilities. Perhaps this was a new address and the ancient tape hadn't yet been updated. *Could he be using a legend?* Given the regime's tight controls over the population, Janson didn't think so. No, it was far more likely that this was the wrong address altogether. Janson deflated. Just like that, he lamented, he could very well be returned to square one.

Nevertheless, he pressed the buzzer for 5B and waited. If no one answered, he'd break into the building and enter the apartment to search for clues.

But following a few silent, uneasy moments, a voice, young and female, squawked through the intercom. Janson leaned in toward the speaker but couldn't make out what the young woman was saying.

He responded by reciting Yun Jin-ho's name, leaving a clear question mark at the end. Then he waited for a reaction.

He expected at the very least a barrage of questions about who he was and what he wanted with the man. Janson had prepared several answers in advance. But the woman surprised him by pressing the buzzer instead. The door came unlocked and Janson opened it, unsure whether this was an auspicious beginning, or he was marching straight into a trap.

He muttered a curse at Berman's obstinacy over not disclosing his source for the address. But then he thought, Does it really matter at this point?

For Janson, there was clearly no turning back now. As he opened the door and started up the stairs, he pictured the bridge that Jina Jeon had pointed out in the demilitarized zone and briefly considered the irony.

Without question, Janson had long ago passed the point of no return.

*   *   *

Stepping into apartment 5B felt like stepping back in time. To the left was a kitchen, clean but cluttered, showcasing appliances that had no doubt lived through the installment by the Soviets of Kim Il-sung as leader of North Korea six decades ago. On the kitchen table, large enough for two, sat a single plate containing half a pancake, kimchi, and an egg, with a small cup of soy sauce on the side.

Janson's eyes wandered around the flat. The interior was every bit as gray as the exterior, with little else to boast about: a tape deck resting next to a stack of audiocassettes; a boxy 12-inch television topped with rabbit ears; a prehistoric sofa that would unquestionably crack under Grigori Berman's ample weight.

The young woman who opened the door stood in front of him with slumped shoulders that rose as she took in the full sight of him. If she was frightened by Janson's presence she had no intention of showing it.

"You are an American," she whispered.

Having just passed a number of gargantuan billboards featuring cartoonish American soldiers dressed in uniforms from the midtwentieth century, all carrying rifles with razor-sharp bayonets pointed threateningly at young children, Janson wasn't sure how to respond.

When in doubt, Janson often went with the truth. As he did now with a single bob of his head.

"You are looking for Yun Jin-ho," she said so softly he could barely hear her. "May I to ask you why?"

For a North Korean, at least, the young woman's English was sublime.

"Are you his wife?" he said, trying to match her volume.

She hesitated then finally shook her head.

"But this is his home," Janson said, motioning toward walls covered in faded gray wallpaper, peeling at both ends.

"No," she said, "this is my parents' home. I live with them." She evidently noticed the subtle change in Janson's features. "Do not worry; they are both at work and will not be home until late."

"They work in Pyongyang?" he said to keep her talking.

"Yes, both my mother and father, they work for the party."

Janson felt something shift in his chest. In North Korea "the party" could only mean "the Workers' Party," the communist party, the party of the late Kim Il-sung, the late Kim Jong-il, and the country's current dictator, Kim Jong-un.

"Are you hungry?" the young woman said, pointing to her small breakfast plate.

Although he was famished, Janson shook his head. North Koreans barely had enough food to eat for themselves. The famine of the 1990s killed off 10 percent of the country's population, and according to a recent United Nations panel, hunger and malnutrition continued to be widespread—and continued to result in untold deaths.

Janson studied his host's face. Like most North Korean women she wore no makeup. She, in particular, needed none. She was a natural beauty, her body slim but healthy. People in Pyongyang ate better than the rest of the country.

Janson fought off the confusion he felt. If this were the delicate dance he'd anticipated, he didn't want to step on her toes. Yet he couldn't account for her letting him into her home, for her offering him breakfast, for her not running away, screaming, the moment she recognized that he was "an American bastard," as the North's ubiquitous propaganda espoused.

He had so many questions. But even in his state of exhaustion, he quickly puzzled together the reason the young woman would not be willing to provide any answers. And why she spoke in such a low voice despite the fact that they were alone.

The home could well be bugged. The Ministry of State Security, North Korea's primary counterintelligence service, was responsible for investigating cases of domestic espionage. If Yun Jin-ho and this young woman were even remotely suspected of spying, the MSS would be listening in.

Janson's eyes instinctively moved to the wall over the television, where three spotless framed photos hung. One of Kim Il-sung, the Great Leader. One of Kim Jong-il, the Dear Leader. One of Kim Jung-un, the Great Successor.

The young woman stepped closer to him. For a moment Janson thought she was about to embrace him. Instead she stood on tiptoes and cupped her right hand behind his left ear.

She whispered, "We should go someplace else to talk, yes?"

Janson nodded but said nothing. He felt embarrassed by how filthy he must be, how awful he must smell. From the hours he spent crawling through the tunnel. From his brawl and firefight in the DMZ. From his unanticipated ride in the fish truck. He'd managed to find a bathroom and clean up some in Kaesong but not nearly enough to make himself presentable.

Her lips went to the side of his head again. "There exists a safe house not far from here."

Janson mustered all his concentration as she softly spoke the street address and apartment number into his ear.

"You should go first," she said. "If we were to be seen to-gether..."

Janson didn't need her to complete the sentence. If they were seen together, the young woman would very likely face the same penalty that Janson would face if he was spotted in the country alone.

THIRTY-TWO

I n the security room on the second floor of the Grand Hyatt Seoul, Sin Bae removed his heavy overcoat and draped it over the man who had been monitoring the cameras. Then he took the dead man's seat and studied the controls. He needed to move quickly. The body of the first guard (whose keys he had taken) was tucked safely away in the dumpster behind the hotel. But there was no way to know whether yet another guard would attempt to enter the security room before Sin Bae could extract the information he needed.

Sin Bae identified the controls that switched the monitors from one camera to another, then flipped through all of the cameras to identify the location of each. He played with the buttons until he figured out how to rewind a specific video feed.

Fortunately, each video was time-stamped. Since Sin Bae had made a note of the precise time Kincaid and Kang Jung had entered the hotel, as well as when the man from the nightclub arrived nearly a half hour later, locating the floor they were assigned to would be that much easier.

Voices in the hallway caused him to pause and turn toward the door. The voices, those of two or more Korean men, increased in volume as they drew near.

Sin Bae rose from the dead man's chair.

But then one of the men broke out into laughter and the second man joined in. Soon the voices faded down the hallway.

Sin Bae sat down and relaxed, determined to get the information he needed quickly so that he could get clear of the security room without killing any more of the hotel's staff.

* * *

KINCAID WATCHED PARK KWAN pace the room holding the cordless telephone provided by the hotel. Her thumb went to her lips of its own accord and she bit down hard, catching both nail and flesh. *Damn*, she nearly shouted. She pulled her thumb from her mouth and examined the fingernail and surrounding skin. Raw but no blood. She cursed herself; this was a habit Janson had drummed out of her years ago. That she was returning to it now while he wasn't here made her even more frustrated.

Where is he now?

Is he safe?

Please, let nothing have happened to him.

She returned her attention to Park Kwan's baritone as he switched seamlessly between English and Korean.

"I see," he said into the phone, his expression giving away nothing. "Yes, please." He stopped in front of the desk Kang Jung was sitting at and picked up a pen and a pad of stationery with the Grand Hyatt logo. "All right. Go ahead."

Kincaid casually wandered over to him, her arms folded across her chest. She peeked over his forearm to see what he had written.

Double damn. Whatever it was, he had written it in Korean.

Finally, he set down the phone.

"Good news?" she said.

"Well..." He was clearly being guarded with his words. He didn't want to get her hopes up. "...it's news, at least. I shall leave it to you to determine whether it is good or bad."

Kincaid nodded, displaying a crooked smile that undoubtedly betrayed her fierce anxiety. "OK, mister. Out with it, then."

"OK," Park Kwan said. "They were able to triangulate the sig—"

The phone on the desk began to ring, sending a startled chill up Kincaid's spine. She reached for the phone but Park Kwan was slightly faster.

She took a step back and listened to him speak to the caller in Korean. Holding the handset against his chest, he turned to her. "Do you know a gentleman named Nam Sei-hoon?"

The name instantly rang a bell. Kincaid recalled Janson mentioning the name during the flight to Seoul from Honolulu.

"One of my oldest and closest friends," he'd said.

She reached out for the receiver.

"This is Kincaid."

"Ms. Kincaid," the voice on the phone said, "I will be blunt. You and the people you are with are in grave danger. I need to bring you in."

"Bring us in?"

"I am told that your pursuers know that you are at the Grand Hyatt hotel. An assassin is on his way. You have ten minutes, fifteen at most."

"We *can't* come in," Kincaid protested.

"Listen to me." The man's voice was stern, authoritative. "You have no choice. You must get out of there as quickly and quietly as possible. There is a safe house just across the road. It is in an eleven-story apartment building. You can see it from the hotel. Take the stairs and go to the top floor. From there you can watch the entrance to the Grand Hyatt. The apartment number is eleven-E. At this moment the door is unlock—"

"I'm sorry to cut you off," Kincaid said, "but we finally have a lock on the boy. And we have to pursue him immediately."

Following a moment of hesitation he said, "My men can handle that, I assure you. Where is the boy?"

"He's..." Kincaid turned to ask Park Kwan but suddenly thought better of it. *Bad security*, Janson would say. If he found out she'd told *anyone*—even an old friend of his like Nam Sei-hoon—where Wyckoff was, she'd never hear the end of it. "He's..." She paused again. "I can't exactly say right now, but I'll know soon."

There was a lengthy silence on the other end of the line. Finally the man said, "All right. Pursue your lead. But please use extreme caution."

"We will."

"And you are leaving the hotel now, I presume?"

"We'll leave right away, I promise."

"Good. Let me give you a number where you can reach me."

* * *

SIN BAE FROZE the screen. There she was, Kang Jung. He was amazed again to find how much she looked like Su-ra.

In the days following their arrival at Yodok, Sin Bae had learned more and more about the ghastly conditions in which he and his family were expected to live. The prison camp stretched for miles in every direction, ten villages packed to overflowing with nearly three thousand people.

Malnutrition was rampant; no one had enough food. A fellow prisoner who possessed little training and no medical supplies played the role of doctor. Many, especially children and the elderly, died of simple colds. And the latrines—outhouses consisting of nothing more than shacks over holes in the ground—were far too few in number. The putrid stench of urine blended with excrement hung everywhere.

As he grew older Sin Bae realized he no longer wanted to live.

But he knew his death would mean the death of his mother and father and eventually his sister, Su-ra. So he exerted himself even harder and grew stronger each year. He ate frogs and salamanders and earthworms for nutrition. He stole clothes from the freezing and rice from the starving. In order to survive he became something less than human.

Because by the age of thirteen, Sin Bae no longer wanted to die.

The phone in Sin Bae's hand lit. He held it to his ear but said nothing.

Ping said, "Change of plans."

Sin Bae looked down at the body at his feet, covered with the overcoat he'd borrowed from the apartment across the street. He frowned in frustration.

Ping said, "You are going to follow them from the hotel. They will lead you directly to the boy. You are not to engage them until the boy is in sight and his identity is confirmed."

"Understood," Sin Bae said softly.

"The little man will take care of the packages you are leaving behind. But you must hurry. The three are leaving the hotel now."

THIRTY-THREE

Just over 120 miles northwest of Seoul, Paul Janson entered the Pyongyang safe house with trepidation. He took a quick look around; the apartment resembled the one in which he'd just met the young woman but was even smaller. After making certain that all of the curtains were drawn, he took a seat at the uneven dining room table and waited.

Several minutes later he heard light footsteps on the stairs outside the door. He stood and ducked behind a wall in case someone came in shooting. After all, thanks largely to Berman's stubbornness, Janson still wasn't quite sure whom he'd met at the other apartment or why he'd been invited here.

But the young woman's voice was the next sound he heard.

"Hello?" she said tentatively.

Janson stepped around the corner. "You never mentioned your name."

"Mi-sook." She didn't ask for his in return.

"You're sure this place is clean?"

"Certain of it. Jin-ho has it checked for the listening devices twice weekly."

"Where is he now?"

"On his way. I alerted him as soon as you left."

Janson tried to keep the puzzlement out of his voice. "Alerted him to what exactly?"

"That you arrived." When Janson didn't reply, she added, "We have been expecting you."

"Expecting me," he repeated.

"Yes, of course."

Janson's mind, moving sluggishly from lack of sleep, tried to process what was happening, but his gaze was repeatedly diverted to the small cot in the rear left corner of the room.

His chin felt all but glued to his chest; his eyelids weighed as much as each of his arms.

"Please," Mi-sook said, motioning to the table Janson had been sitting at before she entered the apartment. "Have a seat. May I to offer you some tea?"

"Just water, please."

He ran his hand up the right side of his face, through two or three days of unchecked growth. He considered how he must look to her. He'd rubbed a handful of fresh powdery snow on his face just before he entered the safe house but otherwise still wore all the scars of his hellish trip through the tunnel, the DMZ, the Reunification Highway, and beyond.

They sat together silently.

Before Janson could finish his glass of water, he heard footfalls in the hallway again. This time the steps were much heavier, sounded much more purposeful.

"It is OK," Mi-sook said, noticing Janson's reaction. "It is only Jin-ho. He was close by when I called him."

Yun Jin-ho entered the apartment with an urgency that sharply contrasted Mi-sook's reasonably laid-back demeanor.

"I cannot believe you are here," Yun exclaimed as soon as his eyes fell on Janson. "I was certain you had been killed trying to enter the country."

"Why is that?" Janson said, wondering for the first time if news of the soldiers' deaths in the DMZ had already reached the palace.

"There were reports that a foreign spy had been executed at a checkpoint on the road to Kaesong."

Janson's heart dropped into the pit of his stomach as he pictured the driver of the food truck being shot and killed on his way back to his family in South Korea. An incredible weight suddenly pressed against Janson's sore shoulders.

"When?" was the only word Janson could manage.

"Two days ago," Yun Jin-ho replied. "The foreigner was carrying false papers he apparently purchased or stole from a South Korean worker at the industrial park."

Janson was struck with a dual wave of relief, first that the man he'd bribed wasn't the victim, and second that he'd heeded Jina Jeon's advice not to enter the North directly through Kaesong.

But this news presented a different quandary. If not Janson, who exactly were Jin-ho and Mi-sook expecting, and why?

Better, Janson decided, to extract that information before telling them who he really was and why he was there.

"Who told you to expect me?" Janson tried.

Yun Jin-ho's pliable facial features scrunched up; doubt entered his eyes. According to Kang Jung's information, Yun was on the back nine of middle age, but life in North Korea had added decades to his face. "The boy, of course."

"The American," Janson said, framing it as fact rather than question.

Yun Jin-ho hesitated. "Yes. The senator's son."

Janson allowed himself to breathe again. "When was the last time the boy got in touch with you?"

"A few days ago," Yun Jin-ho said, his sinewy body full of nervous energy. "I had been expecting another message. When I didn't hear from him again, I was sure something had gone terribly wrong. Then I heard about the incident at the checkpoint in Kaesong and I was sure my worst fears had been confirmed."

"So then you didn't hear about the girl," Janson said, remembering how cut off from the rest of the world all North Koreans were.

Yun Jin-ho shook his head, genuine concern washing over his previously puzzled face. "The young man's girlfriend? No. Has something happened to her?"

"I'm afraid so," Janson said. "The girl was murdered in a hanok in central Seoul."

Yun Jin-ho's eyes fell to the floor as he slowly lowered himself into the seat across from Janson, the nervous energy he'd displayed just moments ago seemingly sucked from his body by news of Lynell Yi's death.

"Murdered," Yun said. But it wasn't a question.

Janson continued. "The boy managed to escape. But he immediately became the primary suspect in his girlfriend's death. He had no choice but to run."

Yun Jin-ho looked up at him with misty eyes. While his hair remained jet black, it was visibly thinning and his hairline was badly receding. "How was the girl killed?" he asked.

Janson said, "She was strangled."

Yun Jin-ho slapped his palm against the top of the wooden table. "I *told* the boy they were in grave danger."

Mi-sook laid a slender hand on Yun Jin-ho's forearm. "It is not your fault, my dear."

Yun Jin-ho said to Janson, "Where is he now, the boy?"

"We don't know. My partner is back in Seoul, searching for him. Needless to say, we're trying to find him before the police do."

Yun Jin-ho and Mi-sook exchanged uneasy looks.

Then, without warning, Yun Jin-ho suddenly cried, "If the boy is not found, then *all is lost*! I possess only *one side* of the equation."

"The equation?"

Yun Jin-ho buried his face in his hands. When he finally removed them, his voice was hoarse, his sallow cheeks wet with tears. "I managed to gain access to plans here in the North. But I know nothing about what is transpiring in the South. It was too dangerous for the boy to send the details at the time."

"The details of what?"

Yun Jin-ho abruptly rose from his wooden chair, which tipped over and struck the floor with a loud *clank*. His sadness had suddenly morphed into complete despair. "*Tell me*. Did he send it with *you*? Did the boy leave you the *flash drive*?"

Janson measured his words carefully and spoke calmly. "All the boy left behind was a brief message. The message said, 'Contact Yun Jin-ho in the DPRK.'"

Yun Jin-ho listlessly rotated his body so that his back was facing the table. Janson stole a glance at Mi-sook, who now had tears in her eyes too.

"Without both halves of the puzzle," Yun Jin-ho said softly, "we are helpless to do anything."

"My partner *will* find the boy," Janson said, hoping the man would be able to rein in his emotions long enough to help him. "So let's start with the half we already have."

Yun Jin-ho glared at Janson over his shoulder. He cleared his eyes of tears. "Before I help you," he said with a new edge to his voice, "I need to know that you will still honor our deal."

Janson lifted an aching shoulder. "I wasn't told about any deal."

As soon as Janson observed their collective reaction, he regretted his words. *Damn* his mind for moving so languorously.

"Who *are* you?" Yun suddenly shouted as his body spun back around. His words now held the unmistakable tone of an accusation.

Mi-sook gently pushed her chair back from the table as though she was suddenly afraid.

Janson stood. Hesitantly, so as not to alarm them. But he needed to be able to defend himself in case one or both of them pulled a weapon.

"My name is Paul Janson," he said. "I was hired by Senator Wyckoff and his wife to find their son."

Mi-sook shook her head sadly.

"So you know nothing of what is happening," Yun Jin-ho said with a heavy sigh. A feeling of futility as thick as the fog in the demilitarized zone had fallen over the entire room.

Janson tried to cut through it. "In the past few days, my partner and I have learned a hell of a lot. We don't have the entire picture yet. That's why I'm here. I need your help."

With narrowed brows Yun Jin-ho said, "And the deal I made with the boy? What of that?"

"If you tell me the terms, I will do my best to honor it."

Yun Jin-ho turned to Mi-sook, who grudgingly nodded.

The spy drew a deep breath and exhaled audibly. Then he bent over and lifted the chair he had knocked over and sat.

"Then have a seat, Mr. Janson," he said quietly. "You and I have much to discuss. And time is not on our side."

THIRTY-FOUR

Quickly," Kincaid said in the hotel room. "We don't have much time. What did your source tell you about where we might find Gregory Wyckoff?"

"According to the signal," Park Kwan said, "it appears the boy is traveling to Beijing."

Kincaid shook her head, nonplussed. "That doesn't make any sense."

She paused to give it more thought. If Gregory Wyckoff suspected that the State Department was involved, he wouldn't be running to the American embassy in Beijing.

"Maybe he anticipated the police getting hold of his image at the mall," she said. "Maybe he's using the phone as a means of misdirection."

Park Kwan appeared doubtful. "If he is, it's an elaborate ruse. It would mean he sent the phone on a train heading west, then bought it a one-way ferry ticket to China."

Kincaid frowned. "But why Beijing?"

"Edward Snowden ran to Hong Kong," Kang Jung interjected.

Kincaid suppressed a smirk. "I think we're dealing with a very different kind of person here. With a very different agenda. Wyckoff's not running because he committed a traitorous act against the most powerful nation on earth. He's running from an assassin and because he's being falsely accused of murder."

Kang Jung pursed her lips but refrained from engaging Kincaid in a debate about Snowden.

"There is other evidence of his intentions, I am afraid." Park Kwan motioned to the phone. "I was told that Wyckoff made several calls from the stolen cell phone, none of which was to his family in the United States."

"Where to, then?" Kincaid said, fearing the answer.

"Most of the calls were to Chinese government officials in Beijing. Two were to an unknown cellular phone in Shanghai." He turned to Kang Jung. "He also visited Chinese government websites."

Kincaid bit down on her lower lip. "Why go west to China when he can just as easily go east to Japan? At least Japan's an ally."

"But," Kang Jung said, "Japan is an enemy to North Korea." She placed her hands behind her back and lowered her head to her chest, pacing as she spoke. "This is beginning to make some sense. Wyckoff's last message to Cy was to find a South Korean spy in North Korea. We assumed it was to *gain* information. But what if Wyckoff was actually trying to *warn* the North? A South Korean spy at the palace may well have been his best and only chance to find someone receptive to the warning. Anyone else in the North would have dismissed it as an American ploy. The only enemy North Korea hates more than Japan is the United States."

"So once that door closed for him," Park Kwan thought aloud, "he went to the next best thing."

Kang Jong nodded. "North Korea's only ally."

Kincaid looked from Park Kwan to Kang Jung and finished their collective thought. "Beijing."

"Precisely," Park Kwan said.

Kincaid placed her thumbnail in her mouth. "But to warn them of what?"

Kang Jung clenched her fists at her sides. "That is exactly what we need to find out. And the only way we are going to accomplish that is by following Gregory Wyckoff to China."

Park Kwan nodded. "The young lady is right."

Kincaid gazed down at the girl. Her first thought was *We can't take this thirteen-year-old to Beijing.* But then, what else could they do? Kincaid was responsible for the kid's safety; they couldn't just leave her in Seoul.

"What did your mother say when you spoke to her?"

"Grandfather's fine. He was never taken to the hospital. He was never even ill."

"I mean *you.* What did she say about *you?*"

"I told her I was safe as long as I remained with you. She's worried, but she trusts me. She told me not to leave your side."

Park Kwan said, "I spoke to her mother too. She's keeping safe, staying with relatives in Jeollanam, and she's counting on us to keep Jung safe as well."

"Then we'd better get moving," Kincaid said. "Because Janson's friend in the NIS just warned *us* that we're in danger."

"You mean . . . ?"

Kincaid nodded. "This hotel has already been compromised."

THIRTY-FIVE

Mi-sook had returned to her parents' apartment, leaving Janson alone with Yun Jin-ho at the safe house. Once Janson summarized his and Kincaid's involvement in the case (from the phone call he received from the senator aboard the Embraer 650 on his way to Honolulu to the moment he arrived at the door to the safe house in Pyongyang), Yun Jin-ho nodded and said, "It is as you suspect. The young translator overheard something that got her murdered. Exactly what that something was, we still need to find out."

"The question is," Janson said, "who can we trust?"

In relaying the events since his and Kincaid's arrival in Seoul, Janson had left out his dealings with Yun Jin-ho's handler, Nam Sei-hoon. In time, he'd ask for the details of how Yun had been recruited and how he maintained contact with the South. But for now, Janson wasn't entirely sure where the spy's loyalties truly lay.

"You mentioned a deal you had with Gregory Wyckoff." Janson

did his damnedest to keep the unequivocal disappointment out of his voice. He'd sneaked into North Korea in the hope of finding answers. Yet all he'd uncovered thus far were more questions. He would have been much more useful had he remained in Seoul, helping to locate the kid he'd been hired to find.

"Yes." Yun Jin-ho lifted his gaze to meet Janson's. "To be frank, I do not know how the boy knew to contact me. At first I assumed he was an American liaison working with the South. But then I discovered who he was. A sitting US senator's son, who was only nineteen years old. I dismissed the possibility that he was an agent for the CIA or some other American intelligence agency. After a few online conversations, I observed how deft he was with a computer, and I thought that perhaps he was a freelance hacker. He later told me that he was a 'hacktivist' with an organization known as the Hivemind."

Janson was thankful that Yun Jin-ho had managed to get his emotions under control. Though he strongly suspected the man could snap in either direction at any time.

He wanted to keep the spy talking until he could figure out his next move. "What else did the boy tell you?" he asked.

"Our conversations were very limited, you must understand. Although we are both fluent in English, we could not be sure who was listening in or watching our monitors, so we were essentially speaking two different languages, each of our own invention."

Janson nodded but said nothing.

"And time, too, was a major limiting factor. He contacted me from Internet cafés, and he had to be very careful. My access to a clean computer with an Internet connection was nearly nonexistent. But I made do. Enough to arrange to meet with his representative here in Pyongyang in order to exchange vital information. That and to come to terms on our agreement. We spoke of nothing else."

"What exactly were those terms?" Janson said. He sensed that Yun Jin-ho was trying to evade the question. Which didn't bode well for Janson.

"I would provide him with top secret information that was apparently relevant to what his girlfriend had learned while acting as an interpreter in the Joint Security Area during the recent four-party talks."

"And in return?"

"He evidently needed to warn me of something. He wanted me to bring something to the attention of the palace. But I made it clear that last was not necessarily part of the deal. I had no intentions of getting myself killed. So, in exchange for the information I provided, his representative—who is now you, I suppose—would do me a significant favor."

Here it was. "And that favor is?"

Yun Jin-ho swallowed visibly and caught Janson in his intense glare. "You must agree to get Mi-sook out of the country within the next twenty-four hours."

Janson instantly thought he'd misheard the spy, that his lack of sleep was now causing him to experience auditory hallucinations.

"You're kidding, right? That's *impossible*. I don't even know how the hell I'm going to get out myself. For all I know I bought myself a one-way ticket to this Stalinist utopia when I entered the tunnel in the demilitarized zone."

Yun's expression didn't change. "You will find a way, Mr. Janson, I am sure."

Janson shook his head. "Even if I do, I couldn't possibly risk bringing Mi-sook. Let's set aside for a second the fact that she would slow me down. If—and since I'm certain of it, *when*—we got caught, your girlfriend would be executed. She'd be charged with conspiring to leave the country with an American. We'd both be lucky to be shot on sight."

Yun Jin-ho sat stoically, his face frozen with resolve. Janson was actually beginning to miss the fireworks of an hour ago.

"This, I am afraid, is nonnegotiable, Mr. Janson." Yun Jin-ho rose from his chair and stared down at him, maintaining a steady pitch as he continued. "Unless you agree, I will *not* provide you the information you need. And without that information, you will be putting at risk millions of lives."

Janson saw an opening. "Just what kind of information did you promise the boy?"

Yun Jin-ho remained steadfast. "Do you or do you *not* accept my terms?"

Janson didn't feel he had much of a choice. "I do."

Slowly, carefully, in the same even tone, Yun Jin-ho said, "If you lie to me, Mr. Janson, if you attempt to leave North Korea without Mi-sook, I assure you that you yourself will not make it out of this country alive. And if that is the case, do not waste your energy hoping for a fast, easy death. Because I promise you, I will make certain you receive nothing of the sort. Even if it costs me my life."

"I give you my word," Janson said forcefully. "Now let's move forward. Get me what I need, and I'll collect Mi-sook and take her south with me."

Yun Jin-ho's thin lips finally turned up in a grin. His grin soon morphed into a humorless chuckle.

"I am afraid it is not so easy as that, Mr. Janson."

"What do you mean?"

"I mean, I am not in possession of this intelligence. I only gained access. I am afraid the task of stealing these secrets must fall to you."

Janson's fortunes in North Korea continued to plummet. "Steal them?" he said. "Steal them how? Steal them from where?"

"From the palace, of course."

Janson clenched his jaw. "And how am I supposed to get near the palace?"

Yun Jin-ho leaned back in his chair and pulled a package of cigarettes from his pocket. He removed one from the pack, placed it between his lips, and lit a match. He held the flame to his tobacco and watched it burn.

After a few puffs he gazed at Janson through the smoke. "That is something I *can* help you with, Mr. Janson. When darkness falls, I will personally escort you into the Forbidden City."

THIRTY-SIX

Beijing Capital International Airport
Beijing, China

S in Bae expertly navigated past the countless duty-free shops
and restaurants in Asia's busiest airport, Beijing Capital International, while reading Ping's encrypted email on his
phone. Because Sin Bae had needed to avoid crossing paths with
Jessica Kincaid at Incheon International, his handler had flown
from Shanghai to Beijing to pick up surveillance from the time the
trio disembarked the plane until Sin Bae arrived on a later flight
from Seoul.

Seeing his head lowered, crowds parted for Sin Bae as though
he were an ambulance speeding down a busy freeway with sirens
blaring. Little did these people know that his awareness was impeccable, at a level higher than any professional athlete who performed in this city's Summer Olympics several years ago. If Sin

Bae crashed into you, it was purposeful on his part, and he'd most likely just relieved you of your wallet or handbag, not for money but for methods of identification or access. Or perhaps he'd planted on your person a phone or a tracking device or something more sinister.

In any case, it was no accident.

Actually, as he breezed through the airport, Sin Bae was not Sin Bae at all, but Song Jin-sung, a South Korean national who worked in research and development at Pfizer Pharmaceuticals' laboratories in Seoul. Song Jin-sung carried a South Korean passport heavily inked with entry stamps from nearly every nation in Asia and several in the European Union, including Tokyo, Singapore, Paris, and Madrid. Song Jin-sung or one of his alternative incarnations had indeed visited each of these cities. Had killed in each of these cities. When he made his exit from each city, he took nothing with him, left nothing behind but the bodies of his victims. And occasionally his calling card: a white-gold cuff link with an onyx gemstone in its center—and a bloodied garrote hidden in its core.

As Sin Bae perused Ping's message, he thought of the teenage girl. He had hoped that Kang Jung would not accompany Kincaid and the man to Beijing.

But she had.

Why did the woman allow the girl to come to Beijing when she knew she was a target? Why make the child a target too? The girl is only thirteen. She should be at her school.

He touched his left temple, where a headache was beginning to form. By the age of fourteen, Sin Bae was no longer in school; he'd been placed on full work duty at Yodok. Because he was large and powerful and possessed incredible stamina, he was given the job of burying bodies on the mountain. In the winter the ground froze and it sometimes took him days to dig a single grave in the frozen earth.

So many bodies.

So many bodies there wasn't room on the mountain to bury them all.

In the winter Sin Bae stripped the corpses of their clothes to give them to members of his family.

In the winter...

In the winter he could find no berries in the hills. No frogs, no salamanders, no earthworms. Corn and rice became short; he and his family edged closer to starvation.

But by then Sin Bae was determined to endure at all costs.

And so he became savage. He began to set secret rat traps all around the camp. Each time he caught one, he immediately cooked it up and devoured it in seclusion. As the food shortages became worse and his family found themselves with even less to eat, he ceased joining them for dinners of rice and corn. For months at a time he consumed only rats.

At the age of fifteen, he became an adult and was warned by his father: *"Be careful, my son. Now that you are a man the guards are permitted to shoot you."*

Newly appointed guards moved into Yodok with their families. They were separated from the prisoners but still resentful of having been stationed in such a hellish place.

Sin Bae often wondered what the guards thought of him. When he was a child, they'd kicked him around for the slightest infractions. As he grew bigger and stronger, they assigned him the most backbreaking work yet seemed to develop a certain respect for him. Respect, or perhaps it was fear. Fear not of his physical stature but of what they saw forming behind Sin Bae's eyes.

Those eyes were now glued to his phone.

According to Ping's email, the subjects had taken a taxi from the airport directly to Tiananmen Square. Sin Bae agreed wholeheartedly with his handler's assessment; the square seemed to both men a peculiar place for Kincaid and her allies to start their search for Gregory Wyckoff.

Perhaps they possessed even more information than Sin Bae suspected. Perhaps they had a precise location on the boy. If so, Sin Bae's stay in Beijing would be brief. In a few hours he might well be right back here at the airport, boarding a return flight to Seoul.

* * *

ONCE KINCAID FINALLY PASSED through the security checkpoint and entered the world's largest square, the text message intercepted from Gregory Wyckoff's stolen phone by Park Kwan's people an hour earlier finally made sense; this *was* a reasonable spot for a clandestine rendezvous, especially if one of the parties was concerned for his safety.

Despite the freezing temperatures, the crowds in Tiananmen Square were as dense as the smog suspended just overhead. Droves of tourists surrounded China's grand monuments, shooting photos with expensive high-tech cameras with all the intensity of the paparazzi at a red-carpet event.

Gazing up through the thick haze at the hundreds of red lanterns decorating the square in anticipation of Beijing's Spring Festival, Kincaid realized that exhaustion was beginning to set in. Attempting to perform the universal cure for drowsiness, she vigorously shook her head from side to side. But it was futile. What she really craved was another shot of adrenaline, like the one she'd received when Janson's old friend called her at the Grand Hyatt in Seoul. She needed to remember that she and Park Kwan and their thirteen-year-old charge were in danger, and that their mission was literally one of life or death.

"Let's start looking for Wyckoff," she said.

According to the incoming text message, Wyckoff wasn't supposed to meet with his unidentified acquaintance for another hour and ten minutes. But Wyckoff's dossier revealed that this would only be his second visit to Beijing in the past decade, so she imagined he'd choose to arrive early rather than risk missing his rendezvous. She suggested that she and Park Kwan split up to cover more ground in less time.

"What about *me*?" Kang Jung interjected.

"You can either come with me or go with Park Kwan," Kincaid said. "Your choice."

Kang Jung shook her head. "What I mean is, three of us can cover far more ground than two."

"I realize that," Kincaid said in a tone she immediately wished she could take back. "But you're not going off on your own. You're too young."

Mercifully, rather than argue, the girl made a face, turned to Park Kwan, and asserted, "I am coming with you."

Kincaid pointed to the tall granite monument in the middle of the square and told them that was where they should rendezvous in just under an hour if they had met with no success. She wished them both good luck then motioned toward the endless line of people waiting to enter Mao's Mausoleum.

"I'll begin with the chairman," she said.

* * *

AFTER PASSING THROUGH CUSTOMS, Sin Bae exited the airport and went directly to the matte-black Audi A7 that was waiting for him in short-term parking. He was pleased to find the windows darkly tinted as he'd requested.

He opened the driver's-side door and slipped into the soft charcoal leather seat. He started the V-8 engine, closed his eyes, and listened to it purr as his mind wandered back to his time at Yodok.

By the age of sixteen, Sin Bae was far from a model prisoner. He caused trouble throughout the camp. He fought. He stole. He had sex with women, which was strictly forbidden at Yodok.

And he was punished.

At one point during his ninth year at Yodok, it seemed as though every other week Sin Bae was being tossed into the sweatbox for punishment of some transgression or another. Punishment for stealing, for fighting, for fucking, punishment for speaking back to a guard. Punishment for not wearing his ragged uniform properly.

In the sweatbox Sin Bae faced total darkness. He was further deprived of food, even his precious rats. He was given so little to eat that he had to snatch whatever he could get his hands on. Centipedes became his breakfast, cockroaches his lunch.

In such close confinement someone of his size was completely unable to move. He crouched on his knees with his hands on his thighs, his heels digging deep into the flesh of his lower back, causing constant, excruciating pain. If he said a word or made a gesture, the punishment was extended.

When finally let loose, no man had ever previously exited the sweatbox on his own two feet. Yet Sin Bae made it a point to do so every time.

Meanwhile, each turn in the sweatbox added five years to his already indefinite sentence.

To this day, every time he closed his eyes, Sin Bae feared he'd somehow wake in the sweatbox. For it was in the sweatbox that Sin Bae had witnessed the most abhorrent event of his life.

Sin Bae opened his eyes. He threw the transmission into reverse and backed out of the space.

The drive to Tiananmen Square would take him approximately thirty minutes.

When he arrived at the square, he wouldn't have to concern himself with parking. One of Ping's other assets would be awaiting his arrival along Bei Chang Jie. Sin Bae would simply exit the car with the engine still running and head to the easternmost entrance of the square, where a guard had been paid well to pass Sin Bae through the security checkpoint without having to answer any inane questions or undergo an intrusive search of his person.

Sin Bae paid the airport lot the nominal fee then peeled the Audi A7 out of short-term parking.

Once on the freeway, Sin Bae regarded his reflection in the rearview mirror with a rare sense of satisfaction. Since he had boarded the two-hour Asiana Airlines flight from Seoul, Ping had also learned the identity of the man now traveling with Kincaid. His name was Park Kwan and he was employed by the Seoul Metropolitan Police, which explained his carrying a gun into the T-Lound nightclub, something not even Sin Bae had attempted.

Thinking of the man and his interference in the coatroom caused Sin Bae to again consider the girl, Kang Jung. For Sin Bae, her death would constitute a particularly cruel irony. For had he not hesitated, had he not suffered that moment of unwanted introspection at the Sophia Guesthouse in central Seoul, the teenage girl who reminded him so much of his sister would not have become involved, and thus would not have become one of his victims.

Yet it was none other than his sister's face that he had glimpsed in the mirror as he strangled the young female translator, Lynell Yi.

Although the interpreter looked nothing like Su-ra (who would forever in his mind remain twelve years old), it was indeed Su-ra who appeared to him that evening.

It was Su-ra's image that had diverted Sin Bae's attention for those several crucial seconds.

Though he had been able to finish the interpreter, Sin Bae's vacillating had afforded Lynell Yi's boyfriend time to escape.

Now the boy—the US senator's son, Gregory Wyckoff—had apparently fled here to Beijing. And Jessica Kincaid and the South Korean cop (and the young Korean girl named Kang Jung) would finally lead Sin Bae straight to him.

It was a bittersweet feeling, a peculiar blend of relief and regret.

For once they led him to the boy, he would have no choice but to terminate the female teen along with the others.

He flashed on Park Kwan in the coatroom and seethed. Because of the cop's interference, Sin Bae's kill count for this mission was about to increase by four, instead of three.

THIRTY-SEVEN

Even in parts of the capital city, the darkness was absolute. Janson had seen numerous satellite photos of the Korean peninsula at night; he'd known that the North remained as black as the seas when viewed from hundreds of miles above. Yet the perfect nothingness of Pyongyang after the sun had fallen still somehow managed to shock him. No streetlamps. No headlights. Not a single window aglow in the towering apartment buildings on either side of the road. It was as though he'd stepped even further back in time. Not just into the early twentieth century but into the Stone Age.

Still, Janson now felt like a soldier on an urban battlefield, no longer just a ghost in the fog. Although the darkness provided consummate cover, the danger of the capital city remained omnipresent. And the situation would only get worse the closer he and Yun Jin-ho came to their destination.

As they pushed through the blackness Janson's heart pounded, his muscles tensed. He was now well rested, even well fed. Working so closely with the regime, Yun explained, had its privileges. Unlike most of North Korea's population, Yun Jin-ho received plenty of food, including expensive imports from South Korea and Japan.

"How did you come to work for the South?" Janson had asked when he woke in the safe house.

Sitting on the cot, Janson could see a map spread out before Yun Jin-ho on the table at which they'd been sitting a few hours earlier.

After several seconds of silence, Yun Jin-ho looked up from his map with a resigned expression. He motioned Janson to the table.

Once Janson was seated across from him, Yun Jin-ho told him his story.

"I had been a defector," he began.

Before defecting, Yun Jin-ho had served as one of General Kim Jong-il's loyal deputy directors. It was a highly prestigious position, one of the most coveted roles in the country. It had taken years of hard work and education for Yun to rise in the ranks under the Dear Leader's father, Kim Il-sung.

"I had drunken the Kool Whip," Yun Jin-ho conceded. Janson didn't correct him.

Yun Jin-ho, like all his fellow countrymen, had worshipped Kim Il-sung. *He was our deity*, Yun said. No North Korean, not even the educated, thought of the Great Marshal as a mere mortal, a man made of flesh and blood. According to official state history, Kim Il-sung was one of the world's great warriors, a liberator of the Korean people who had literally fought a hundred thousand battles during the Japanese occupation. State propaganda portrayed Kim Il-sung as more virtuous than Confucius, more benevolent than Buddha, more just than Muhammad, more loving than Christ.

"No one," Yun Jin-ho said, "including me, knew him for what he was: a figurehead. A puppet handpicked by Soviet intelligence while they temporarily occupied the North following the Second World War." He closed his eyes as a joyless smile appeared on his face. "You should have witnessed my astonishment after my defection when I learned that our Great Leader had been fluent in Chinese and proficient in Russian, but could not speak Korean well at all when Stalin first placed him in command of our people."

When in 1994, Kim Il-sung died at the age of eighty-two, all of North Korea was stunned, Yun Jin-ho included.

"It was unthinkable," he said, looking into his past. "How do *gods* die? And what on earth do you do when yours does?"

Like his countrymen, Yun Jin-ho had never felt so sad and frightened in all his life. He joined the millions who flooded the nation's streets, overcome by panic, overwhelmed with grief. Many committed suicide by jumping from tall buildings. Others incessantly banged their heads against concrete sidewalks and walls, spilling their own blood, right up to the moment they lost consciousness or died. It was as though the entire nation joined in a collective, unending scream. Millions of mourners swarmed around the more than thirty thousand statues already erected in Kim Il-sung's honor. They wept, they passed out from the heat, from their shock. But most of all they prayed.

"We were told that if we prayed hard enough, if we cried and screamed at the top of our lungs, if we pulled our hair from our heads and pounded our chests till they bled, then maybe, just maybe, the Great Marshal would be resurrected, maybe he would return to us, ride down from the sky on a winged horse to once again lead his people."

Instead the people of North Korea were given his son.

* * *

KIM JONG-IL HAD BEEN introduced to the North Korean people as his father's successor twenty years before Kim Il-sung's death. A mercurial figure, Kim Jong-il possessed none of the military experience or charisma of his father. Yet, largely because of the regime's iron grip on its people, the transition of power went smoothly. And the cult of personality continued without a hitch.

However, some officials inside the palace, including Yun Jin-ho, were weary of the son. His various voracious appetites were well-known among those in the palace, and though nothing was ever spoken aloud, the son's need for abundance in all things was often viewed with disgust.

Although Kim Jong-il was a recluse, he demanded the constant company of young Norwegian models to entertain him. His significant paunch betrayed his love of food; his spirits cellar gave away his expensive tastes in wines and liquors.

While his people starved, Kim Jong-il went on international spending sprees that made Yun Jin-ho's stomach turn.

"He'd send his personal chef to Japan to buy thousands of pounds of the most expensive sushi and squid," Yun said with revulsion. "To Thailand for the top papayas and mangoes. To Denmark for the world's best bacon. To Iran and Uzbekistan for pistachio nuts and caviar." Yun shook his head sadly. "While his people died of malnutrition in the streets, their Dear Leader would purchase cases of Perrier water from France, kegs of Pilsner draft beer from Czechoslovakia. He was the world's single largest customer of Hennessy Paradis cognac."

Although he maintained appearances, it wasn't long before Yun Jin-ho no longer enjoyed serving the regime. He no longer loved his work. He no longer loved his country because he no longer loved its leader. Even as he ascended in rank within the palace walls, Yun Jin-ho began seeking a way out.

Not just out of the palace, but out of North Korea, forever.

He saved his money. Spent what little free time he had studying maps. Spoke of none of this to anyone, not even his closest and most trusted friends in the palace. Silence, he knew from the very beginning, would be key.

Yun Jin-ho continued to perform his job well. He watched quietly as Kim Jong-il obsessed over obtaining nuclear weapons, even as his own people starved and rotted in North Korea's scattered labor camps.

After years of bearing witness to Kim Jong-il's crimes and atrocities, after years of observing firsthand his utter indifference to and neglect of his people, Yun Jin-ho decided he could wait no longer. It was time to make his move.

And he did. Knowing full well that it could cost him his life.

* * *

IN ORDER TO RECEIVE substantial time away from his position at the palace, Yun Jin-ho feigned a protracted illness. It was risky. He'd had to bribe his doctor with most of the small fortune he'd saved up in order to be given the desired diagnosis. If the palace ordered a second doctor to corroborate the findings of the first, Yun Jin-ho and his doctor would have both been publicly executed.

He could have simply run, but he badly wanted the opportunity to return to the palace if his escape somehow went awry. Yun Jin-ho knew that if he found life in North Korea intolerable now with his prestigious position and all the perks that came with it, he would not survive a month as an ordinary citizen, let alone as a prisoner in one of Kim Jong-il's labor camps.

Yun Jin-ho paid an old friend to drive him to the mining town of Musan in the central North Hamgyong Province. Of course, Musan's mines and factories had closed down during the economic collapse of the nineties, so it now resembled a ghost town from America's Wild West. Populated with outlaws, Musan had become a launching point for North Koreans desperate to cross the border into China. Some, like Yun, were defectors; others were entrepreneurs who bought and sold everything from rice and corn to virgin brides on North Korea's burgeoning black market.

But the most lucrative business by far was smuggling people: serving as guides; obtaining false papers; bribing soldiers and train conductors in North Korea, and bandits and police on the Chinese side of the border. Because of the town's location (near one of the narrower stretches of the Tumen River), smuggling people from Musan had become a booming industry.

Yun Jin-ho crossed the river at midnight. From there, his guide led him down a dirt road farther into China.

He remained only one day in a village in China's Jilin Province before continuing his journey north. Although his ultimate destination was Seoul, to get there he'd have to make it to Mongolia undetected. If he were to be arrested in China, Chinese authorities would return him to North Korea, where he would be sent to a gulag or executed for his attempt to defect.

Fortunately, the landlocked nation of Mongolia had much different laws. Unlike China, Mongolia permitted the South Korean embassy in Ulaanbaatar to accept defectors from the North. So from the Mongolian capital, Yun Jin-ho was put on a plane to Seoul.

Once he arrived, Yun Jin-ho spent weeks being debriefed by South Korea's National Intelligence Service. Yun quickly came to realize that because of his position with the North Korean regime, he was a high-value defector. He wasn't sure whether this was a good thing or a bad thing.

"It would be a long time," he conceded, "before I figured it out."

Immediately following his lengthy debriefing, Yun Jin-ho was introduced to a small man by the name of Nam Sei-hoon.

"Weeks earlier, when I had finally touched down in Seoul following my long arduous journey through China and Mongolia, I never dreamed I would ever return to Pyongyang," he said. "But Nam Sei-hoon, he had his own designs on my future. Soon he made me an offer I couldn't refuse."

* * *

NAM SEI-HOON PROMISED Yun Jin-ho riches beyond his wildest dreams.

"Give me just one year of your life," Nam said, "and I will give you a life that will put Kim Jong-il's to shame."

"That was nearly five years ago," Yun Jin-ho told Janson at the table. "After the first year expired, he told me it was too dangerous to attempt an exfiltration just then. He told me to 'hang in' for another few months, so I hung."

Nine months later Nam Sei-hoon continued to stall. By then Yun Jin-ho realized he was being played by his handler in Seoul. He began making plans to escape on his own yet again. Only this time, using his unique knowledge, he would cross the demilitarized zone straight into South Korea. Once he made it back to Seoul, he'd sound the alarm about Nam Sei-hoon. Yun Jin-ho would have his revenge against the man who had attempted to shanghai him.

But as Yun Jin-ho planned his second escape from the North, he was approached by one of the Dear Leader's personal guards, a member of the Guard's Command.

"If you attempt to leave Chosun," the soldier in the mustard-colored uniform warned, "you will be taken to General Kim's residence, where you will be slaughtered like the pig that you are."

Yun Jin-ho knew immediately that the bodyguard was being run by Nam Sei-hoon. Had he been loyal to the regime, there would have been no threat, there would have been no warning. Yun would have simply been taken to a hard labor camp and subsequently executed.

From that day on, Yun Jin-ho knew he was constantly being watched. He vowed to deliver no more information to Nam Sei-hoon's goons in the South.

But that vow didn't last long.

"This time the message was delivered by a member of North Korea's Ministry of State Security: 'Continue providing intelligence from the palace,' he told me, 'or *she* will be carved up and fed to the prisoners at Senhori.'"

Yun Jin-ho need not ask which "*she*" the brute was referring to. Months earlier, Yun had begun a clandestine relationship with a young woman in Pyongyang.

Her name was Han Mi-sook.

* * *

OVER THE NEXT FEW YEARS, Nam Sei-hoon used a combination of carrots and sticks to keep Yun Jin-ho under his thumb.

He dangled in front of Yun Jin-ho a dazzling life for him and his new bride, a life of leisure and luxury in the most prestigious section of Seoul.

In rare communications, he told Yun Jin-ho how he would be perceived as a hero when he finally returned to South Korea, how he would be given the key to the capital city, how he and Mi-sook would dine with the president at the Blue House as often as they liked.

When Yun Jin-ho saw through Nam's charade and called him on it, the little man became cruel.

He had Yun's entire savings stolen from his home so that he could not afford the bribes necessary to defect.

He threatened to plant evidence that would show Mi-sook to be a spy for the American bastards.

Nam Sei-hoon even went so far as to doctor photos depicting Yun Jin-ho in the embrace of another woman.

"If you stop providing intelligence from the palace," Yun was told, "Mi-sook will come home one evening to find these photographs waiting for her on her doorstep. Then she will know you for the filthy rat that you are."

Following a particularly nasty confrontation with one of Nam Sei-hoon's spies in the Guard's Command, Yun Jin-ho finally decided that his only way out of North Korea was to take his own life.

But it was as though Nam Sei-hoon, from nearly two hundred kilometers away in Seoul, managed to read Yun's mind.

For the first time, Mi-sook was threatened directly. She was told by a member of the North's Ministry of State Security: "If Yun Jin-ho takes his own life, you will witness your parents being dealt a death so horrible that your eyes will melt in your skull."

When Mi-sook told him, Yun Jin-ho had no choice but to come clean. He confessed everything. From his initial defection to the constant surveillance and threats.

Mi-sook took the news better than Yun Jin-ho ever expected. In the end it was her decision that the couple stay strong and plan against all odds to defect—so that one day Yun would be afforded the opportunity to take his revenge against the little man in Seoul.

* * *

IN THE DARKNESS Janson felt Yun Jin-ho's presence at his side. They were linked in more ways than Janson had initially imagined. He now felt affection for the man.

They had both lived the double life of a spy.

They had both selflessly served their nations.

They had both been used as pawns.

But what really mattered to Paul Janson, as he and Yun Jin-ho made their way silently through the blackened streets of Pyongyang, was that they shared a common enemy.

They had both been betrayed by Nam Sei-hoon.

THIRTY-EIGHT

Tiananmen Square
Dongcheng District, Beijing

Kincaid wished Janson were here with her. His ability to see through mobs of people for the one face he was looking for nearly matched his proficiency at blending in. Kincaid, though skilled in other ways, wasn't nearly as adroit at either.

She'd burned Gregory Wyckoff's image into her memory days ago. She'd placed a hat on him, given him sunglasses. Even colored his hair a jet black. Still, she had to examine each individual feature on each individual face she surveyed before moving on to the next. She just couldn't quite grasp the complete picture the way Paul Janson had tried to teach her.

As she continued to work her way down the infinite line of people waiting to gain entrance to Mao's Mausoleum, Kincaid became acutely aware of the clock. Wyckoff's meeting was scheduled to take place less than forty minutes from now.

The clock is always ticking, she reminded herself.

The faces she examined turned their gazes back on her. Since visitors couldn't enter the exhibit carrying anything, they'd had to lock their cameras and handbags and smartphones—even their *coats*—in a group of lockers a few hundred feet away. So the people Kincaid studied were incredibly bored. Bored and cold and frustrated and annoyed. Particularly annoyed, it seemed, at this American woman who scrutinized their expressions as though she were preparing to paint a mass portrait without their consent.

Nevertheless, Kincaid maintained her intense focus. She dismissed Asians without hats and sunglasses but had to examine those who she thought could have been Caucasians in disguise. A surprisingly high percentage, she soon realized.

She experienced a strange sensation, felt the slightest tickle at the back of her mind.

Something about her thinking was decidedly off.

Something.

But what?

She peered into a young Korean man's eyes and finally realized where she'd gone wrong. She shouldn't have just been searching for Gregory Wyckoff. There continued to be a threat not just to her and Park Kwan and Kang Jung, but to Wyckoff as well.

She should have been watching for someone like herself.

She should have been watching for a Cons Ops agent.

She should have been watching for Sin Bae.

A high-pitched shout suddenly spun her around. Her eyes immediately fell on a young woman who'd just been knocked to the ground.

Looking past the woman, Kincaid spotted the back of a young

man in a brown leather jacket, running for all he was worth. *Sprinting* toward the security checkpoint at the closest entrance.

The crowd near the entrance instinctively began to disperse. Kincaid could no longer see the runner, but she became acutely aware of two distinct sets of footfalls over the surprised cries of dozens of bystanders.

She locked on a second man obviously chasing the first.

Cursing herself under her breath, she bolted after them both.

*   *   *

SIN BAE MOVED LIKE LIGHTNING. Where had his impeccable awareness been just now?

He had screwed up yet again. After a career boasting five dozen flawless kills, he suddenly seemed to be falling apart at the seams.

He had no choice but to make things right. This time there would be no second chances. With Ping nearby in the city, he knew he would pay the ultimate price for his failure. If the American boy lived, Sin Bae would pay with his life.

He pushed himself harder. Knocked over an old man then a child but did not dare slow down.

As he ran after the boy in the brown leather jacket, he could not help but analyze what had gone wrong back in the square. But it was simple. Instead of hunting the boy, he'd had his eyes on the American woman who had been searching the long line at Mao's Mausoleum. He had been *distracted* when he suddenly heard a female shriek.

He'd spun and found that a young woman had been knocked to the ground, her attacker already twenty yards away in a dead run.

The boy, he thought. He recognized me.

It was something Sin Bae would have thought an impossibility.

The hanok where he had killed the girl was as black as pitch. The boy had been asleep.

True, when Sin Bae saw his sister's image in the mirror across the small room, he hesitated. And when he hesitated, the girl managed to kick over a lamp.

But as soon as it happened Sin Bae had clutched the girl by her throat and squeezed, turning away from both the boy and the mirror in two seconds flat.

He *knew* he hadn't been seen.

When the boy came at his back to help the girl, Sin Bae had simply thrown an elbow, catching the kid square in the face.

By the time the boy got back to his feet the girl was already dead. The boy had been left with no choice but to run.

How was it possible that the boy had seen him that night? Seen him so well as to be able to recognize him in the smog-drenched throngs of Tiananmen Square?

No matter, he thought now, as he sprinted down the bicycle lane chasing the boy.

All that mattered now was that he catch him. Kill him.

Kill Kincaid and Park Kwan and, regrettably, Kang Jung.

Then Sin Bae would turn his attention to Janson. Killing Janson would be fun.

THIRTY-NINE

More goddamn tunnels? Janson had thought when he first heard Yun Jin-ho's plan. But now, from up high on a dark hill in the northern outskirts of Pyongyang, he saw only the idea's genius.

The moment he caught a glimpse of the five-square-mile leadership complex in the Ryongsong district, Janson realized there was no other way inside. The compound burned so bright, he wondered whether it could be seen from space, a solitary bulb in an ocean of darkness.

Back at the safe house, Yun Jin-ho had warned Janson of the palace's defenses. The complex was surrounded by an electrified fence (the capabilities of which were still fresh in Janson's mind). Of course there were more landmines. And checkpoints every few thousand yards.

"There is an underground headquarters," Yun Jin-ho had told him, "for use in a time of war. The walls are protected with iron bars, and their concrete is covered with lead in case of a nuclear attack."

"The American bastards?" Janson said with a half smile.

Yun Jin-ho didn't look up from his map. "Exactly."

"What kind of firepower do they keep up there?" Janson asked.

"Mass-scale conventional weapons for certain. I suspect more."

"Chemical? Biological?"

Yun Jin-ho shrugged as though Janson had asked whether the residence contained an adequate number of restrooms. "There are a dozen military units ready to fend off any threat. I do not think they will need to use mustard gas against one individual. Even if he is American. Even if he is Paul Janson."

"You'd be surprised," Janson said with a straight face.

Yun Jin-ho lifted his head and studied his guest. "I like you, Mr. Janson. You are not bad." He looked back down at his map. "For an American bastard."

Now as he peered at the complex through his field glasses, Janson thought he could make out some of the on-campus structures Yun Jin-ho had described, including large houses hiding among massive administrative buildings made of concrete.

Every structure represented an achievement in architecture, something Janson could be confident of even with his amateur eye.

Surrounding the residences were perfectly manicured gardens. Artificial lakes dotted the entire property.

On his haunches Janson peered at the elaborate swimming pool, which according to Yun Jin-ho's map was 50 feet wide, 160 feet long. At its center stood the most immense waterslide Janson had ever laid eyes on. There were horse stables, a running track, and an athletic field. Janson lingered a moment on the shooting range then took in the racecourse that could have been designed for Kyle Busch or Danica Patrick or some other hotshot NASCAR driver.

"I've seen enough," Janson said, pocketing his field glasses. "I'm ready to join Kim Jong-un for a late supper."

Yun Jin-ho turned to him with a smile Janson could barely see in the moonlight. "I am afraid that American bastards must use the designated entrance, underground."

Janson stood. "Well, what are we waiting for, then? Lead me to it."

* * *

YUN JIN-HO LED Janson belowground.

"This is a station," Yun said, "that very few North Koreans have ever seen. You are the first foreigner to enter, and you are very likely to be the last."

Janson was thankful that his eyes had adjusted to the darkness aboveground. Because this underground station was every bit as dark as the bottom of the sea. He slowly followed Yun Jin-ho along the tiled wall.

"This particular station," Yun said, "has been closed for some time."

"What was it built for?"

"It was built to transport North Korea's First Class passengers around the country."

Janson's brow furrowed in the darkness. "First Class passengers?"

"There have been three First Class passengers in the history of North Korea: Kim Il-sung, Kim Jong-il, and Kim Jong-un. Four, if you count Kim Jong-il's tiny white Maltese."

"Kim Jong-il had one of those little toy dogs?"

"He received him as a puppy. That puppy was the only true love in the Dear Leader's life once his father died. Seeing Kim Jong-il playing with that tiny white dog, it was the only time I ever felt any compassion for the man."

"I guess that makes sense," Janson said. "Hitler, after all, had a female German shepherd named Blondi."

"The difference, I would imagine, is that Blondi was not the only dog in Germany that was not ultimately made into a meal for the starving."

Janson felt an uneasiness splash around in his stomach as they continued along the wall.

"Stop here," Yun Jin-ho said. "This is where you will jump down onto the tracks."

Janson reached into his pocket and removed the miniature Maglite but didn't turn it on.

Yun said, "And this, I am sad to say, is where we must part ways, Mr. Janson."

Janson offered his hand but Yun Jin-ho instead pulled him forward by the shoulders and gripped him in a tight embrace.

"Godspeed, Mr. Janson." His voice was quivering. "Once you have what you seek, you will head out of the compound at the northernmost checkpoint, as we discussed."

"You're absolutely certain I can trust the guard at that checkpoint to let me out?"

"Sure as shit, as you American bastards say."

"I don't think anyone says that. At least not very often."

"Whatever floats your balloon, Mr. Janson." Yun Jin-ho took a step backward. "Once you are out of the compound, you will find a military jeep waiting for you on the far side of the road. It is painted black. Mi-sook will be behind the wheel. She has been instructed not to use headlights under any circumstances. The taillights have been removed."

Janson didn't like this part of the plan. "Without headlights—"

"Believe me, Mr. Janson, as I told you before, it is the only chance you have, the only way to make certain that they will not spot you and kill you on the road. Mi-sook has been practicing driving these roads blind for months." Yun's voice began to fade. "She knows what she is doing. Trust her and you will be fine."

"You never explained to me why you won't be coming with us," Janson said. "If you and Mi-sook are under surveillance, they're going to realize she's gone. And when they find out, they're going to come to collect you. They're going to kill you." Janson sighed. "Please, reconsider coming with us."

In the darkness, Janson listened but there was no reply. Even Yun Jin-ho's footfalls had faded into silence.

FORTY

With Wyckoff and Sin Bae popping in and out of her sights, Kincaid sliced through the smog, her arms pumping at her sides, her heart jackhammering in her chest. Gregory Wyckoff's dossier raved about his intellect but provided little about his physical abilities, suggesting there wasn't much to tell. Regardless, she strongly suspected that Sin Bae was in far better shape, and that the assassin would catch Gregory Wyckoff sooner rather than later. So Kincaid kicked it into high gear, giving the chase every last bit of strength she had.

But it soon became clear that it wouldn't be enough.

As she ran, bicycles whizzed past her on either side, nearly every rider shouting expletives for her sprinting against traffic in their bike lane.

Her body acted before the thought even reached her mind. A good thing since had she given the notion even the slightest reflection, she very likely would have decided against it.

But just then her body was running the show. Kincaid's left arm shot straight out from her body in a clothesline milliseconds before a bicycle blew past her. The moment she felt impact she closed her fist around a stretch of material and yanked as hard as she could.

For a moment she thought her arm would be ripped right out of its socket, the momentum was so great. But instead, the male cyclist was severed from the bicycle and both he and the bike were thrown into a circular skid.

Although Kincaid genuinely hoped that the helmeted cyclist was all right, she didn't stop to ask.

She snatched the bike off the ground and propped it up on its wheels. Then she faced it in the opposite direction, gave herself a running head start, and hopped aboard, pedaling as though she were the team leader in the Tour de France.

After a few seconds she had both predator and prey in her sights again. Sin Bae, as she'd assumed, was quickly closing the gap. She didn't have much time to catch up.

Shit. Wyckoff was approaching an intersection, where he'd have to stop or risk getting struck by traffic.

Kincaid leaned forward, lifted her rear end from the seat, and pushed even harder.

She eyed both men through the smog. Wyckoff was slowing, Sin Bae was preparing to pounce.

From the corner of her eye she caught a black Audi A7 careening down the near lane, moving faster than any of the other vehicles on the road.

Wyckoff apparently locked on the Audi with his peripheral vision as well. Just before entering the intersection, the kid dropped to the ground like he'd been shot.

But Sin Bae's reflexes were just as good. The assassin stopped on a dime, and in one liquid motion he reached across his body for his left wrist.

Kincaid saw the glint of the white-gold cuff link as Sin Bae yanked it from his sleeve. The razor-sharp wire that trailed was barely visible but Kincaid knew it was there, knew that in a moment it would close around Gregory Wyckoff's throat just as it had around hers.

Her muscles went to war with her mind, which demanded she squeeze the brakes immediately. Instead Kincaid opened her fingers wide and steered directly at Sin Bae.

As soon as the bicycle collided with the assassin, it toppled end over end; the unforgiving sidewalk leapt off the ground to strike Kincaid in the head.

As she hit the concrete, she tried to keep her eyes wide open, her gaze fixed on Sin Bae.

The assassin had been caught completely off guard, his body thrown into the roadway just as the black Audi A7 reached the intersection.

Sin Bae's body bounced atop the hood of the car, shattering the windshield completely. The Audi shrieked to an immediate halt, flinging Sin Bae's bloodied form forward at least thirty feet, where it hit the road and rolled to a stop.

Other vehicles approaching the intersection screeched to a standstill; several were rear-ended.

Kincaid heard shrieks like dying birds rise all around her. She tuned them out and turned her focus on Wyckoff.

With her ears ringing, she helped the boy up onto his feet and shouted, "It's going to be all right. I'm Jessie, I was hired by your father. You'll be safe with me."

Wyckoff, though clearly in a daze, looked into her eyes and nodded carefully.

Kincaid gripped his arm, said, "Let's get the hell out of here."

Then together they vanished into the chaos and smog.

FORTY-ONE

An hour and a half after Yun Jin-ho left to return to the surface, Janson spotted the door he'd been searching for.

It had been a rough ninety minutes, Janson navigating the maze of underground tunnels using nothing but the miniature Maglite and his memory of a crude map Yun Jin-ho sketched at the table back at the safe house.

Now that he'd finally reached his destination, Janson extinguished the Maglite and dropped onto his haunches to search his go-bag for the items he needed for the next phase of his mission.

No killing anyone who doesn't try to kill you can be a tricky rule. Obviously, had Janson not tunneled across the border in the demilitarized zone, the two soldiers he'd killed would still be alive. But then, in Janson's world not everything was black-and-white.

The gauge he found himself increasingly using was: *Is this for the greater good?*

Whenever feasible, of course, Janson used nonlethal force.

Toward that end he removed from his bag a dart gun containing the incapacitating fluid known as carfentanil. An analogue of the synthetic opioid analgesic fentanyl—a popular painkiller frequently prescribed in patch form—carfentanil had a potency ten thousand times stronger than morphine and a hundred times stronger than fentanyl itself.

Janson double-checked the .33-gauge needles and 1-millimeter vials of carfentanil citrate. The dosage was sufficient to take down a bear. Janson had earlier worried that it would be lethal to North Korean soldiers whose growth had been stunted by the Great Famine of the nineties. But there were few alternatives. In the end he'd decided carfentanil citrate was by far his safest bet—and theirs.

With his go-bag on his back and the dart gun in his hand, Janson reached for the door handle in the darkness. When the handle began to twist under the weight of his fingers he experienced a mixed sensation of relief and apprehension. He was about to enter the palace.

He turned the handle and swung the door open, raising the dart gun as he stepped into the frame.

The door opened onto a long, narrow hallway, as white and sterile as a hospital wing. At the far end of the hallway, a single soldier from the Guard's Command sat on a metal folding chair, his head leaning back against the white wall behind him. His eyes were closed. And he was snoring.

Janson gently closed the door behind him and started up the hallway. Of course, he couldn't leave it to the Sandman to determine when the guard awoke, so as Janson drew near, he fired a dart into the center of the guard's chest.

The guard stirred for a few seconds, just long enough to open his eyes and look up at Janson.

"I'm just a dream," Janson whispered.

The guard's eyelids fell shut and his breathing became shallower.

Janson plunged his fingers into Sleeping Beauty's front shirt pocket and relieved him of his key card. Then he checked the guard's pulse—*you'll be just fine, buddy*—and moved on.

He turned right down the next hallway, at the end of which was a closed metal door with a card reader. He casually slid the guard's card through the reader as though he were purchasing a pack of gum with a debit card at the local 7-Eleven. Then he cautiously opened the door.

As he entered another short corridor, he immediately heard multiple sets of footfalls. Quickly he pressed his back against the far wall.

The two men who were approaching seemed to be making chitchat, but of course Janson couldn't make out a word they were saying. According to the layout Janson had memorized, they could only be coming to check on Sleeping Beauty.

Both men laughed as they turned the corner.

Janson threw his left arm around the throat of the man closest to him and fired a dart into the other.

As that second guard dropped to his knees, Janson fired a dart into the lower back of his captive.

The guard instantly slumped in his arms.

As Janson was setting him down he noticed a blue-and-white metal canister slipping from the fingers of the guard's left hand.

He tried to pluck it from the air but the metal canister hit the ground from about two feet up and rolled all the way to the opposite wall.

Janson grimaced at the noise and backed up against the wall, ready to fire again.

After several tense seconds his pulse began to slow. He knelt next to the canister and immediately identified its contents.

Xpec3 shaving foam manufactured in South Korea.

Janson absently ran his hand through his beard. Then he turned over one of the fallen comrades and found a small green feather duster jutting out of his mustard-colored waistband.

Janson smiled as he considered the prank that the two guards were about to play on Sleeping Beauty.

Maybe you're not so different from us American bastards after all.

He pushed himself to his feet and continued up the new corridor.

Stepping through another door, he entered a hall in which the lights were dimmed. At the end of the hall stood a red steel door. There was no guard in sight. He took a deep breath and moved quickly.

Once more Janson slid the card through the card reader. The door came unlocked. Janson swung the door open.

On the other side a large guard went for his weapon.

Janson fired a dart before the guard could get a shot off.

The dart struck the man in the side of the neck. He crumpled immediately.

Janson stepped into the anteroom.

This is it, he thought.

At the opposite end of the room was a final door. On the wall to its left was a metal keypad.

Janson moved briskly across the room and entered Yun Jin-ho's six-digit pass code from memory. The electronic lock clicked.

Janson opened the door. And stepped forward into Kim Jong-un's War Room.

FORTY-TWO

At the Shangri-La China World Hotel in Beijing, Kincaid closed the door to their luxury suite and told Gregory Wyckoff to relax and have a seat. But when she turned and entered the room the boy was already sprawled out atop the exquisite red-and-gold comforter on the king-size bed, fast asleep.

Poor kid, she thought. Kincaid knew what it was like to be running for days. And she could certainly sympathize with anyone who was being chased by Sin Bae. Had it not been for Park Kwan spotting his gun on the floor of the coatroom in T-Lound, Kincaid would have already been counted as one of his victims.

Like Lynell Yi, she thought, the kid's girlfriend. From what Kincaid knew about their relationship, Gregory and Lynell had been closer than close, a young couple experiencing the world together as though they owned it. And when you were that much in love, that's exactly what life felt like.

That was how Kincaid felt when she was with Janson.

I should have heard from him by now, right?

Not necessarily. If something had happened to him in North Korea, she would have learned about it. At least that was what she kept telling herself.

Kincaid sat in the room's soft leather chair and planted her elbows on the oversize mahogany writing desk. She stared at the phone. She needed to reach out to Senator Wyckoff and his wife, to let them know their son was safe. But she'd lost her own phone and, as gorgeous and modern as it was, she didn't trust the hotel to provide her with a secure line. Especially in China.

She also wanted to call Park Kwan. He and Kang Jung would be worried about her. Surely they'd connected the incident outside Tiananmen Square with her missing their rendezvous. But she wanted to get in touch with them to make sure that they were safe and to let them know that she and Wyckoff were alive and as well as could be expected. Still, she harbored little doubt that both their phones were hot. By calling them, she could be giving away her and Wyckoff's location, and putting Park Kwan and Kang Jung in further danger. No, she couldn't do that. Park Kwan was a cop, a *smart* cop, and she had to trust him to take care of himself and Kang Jung.

Instead she phoned the Embraer 650, which as far as she knew was still sitting on the tarmac at Incheon International.

"CatsPaw. Kayla speaking."

Kincaid made a face and mimicked the words silently. *CatsPaw. Kayla speaking.*

"*Hell-o?*" Kayla said.

"Hey, Kayla, it's Kincaid."

"Oh, *Jessie*," she said, "it's so good to hear from you. Are you and Paul all right?"

Kincaid swallowed the bitterness in her throat. "Janson and I are fine. Listen, I need a favor. I need you to contact our client via a secure line. The number is in the file."

"OK, sure. What's the message?"

"Tell the client we have the package and we're going to deliver it to Washington safe and sound as soon as possible. Details to follow."

"Got it," Kayla said. "Anything else?"

"Yes. Tell the pilots we need the Embraer in Beijing right away. The IATA code for the airport is PEK. Terminal three. Have the jet prepared for a flight to DC. File a zero-one flight plan."

"A zero-one?"

"They'll know what I mean. Be ready to depart PEK six hours from now."

Once Kincaid hung up the phone, a weary voice tapped her on the shoulder.

"I don't have to return to Seoul, do I?"

Kincaid spun in her chair. Gregory Wyckoff was sitting up on the king-size bed. Dark, puffy flesh engulfed his eyes.

"No," Kincaid said with a slight smile. "I wouldn't send you back there. I know you're innocent."

Wyckoff bowed his head. "Thank you."

Kincaid folded her hands in her lap. "Do you feel up to talking about all this?"

"If I'm leaving Beijing in six hours, I suppose we'd better."

"OK," she said, leaning forward. "Why don't you start with Lynell?"

Wyckoff cleared his throat and began speaking softly.

"A few days ago—Christ, I've really lost track of time."

"It's all right."

Wyckoff intertwined his fingers atop his head and closed his eyes to collect his thoughts. When he opened them, he said,

"Lynell came home—and by home I mean our apartment in Seoul—one night and seemed all bent out of shape, as though she was preoccupied with something. I knew she'd been going through a particularly tense time at work."

"She was working as a translator," Kincaid said to help move him along.

"Right. She was a contractor, hired just six months ago, specifically for the four-party talks. She worked out of an office at the US embassy, but the actual talks are being held at the Joint Security Area in the demilitarized zone. That was where she'd been that day."

"Go on."

"She worked directly for the US envoy. For the past half year they've been negotiating a host of issues, from the UN sanctions to the North's nuclear program. The chief US negotiator had been complaining recently that as soon as they make a few steps toward progress, the North begins moving the goalposts and acting erratically."

"How so?"

"Well, for instance, the North is currently holding three US citizens on vague charges of espionage. Each of the individuals was in the country on a tourist visa, and they *were*, in fact, tourists. The US would make some concessions, offer to ease some restrictions, and the North would agree to release the—for lack of a better word—hostages. But then the next day, joint US-ROK military exercises that were scheduled nine months in advance would take place, and the North would suddenly go nuclear, no pun intended. They'd renege on the agreement and all parties would have to return to Go without collecting their two hundred dollars."

"I assume that's a Monopoly reference?"

"Sorry, yeah. What I'm trying to say is that things have been getting intense recently, from what Lynell had been telling me. So when she came home upset, I thought maybe she'd made a mistake, ya know. In the translation. I figured she got reamed out, maybe by the chief US negotiator, maybe by Ambassador Young, who could be a real dick. But after a couple of hours, I realized it was much more than that. Something was definitely wrong; something weighty was on her mind."

"Did you press her on it?"

"I asked, but Lynell wouldn't tell me anything at our apartment. At first I figured she simply didn't want to talk about it. I was resolved to try again in the morning. If she wouldn't give by then, I'd wait until she came home from the Joint Security Area the next day to see whether the mood had passed, or something was continuing to trouble her."

Kincaid nodded but said nothing.

"At around eight that night I went to the bathroom to get ready for bed. When I came out, there was a sheet of paper on the coffee table. There was a message scrawled in Lynell's handwriting; it just read, 'Not in here. O/s.'"

"O/s?"

"'O/s' was her shorthand for 'outside.' So I went outside and she started talking right away. She said she inadvertently overheard something Ambassador Young was saying. She said she only heard bits and pieces." As he spoke, Wyckoff looked past Kincaid as though staring through the wall into the room next door. "The ambassador had been speaking to someone Lynell never met before. Someone from the South Korean delegation. A younger man, she said, maybe thirty or thirty-five years old. She heard Young use words like 'provocation,' 'incursion,' and 'ground war.' Then she heard them discussing troop numbers from the United States." Wyckoff shook his head sadly. "That was essentially it.

That and the name of some operation. The operation was called Diophantus."

"How long had she listened?"

"Not long," Wyckoff said. "No more than thirty or forty seconds. But when she spun around to leave she walked straight into Ambassador Young's chief aide."

"Jonathan?"

"Jonathan Day. He's Young's lackey. He had a thing for Lynell awhile back and she rejected him. He'd been giving her angry glares ever since." Wyckoff looked Kincaid in the eyes. "She started to move past him, and he grabbed her by the arm, accused her of eavesdropping. He actually used the words 'espionage' and 'treason.' Lynell pulled away, but she was sure Jonathan was going to report what he'd seen to the ambassador."

Kincaid prodded him to go on.

"Neither of us was very concerned for her job. 'Let them sack me,' she said. But we *were* concerned about what might happen to her if they discovered *what* she overheard. She was afraid that they'd subject her to a polygraph. *That's* why she'd been so reluctant to tell me at first. Because they'd ask her if she'd told anyone else. And she didn't want to have to give them my name."

Wyckoff shrugged, his stare floating toward the ceiling. He was clearly trying to keep the emotion out of his voice. "But she loved me," he said. "She never kept anything from me. And Lynell had always said I was the smartest person she knew. Even though I knew that was bullshit, it meant a lot to me given her own education and family background."

"Did she know you'd use the information?"

"She knew that I'd dig deeper," Wyckoff said, once more with that far-off look in his eyes. "And I did."

Kincaid canted her head.

"I'm kind of good with computers," he said.

"From what I understand, that's the understatement of the millennium."

For the first time since she met him, Wyckoff managed a tired smile.

"OK," he admitted. "I'm a hacker. Or what you might call a *hacktivist*."

"You moved on the information right away?"

"I didn't waste any time. I immediately got myself to a secure computer and entered the State Department's email system. Months earlier I had socially engineered a young female aide in order to gain access. I didn't want to risk breaking into the system using Lynell's account. But as it turned out, the backdoor I'd installed using malware months before was still open."

"What did you do once you were in?"

"First thing I did was run a search for 'Diophantus.' I made a mental list of every email user who had typed the word into a message. There weren't many names. But the names that *did* appear were all huge political players. Ambassador Young, of course. The director of National Security, Sanford Hildreth. The director of the Defense Intelligence Agency, Douglas Albright. A deputy director of the CIA's Clandestine Service named Ella Quon. A chief systems engineer named Eric Matsumura. And someone I'd never even heard of—neither had Lynell. His title was listed as undersecretary of state but I couldn't find his name anywhere else in the database or even on the web."

Kincaid realized she'd been chewing on the pad of her thumb. She pulled it out of her mouth and said, "Let me guess. His name was Edward Clarke."

Wyckoff nodded. "Yeah, who is he? How did you know?"

"He's the director of Consular Operations."

"Cons Ops?" Wyckoff scoffed. "I thought Consular Operations was just a myth. You mean to tell me it really exists? The State Department runs its own black ops?"

Kincaid nodded.

Wyckoff's mouth dropped open; his tired eyes grew wide. "Are you...Are you serious?"

"Believe me," Kincaid said. "Consular Operations is my former employer."

Wyckoff shook his head sadly. "Every day I wake up, I realize I know less and less about my government."

FORTY-THREE

According to Yun Jin-ho, Janson had ten, fifteen minutes, tops, before the Guard's Command ascertained that their sentries were down and ordered reinforcements to move in to intercept the intruder and reestablish control over the premises.

Janson promised himself he wouldn't waste a second of that precious time. He marched straight to the center of the War Room, the design for which had apparently been stolen from the bridge of *Star Trek*'s original *Enterprise*.

He sat in the captain's chair and worked the attached keyboard with his fingers as quickly as he could. Yun Jin-ho had told him precisely where to look. After navigating past several screens on the sizable monitor in front of him, Janson pulled up a file designated "15-4-1912" (Kim Il-sung's birth date) and clicked "Enter." At the prompt Janson entered Yun Jin-ho's fourteen-digit pass code from memory.

In the glow of the monitor, Janson's eyes slowly widened. A deep chill ran up his spine. He shivered, felt the fine hairs on his arms rise like a synchronized army.

No, he thought. This can't be.

* * *

"ONCE WE LEARNED who the players were, Lynell and I decided it was too dangerous to return to our apartment. So we registered at the Sophia Guesthouse, a hanok in central Seoul."

"I paid the hanok a visit when we first arrived in the city," Kincaid said.

"We'd talked about switching off, with one of us sleeping and the other keeping awake and alert. In the end, we were both too exhausted. We had spent the past few hours planning how to get the hell out of South Korea and where to go—and the last half hour arguing like hell over all of it."

A wall of water formed in front of Wyckoff's already glazed eyes. "I woke up when I heard a crash. Lynell had knocked over a lamp. It was the first thing I saw. At first, I didn't think much of it. I couldn't really *see* anything, just shapes and forms." He rubbed the heel of his palms against his temples. "Then my eyes adjusted and I saw Lynell in the corner of the room. It looked as though she were being lifted off the ground by some invisible force. She was still kicking her feet. It was the most frightening thing I'd ever seen. Like something out of a horror movie."

Wyckoff was breaking down.

"Take it easy," Kincaid said, reaching out, placing a hand on his knee. "If you need some time, I'd understand. Would you like a glass of water? Some tissues?"

Wyckoff waved her offer away with his hands. "The guy who

was holding her, as soon as he saw me lift my head, he spun his body around so that his back was facing me. I jumped up from the mat and ran at him. He smashed his elbow into my nose, and I hit the floor like a stone. I thought my nose was busted; I felt so much blood spilling out of me."

Wyckoff stood. Paced over to the curtained sliding glass door and turned back. "When I finally managed to pick myself off the floor, the guy was still holding Lynell up by the throat but she wasn't kicking anymore. She wasn't doing anything; her body was entirely limp. I knew right away she was dead." He paused to wipe away his tears and clear his throat. When he spoke again, his voice was little more than a rasp. "So I spun around and opened the door. Just as I did, I heard her body drop to the floor. But I didn't look back. I ran as fast and as hard as I could across the courtyard. Lynell's killer started running after me. I heard his feet slapping against the pavement. He was so fast. I was sure he was going to catch me."

"What did you do?" Kincaid said gently.

"I remembered seeing a fire escape on our way to the hanok. I headed straight for that building. I turned down the alley, pulled myself up on a pipe, and reached for the ladder. I ran up the fire escape as quick as I could until I heard him coming again. I froze in place somewhere between the second and third floors. I figured that was my only chance. Sure enough, he slowed down, checked the alley. He even looked up, seemed to look right at me. But it was so dark, he didn't notice me. I waited for him to grab hold of the pipe to pull himself up. But he didn't. Instead he ran out of the alley and kept going. As soon as he did, I climbed up to the roof. It was freezing up there, but I stayed until morning."

Kincaid's eyes narrowed. "You said it was pitch black in the hanok. Yet you recognized him today at Tiananmen Square, didn't you?"

Wyckoff nodded. "I only saw a flash of his face before he turned around. There was just a hint of moonlight seeping in through the shades. But it was all I needed. I have..." He paused for several seconds, gazing up at the ceiling as though he was contemplating the nature of the universe, then said, "I have a photographic memory."

"A photographic memory? Really? That wasn't in your dossier."

He smiled sadly. "No, it wouldn't be. It's not something I boast about. My dad calls me a slacker as it is. If he knew I had a photographic memory, he'd expect me to become a brain surgeon or run for president. Probably both. No one really knows about my photographic memory. In school, I didn't want to risk being labeled a freak. Only Lynell knows." He paused again, a fresh wave of tears spilling over his lower lashes down his cheeks. "*Knew*," he corrected himself. "Only Lynell *knew*."

Kincaid waited for him to calm himself. When he seemed to have control over himself she asked, "How did you learn of Yun Jin-ho?"

Wyckoff lifted his bloodshot eyes in surprise. There were questions in those eyes, but he didn't ask them.

"When Lynell and I first moved to Seoul, I hacked into the government's servers, looking for secrets. Specifically, I wanted to find South Korea's intelligence on the North's nuclear program. Everyone wants us to believe that North Korea is on the verge of becoming a nuclear power. Washington and Seoul want us to believe it to demonstrate that the Kim regime is a threat to the region and to justify suffocating economic sanctions. Pyongyang wants us to believe it because they're afraid of a future US-ROK invasion aimed at regime change. I think the claims being made by both sides are highly exaggerated, if not complete bullshit. Of course, the only ones suffering as a result of all the lies are the North

Korean people. I thought if I could expose the actual intelligence Seoul has on North Korea's nuclear capabilities, the United Nations would have no choice but to lift their sanctions and allow the North's economy to collapse or thrive on its own."

Wyckoff sat back down on the bed. "I engaged the help of the Hivemind and together we found nothing to prove or disprove my theory. But we *did* discover what appeared to be a list of agents the NIS is running in Pyongyang. Spies. In North Korea's Ministry of State Security, Kim Jong-un's Guard's Command, even one deputy director in the palace."

Kincaid said, "Yun Jin-ho."

Wyckoff nodded. "Code name: MALTESE. It took some work to figure out his true identity. But once I did I realized he was someone who might be willing to sell secrets to a third party like myself."

"What made you think that?"

"There were extensive notes in his electronic file. Yun Jin-ho was obviously a reluctant spy. Not for ideological reasons—he clearly despised the North Korean regime—but because he didn't trust his handlers in Seoul. They'd apparently made him promises they hadn't kept."

"What types of promises?"

"Promises to bring him in from the cold. Promises to get him and his fiancée safely out of Pyongyang and return them to Seoul, where Yun Jin-ho had originally defected to five years ago."

Kincaid nodded as she took it all in. "So you made contact?"

"I first contacted him months ago, long before this happened. He was wary of me in the beginning, but that was perfectly understandable. I gave him time to check me out for himself. Eventually, we sort of became friends.

"The morning after Lynell was killed I snuck into a high school to use a computer. I hacked into the DIA's email system and pulled up the director's account. Albright had been a lot less secure than Ambassador Young. The details were sketchy but within a half hour I had a good idea of what Diophantus is all about. And why Lynell was killed for overhearing what she heard. I sent Yun Jin-ho an encrypted email, which is how we usually communicated."

"You told him about Diophantus?"

"Actually, he had recently told me that he discovered something at the palace that might be of interest to me. He refused to turn it over to his handlers in Seoul. He said it was too big, too important to entrust to NIS. But he believed I was the perfect vehicle to deliver this particular intelligence. He told me if I published what he had, I could literally change the world. But he insisted on *selling* the secrets to me. They wouldn't be free."

"What was his price?"

"He said, 'Get my fiancée out of Chosun'—that's what they call Korea in the North—'and I will give it to you.' Now I told him I had information for the palace too. I said, maybe we could trade. He refused. He just wanted me to send someone to help his fiancée escape. I figured it was the only way to get whatever information he had and to pass on the warning about Diophantus to the palace. So I did."

"You sent someone to collect his fiancée?"

"I quietly hired an American expat I knew. A former Navy SEAL. He'd been a contractor with the Central Intelligence Agency in Kandahar after nine-eleven. Then he worked for Blackwater in Iraq. A few days ago he went up North, but I never heard from him again. I'd paid him half up front; he probably took the half I gave him and made himself scarce."

"If you don't mind my asking, where did you get the money for something like that?"

"I took out a cash advance on a credit card number I stole on-line." He looked up. "Don't worry, it belonged to a bad person."

"So, you never learned what information Yun Jin-ho discovered in the North."

Wyckoff shook his head. "And he never received my warning about Diophantus."

Kincaid felt her pulse begin to race. "What is it? What is Diophantus?"

"Like I said, initially I didn't know. There were very few details about the operation in Young's emails. But it seemed clear from the messages that Diophantus was purposefully shrouded in secrecy. And that there was a significant risk attached to it if someone found out."

"Which you did the next morning." Kincaid heard the impatience in her own voice. "So tell me, Gregory. What *is* Diophantus?"

Wyckoff took a deep breath then swallowed hard.

"In short, it's a plot to start a second Korean War," he said. "A war meant to collapse the North Korean regime and reunify Korea."

Kincaid took in his words. Was about to speak but Wyckoff beat her to the punch.

"I know what you're thinking," he said. "That regime change in the North may not necessarily be a bad thing, especially for the North Korean people. I thought about it too. The problem is that this war would inevitably result in the loss of millions of lives, including the lives of thousands—maybe *tens* of thousands—of American troops." He paused. "And the war wouldn't have the support of the American public. Regardless of your view on Iraq, this without question *would* be a war that the American public was duped into."

FORTY-FOUR

J anson couldn't believe his eyes. As he attempted to print the forty-five-page document, he tried simultaneously to comprehend its contents and calculate its consequences.

The invasion would commence with special forces, of which the Korean People's Army numbered almost two hundred thousand.

They would start with predawn airdrops and shore landings. As the soldiers struck land, they would immediately begin sabotage operations. They'd hit power stations and telephone lines, bring down cell and Internet networks.

While panic rose like a tsunami over the ten million citizens of Seoul, the North would strike with artillery at a rate of hundreds of thousands of rounds per hour.

All arteries out of Seoul would be choked with traffic as the South Koreans attempted to flee their city under fire.

Meanwhile, hundreds of chemically armed Scud missiles

would be launched at targets ranging from Incheon International Airport to Seoul Station, making escape impossible.

To slow down US reinforcements, hundreds of Nodong missiles carrying chemical weapons would be targeting Japan.

Torpedoes launched from North Korean submarines and semisubmersibles would strike US ships carrying personnel and supplies to the peninsula, leaving the South Koreans' puppet masters with fewer than thirty thousand troops on the ground.

The printer paused for no apparent reason.

Goddamn it, Janson thought. Not now, not a fucking paper jam.

He cracked open the casing and ripped the offending sheet from around the toner cartridge. He slammed the tray shut, and the printer resumed printing.

Janson turned back to the screen. Here it was, right in front of him, the strategy for the actual invasion: 750,000 troops, 2,500 tanks. Hundreds of *drones*.

Drones. And not just the toy planes that US and South Korean intelligence *knew* the North possessed. Not just surveillance drones, but drones that could carry a 450-pound payload. Drones that could carry out attack missions, dropping Hellfire-style missiles from the sky like rain. Attacks like those being carried out by the US military in places such as Yemen, Afghanistan, and the tribal areas of Pakistan—only these deadly attacks would indiscriminately target heavily populated South Korean cities, slaughtering millions of innocent civilians.

Auster, Janson thought. Cal Auster. That's why the son of a bitch is in South Korea, so close to the demilitarized zone.

What had Auster said to Janson when they first met in Afghanistan?

"I serve a basic human need, man. You think votes are going to change the course of a nation like Afghanistan, you naive mother-

fucker? Hell no, not votes. The only things that are ever going to change this fucking country are bullets and more bullets. Lots of fucking bullets and bombs and bunker-busters. It's a new war, Paul. A new world. And I'm going to fucking arm all of it."

Janson scrolled down. *Not much time now.* He had to get the hell out of here or he never would. Janson had to warn the South, he had to warn the Blue House.

Christ. Not just the Blue House, but the White House as well. According to these documents, the latest version of the DPRK's Taep'odong missile had the capacity to reach the United States. Not just Hawaii and Alaska but also the continental United States, from the southern tip of California up to Washington State.

This wouldn't just be a second Korean War. Once China became involved, this would become the Third *World* War.

And the North would commence this operation at the slightest provocation. They'd have to ensure China's involvement, and in order to do that they'd need cover. They'd essentially need to say, *Look, the South started it.* But given what China had at stake—namely their border with North Korea—it wouldn't take a hell of a lot. Maybe nothing more than a stray bullet that crossed the demarcation line in the dead of night.

Somewhere in the residence an alarm sounded.

Janson grabbed his stack of documents and stuffed them into his go-bag. He replaced the dart gun with his Beretta—the dart gun would be useless against the number of gunmen he was sure to encounter—and raced for the door.

He burst into the hallway and found no one. He took the stairs as he'd been directed to by Yun Jin-ho, still picturing the spy's crude map in his mind.

As he ascended, two soldiers from Kim's Guard's Command

were hurrying down the stairs carrying firearms. When they spotted Janson they stopped and fired. Janson took cover then carefully placed two bullets in each of them and let their bodies tumble past him on the stairs.

He wouldn't be caught.

He wouldn't be killed.

Not here, not tonight.

He needed to make it to Seoul.

Janson burst through the door to the outside and immediately heard the crackling of at least a dozen AK-47s.

But there was mercifully little light. Janson looked up and saw that most of the floodlights above him had been destroyed.

He sprinted forward in the direction of the designated checkpoint, thinking, *There's no way this guard's going to let me pass, no matter how much he's been paid. He'd be shot dead alongside me.*

As he neared the checkpoint Janson saw something strange. Two bodies lay on the ground within a few yards of the booth.

Janson ran harder, faster, maybe harder and faster than he'd ever run before in his life.

Soon the lone remaining guard's face came into view.

It was Yun Jin-ho, a wide, crazy smile spread across his visage.

"This way, Janson," he cried.

Yun Jin-ho. He'd taken out the guards. He'd taken out the lights.

"You're coming with me," Janson called on the run, ducking below the bullets buzzing by them.

"Impossible," Yun Jin-ho shouted.

As Janson passed the middle-aged spy, he looked back and saw at least two dozen North Korean soldiers coming at him from behind.

In front of him stood a wide-open gate.

Janson ran past it and spun around, hoping to persuade Yun Jin-ho into accompanying him.

But it was too late.

The soldiers were almost on him.

Yun Jin-ho had slowed them down by raising a hand grenade high above his head.

Several soldiers stopped to fire at him; others swerved past him in order to reach Janson before he made it to the road.

Yun Jin-ho pulled the pin.

As the soldiers riddled Yun's body with bullets, he screamed, "For *Mi-sook!*" then spiked the grenade against the pavement like a football in the end zone.

The blast knocked Janson off his feet.

His head smacked the blacktop; he was sure he'd suffered a concussion. He lifted his hand over his eyes to block out the ferocious heat from the explosion.

From his spot on the ground he could tell that nearly every North Korean soldier was either dead or critically wounded. Most had been shredded to pieces by the grenade.

Janson wasted no time. Pushing himself to his feet, he hobbled across the road and quickly spotted the black jeep.

Staggering, he crossed in front of the vehicle and ducked into the passenger side.

"*Drive,*" he shouted to Mi-sook.

Blindly with no headlights she pressed down on the accelerator, tossing Janson back against the hard vinyl seat.

"Are you all right?" Mi-sook said, glancing at his face.

He was about to tell her to keep her eyes on the road, but what was the point? She was literally flying blind.

"I'm fine," Janson lied.

From the backseat Janson heard a strange noise. A wail, like the crying of a small infant.

He swung around in his seat and looked in the back. His eyes widened in surprise.

Shooting a stunned look at Mi-sook, he shouted, *"What the hell is that?"*

* * *

JANSON HAD DRIVEN blind before. A long time ago. While he was still training to become a Consular Operations agent.

The training had taken place at a facility known as The Point, located on a peninsula in Perquimans County, North Carolina, along the Albemarle Sound. Owned by the Department of Defense, The Point was a sister facility of The Farm, training grounds of the CIA's National Clandestine Service. The Farm was located at Camp Peary, a nine-thousand-acre military reservation near Williamsburg, Virginia. There was a time when The Farm hosted Cons Ops trainees as well. But that was before. Before Jason Bourne. Before Cons Ops became known as the black sheep of US black ops.

But from all accounts, training for Consular Operations differed little from that for the Clandestine Service. Both included a defensive-driving course called "Crash & Burn." In addition to learning evasive techniques, reverse driving, and how to smash through barriers, all trainees had to prove proficiency in navigating a motor vehicle blindfolded.

Janson remembered a series of traumatic tests that involved maneuvering through simulated border crossings and hostage situations while behind the wheel of a gray Monte Carlo with a burlap hood securely fastened over his head. He also remembered complaining to a fellow student that these bizarre exercises were a complete waste of time. Because *"When the hell are we ever going to find ourselves in that fucked-up a situation?"*

Well, lo and behold, it was Janson who was now behind the wheel, blindly punching through obstacles as Mi-sook sat in back, cradling her baby. When Janson realized the infant was on board and that the old jeep was equipped with neither air bags nor a child safety seat, he insisted Mi-sook pull over so that he could take over driving duties. Now, twenty minutes after he lost what he hoped would be the last of their pursuers, the jeep raced blindly north up National Highway 65 toward the city of Hyesan.

Hyesan would provide them with two distinct paths out of North Korea. One, crossing the frozen Yalu River on foot, was risky. It was a well-known route that would lead Janson and Mi-sook and her baby into Changbai, China's autonomous Korean region. Janson had little doubt that North Korean soldiers would have set up a roadblock in the vicinity of the Changbai-Hyesan International Bridge, making crossing the river undetected a practical impossibility.

The other path—which Janson considered Plan A—was nearly as dangerous because it hinged on the cooperation of at least two other individuals. They were both friends of Yun Jin-ho and they were expecting Janson and Mi-sook's arrival. But if alarms had sounded from the palace, it was possible these North Korean soldiers would decide not to put themselves at risk—especially if they had already learned that their friend Yun Jin-ho was dead.

Janson hoped that the infant would warm their hearts enough to persuade them to assist. If that didn't work, Janson was ready to provide them with vast sums of cold, hard cash. If that didn't work...

Well, Janson was still armed to the teeth.

* * *

HOURS LATER, JANSON and Mi-sook arrived at Hyesan Airfield. A military airport with a single gravel runway, Hyesan Airfield underwent perpetual construction. So there were few lights and fewer personnel on-site in the wee hours of the morning.

As Janson rolled the jeep past the southern gate, they were given the all-clear signal by the first of the two accomplices supplied by Yun Jin-ho before his untimely demise. Mi-sook, who had moved to the front passenger seat with her child, rolled down her window and spoke to the guard in Korean.

She turned to Janson. "He says that KPA units are stationed along the Yalu River in Hyesan and along the Tumen River in Musan."

Janson said, "Is the plane fueled up and ready to go?"

Mi-sook spoke to the guard again, then looked back at Janson. "It is a very small plane, but yes."

"What kind of a plane?"

Janson heard the guard say, "Antonov An-Two."

"Christ," Janson said.

Mi-sook looked a question at him. "You have heard of it?"

"I've read about it," Janson said. "In history books."

The Antonov An-2, or "Annie," was a mass-produced single-engine aircraft designed by the Soviets in the 1940s. It was designed for light utility transport and agricultural work like crop spraying. It was notoriously slow.

Mi-sook said, "We can leave the jeep. Chang-bo will drive it north and destroy it somewhere south of the Chinese border."

As Janson and Mi-sook exited the vehicle, Janson got his first look at the Annie. It was the Y-5 version, built by license in China. North Korea possessed a number of them. If Janson's military history was right, they'd flown them during the Korean War, for parachute missions and sabotage operations behind enemy lines. They were equipped with wooden propellers and canvas wings, which gave them a low-radar cross section and thus a narrow degree of stealth.

Looks like Snoopy's archnemesis, the Red Baron, he thought as they crouched behind a troop transport to remain hidden from the two soldiers in the control tower.

"How are we going to make it to the runway without the air controllers spotting us?" Janson asked.

Once Mi-sook translated, Chang-bo removed a walkie-talkie from his belt and spoke into it. Suddenly the Annie's lights flared brightly, and Janson noticed they were aimed directly at the control tower. Over Chang-bo's walkie, Janson could hear the air controllers squawking loudly about the pilot's error.

But it was no error. The pilot had purposefully blinded them.

Janson grabbed Mi-sook and together they hustled toward the Annie, the infant wailing in Mi-sook's arms.

Once they were aboard, the Annie began moving backward until the plane's lights were no longer directed at the control tower. Janson and Mi-sook strapped themselves in, Mi-sook gripping her child tightly.

The plane started down the small gravel runway. The jarring bumps and jolts were instantly forgotten once the Annie lifted them into the air.

Moments later the pilot turned and pointed the plane's nose in the direction of China. The brief flight would take them to Shenyang, where they'd board a commercial airliner to Seoul.

Only once the pilot announced that they'd crossed into Chinese airspace did Janson finally lean back in his tiny vinyl seat and exhale.

Still not quite as bad as flying coach, he thought.

* * *

KINCAID DUG THE TELEPHONE NUMBER out of her pocket. She unfolded it and set it on the oversize executive desk in her room at
the Shangri-La China World. She lifted the phone and dialed.

Nam Sei-hoon picked up on the first ring.

"Mission accomplished," she told him.

"Good, very good." He paused for a moment. "Have you spoken
to Paul?"

"I haven't heard from him yet. I'm concerned that something
might have happened up north."

"I am sure he is fine. I will put out some feelers and let you
know as soon as I hear anything."

"Thank you," she said.

"It is my pleasure, Ms. Kincaid." He cleared his throat. "I assume you will be returning to Seoul with the information you
obtained from the Wyckoff boy?"

"I will, immediately. Do you have a place for us to meet?"

"There is a safe house in Gangnam. Let me give you the address."

PART III

On the Brink

FORTY-FIVE

The Westin Chosun Seoul
Jung-gu, Seoul

Janson moved quickly through the ultramodern lobby of the Westin hotel. Standing in the elevator bank, he waited for an empty lift. When one opened, he stepped on and punched the button to close the doors. As the doors moved toward each other, an old woman hurried toward them, a look on her face begging Janson to hold them open for her. He looked away and exhaled when they left her on the other side.

She'd thank me if she knew how I smelled, he thought as the elevator ascended to the seventeenth floor.

Standing outside room 1708, he rapped on the door in the manner in which they'd agreed. When the door finally opened, Jina Jeon's expression told him all he needed to know about the sight of him. Her eyes drifted to his hairline, where he'd sustained a significant laceration following the blast from Yun Jin-ho's grenade.

His heart ached as he recalled the image of the North Korean pulling the pin high over his head, about to sacrifice his life for Janson and Mi-sook.

"How is she?" he said as he stepped past her.

"Doing better," Jina Jeon assured him. "She's a bit overwhelmed."

That was more than understandable. The culture shock alone no doubt landed a number of defectors in the hospital beds of Seoul. Even Janson, who'd traveled widely on every continent except Antarctica, felt as though he were standing on a different planet than the one he was on just twenty-four hours ago.

Janson glanced into the bedroom of the executive suite and saw Mi-sook sleeping sideways, fully clothed, atop the California king-size bed, the bassinet provided by the hotel right at her side. He closed the door and moved back into the sitting room, where Jina Jeon was on her knees, collecting a couple of cold bottles of water from the minibar.

She handed one to Janson, who twisted the cap and drank hungrily.

"Mi-sook's papers worked perfectly," he said. "Thank you."

Jina Jeon sat at the square wooden table near the sliding glass door that led out to the lanai. Though the curtains were closed the room was brighter than Janson's eyes could stand, so he dimmed the main overhead light before sitting across from her.

"I'm sorry about the house," he said.

Jina Jeon rolled her eyes and smiled. "You say it as if you soiled my white carpet by stepping inside with mud on your boots."

"I did," Janson said, with a painful attempt to return the smile.

"That's why I'm apologizing. The house blowing up, that was all done in order to cover up my initial faux pas."

Jina Jeon laughed; it was the most pleasant sound Janson had heard in days.

"You and your mom will be reimbursed," he said. "For everything and more. Just toss out a number and give me the name of your bank and I'll have the amount wired to you within forty-eight hours."

"Who will the wire be from?"

"My business."

"CatsPaw?" she said. "Or the Phoenix Foundation?"

Janson masked his surprise; not a difficult task since he was too exhausted to exercise his facial muscles.

"I only just found out," she said.

Janson didn't ask how. He assumed she obtained the news from the same source who provided her the documents that allowed Mi-sook into the country. Without the false South Korean passport, Janson would have had to leave Mi-sook and her baby in Shenyang, something that would have broken his heart under the circumstances.

"I initially thought we had lost more than just the house," Jina Jeon said following minutes of silence. "I thought we had lost you."

Janson saw clearly the emotion in her eyes.

She said, "When I finally learned you were alive, I became afraid that it looked as though I betrayed you."

"The thought never once crossed my mind," Janson lied.

Ultimately, though, he *had* rolled the dice on the chance that Jina Jeon hadn't betrayed him—even before he'd realized that it was Nam Sei-hoon who stabbed him in the back. Before Janson watched Kang Jung get attacked in her own home by a female Cons Ops agent, he had no idea whether it was Jina who had tipped off Cons Ops or not—and he'd been heading straight for the tunnel suggested to him by Jina as his best opportunity to infiltrate North Korea.

Nam Sei-hoon. Putting Janson in danger was one thing; Janson was and always would be a soldier. Janson was in the fight. But to allow a thirteen-year-old girl to be killed, that was quite another thing. Even if Janson could push aside his own betrayal, even if he could forget Yun Jin-ho's story, even if he could erase the memory of Yun dying to saving his and Mi-sook's lives, he could never forgive the little man for putting Kang Jung's life at risk, if not directly ordering the attack himself.

Regardless of what happened in the next forty-eight hours, Janson would make certain that Nam Sei-hoon met a bad end.

One person, one mission, one redemption at a time.

Just now there were more pressing matters. He'd been in touch with Kayla. Gregory Wyckoff was alive and well and sleeping aboard the Embraer on his way back to the United States. Kayla had also heard from Kincaid, which relieved Janson as much as any news he'd received in his life. Kincaid had called Kayla from Beijing, which meant that, at least for the time being, she was safe. He'd immediately called Park Kwan, who told Janson that he was also in Beijing—along with Kang Jung. Janson's anger over the thirteen-year-old's continued involvement quickly subsided as he realized she was probably much safer with Park Kwan and Kincaid in Beijing than she would be with her mother or father back in Seoul. At least until this was over.

What bothered Janson most, however, was that they'd been separated from Kincaid in Beijing and didn't know where she was. Park Kwan told him what he knew about the excitement just outside Tiananmen Square, which was very little. But he did know there was blood. Fortunately, when Janson put the time line together in his head—when Kayla heard from Kincaid and when the incident occurred near Tiananmen Square—he knew she'd survived that particular incident. And that she'd ultimately gotten Gregory Wyckoff safely to Beijing Capital International, though she wasn't there when the Embraer lifted off to take Wyckoff to the United States.

So, where is she now? And why hasn't she called?

He made a few assumptions. One, that Kincaid didn't know Janson had made it back to Seoul. Two, that she was on her way back to Seoul anyway and didn't want to risk using an unsecure line from a plane, even if only to check in. Three, that she'd assumed her call to Kayla would be sufficient to alert Janson and anyone else who mattered that she was alive.

Still, he wished Kincaid hadn't lost her phone. His missing her aside, he felt the need to at least touch base. To keep her apprised. And to finally learn what Gregory Wyckoff knew about Diophantus.

Keep her apprised . . .

"Something wrong, Paul?" Jina Jeon's voice was laced with concern. But he didn't turn to look at her. His mind was grasping for something. Something important. Something vital.

He tried to conjure up a timetable for the hours between Jina Jeon's house exploding and his entering the tunnel.

He'd been cut off from Kincaid and the rest of the world since then.

He had spoken to Kincaid following the attack on Kang Jung, but only to ask her to grab the girl and haul her to safety.

Christ, he thought as his head fell into his hands. He hadn't yet warned her about Nam Sei-hoon.

If something happened to Jessica Kincaid, Janson would never be able to forgive himself. If she were hurt or killed because he'd neglected to caution her, he might as well begin digging his own grave.

He leapt out of his seat and rushed toward the phone but stopped dead.

Whom could he call?

For the time being, at least, Kincaid remained just out of his reach.

FORTY-SIX

At the little man's "safe house" in Gangnam, an austere two-bedroom apartment in a modest building set away from the flashy clubs and designer boutiques of Apgujeong, Sin Bae circled the chair he'd placed in the center of the living room. As he did, his hatred for the woman swelled. He wasn't quite sure why, since it had been *his* mistakes and failures over the past few days that put him in this precarious situation. This woman had only been acting in accordance with the nature of all living things. She'd simply been trying to survive.

Yet he was incensed by her mere presence. Never before had he taken his work so personally. But then, never before had he failed so egregiously in his tasks. These emotions, not only this rage but his reluctance to terminate the young girl, were unquestionably to blame. Whatever he experienced while strangling the translator at the Sophia Guesthouse, whatever had jumped at him like a plastic ghost in a haunted house, had incited this precipitous downfall.

Sin Bae wanted to slit Kincaid's throat and get it over with. But he'd been instructed by Ping to wait for a call. The little man was not pleased that Kincaid had come alone. It meant that there were many loose ends left to be snipped. The police officer Park Kwan, the teenager Kang Jung. The senator's son. And Paul Janson. Maybe even the former Cons Ops agent Jina Jeon.

As he circled Kincaid's chair, his message indicator blinked on. He retrieved his phone from the folding table and read it:

Find out location of the others.

Sin Bae ran a hand through his damp black hair. The pain in his upper back was growing worse, radiating into his shoulders. The opiates Ping had passed to him following the incident in Beijing were causing him to itch; they were making him sweat. Irritably, he tossed the phone to the hardwood floor, where it landed with a splat. If the little man did not know how to locate the others, Sin Bae should have received this message an hour ago, when the woman first stepped into the apartment.

He grinned as he recalled the look on her face when he closed the door behind her. She moved quickly but Sin Bae raised the stun gun and incapacitated her before she could attack. Then he tied her up.

He hated how she now fixed her gaze on his face, inspecting with glee the cuts and bruises she'd caused him back in Beijing. She had probably thought him dead. Probably thought when she first saw him behind the door that she was beholding a ghost.

Perhaps she still did. He wondered whether she believed in such things. Pondered on whether an apparition could make this woman scream.

* * *

KINCAID WAS MORE TERRIFIED than she'd ever been in her life. But she'd be damned if she was going to give this son of a bitch the satisfaction of knowing it.

No matter what happened, she would remain strong.

She would die the way she'd been taught to die. With her dignity intact.

She would die the way Janson would die.

Kincaid watched her captor's face as he circled her. Why hadn't he killed her yet? Sin Bae was a professional. He was Cons Ops. What was he doing wasting time with theatrics? It could only mean that he'd been instructed not to kill her—yet. Clearly he'd been ordered to wait.

But why?

With so much fear running rampant in her mind it felt impossible to uncoil the logic.

Janson, she thought. He's still alive. He made it back from the North and now they need to use me as bait.

But, no, there were other loose ends as well. Park Kwan and Kang Jung, whom she'd left in Tiananmen Square. She'd had no choice. And now both the cop and the girl were better off for being deserted in Beijing. Sin Bae could torture her all he wanted, she didn't know where they were. Didn't know where the hell Janson was.

What about the boy?

By now everyone must know that Gregory Wyckoff had been put on Janson's private jet and sent back to the States.

She watched her captor curl his fingers into a fist and felt an entirely fresh wave of terror.

"Where is the cop?" Sin Bae demanded.

Kincaid could hear the slur in his voice. He'd lost some teeth or bitten through his tongue; he sounded as though his tongue were swollen to ten times its normal size. She almost smiled as she re-called steering the pilfered bicycle into him, launching him in front of that speeding black Audi.

Sin Bae suddenly struck her with a closed fist.

The blow fractured her left cheekbone. Her head swung so hard to the right that she thought he'd broken her neck.

*   *   *

Sin Bae watched as blood poured from between her lips. She was so dazed from the strike that he thought he might have knocked her unconscious. If he had, there would be consequences. There would be repercussions if he wasn't able to extract the information they wanted from her.

He needed to calm himself. This rage would only cause him to make yet another critical error. He rubbed his knuckles and committed himself to not hitting her so hard next time. Had he aimed for the temple, a slug like that would have killed her in-stantly.

His eyes fell on the phone he'd thrown to the floor. The light was blinking. There were so many flashing lights in South Chosun. What would Su-ra have thought if she'd seen Seoul?

Su-ra, he thought. Why continue to haunt me?

"Because you left me, big brother. Because you left me to die."

I was just a child then. Just a child, like you.

By the time Sin Bae escaped from Yodok, he'd seen so many bodies that death no longer affected him. One year earlier, a young man he'd grown up with in Pyongyang became a prisoner at the camp. Like so many new prisoners, the guards quickly recruited him to be a snitch. By then, Sin Bae had no tolerance for snitches. So he'd invited his old friend for a walk near the foot of the mountains one late afternoon. They spoke for hours like old friends. Once darkness fell, however, Sin Bae casually lifted a rock and struck the young man in the back of the head. He buried the body where he'd buried so many before.

But nothing could have prepared him, could have deadened him enough for what was to come.

Several months after he murdered his old friend he was sentenced to the sweatbox for stealing corn. While he was inside, the guards taunted him like never before, tossing lit matches atop his box, pissing through the slats, defecating just feet from his locked door.

Then one gray and rainy morning, the guards grabbed little Su-ra as she passed by his box on her way to the factory.

Although he could not remember what they did to her, where they touched her, how she'd screamed, he still saw clear as day the moment their father tried to come to her rescue.

Father had picked a handful of dirt up off the ground and smashed it into the face of one of the offending guards.

Immediately another of the guards knocked Father to the earth with the butt of his gun. Then he and his humiliated colleague dragged Father through the dirt, threw him up against Sin Bae's sweatbox. Father, emaciated and dazed, turned and looked through the slats at his son.

Father managed to say only the boy's name before the guard placed the muzzle of his gun to the back of his head and pulled the trigger.

Before Sin Bae could fully register what was happening, he was drenched in his father's blood.

Days later when Sin Bae was finally released from the box, he stood on his own two feet and walked home.

As he washed the blood and bits of skull and brain from his

body with contaminated water from the prison well, he resolved to leave Yodok one way or the other.

Soon.

* * *

STANDING IN FRONT of a barely conscious Kincaid, Sin Bae's eyes were drawn to the still-blinking phone.

He ignored an incoming call. Instead he leaned into Kincaid's battered face and in a near whisper said, "Tell me. Where is the girl?"

Kincaid said nothing.

Sin Bae suppressed the urge to strike her again. He swiftly moved across the room and retrieved his phone from the floor. The missed call was from Ping. No message, of course. Sin Bae would be expected to return Ping's call immediately. But Sin Bae was tired of hearing the little man's whims. His last order was to learn the location of the others, and that was just what he'd do. He'd take matters into his own hands. He'd begin with Janson. Instead of running around Seoul, trying to hunt him down, Sin Bae would make it so that the bastard came to him.

He dialed the number Ping had given him earlier.

The phone rang four times before a woman answered.

"CatsPaw Associates," she said.

* * *

QUINTISHA UPCHURCH felt her skin crawl the moment she heard the slurred voice on the other end of the line. Quintisha had been the general operations manager for both CatsPaw and the Phoenix Foundation since their inception. She was known around both organizations as the only person in the world who could find Paul Janson, day or night. In the time she'd worked for Janson, she'd pretty much heard it all. Often with her heart in her throat. But the tone of this call was different somehow. She experienced a level of dread she'd never felt before. As though all calls leading up to this one were merely rehearsals.

"Tell him that I have her," the voice said. "If he wants for her to leave this place alive, have him call the little man within the next half hour. No later. Because in thirty-one minutes, she dies."

That was the entire conversation. Roughly three dozen words in all. Not a single name was mentioned during the call. But Quintisha Upchurch understood the message perfectly, and she wasted no time. She touched her finger to the flash button and speed-dialed Paul.

"Mr. Janson," she said as soon as he answered, "we have a situation."

FORTY-SEVEN

Nam Sei-hoon reached across his desk and lifted the ringing phone, expecting to hear Ping's voice when he held the receiver to his ear.

The voice greeted him in clearly spoken Korean, but Nam could detect a definite accent. A Western accent. Maybe even American. Which was odd because Americans, in his experience, sorely lacked an aptitude for foreign languages. Surely a dolt like Edward Clarke had not attempted to learn Korean. Surely not so much as a greeting.

Yet this was Nam's very personal, very private line.

"To whom am I speaking?" Nam said in English.

"The man who is going to put a bullet into your fucking traitorous skull."

Nam Sei-hoon suddenly began to sweat. His hands became so wet so fast, the phone nearly slipped from between his fingers.

"Janson?" he managed through quickening breaths.

"I would say you're a disgrace to your country, Sei-hoon, but that wouldn't suffice. You are a goddamn stain on all of humanity."

Nam stood from his chair, found himself weak in the knees. He was suddenly overcome by a certainty that Janson was somewhere inside the building.

Impossible, he thought. But then, if anyone could penetrate NIS it was Janson.

"Is this some kind of a joke, Paul?" he said, his voice thick with fear.

"Where is Kincaid?"

"Your partner? I do not know. I have not heard from her. Has she gone missing? Is there some way that I can help?"

"Right now," Janson said, "you can only help yourself."

Nam Sei-hoon carefully lowered himself back into his chair. Janson knew. Playing stupid was not going to save him. Still, he couldn't bring himself to allow a single concession just yet. So he said nothing.

"The only way you live," Janson said, "is if I die first. And I'm going to give you that chance, Sei-hoon."

"Paul, I . . ." He swallowed the bile rising in his throat.

"Shut up and listen carefully," Janson said. "Because I am going to make you an offer that will only be good until I hang up this phone. And if I hear one word from you that I don't like, I'm going to hang up without warning. And then I'm coming for you. Understood?"

"I . . ." Nam realized there was no use. "Yes, Paul, I understand."

"Good," Janson said. "Because I am going to trade you my life—and, thereby, yours—for Jessica Kincaid's."

* * *

NAM SEI-HOON BELIEVED Janson when he said that Kincaid didn't know anything about Nam's involvement. Of course she didn't. Had she known, she never would have shown up at the safe house in Gangnam. And surely with Sin Bae hovering over her, she hadn't spoken to anyone since.

But Kincaid did know about Diophantus. Assuming that Gregory Wyckoff knew, of course. And that was the assumption he demanded everyone make. Which meant that Kincaid would still have to be eliminated.

But that could wait until after Janson was dead.

Nam Sei-hoon knew that Janson wasn't bluffing when he offered to trade his life for Kincaid's. Even if he hadn't loved her, that was a trade Paul Janson would make. That was the kind of man Janson was—or at least the kind of man Janson had become.

When Nam first met Janson, he was a frogman, a US Navy SEAL, a green-faced killing machine who stood out among his teammates during joint US-ROK live-fire training exercises at Rodriguez Range, roughly fifteen miles south of the Korean Demilitarized Zone. Nam had been so impressed with Janson that he insisted on meeting the man. During Janson's stay, they dined together regularly, discussing the Forgotten War over drinks. Nam quickly realized that Janson was as smart as he was strong, and the two became fast friends. They had been close ever since.

Over the years, Nam followed Janson's career the way most men follow professional sports. When Janson disappeared in Afghanistan, Nam Sei-hoon mourned. Eighteen months later, when Nam learned of Janson's daring escape from Kabul, he celebrated. When Janson joined Consular Operations, Nam offered his support anywhere in the world it might be needed. When he learned of Janson's falling-out with Cons Ops, Nam Sei-hoon offered him sanctuary in South Korea.

Soon after, Nam heard that Janson considered himself "re-formed." He'd gone into business as a private security specialist. But his objective was not the accumulation of wealth; it was to aid former covert government agents like himself. Nam Sei-hoon didn't know what to make of it. But in recent months it had become clear that Janson was no longer the man he'd been. The Machine had regrettably gone soft. And now that Janson's interests conflicted with his own, Nam Sei-hoon only did what had to be done.

Still, he knew Janson to be a man of his word, whether that word was posed as a promise or a threat. So Nam would have been a damn fool not to take Janson up on his offer. Had he not jumped at it, Nam would have instantly been reduced to a walking corpse.

Now Nam Sei-hoon had calls to make.

His first call was to Clarke's man, Ping. He again warned the handler not to allow Sin Bae to kill Kincaid. There was going to be a trade, he told him. Nam would call Ping back in ten minutes with further instructions.

His next call was to Edward Clarke himself. Nam knew better than to divulge any details to Clarke about the goings-on in Seoul. He simply wanted to instruct him on what needed to happen in the United States.

"The jet will be landing in Honolulu to refuel," Nam said. "And I am told that the senator and his wife are still in the islands."

"That's correct," Clarke replied.

"That boy can never make it to the mainland. He can never even make it into his father's arms."

"I assure you," Clarke said, "Gregory Wyckoff will be taken care of. We've already jammed all the Embraer's communications. And I have a plan in place on the ground at Hickam Field."

"Good. Keep me informed."

Nam Sei-hoon hung up the phone and studied the timetable for Diophantus. He needed more time. Not much, but enough to ensure that the operation would move forward without a hitch early tomorrow morning.

He picked up the phone and redialed the number for Ping.

When Ping answered he said, "Do not talk. Just listen. Sin Bae is about to receive a new guest."

FORTY-EIGHT

Nam Sei-hoon would attempt a double cross, Janson was sure. But it wouldn't involve killing Kincaid right away. Instead he'd have her followed. He'd make certain Janson was dead before moving on her again. Nam Sei-hoon may have been a two-faced prick. But he wasn't stupid by any stretch of the imagination.

Janson gazed up at the windows high above the neon city. How many snipers had their scopes trained on him this evening? Were they Nam Sei-hoon's men? Or Edward Clarke's agents? Or both?

He supposed it didn't matter.

Janson's phone finally buzzed in his hand. He pressed it against his ear. As he listened to the voice, he could feel the presence of two men approaching him from behind.

As instructed, Janson took two steps forward so that he was standing on the edge of the curb.

The men who came up behind Janson began to frisk him. He

raised his arms out at his sides and spread his legs just enough so that they could check his inseam. This part didn't matter; he was clean. Janson was sure Nam Sei-hoon knew that he wouldn't risk Kincaid's life by showing up armed. Nam would know this was no ruse.

The voice on the phone said, "There is a black van approaching from your left. Hang up now and await a call from the female. You will have precisely six seconds. As you speak to her, the van will pull up directly in front of you. When the six seconds are up, the phone will be taken from you and you will step inside the van."

With his thumb, Janson ended the call. The moment he did the phone vibrated in his hand again. He pressed it to his ear.

"Paul?"

Her voice sounded nasal, as though she'd been struck in the face. Anger as sharp as a nail rose in his throat. He drew a deep breath. His heart pounded in his chest. She was alive, at least. Kincaid was alive and her voice still sounded sweeter than the most beautiful music he'd ever heard.

In his peripheral vision, he saw the van pulling over to the curb.

"Are you safe?" he said.

"Paul, don't do this! It'll be for nothing. I won't be able to liv—"

The van rolled to a complete stop directly in front of Janson.

"We have *three seconds*, Jessie. *Are you safe?*"

"Yes. I'm in a public pla—"

As the phone was ripped from Janson's hand, he was struck in the back of the head. His knees buckled beneath him. He became dizzy and had started to fall when multiple sets of hands grabbed hold of him. A hood was draped over his head. Barely conscious, Janson was hefted into the back of the van.

The panel door slid closed as the van merged back into traffic.

Behind the hood, Janson closed his eyes; he dreamed again of Jessie, in her red two-piece, on the soft warm sands of Waikiki Beach.

* * *

WHEN THE HOOD was finally pulled off his head, Janson kept his eyes closed to allow them time to adjust. But instead of the peach hue he expected to see displayed on the backsides of his lids, he saw only a gunmetal gray that reminded him of the sky over Pyongyang. Slowly, he opened his eyes and gazed up at the badly damaged face of Sin Bae.

Good for you, Jessie, he thought.

"Before now," Sin Bae said softly, "we only knew each other by reputation."

Janson tested his restraints; his arms were securely fastened behind him, his legs to the legs of the sturdy wooden chair on which he was seated.

"You're much uglier than I expected," Janson said, looking into the killer's eyes. There he saw a flicker of light that he hadn't found in the eyes of many active Cons Ops agents.

Sin Bae half-smiled. One of his top front teeth was missing; it looked like a recent adjustment to his face.

Jessie really did a number on you, didn't she? That's my girl.

"You are much more human than I expected," Sin Bae said.

For a moment Janson had the eerie feeling that Sin Bae was reading his mind. But no, here Janson had the advantage. Because he had only hours ago read a complete dossier on his captor, courtesy of Grigori Berman.

"I had been told you were the Machine," Sin Bae continued. He took a step forward and leaned into Janson's face.

Janson could smell the stench of blood on him.

"But if you are a machine," Sin Bae said, "then you are an old, broken-down machine at best. You are a printing press. A typewriter, maybe. A pay phone. A fax machine. Whatever you are, Paul Janson, you are obsolete."

Janson said nothing. He thought briefly of a man named Doug Case. A former Cons Ops agent whom Janson had found in a broken-down secondhand wheelchair at the mouth of a filthy abandoned railroad tunnel in Ogden, Utah.

Doug Case had been Janson's first.

First recruitment.

First student.

First graduate of the Phoenix Foundation.

Doug Case had been the first covert government agent that Janson saved.

When Janson first dreamed up Phoenix, he knew it wouldn't be easy. Janson's skill set was specific. And if he wanted to atone, he had no choice but to make use of those skills. In order to rescue other covert government agents—in order to give them new lives—he'd need money, and plenty of it. In order to earn that money, he'd have to take on dangerous jobs, and dangerous jobs often required the use of force.

Sometimes *lethal* force.

Janson was never under any illusion. He knew he'd be tested on every mission, that he could fail in his task with a single pull of the trigger. His business, after all, was rife with moral conundrums, not the least of which was the necessity of atoning for violence with violence. Hence, the Janson Rules.

No torture.

No civilian casualties.

No killing anyone who doesn't try to kill us.

But regardless of the difficulty, Janson had been determined to evolve. The Machine had resolved to become human.

That, Janson was convinced, is what Sin Bae sees now. That is what's hopefully frightening the living hell out of him.

Janson watched Sin Bae twist his left cuff link between his thumb and his index finger. According to the extensive dossier Janson read on Sin Bae back at Jina Jeon's suite at the Westin, the gesture was the assassin's tell. It meant that Janson would be dead within thirty seconds.

"It's not too late, you know," Janson said as casually as he could manage.

Sin Bae's expression was one of mild amusement. "Too late for what?"

"It's not too late to atone."

The assassin smirked. "Are you a priest?"

"No," Janson said, lifting his head and leveling his gaze at him. "There's no religion for men like us. Let's not pretend like there is."

Sin Bae stepped slowly around to the back of Janson's chair.

Janson said, "I was just there, you know."

"Just where?"

"Pyongyang. The city where you were born. The city you and your family were snatched from in the dead of night when you were just seven years old. The last place you saw before Yodok."

Janson held his breath, waited for the garrote to close around his throat. He closed his eyes and summoned an image of Kincaid. But instead of Jessie's smiling face he saw her shouting at him from a distance.

"Paul, don't do this! It'll be for nothing. I won't be able to liv—"

"Tell me," Janson said slowly. "When you escaped from Yodok, when you fled the North, when you found the American embassy in Beijing, did you tell them that you had left your baby sister behind?"

Silence.

Janson said, "Did you tell the Americans that Su-ra remained at Yodok? That she was close to dying of malnutrition? Did you tell them that?"

Further silence.

"Did you ask for help? Did you ask the Americans to help you rescue your sister? Did you tell them that you had promised her? That you promised you'd be back for her? That you cut yourself and bled for her so that she'd believe—so that she'd *know*—you were coming back to save her?"

Janson could feel Sin Bae hovering over him, could hear the assassin's heavy breathing, like the sound of a sick and dying animal.

"What did they do, Sin Bae? What did they do for your sister? What did they do for you?"

When Sin Bae remained silent, Janson said, "I'll tell you what they did. They did for you what they did for me. They turned you into a killer."

Sin Bae leaned in behind him. Janson could smell his breath, could again smell the stench of blood on him.

"Do you even know why you're about to kill me?" Janson said. "Do you know why you were going to kill Jessica Kincaid?"

"Because you are traitors," Sin Bae muttered.

"You think so?" Janson said softly. "Really? And what about the thirteen-year-old Korean girl they tried to kill? Is she a traitor too?" Janson's voice rose several octaves along with his anger. "Tell me, Sin Bae. Who did *she* betray? What has that little girl done that *she* deserves to die?"

Sin Bae said nothing.

"We are *all* machines to them, Sin Bae. We are *all* just machines to Consular Operations. We are *all* just machines to Director Clarke. We are *all* just machines to be turned on and off at will.

We are *all* just machines awaiting instructions to kill. And when we don't serve their purposes any longer—when *we become obsolete*—then they terminate us. They'll do it to you, Sin Bae, just as they're doing it to me."

Janson could hear the assassin slowly extracting the garrote from his cuff link, like the reeling in of a fishing line. It was too late, he realized. The Korean was too far gone. Janson had never turned, never *saved* an agent from a position of such vulnerability. What could he say? What could a dead man have to offer the living?

"We are *all* just weapons to them," Janson said quietly. "We're all just guns and garrotes. How much did *you* mourn the last time you lost one of those cuff links? How much did *you* mourn the last gun you had to leave behind in some nameless city? That's how much they'll mourn for you, Sin Bae, when you become lost or obsolete. That's how much they'll mourn for me."

The wire began to close around Janson's throat.

"I was just like you," Janson breathed. "Then I woke up one morning in a cold sweat thinking about all the people I killed for all the wrong reasons. *That* was the morning I realized I was nothing more than a sanctioned serial killer. *That's* the morning I ceased to be a machine. *That's* the morning I became human."

"It is too late for me," Sin Bae said as the garrote sliced into the outer layer of flesh around Janson's throat.

Janson felt his face burn red, felt every part of his head turning to fire from his neck to the top of his scalp.

This was it, he knew. This was the end.

"You should *know*," Janson said, struggling for breath, "why you're about to murder me. You should *know* why you were asked to kill Kincaid and the thirteen-year-old girl. You should *know*..."

Janson struggled to get out the final few words of his plea.

"You should *know*... about Diophantus."

FORTY-NINE

Director Edward Clarke stepped into the sumptuous ban-
quet hall and turned 360 degrees, gazing up at the two-
story ceilings with their dangling crystal chandeliers, the
spotless egg-white walls that seemed to be a football field apart
from each other, taking in all the empty space.

Christ, he thought. Our voices are going to echo in here as
though we're in the goddamn Himalayas.

In the center of the room stood a great round table, topped with
fine china and crystal water glasses. Seven men and one woman
sat around the table exchanging silly banter. With a head of steam,
Clarke finally approached.

"Whose fucking idea was all of this?" he said, motioning around
the hall.

Bruce Javers, the thirty-something blowhard who'd founded
Jupicon, Ltd., a multinational software company headquartered in

Silicon Valley, jumped out of his seat, exhibiting a smile as wide as his ass.

"What are you talking about, Eddie? This place is fantastic." He placed his rhino's leg of an arm around Clarke's shoulder, and it was all Clarke could do not to twist it into a pretzel and keep twisting it until the loudmouth squealed like a pig.

"First of all, Bruce, don't call me Eddie." Clarke spoke loud enough for those at the table to hear. He didn't want to repeat this conversation. And he didn't want a repeat of this abomination to secrecy and security when it came time for their post-operation meeting in a few days.

"Has history taught you people *nothing*?" Clarke squawked.

Milhouse Hastings, CEO of defense contractor Leverton-Wells and another heart attack waiting to happen, looked up in surprise.

"You people?" Milhouse said. "What do you mean by 'you people'?"

Clarke had fucking had it. This was a long time coming. "I mean you filthy-rich, white-bread dumbfucks who hold clandestine meetings that make the royal-fucking-wedding appear unpretentious."

"What are trying to say, Ed?" This from Jacob Paltrow of Norvo Incorporated, the biotech giant that would one day make environmentalists consider giving Monsanto the Lady Bird Johnson Award.

"What I'm saying is," Clarke shot back, "did all of you *sleep* through the forty-seven percent debacle? Look at this goddamn room. For all we know, Jimmy Carter's grandson could be sitting behind that wet bar, taping this entire meeting for *Mother Jones*. Hell, he could be standing there in plain sight, and we wouldn't be able to see him without binoculars given the size of this fucking place."

Bruce Javers laid one of his beefy hands on Clarke's shoulder again. "Relax, Eddie, we had the place swept half an hour ago. It's cleaner than the Duchess of Cambridge's va—"

"*Shut up, Bruce!* We already have *one* international incident on our hands." Christ, the guy was drunk; Clarke could smell the bourbon on his breath. "And *don't* call me Eddie."

Clarke moved past him toward the table.

The place was swept, fine. Then let's get this the hell over with.

* * *

"Firstly," Clarke began ten minutes later, "I want to thank everyone at this table for their patriotism."

What a crock of shit, he thought as he continued with his preamble. The titans of industry sitting around the table—Bruce Javers, Milhouse Hastings, Jacob Paltrow—had lent their financial support to this operation for one reason and one reason only: to advance their bottom lines. Granted, Clarke agreed with their conviction that the current administration wasn't doing enough to combat the systematic data theft and cyber-espionage being committed against their corporations by the Chinese government. The three American companies represented at this table alone had been victimized to the tune of hundreds of billions of dollars. Hence, Diophantus. Collapsing once and for all the North Korean regime would create a unified Korea, one governed by an American ally, the democratically elected administration in Seoul. Once Korea became whole, the United States would have a friendly nation right on China's border. A strategic boon for America, a nightmare for the Chinese. No longer would their cybercrimes against US industry go unchecked. But even then, to call these three patriots, well, that was almost laughable.

"Without your support," Clarke continued, "this operation would never have been possible."

Clarke considered himself the only patriot in the room. Sandy Hildreth, the NSA director, was being paid handsomely for his role. Ella Quon was gunning for the position of director at the Central Intelligence Agency, and Douglas Albright, well, he simply wanted war. He'd been the administration's loudest critic when the president announced budget cuts for the Department of Defense. Albright was banking on becoming defense secretary once the right party took office, and he wanted to inherit a military that could fight *at least* two wars at a time. For years, Albright had been eyeing North Korea and Iran, quietly advocating military force to remove the regime in each. Word around the DOD was that Albright also had his sights set on Pakistan and half the Middle East.

Clarke cleared his throat and took a swallow of ice water. "Now, as you all know, we are not at this table to celebrate. That would be premature. However, we *are* here to discuss the *next* phase of Diophantus, which is just as, if not more, crucial to our success."

Opposite Clarke, the blowhard Bruce Javers looked to be tuning out. But it didn't matter. He had a seat at the table because of his money, not his mind. With Congress watching every last penny being spent, an operation like Diophantus would have been impossible to keep secret otherwise. And, of course, it *needed* to be kept secret. Because even the goddamn neocons, who never met a war they didn't like, were opposed to military action in North Korea. At least out loud. Their pipe dream was that the regime would fall on its own. But if it didn't fall during the Great Famine of the nineties, when millions of North Koreans died of starvation and malnutrition, Clarke held out little hope that the leadership would collapse under its own weight anytime soon.

After all, how would it? The people of North Korea certainly weren't going to stage a revolution. Nothing like the Arab Spring was remotely possible in the DPRK. There was no freedom of assembly. There was no Internet, no social media platforms that could help citizens organize. And protestors wouldn't face just tear gas, rubber bullets, and fire hoses; they'd be shot dead in the streets. No, the people of North Korea weren't capable of collapsing the Kim regime.

And the regime *needed* to collapse, to be sure. Twenty years of failed diplomacy had gotten America and her allies absolutely nowhere. Administration after administration did *nothing* while the Kim regime advanced its nuclear weapons program right under their fucking noses.

What few seemed to comprehend was that the DPRK wasn't just a threat to the region; North Korea constituted a threat to the entire globe. As badly as that country needed money, who in the rational world could seriously doubt that Kim Jong-un would sell some of his nukes to al-Qaeda or Hezbollah or ISIS or some other terrorist organization hell-bent on spreading Sharia law to every nation in the world?

"As we've discussed before," Clarke said, "we're looking at a hard landing in Korea. Once the Kim regime falls, we're going to face a humanitarian crisis of biblical proportions. We're going to need to help Seoul deal with the flood of refugees. These people are going to need food, clothes, shelter, and they're going to need counseling. Integration isn't going to be easy. These folks have been brainwashed their entire lives. All that brainwashing is going to need to be undone. And once our boys take Pyongyang, the North is going to need a Marshall Plan. This is a war we're going to win, but war isn't pretty. We'll need to rebuild. We don't have a crystal ball; we can't see into the future. Nothing's a guarantee. But while we can't count on much, the one thing we can be damn certain of is that the American taxpayer isn't going to want to pay for the aftermath of the second Korean War."

Edward Clarke folded his hands on the table in front of him and looked at Javers, Hastings, and Paltrow, one at a time. "And that, once again, is where you gentlemen—and your checkbooks—will come into play."

FIFTY

J anson is dead."

Nam Sei-hoon took a deep breath and savored Ping's words. He received no pleasure from having his old friend killed. Only relief. Because Janson had made it clear that if he lived, Nam would die. And Nam Sei-hoon's country needed him. His life was only now getting started. In a few months, maybe even in a few weeks, Nam could finally emerge from the shadows and take his rightful place in history.

"Thank you," he said into the phone. "Now we must deal with Kincaid."

"Sin Bae informs me that Kincaid has returned to the area. She has the building under surveillance. But she has brought the Seoul police officer. In Sin Bae's condition, he cannot eliminate them both. He will need assistance. In fact, he should immediately be extracted. We believe he suffered broken bones in the accident, maybe even serious internal injuries. Besides, too many

South Koreans have seen his face. Now that the cop is involved, I would like to get him out of Seoul as quickly as possible."

Nam Sei-hoon sighed. "Very well. I will contact Clarke and have him send two of his people to the location."

"And Sin Bae?"

"He is to remain until they arrive, of course. Then he may return to Shanghai for medical attention."

* * *

"THE LITTLE MAN will have Clarke send two agents to clean up."

Sin Bae stretched his neck as he listened to Ping over the phone. The pain from the injuries he received in Beijing was getting worse, and he told Ping so.

"Once the agents arrive," Ping said, "you may return to China. I will meet you in Shanghai and get you the medical attention you need." There was a lengthy pause, followed by a barely audible sigh. "Once again, I apologize. The agent who was driving the Audi will be punished accordingly."

"I would like for him to be in Shanghai when I arrive."

"It will be arranged," Ping said. "But I urge you to consider who is to blame. It was the woman with the bicycle who caused you to be in the road. Our man was only attempting to assist you in the capture of the boy by cut—"

"I asked for no assistance," Sin Bae huffed and hung up.

* * *

NAM SEI-HOON SAID, "Absolutely not. Do not even *consider* leaving Seoul."

Ambassador Owen Young remained quiet on the other end of

the line. Then he said, "With due respect, we discussed this a long time ago and—"

"That was before you permitted one of your translators to overhear our plans."

"You just finished telling me that everyone has been dealt with," the ambassador cried. "I *beg* you. At least allow me and my chief aide to take leave. Jonathan is the one who caught our eavesdropper in the first place. Without his help, we would not even have known Diophantus was in jeopardy."

"It is far too risky at this point. If the American ambassador is seen fleeing Seoul less than twenty-four hours before the conflict, it will implicate us all."

"You speak of *risk*," Young hissed. "You are putting our very *lives* at risk by not allowing us to leave the capital."

"Do not be absurd, Ambassador. With the aid of American forces, this war will not last a week."

"But it *is* war. And I have *family*, goddamn it. I have *children*."

"And they will be safe, Ambassador, because the North will never get anywhere near Seoul."

"We do *not* know all their capabilities."

"You are wrong. *You* do not know all the North's capabilities. *I* do. You are speaking to the National Intelligence Service's head of North Korean Affairs, or have you forgotten?"

"North Korea is an *intelligence black hole*."

Nam Sei-hoon wanted to reach into the phone and grab Young by the throat.

"Do you really believe that, Ambassador? What if I were to tell you that I have been running a deputy director in Pyongyang for the past five years?"

Ambassador Young fell silent once more.

Nam Sei-hoon felt something shift in his gut. This was a secret he had kept close to the vest since the very beginning. Other intelligence agents in North Korean Affairs knew about Nam's people in the Guard's Command and the Ministry of State Security. But no one knew he had someone in the leadership at the palace.

Nam hung up the phone.

He stood and walked over to the wall that displayed a map of Korea. The map would soon need to be replaced. The demarcation line would be erased, the demilitarized zone known by a new name. After a century of occupation and division, Korea was once again about to become whole.

And Nam Sei-hoon would be the man responsible for returning the peninsula to its long-forgotten glory.

FIFTY-ONE

Kincaid badly wanted to see Janson. But it would have to wait. Just now she was needed as a lure. Sitting in a plush chair in room 1708 at the Westin hotel, she leaned her head back so that Jina Jeon could get a better look at her nose. In the bedroom of the suite, the baby began bawling.

"Sorry," Jeon said as she went to check on the child.

Kincaid lifted her head. "Where did the mother say she was going again?"

"She didn't," Jeon called back to her. "Not really. She just said she'd be back in thirty minutes. That was three hours ago."

"Maybe she got lost."

"Doubtful," Jeon said as she reentered the room. "I gave her one of my two phones with my other number and the number of the hotel plugged in. She would have called if she were lost."

"Did you try calling her?"

"Twice. Both calls went straight to voice mail. The phone's shut off."

"You think someone took her?"

"No, I don't. What I think is . . ." Jina Jeon trailed off.

"What?" Kincaid prodded. Every time she spoke, the left side of her face felt as though it were on fire.

"I think she was under the impression that she couldn't be a good mother to her daughter here in Seoul. I think she looked around the city and felt like she'd landed on another world. I think she was scared."

"So what are you going to do?" Kincaid said. She had been certain she wasn't going to like Jina Jeon, but she'd been wrong. And she was kind of disappointed about it.

"Nothing. Until I know for sure." Jeon returned to her position behind Kincaid's chair. "Lean your head back again."

Before Kincaid could comply, the hotel phone began to ring. Kincaid leapt from her chair to retrieve it.

Hearing Park Kwan's voice felt like ten milligrams of Valium melting under her tongue. "Kang Jung and I are both safe and sound and back in Seoul," he said.

"Thanks so much for returning my call so quickly."

"Would you like us to come to the hotel?"

"No," Kincaid said. "Just continue taking care of Kang Jung until all this blows over."

Kincaid gave Park Kwan the number to Jina Jeon's phone.

She hung up the phone and retook her seat.

"Lean your head back," Jina Jeon said.

There was a knock on the hotel room door. Kincaid hopped off the chair again. "I'll see who it is."

"It's my mother," Jina Jeon said as Kincaid put her eye to the peephole.

"It's your mother," Kincaid said as she opened the door.

Jina Jeon's mother gave Kincaid a hug and asked her how she was feeling.

"Fine," she lied.

"Great. Now where's my little girl?"

"Right here, Mom."

"Not you, silly. The baby."

"She's sleeping in the next room."

"Let me go have a look at her."

Jina Jeon pointed at the chair. "Jessie?"

Kincaid pointed to her watch. "No time. We have to go."

* * *

KINCAID MOVED ON the signal. She crossed the street toward the apartment complex, her eyes darting left and right. The image of Sin Bae's body bouncing off the Audi A7 in Beijing remained fresh in her mind.

As she entered the courtyard, her nerves began to rattle. She kept herself from checking Jina Jeon's position for fear of giving away her cover. But she surveyed the bushes, the trees, expecting someone to jump out at her at any time the way Sin Bae had back at Dosan Park.

Halfway through the courtyard, Kincaid heard a thump.

She hurried to the door of the building and found it propped open with a crushed can of Hite Queen's Ale.

I sure could use a beer or twelve when all this is over.

She opened the door and heard a second thump from behind her.

Then in her ear, Jina Jeon's silky voice.

"All clear."

* * *

UPSTAIRS IN THE master bedroom of the safe house, Kincaid stared at one of the Cons Ops agents, who was out cold, restrained to the chair she'd been restrained to just hours earlier.

He was dark-skinned. Maybe Indian. A pair of pewter eyeglasses lay on the nightstand on the left side of the bed. Round frames, like John Lennon's. Only this guy didn't look like he was about to wake up and belt out a couple of verses of "Imagine."

She stepped out of the room. And came face-to-face with Sin Bae.

She stared into the assassin's eyes with a hatred reserved for a select few.

She stepped aside to the right and walked past him. She entered the kitchen and found Jina Jeon filling a bucket of water from the tap.

When Jina Jeon saw her, she shut off the faucet.

"I don't trust him," Kincaid said, touching her fingers to her throbbing cheek.

Jina Jeon tilted her head and looked at Kincaid with sympathetic eyes. Finally, she sighed. "Your presence has been requested in the second bedroom," she said, lifting the heavy bucket out of the sink.

Kincaid bit down on her lower lip. She wasn't *entirely* sure she trusted Jina Jeon either.

Silently she moved to the back of the apartment, tapped on the door to the second bedroom, and entered without waiting for a response.

The second Cons Ops agent, tied up to a similar chair as the first, was just beginning to stir. He lifted his head groggily before it fell forward against his chest.

This agent was Caucasian, young, with olive-colored skin that Kincaid guessed was either Greek or southern Italian.

He lifted his head again. This time his eyelids fluttered open. He stared up at the man standing before him.

With the croak of a lifelong smoker he said, "You're supposed to be dead."

Janson said nothing.

*   *   *

AFTER TWENTY MINUTES of interrogating the two dazed Cons Ops agents, the four of them—Kincaid, Jina Jeon, Sin Bae, and Janson—regrouped in the living room to discuss a new strategy.

Sin Bae was the first to speak. "We know their training. They will tell us nothing unless we break them."

Jina Jeon said, "I prepared a bucket. It's in the kitchen."

Kincaid swallowed hard and turned to Janson.

"No way," Janson said. "No torture."

Kincaid's eyes fell on the cuts around Janson's throat. Following Sin Bae's attack in the coatroom she'd suffered similar lacerations, but fortunately she'd been spared the sight of them until they had sufficient time to scab over.

Jina Jeon said, "Paul, they're leaving us no choice."

Janson shook his head. "There's always a choice."

Kincaid glanced at Jina Jeon. Was she really going to protest against the Janson Rules? She was a Phoenix Foundation graduate. She should know better.

Sin Bae stepped away from the conversation. Kincaid remained unclear as to just how Janson had turned him. Janson had only told her, *"He's a lot more like you and me than either of us could have imagined."*

Jina Jeon said, "What about protecting Seoul? What about the greater good? We know the *what*. But it does us no good without knowing *when* and *how* and precisely *where*."

"No civilian casualties," Janson said. "No killing anyone who doesn't try to kill us. No torture. *No* exceptions."

Janson folded his arms across his chest. A sure sign, Kincaid knew, that he wasn't about to budge on this issue. Although she understood him, probably understood him better than anyone else in the world— at least as well as anyone *could* understand Paul Janson—she had to admit, their options were few and time was fast running out.

"Maybe they don't even know the details of Diophantus."

Janson shook his head again. "One of them does. Probably Vik Pawar. I know Clarke. He's not going to have trusted Nam Sei-hoon well enough to leave the entire operation in his hands, especially if he was allowing Nam to control some of his agents. Believe me, Clarke isn't unrepresented here in South Korea."

"What about Sin Bae?" Kincaid said. "They haven't seen his face. They don't know you turned him."

Janson gave her a sideways glance that said, *We can't trust them alone together.*

Kincaid understood. Sin Bae may have turned but he was fragile. With the right psychological pressure, an experienced agent like Vik Pawar could turn him back.

No one spoke for several minutes. Finally, Janson unfolded his arms and turned to Jina Jeon.

"Get me the bucket," he said.

* * *

JANSON DIDN'T SO MUCH AS glance in Vik Pawar's direction as he stepped into the room and set the bucket down on the floor. His body language, however, exuded reticence. Any objective observer could see that Janson was uncomfortable with what he was doing. Disgusted, even. There was a self-loathing in his eyes, an inwardly directed anger evident on his face.

His sluggish movements as he tossed the double mattress aside betrayed the turmoil in his mind. As he separated the plywood from the rest of the bed frame, he mouthed a silent curse at himself. Shook his head like a drenched dog, as though he were attempting to free himself from whatever was weighing him down.

After testing its strength, Janson arranged the plywood lengthwise at a moderate angle, then lifted the heavy bucket of water and set it down next to the plywood's lower edge. He took a step back to appraise his work, a tear plainly forming in the corner of his left eye, his mouth set in a severe frown.

"I'm not going to lie, Vik," he said quietly without looking at his prisoner. "I'm not going to pretend you have this coming in order to appease my own conscience. *No one* has this coming."

Janson finally gazed up at Vik Pawar. He looked at him as he'd looked at so many others during his years in Consular Operations. Expressionless. Not like a human being beholds another. But like a machine.

Janson said, "But I'm also not going to pretend that I have all the time in the world to convince you to talk. Because I don't. You know that at least as well as I do."

Janson stepped over to the bedroom door and rapped on it three times. "My conscience," he said to Vik, "will just have to accept that I'm doing this for the greater good."

Jina Jeon entered the room and handed Janson a stack of clean forest-green towels. Janson thanked her and said, "In two minutes, bring in Sin Bae and the rope and cords. This is a three-person job.

If we do it right, Vik lives. If we do it wrong, he dies. Let's agree to try to do it right."

When Jina left the bedroom, Janson turned to Vik with something close to compassion in his eyes. "Ever do this before?"

Vik's head moved to the side ever so slightly.

"Ever have it done to you?"

Again, Vik's head twitched almost imperceptibly. But he refused to look at Janson. His eyes instead remained fixed on the door.

"Me neither," Janson said. "This will be a first for both of us. Like two virgins on prom night. Only I bet we both wish our dates were a hell of a lot prettier."

Vik Pawar said nothing.

"I've seen it done, though," Janson continued. "I know enough not to buy into the official lie. That it merely 'simulates' drowning. That's complete bullshit. You'll only feel like you're drowning because I'll be *drowning* you. I won't be simulating jackshit. CIA lawyers can argue the point until they're blue. But there's no truth to it. Not a shred. I think it was Christopher Hitchens who said, 'If waterboarding does not constitute torture, then there is no such thing as torture.'"

Their eyes finally met.

Janson said, "See these cuts around my neck? They're from just a few hours ago. I was sitting right there in the chair you're sitting in now. Sin Bae had a garrote around my throat. He was strangling me to death." Janson paused. "Want to know what changed his mind?"

Vik Pawar said nothing, so Janson answered for him.

"Sure you do. I told him what little I knew about Diophantus. About how many innocent civilians are going to die. On both sides of the demarcation line."

Vik's gaze moved back to the door.

Janson followed it. "That son of a bitch out there is a monster," he said. "He was going to kill me, he was going to kill Kincaid. He was even going to kill a thirteen-year-old girl. But Diophantus, that was too much for him to stand. Even he had to draw a line."

There was a rap on the door.

"Thirty seconds," Janson called out.

He turned back to Vik Pawar and lowered his voice again. He spoke as softly as he would in a church or a library. "That's how I know I'm doing the right thing here. With you, I mean. Because you *know* the consequences of Diophantus. And of the ten million people in this city, you're the only one with the power to stop it. That you won't makes you even more of a monster than Sin Bae. And *that's* why I can set aside my convictions tonight and pour water down your throat and nostrils, maybe until you drown."

Vik finally looked Janson directly in the eyes. But there was nothing in those eyes. Certainly no life, no humanity. Janson's eyes appeared completely dead.

"I'm sorry for what's about to happen, Vik," he said in a mechanical voice. "I truly am, no matter how much of a monster you are."

Another rap on the door.

"Ten seconds," Janson called out.

He looked back at Vik. "I'm sorry that I am about to torture you. And I'm sorry that you're going to die tonight. Because as much as I'd like to con myself into believing otherwise, I know that's the only way this night ends. In five seconds, once Sin Bae steps through that door and allows you to see his face, I know there is no way in hell he's going to let you leave this room alive. That's something I'm just going to have to live with. Tonight and every night until I die."

Janson shrugged and hung his head. "So what, right? It's no secret that I already live with a whole hell of a lot worse."

FIFTY-TWO

S everal minutes later Janson emerged from the bedroom. "We have to move. Quickly."

Kincaid said, "Where to?"

He took a deep breath. "The demilitarized zone." Turning to Jina Jeon, he said, "But first we have a stop to make."

Jina Jeon looked at him, a question mark on her face.

"Chuncheon," he said.

After finishing with Vik Pawar and Max Kolovos, they "borrowed" two vehicles from Seoul residents, crossed the Dongho Bridge, and took the Seoul-Yangyang Expressway north toward Chuncheon.

Janson drove with Kincaid seated next to him. Jina Jeon traveled with Sin Bae.

The drive would take roughly forty minutes.

As Janson maneuvered to pass a slow-moving vehicle, he turned to Kincaid. He'd wanted to talk to her ever since they'd reconnected at the Gangnam safe house. But he hadn't had the chance to be alone with her until now.

"It's not what you think," Janson said.

Kincaid turned to him. "What do you mean?"

"With Vik. It's not what you think."

"You did what you had to do," she said.

Janson glanced at her. "There are no exceptions to the rules," he said. "Not for you, not for me, not for anybody."

"You don't have to justify it to me, Paul."

"Jessie, listen to me. I did *not* torture Vik Pawar."

Kincaid said nothing.

"I used the *threat* of torture," he added softly. "But I wouldn't have gone through with it if he didn't talk."

The taillights of the vehicles in front of him became red blurs as water welled before his eyes.

"Even that was farther than I'd wanted to go," he said. "But it worked. Vik knew me back in the day. He didn't think for a second that I wouldn't go through with it. Even after he cooperated, when I was dosing him with carfentanil citrate, he was convinced I was poisoning him. Even then he begged for his life."

"Is that what's bothering you?"

"More than I would've ever thought."

Why it was troubling him though, Janson couldn't quite put his finger on. He *knew* what he'd been when he worked for Consular Operations. He *knew* his reputation as the Machine. Tonight he'd simply used it to his advantage.

"What bothers me, I think, is that Vik had heard the rumors about me, about Phoenix. But he didn't believe them. Vik didn't believe I could have changed all that much."

"But you have," Kincaid said. "Completely, totally."

Janson kept his eyes on the road. He envisioned the two North

Korean soldiers he'd encountered in the demilitarized zone. The one who had fried on the electrified fence. The one he'd shot through the head. His greatest concern at the time was how badly he'd damaged the windshield on the jeep.

He heard Heath Manningham's voice in his head.

"Walked away, did you? Tell me. How many have you done since you 'walked away'?"

"Sometimes I wonder just how much," he said.

* * *

IT WAS 3 AM when they finally reached Chuncheon. Janson pulled the car into the gravel lot in front of Cal Auster's place, with Jina Jeon directly behind him.

Janson got out of the car. "Stay here," he told Kincaid. "This should only take a few minutes."

As he started up the drive, Jina Jeon fell in beside him. "What's the plan?" she said.

"Well, the equipment we bought from Cal was defective, so I'm going to ask him nicely to replace it."

"How was it defective?"

"Cons Ops took it all after they blew up your house. Or were you holding out on me when you told me that?"

"No, they took every last thing you'd stashed in the barn. In hindsight, I'm very sorry I made you keep your equipment out there."

"As far as I'm concerned, Cal insured me against theft."

"And if he disagrees? If he refuses to replace anything?"

Janson lifted a shoulder. "I'm confident he'll eventually come around."

Janson pressed the doorbell several times; the chime was good and loud.

"By the way," he said to Jina as they waited, "what were you and Cal discussing in private when I went topside? You two have a thing together?"

"God, no. He asked me if I'd reconsider."

"Reconsider *him*?"

"Reconsider *working* for him."

When the door opened, Cal Auster stood in its frame, with his arms out. He wore an open terry bathrobe over flowery-patterned boxer shorts. Salt-and-pepper chest hairs poked out over a badly stained white tank top.

"What the fuck is this?" he barked. "Do you have any fucking idea what time it is?"

"Time to open the store," Janson said, pushing past him.

"*Hey*," Cal Auster shouted. He reached into the side pocket of his bathrobe and came out with a subcompact 9mm, what some referred to as a pocket pistol.

With his back to Cal, Janson swung his left leg around in a wide arc, the heel of his combat boot connecting with Cal Auster's knuckles. The pocket pistol flew in the direction of the front door and Jina Jeon swiped it from the air. She tossed it underhand to Janson.

"*Fuck*," Cal Auster cried, baring his yellowed teeth. "You broke my fucking *fingers*."

"You should have thought of that before you pulled a gun on me, Cal."

"What do you *want*, anyway? What are you here for, Paul?"

"The equipment I purchased from you, it was stolen from me."

"How is that *my* problem?"

"It's not your problem," Janson said calmly. "*I'm* your problem."

Janson raised the gun. "You gonna help me, Cal?"

Cal Auster cackled. He looked from Janson to Jina and back

again. "What are you going to do, *kill* me? You're not going to kill me, Paul. Maybe ten years ago. But now? Now I've got your number. You're a fucking *Boy Scout*. Hell, you're a goddamn *Brownie*."

"I don't have much time," Janson said. "Which means you have even less. Take me to your stash, or I promise you, I'll make you regret ever being born."

Cal Auster grinned. "Make me regret being born, huh? And how exactly are you going to do that, Paul? Don't you remember your own rules?" He raised his left hand, which had its fingers still intact, and began counting off. "No killing civilians. No torture. No killing anyone who doesn't first take a shot at you."

Auster took a step forward. "According to your own code, Janson, Uncle Cal is fucking bulletproof."

"Tell me, Uncle Cal. Have you sold Chinese-manufactured AK-47s to the North Koreans recently?"

"What the hell business is that of yours?"

"Come on, Cal. You know I have a soft spot for weapons dealers. Don't make me do this."

"*Fuuuck* you, Paul," Auster said, lowering two of his three fingers.

Janson drew a breath, narrowed his right eye, and aimed at the last finger standing.

He squeezed the trigger.

Cal Auster screamed, louder and longer than the soldier who'd fried on the electrified fence in the DMZ. Blood spurted uncontrollably from Auster's hand.

Janson's eyes fell on the middle finger sitting on the floor.

"Jina," Janson said, "you want to help him with all that blood?"

As she ran into the kitchen for towels, Auster cried, "What the fuck did you go and do that for?"

"*Your* weapons fired on me in the DMZ. *Your* AK-47s tried to kill me, Cal. Therefore, the Janson Rules don't apply." Janson took a step toward him, placed a hand on Auster's stooped shoulder. "Now, when Jina comes back, she's going to help stanch the bleeding. Then you and I are going straight to your stash. Or else."

Tears streamed down both sides of Auster's face. "Or else *what*? You gonna shoot another finger?"

"No," Janson said evenly. "Next time I'm going to aim substantially lower, at something slightly skinnier and a whole lot shorter."

FIFTY-THREE

On the drive north toward the DMZ, Jina Jeon's cell phone rang from the backseat. Janson looked in the rearview. All four of them were traveling in Cal Auster's black Cadillac Escalade.

After a few moments, Jina Jeon held her hand over the phone and said, "It's Mi-sook."

"Tell her to get back to the hotel," Janson said. "She can't abandon her baby. She can't abandon Jin-ho's child."

Jina Jeon repeated Janson's words verbatim. She listened a moment then said, "Me? No. No, I can't take care of your baby, I'm sorry. No. No, my mother can't either. She's seventy-four years old. What about *your* parents?"

Janson continued driving. After a few minutes, Jina Jeon put down the phone.

"What did Mi-sook say?"

"She insists she's not abandoning her baby. She said she just needs to take care of something before she returns."

"You mentioned *her* parents?"

"Yeah, I wasn't thinking. Of course she's not going to return her baby to North Korea. And her parents aren't coming here. Her father's a general in Kim Jong-un's army."

Janson accelerated. There was little time. Back at the Gangnam safe house, Vik Pawar had finally divulged the details of the Diophantus operation.

"Inside the demilitarized zone," Vik had said breathlessly as Janson stepped over to the door to allow in Jina Jeon and Sin Bae.

Janson held the knob tightly in his fingers but didn't turn it. "Inside the demilitarized zone, *what?*"

"Inside the DMZ, several Cons Ops agents are embedded with the ROK soldiers protecting the border."

"What are they going to do?" Janson said, fearing he already knew the answer.

"They're going to make a brazen incursion over the border. They're going to engage the North."

Christ, Janson thought. He knew there had been hundreds of incursions over the past sixty years—just about every one of them committed by the North. In the 1960s a series of skirmishes resulted in the deaths of 750 soldiers, including 43 Americans. In addition, North Korean commandos disguised as ROK soldiers had crossed the border numerous times in attempts to raid the Blue House; none had succeeded, and very few had even survived. And that was just scratching the surface.

"When?" Janson demanded. "When is this supposed to go down?"

When Vik Pawar said nothing, Janson walked back to Vik's chair and grabbed him by the lapels of his shirt.

"When, Vik? *When?"*

"Just after dawn."

Now as Janson sped north, he couldn't tell if the sky was lightening or whether it was his imagination, and he didn't dare ask anyone else in the car for fear of the answer.

While none of the previous incursions had escalated into full-scale war, this operation had war as its very objective. It was a perfect storm. As part of its new zero-tolerance policy, the South Korean president had vowed to launch ballistic missiles at Pyongyang if the North fired so much as one shot over the border. Now rogue US agents planned to provoke North Korean soldiers into doing just that.

What Nam Sei-hoon, Edward Clarke, and the other imbeciles involved in Diophantus didn't know was that the North was prepared to respond to force with force—a level of force no nation on earth could have anticipated from the hermit kingdom.

"What will happen if we're too late?" Kincaid said as they neared the DMZ.

Janson drew a breath. "Once the North retaliates, hostilities will escalate, and the South will take advantage of the United States' security guarantees, drawing the world's only superpower into a second Korean War.

"Once the US is involved," Janson went on, "China will issue a statement condemning the action. Then they'll act in a way consistent with Chinese interests, which include not having the US or her ally sitting right on the Chinese border. China will enter the conflict, and hostilities will immediately spiral into a proxy war between the first and third most powerful militaries in the world."

It was a war the United States would ultimately win.

But at what cost?

Having studied the plans he stole from the palace, Janson knew at least part of the answer to that question. Early in the conflict, the North would attempt to take Seoul. Failing that, they'd burn the city of over ten million to the ground.

Once the war became unwinnable for the North, the regime would turn their weapons on Pyongyang and their own people.

Millions would die. If the North successfully launched its nuclear weapons, *tens* of millions.

Because no one in the West except Paul Janson knew that the new Supreme Leader of North Korea, Kim Jong-un, had secretly adopted the ultimate scorched-earth policy.

FIFTY-FOUR

Janson slashed through the dense mist hanging over the demilitarized zone, one of Cal Auster's M15s slung over his shoulder. He listened for shots but heard only Kincaid's footfalls as she thudded against the dampened earth just behind him.

In the distance Sin Bae and Jina Jeon were swallowed by the fog. Janson wished for a moment that they hadn't separated. But it was the right call. Dawn was fast ascending on the horizon, and they needed to find the embedded agents before the first shots were fired.

In less than ten minutes, however, Janson realized it was an impossible mission. There were too many soldiers, spread out in too many directions. There was too much ground to cover in too little time. The darkness and fog were working against them. It was difficult enough to see a few feet in front of them, let alone spot an individual soldier who looked as though he was on the verge of firing. Even if they did spot him, could they stop him in time? Only with a perfect shot in far-from-perfect conditions.

The team regrouped, all four of them breathing hard.

"It's no good," Janson said. "We'll never find them in time."

"What do we do?" Kincaid said.

Janson thought about it with his hands on his hips. "We've got to warn the North. If we can't stop the incursion, the only way to prevent a full-scale war may be to keep it from escalating."

"How the hell do we do that?"

"Pyongyang. Look, the palace doesn't want a regime change. They may be prepared to invade on the slightest provocation, but if they knew about Diophantus being a product of a rogue US intelligence agency, they'd know it was a fight they ultimately couldn't win. Sure, they might burn Seoul and eventually Pyongyang to the ground, but they'd die in the fire. They don't want that; they want reunification with Kim Jong-un as the Supreme Leader of all Korea. The North's invasion plans are predicated on theirs being a surprise attack. If they know the South is ready for them, they'll hold back. At least I hope so. As I see it, it's the only chance we have."

"How are we going to warn the palace?"

"Jina," Janson said, "call Mi-sook back. Ask her what her father's full name is and where he might be located at sunrise."

"What are you thinking?" Kincaid said as Jina Jeon dialed Mi-sook.

"I crossed into the North before," Janson said. "I can cross into the North again."

Jina Jeon spoke a few words in Korean, then lowered the phone. "Her father's name is General Han Yong Chol. This morning he should be somewhere near the Joint Security Area."

Janson nodded as he contemplated what that meant. No tunnels; the tunnel would eat too much time off the clock. That was a relief. If Janson never set foot in another tunnel the rest of his life, he'd be content.

The Joint Security Area was convenient given their current position. But it was highly dangerous territory. He'd likely be shot at from both sides of the border. He'd need some sort of a diversion.

He looked from Jina Jeon to Sin Bae to Kincaid. He made a decision.

"Jina, you're with me."

Kincaid shot him a look.

"Sin Bae, I need you and Kincaid to provide cover."

"Why am I remaining behind?" Kincaid protested.

"Because, unless you speak fluent Korean, General Han is going to be carrying two dead Americans back to the palace instead of a warning."

* * *

THROUGH HIS FIELD GLASSES Janson watched the Joint Security Area with growing unease. Crossing the demarcation line there looked to be an impossibility. Even with Kincaid and Sin Bae providing suppressive fire, North Korean reinforcements would be on him and Jina in seconds.

He lowered the field glasses and sighed. "We can't fight our way through. And a simple diversion won't work."

"So what do we do?"

"That leaves us only one option, Jina."

"And that is?"

"Surrender."

* * *

Approaching the Joint Security Area, Janson looked to the east where a sliver of sun was now visible over the low mountain range. He couldn't help but think, This is where it all started. At the "Truce Village" where the four-party talks went the way of all others. Maybe critics were right, that diplomacy here was impossible. Sixty years ago two superpowers—the United States and the Soviet Union—had divided a nation along a line that held no significance to the people on either side of it. One side prospered, the other failed famously. To Janson, reunification *did* appear to be the only way to save the twenty-five million people who, through no fault of their own, were born and brainwashed on the wrong side of the line.

But, no. Even if reunification was the only solution, it shouldn't be the result of secret actions taken by rogue factions of US and ROK intelligence agencies. That was where Edward Clarke and Nam Sei-hoon were wrong. If the past decade and a half had taught Janson anything, it was that you can't trick a public into going to war and expect a positive result. Transparency was necessary. Truthful dialogue and civilized debate were key. Those were the principles critical to democracy. Those were the principles that Americans died for in every war they fought from the creation of the republic through Afghanistan.

Transparency was what Lynell Yi had died for.

What Gregory Wyckoff continued fighting for.

What Janson would give his life for, if need be.

He raised his hands high in the air and Jina Jeon did the same. Within seconds of doing so they were spotted by a soldier from the Republic of Korea. The soldier lowered his binoculars and turned to a superior officer, who immediately lifted a walkie-talkie to his mouth.

Three more soldiers materialized from around the corner of the blue building.

"Remember," Janson said quietly, "our objective is to get as close to the demarcation line as possible. Close enough so that we can run to the other side without getting tackled. Or shot."

"What if the South Koreans arrest us before we can get close enough?"

"We're not going to give them the opportunity. On my mark, we split. You go left, I go right. Just be sure to keep your hands visible and hopefully we won't get ourselves gunned down on this side of the line."

"And the other side?"

"You can communicate with the North Korean soldiers. Just tell them that you're a defector and you want to surrender yourself."

"And you?"

"A fair question," Janson said. "I'm just going to play it by ear."

Janson was pleased to see that the ROK soldiers were not approaching. As long as they remained in the Joint Security Area at their posts, getting to the demarcation line shouldn't present a problem for either of them.

Glancing over at Jina, Janson noticed that her raised hands were trembling. He felt a similar sensation in his stomach, but it hadn't yet manifested itself to watchful eyes.

The ROK soldiers remained frozen in place, though the two on the outer flanks had raised their weapons.

"Just a precautionary measure on their part," Janson tried to assure her.

But the truth was, he didn't know their orders.

A soldier stepped forward with his right hand held out in front of him and shouted in Korean.

"He's telling us to stop," Jina said.

"Yeah, I gathered that."

"We're too far away."

"Wait for my mark."

The soldier with the raised palm called out to them again. When they didn't respond he too raised his assault rifle. In the distance Janson could see the three North Korean soldiers standing at attention, watching their counterparts' interaction with the trespassers.

To Jina, he said, "Tell them that we—"

Janson never finished the sentence. Because the soldier who'd just raised his weapon fell down dead, a wide entry wound visible just below his left eye.

Janson looked around; he had no idea where the shot had come from.

He and Jina lowered their hands.

"Run," he told her.

They ran.

A few moments later all hell broke loose.

FIFTY-FIVE

This week most of Nam Sei-hoon's colleagues at NIS had become accustomed to seeing him arrive at the office before daybreak. So as not to arouse suspicion, he made this morning no different.

Once he walked into his office and closed the door behind him, he sat at his desk and logged on to his computer. As he did most days, he went directly to his email client and entered his seven-digit pass code. There were nine new messages, most of which were addressed to the agency at large as opposed to him personally. One, however, instantly caught his eye. This email, addressed directly to him, was from his deputy.

Since he'd become involved in Diophantus, Nam Sei-hoon had taken a decidedly less hands-on approach to his job. He'd delegated many of his duties to his deputy, Jae-suk. Prior to Diophantus, Nam had gotten great pleasure out of debriefing North Korean defectors. Many were diplomats or high-level officials who had received permission to exit the country temporarily—and therefore could be sent back. Under Nam Sei-hoon's control, of course. In the past decade, Nam Sei-hoon had recruited a number of members of the North Korean Guard's Command and even a few agents from the Ministry of State.

Because the palace in Pyongyang was so compartmentalized and secretive, these agents seldom provided much actionable intelligence. After a year, Nam Sei-hoon would typically let them off the hook and bring them back to Seoul, providing them with an additional $20,000 to start their new lives. Once in a long while, Nam Sei-hoon caught a very big fish, someone in Kim's inner circle. And when he did, he *never* let them go.

Now Jae-suk was alerting him to a new defector, whom Jae-suk referred to as "the wife of a deputy director." He nearly dismissed it. After today, he would have far greater things to concern himself with, not the least of which was the reunification of the country. But then he realized how foolish it was to think that way. Once Diophantus was in play and the conflict began, he would need intelligence from the North more than ever. Even once the conflict ended, intelligence would be crucial to easing the inevitable pains of reunification.

Nam Sei-hoon picked up the receiver and dialed the campus where the defectors were kept. After identifying the defector by name and number, he instructed the official to have her brought to the NIS.

"I would like to conduct the brief here in my office," he said.

"Very well, sir. Is this afternoon convenient?"

"No, no," Nam said, glancing out the window at the approaching dawn. "Bring her now."

* * *

AT HICKAM FIELD on the Hawaiian island of Oahu, Lawrence Hammond ended his call. He hesitated several seconds before rising off the couch in the otherwise empty office. He walked toward the refrigerator. Halfway across the room he stopped, his head rushing with thoughts that made him woozy.

It was one thing to provide information. It was quite another thing to kill.

Could he actually go through with this?

Hammond's eyes welled with tears as he considered his options.

There *were* no options, were there? Clarke had made it clear enough: it was either the kid or Hammond himself. What had started as a simple deal to make a few extra bucks providing ammunition to the senator's political adversaries had become Lawrence Hammond's worst nightmare.

It would seem to be a great leap from collecting opposition research against his boss to murdering that boss's only child. But it had all happened so fast that there had never been a moment to reflect on where all this was heading.

But now he knew.

Now he had no excuse.

This had been their plan all along, to use him for whatever their needs were, however diabolical they might be. Once Hammond accepted that first envelope, he'd surrendered the life of which he had dreamed.

He opened the refrigerator and collected the bottle of Snapple Green Iced Tea, Gregory's favorite drink. Then he moved to his briefcase and set it on the desk.

He unlocked the briefcase using his four-digit code and extracted the vial of arsenic.

As he stared at its contents, his cell phone buzzed on the desk.

Grudgingly, he answered.

The plane, he was informed, was beginning its descent. It would touch down at Hickam in roughly a half hour.

FIFTY-SIX

Janson and Jina Jeon darted, unarmed, across the Joint Security Area as the sound of automatic weapons fire cut through the bitterly cold air. In the mix of confusion and fog, they were mercifully ignored by the soldiers on both sides.

As the bullets flew, Janson felt as he'd felt during firefights in Afghanistan. Felt as though he was caught in the middle of a war no one would ever fully understand.

As they approached a large hill, Janson slowed down, taking Jina's arm as he did. Peering at its peak he saw a mass of North Korean soldiers charging forward, breaking through the thick predawn mist.

"*Hands up*," he shouted to Jina. "Start calling to them. Tell them we surrender."

Janson quickly withdrew a white hankie and swung it high above his head.

As soon as the soldiers spotted them, they raised their weapons.

For a moment Janson thought this was the end.

Then Jina Jeon shouted out in Korean. Though they shared a language, Janson knew that the North and South possessed two distinct dialects. He hoped like hell that these soldiers would understand her.

Several of the soldiers at the front of the line halted. They dropped to their knees and gazed into their sights.

Janson watched in horror. He and Jina Jeon were facing a firing squad.

Two troops emerged from the pack and moved forward, their weapons still raised.

As they neared, they spoke words Janson didn't understand. Without turning his head, he glanced in Jina's direction for the translation. But she was already engaged in a conversation with them. He listened carefully. Heard her utter the name Han Yong Chol.

The moment she did, one of the two soldiers looked back at his group. Then both shouted at Janson and Jina, Jina suddenly screaming in Janson's ear, "*Get down.*"

Janson dropped flat on his stomach. One of the soldiers helped him along, pressing him hard into the ground, stepping on the back of his neck. He heard Jina cry out in pain and he immediately burned with a desire to pick himself off the ground and kill the two soldiers with his bare hands.

Once they were thoroughly frisked and found to be clean, the soldiers shouted out new commands. Janson looked hopefully to Jina Jeon.

"Stay down," she said. "They're bringing General Han."

General Han Yong Chol was a large man by North Korean standards. He stood a full six feet tall. With broad shoulders, a wide chest, and a uniform every bit as crisp as the January air, he exuded authority. His booming voice did nothing to dispel the effect.

Although Janson was entirely comfortable with Jina Jeon doing the speaking, she immediately made clear that she intended to translate instead.

"The general wants to know why he shouldn't shoot us."

That wasn't the question Janson had been expecting.

Still lying flat on the ground, Janson said, "Tell him we're friends of his daughter, Mi-sook."

Jina translated Janson's words, then the general's response. "He says, 'Where is she? What have you done with her?'"

"Tell him she defected."

General Han didn't wait for Jina's translation. "You *lie*," he shouted in English. "She would *never* betray the Fatherland."

"She didn't do it for herself," Janson shouted back, "she did it for your granddaughter."

The general pulled a handgun from its holster, knelt, and held the gun to Janson's head.

"Jina," Janson shouted, "do you still have your phone?"

"Yes."

"General Han, you can speak directly to your daughter. We can call her right now."

Han kept his weapon trained on Janson but held his other hand out for the phone. Jina cautiously pulled it from her pocket and set it in his outstretched palm.

"We're here to *warn* you," Janson said. "The firefight in the Joint Security Area, it was planned. The first shots were fired by US intelligence officers acting on the authority of the director, without the White House's knowledge or consent. They're trying to draw you into a war that will ultimately collapse your regime."

Janson dared to look up. The gun was still leveled at his head. But the general had Jina Jeon's phone to his left ear.

"Mi-sook?" Han said.

As the general spoke to his daughter in Korean, Janson listened for familiar words. Hearing Yun Jin-ho's name, Janson felt as though his heart might break into two.

When General Han ended the call a few seconds later, Janson didn't know what to expect, a bullet or further dialogue. He tried to prepare himself for either event.

Han said, "According to Mi-sook, this war poses an existential danger to both Chosun *and* South Chosun."

"It's true," Janson said. "If Pyongyang retaliates for this morning's incursion, it will draw US forces into the conflict. In days North Korea will be leveled."

"*Up*," Han shouted.

Janson slowly rose to his knees, then to his feet.

"What do we do?" the general said.

"We need to get to Pyongyang before this gets too far out of hand. We need to get to the palace."

The general shook his head. Lowered his voice even though none of his soldiers was in earshot.

"Surely you know that the Supreme Leader is a madman," Han said. "He will never listen to us."

"Even madmen respond to psychology," Janson told him. "If Kim Jong-un knows he's being tricked into going to war, he'll respond to that. We can get him on the phone with the US president."

"You *know* the US president personally?"

"Let's just say, I have contacts." When Han didn't respond, Janson added, "It's our only chance, General. It's our only hope to avoid a second Korean War that will lead to the destruction of both Seoul *and* Pyongyang and the deaths of millions of Koreans on either side of the thirty-eighth parallel."

After a moment of silence, Han said, "You may have direct access to your White House, but I do not have access to the palace. The Guard's Command would never permit us to enter, especially after the incident that occurred at the Ryongsong residence earlier this week."

"Just get us to Pyongyang," Janson said. "*I'll* get us into the palace."

"*You?*"

"Yun Jin-ho showed me the way. You have to trust me, General. I know what we have to do."

FIFTY-SEVEN

Twenty minutes later Janson was back on the Reunification Highway on his way to Pyongyang. This time, however, he and Jina Jeon rode in the rear of a troop transport with two dozen North Korean soldiers under General Han's command. The troop transport breezed past the numerous KPA checkpoints without incident.

"We have reached the city," the general announced in English over a walkie-talkie Jina Jeon held in her hand.

She nodded to Janson, who pulled Han Yong Chol's smartphone from his pocket. As a general, Han was one of the privileged few in the Korean People's Army who could make calls outside North Korea with his cellular phone.

Janson dialed Park Kwan, who immediately turned the line over to Kang Jung.

"Eagle has landed," Janson said. Kang Jung had insisted on the use of the code.

"Acknowledged," she replied. "T-minus one eighty."

Janson glanced at his watch. To Jina he said, "In three minutes Kang Jung is going to shut down the grid."

Because rolling blackouts were a regular occurrence in North Korea, the palace and other elite areas operated on a separate electrical grid. To which, thanks to North Korea Uncovered, a Google Earth project made public by the US-Korea Institute at Johns Hopkins, Kang Jung knew the precise coordinates.

"Amazing kid," Jina said.

Janson slipped General Han's phone back into his pocket. "Yes, she is."

* * *

WITH THE ELECTRIFIED FENCE unelectrified, General Han's troop transport crashed through the gate, sending unsuspecting soldiers and guards fleeing for their lives.

A hundred yards inside the compound the vehicle screeched to a stop. The tailgate opened and out spilled the two dozen troops under Han's command.

Leading the way with smoke grenades, Han's soldiers moved briskly and brazenly toward the palace.

When they reached the palace doors, General Han demanded that the Guard's Command throw down their weapons and surrender—and they did. Janson had seen nothing like it since the First Gulf War, when the Iraqi army surrendered to American military forces immediately upon their arrival in the deserts of Kuwait during Operation Desert Storm.

Once the Guard's Command surrendered, Han summoned Janson and Jeon to the front. He ordered several of his soldiers to stand guard outside the palace doors, then commanded his remaining troops to drop their weapons.

"We're going inside the palace *unarmed*?" Jeon exclaimed.

"Repeated attempts on the lives of Kim Jong-il and Kim Jong-un by their own bodyguards have resulted in a new palace policy," Han explained. "No weapons allowed in the same building as the Supreme Leader. No exceptions." Marching forward, he continued speaking over his shoulder. "Rest assured, we will not meet with any armed resistance inside the palace walls. In fact, if our experience on the grounds *outside* the residence is any indication, we should not meet with any resistance at all."

* * *

KINCAID AND SIN BAE lowered their weapons and dropped back even farther once they received word from Park Kwan that Janson and Jina Jeon had made it to Pyongyang.

Kincaid couldn't help but look on Sin Bae with revulsion. His mere image stirred up the fear and anger she'd experienced sprinting through Dosan Park. The helplessness she felt diving into the rear of the taxi, ducking down into the subway station, disguising herself in the dressing room of that Seoul department store.

She glanced at him over her shoulder and saw him as he was when he entered the T-Lound nightclub. Though the sounds of automatic weapons fire replaced club beats, he appeared as he'd appeared on the upstairs dance floor—ruthless and relentless.

This is the same monster, she thought. The same monster who'd nearly sliced through her windpipe with the garrote he extracted from his cuff link. The same monster who would have ended her life without a scintilla of remorse had Park Kwan not stepped into the coatroom and spotted his gun at the exact moment that he did.

"He's a lot more like you and me than either of us could have imagined," Janson had said.

Speak for yourself, she thought. But then, that was exactly what Janson had been doing.

Janson saw *himself* as a monster, Kincaid realized. Still, after all this time severed from Consular Operations. He'd said as much in the car on the way to Chuncheon this morning.

She suddenly felt for Janson something she'd never dreamed she'd feel for him. Had never dreamed there would ever be a need. Never dreamed there would ever be so much as an excuse, even if she'd wanted to.

Pity.

For the first time in her life Kincaid pitied the man she loved.

The most beautiful, most intelligent, most caring man she'd ever met didn't believe he was a good man, didn't believe he was a man at all. He thought he was a monster. Like Sin Bae.

"He's a lot more like you and me than either of us could have imagined."

Janson still thought of himself as a Machine.

* * *

IN A MAGNIFICENT ROOM of vaulted ceilings and green marbled walls, Janson stood rigidly with General Han Yong Chol on his left and Jina Jeon on his right.

Following their forced entry into the compound the last thing Janson had thought would become a priority was proper decorum. But the enigmatic hermit kingdom continued to live up to its reputation.

A white-haired official stepped into the room, followed by two members of the Guard's Command. He issued orders to the three visitors, orders that Janson, of course, couldn't under-stand.

"You have to remove your watch," Jina Jeon whispered.

The official shouted at her. She responded in Korean, appar-ently informing the official that Janson spoke only English.

This is surreal, Janson thought. If someone told him last week that in a few days he'd be standing in Kim Jong-un's palace, he'd have tried to smack them out of their derangement.

Janson waited for one of the Guard's Command to pat them down, but no one else approached. He supposed visitors to the palace never made it this far without getting frisked, maybe not without enduring a full-body cavity search.

Bad security, he thought.

Janson regretted not snatching one of the handguns from the troop transport. He'd known that with the grid down, the entrance metal detectors wouldn't be functioning. But he presumed the Guard's Command would fall back on wands. And there was some-thing far more important Janson needed to get past security. Some-thing largely made of plastic that alone probably wouldn't have set off a metal-detecting wand. So he hadn't wanted to risk inviting ad-ditional scrutiny. After all, foiling Diophantus was far more press-ing than his own personal safety, or even Jina Jeon's.

Ten full minutes later—ten full minutes of standing, ten full minutes of silence—a second official entered the room, followed by six others. Janson couldn't help but notice that each official who entered was several inches shorter than the last.

Janson thought of Nam Sei-hoon; immediately he felt an over-whelming heat rise up his neck till it colored his cheeks and the tops of his ears.

He took several deep breaths and waited for his pulse to slow.

Once the seven dwarfs were lined up against the wall in size order, the original white-haired official walked to the middle of the grand room and spoke in a voice majestic enough for Yankee Stadium.

"The chairman of the Presidium of the Supreme People's Assembly of the Democratic People's Republic of Korea will now enter."

Janson glanced to his left at Han Yong Chol, who whispered, "Officially, he serves as head of state, the Supreme Leader's number two."

"And in reality?"

"In reality, he is Kim Jong-un's puppet, his mouthpiece. Nothing more than a stooge."

FIFTY-EIGHT

Lawrence Hammond gazed out the office window and watched the Embraer 650 touch down at Hickam Field. He'd convinced the senator and Mrs. Wyckoff to allow him to board the jet first. For their safety, of course. Hickam had lost communications with the Embraer long ago, and they didn't know quite what to expect. The senator suggested that a pair of soldiers greet his son on the plane, but Hammond argued that a military presence would only frighten Gregory after all he'd been through. The senator and Mrs. Wyckoff finally agreed—Hammond would take the lead.

Watching the jet taxi along the runway, Lawrence Hammond lightly shook the contents of the bottle of Snapple Green Iced Tea.

The knock at his door meant that it was time to step onto the tarmac.

* * *

THE KNOCK AT Nam Sei-hoon's door meant that his interviewee had arrived. He straightened his tie. Removed his glasses and cleaned the lenses. Checked his email for updates, but there were none.

Initial reports had come in. There had been an incident at the DMZ. But details were murky at best. Nam had ordered his deputy Jae-suk to keep him informed. If the situation worsened, Nam Sei-hoon would take a motorcade to the Blue House to consult with the president.

"Enter," Nam said in Korean.

The door opened. In its frame stood two guards, between them one of the most beautiful women Nam Sei-hoon had ever laid eyes on.

Nam remained seated. Not out of impoliteness but because he was ashamed of his height, especially around beautiful women.

He motioned to the leather chair opposite his desk and asked the woman to have a seat. Then he dismissed the guards. One began to protest, but Nam shot him a look that made it clear this was not an issue subject to debate.

When the door closed behind the guards, Nam said, "Let me be among the first to welcome you to the Republic of Korea." He bowed his head. "Please allow me to introduce myself. My name is Nam Sei-hoon. I am the director of North Korean Affairs here at the National Intelligence Service."

A lovely smile materialized on the young woman's face.

"I know who you are," she said.

* * *

NINE MEMBERS of the Guard's Command preceded three high-ranking military commanders whom Janson didn't recognize.

Only once everyone was standing at attention did an old man in a black suit appear in the frame of the double steel doors. He wore a steel-gray tie, small gold-rimmed glasses, and his hair (what little was left of it) was dyed jet-black.

As the chairman stepped forward the line of Guard's Command members parted to allow him through. He was followed by one of his military commanders, who Janson could now see held the rank of general.

As the pair moved forward the general touched a finger to his right ear.

The old man halted roughly ten feet from Janson, Jeon, and General Han. From this distance, Janson realized the chairman had to be approaching his nineties, if he wasn't there already.

"I am General Jang Yong-sun," the uniformed man said in English. "You are standing in the presence of the chairman of the Presidium of the Supreme People's Assembly, Comrade Tak Dong-gun."

On either side of him, Han and Jina bowed, so Janson did too.

"State your business," General Jang ordered.

Janson glanced at Han but immediately realized all eyes were on him.

"My name is Paul Janson," he said. "I am a former covert agent for the United States government. I presently work as a private security consultant. I was recently hired by United States senator James Wyckoff of North Carolina to locate his teenage son, Gregory Wyckoff, who has been falsely accused by the South Korean government of murdering his girlfriend, Lynell Yi.

"Ms. Yi had been working as an interpreter for the US envoy in connection with the four-party talks currently being held in the Joint Security Area of the Korean Demilitarized Zone. I'm here because my colleagues and I, in the course of our investigation, learned that Lynell Yi was murdered by an agent working on behalf of a rogue faction of a United States intelligence agency.

"Gregory Wyckoff was subsequently put in the frame in order to remove him from the equation. Ms. Yi was murdered because she overheard a conversation between the US and South Korean envoys. The conversation was about a clandestine operation called Diophantus. The objective of Diophantus, we have since learned, is to provoke the North into starting a second Korean War that would ultimately collapse the current regime here in Pyongyang.

"*That* is why shots were fired across the border in the demilitarized zone this morning. And that, General, is why you *must* refrain from escalating hostilities. Rogue US factions, in cooperation with rogue factions within South Korea's National Intelligence Service, *want* you to respond with an attack on the South, so that the United States military will be drawn into the conflict in accordance with US-ROK security agreements.

"Once the United States is involved, this war—as you know, General—will result in the slaughter of your military and, eventually, your civilian population."

General Jang remained expressionless as he placed a finger to his right ear. At his side the chairman appeared profoundly bored.

"Comrade Chairman?" Janson said to the old man.

It was General Jang who responded. "We find it difficult to believe that the United States government is unaware of this so-called plot, Mr. Janson. What you describe would cost massive sums of money, particularly if, as you suggest, the ultimate objective is to remove the regime here in the Democratic People's Republic and reunify Korea. All of us on the peninsula appreciate the fact that reunification, no matter how desperately we want it, will cost *billions* of your US dollars."

Janson narrowed his eyes. It was something he'd lost sight of in all this. The financial cost. He'd been so caught up in the human price that would have to be paid to reunify the peninsula that the monetary aspect had escaped him entirely. The United States' black budget had recently been exposed. And Congress was tracking every penny. How could he have missed this? Someone else—another nation?—had to be backing this operation. But who?

"*Cui bono?*" Janson said aloud to himself.

General Jang appeared nonplussed. "Excuse me?"

"*Cui bono?*" Janson repeated. "It's a Latin adage, General. It essentially means 'Who benefits?'"

There *had* to be a hidden motive beyond regime change. When Janson started his career with Consular Operations, an agent's worst enemy was often his own government—directors like Derek Collins who were so goddamn certain of their cause, they cared nothing of the cost of collateral damage. But these days, with slashed budgets that could be exposed by wayward NSA contractors, intelligence directors couldn't wield that kind of power. At least not without help.

But help from whom?

Today nothing made sense unless it made *financial* sense. Violations of human rights—even the worst atrocities—only spurred action when they affected someone's bottom line.

Shanghai.

In his mind he heard the shots ring out, felt the pounding of his heart in his chest as he tried to lose himself in the crowd. Picturing himself in the sights of a sniper's rifle as he pushed his way to the taxi stand, he thought of Silent Lynx, and of his own narrow escape from the People's Republic of China.

He flashed on his client, Jeremy Beck. Jeremy Beck, who'd spent millions just for *evidence* of the Chinese government's ongoing campaign of cyber-espionage and data theft.

"*Who else is going to do it?*" Beck had said when he first hired Janson. "*Certainly not the Justice Department. Certainly not the US Congress. Washington won't go to war with Beijing over this. At least not in the current geopolitical climate.*"

"So?" General Jang said. "Are you going to answer the question? Or are you posing it to us? *Who* benefits, Mr. Janson?"

"Governments no longer wield absolute power, General. Global corporations do. They've been running countries for decades. Now they're running superpowers."

The general held a finger to his ear.

Janson continued. "Once the North Korean regime is gone and Seoul has control over the entire peninsula, the United States will have an ally directly on China's border. Beijing's days of stealing billions of dollars' worth of trade secrets from US corporations, including the military industrial complex, will be over."

* * *

THE BABY-FACED private first class who had days ago driven Lawrence Hammond and his guest Paul Janson from the tarmac to the very administration building in which he was now standing knocked again at the door. There was still no response from the senator's chief aide, and Senator and Mrs. Wyckoff were getting antsy. Understandably so. Given what they'd been through over the past few days, the private's own parents would have been antsy too.

He glanced down the hall and knocked once more.

"Mr. Hammond?" he called out.

Finally he twisted the door handle to the office and poked his head inside.

"Mr. Hammond?" he called again.

The first thing the private noticed was the shattered bottle on the floor near the refrigerator. It appeared to have been a bottle of Snapple Green Iced Tea.

Then he saw Hammond's hand lying open on the floor. He followed it up Hammond's arm, past the shoulder, all the way to his face.

"Mr. Hammond?" he said quietly, though he knew it was unnecessary.

The private recognized a dead man when he saw one. He'd seen dead men before.

* * *

"You PRESENT AN interesting set of facts, Mr. Janson," General Jang said. The chairman had yet to utter a word. "But it is for the very reason you state that the Democratic People's Republic of Korea will never fall to the American bastards and their puppets to the south. Our neighbor China has far too much to lose to ever allow it."

Janson said nothing.

"You see, Mr. Janson, South Chosun is not the only nation on the peninsula with security agreements in place."

"China will never enter a war started by the North," Janson said.

"Indeed, you are right. And what transpired in the demilitarized zone this morning is insufficient cause to escalate the conflict. Which is why, within the next ten minutes, our covert agents in the South will launch a ballistic missile at Pyongyang."

Janson and Jina Jeon exchanged nervous looks.

"Of course, we have nothing to fear," Jang said with a tight grin. "The missile will land harmlessly in a field hundreds of kilometers from here. It will only *appear* as though it was fired at the palace."

"You son of a bitch," Janson said, looking the general directly in the eyes. "You've been waiting for this."

General Jang said, "We are well aware, Mr. Janson, that the world will not accept a unified Korea born of a successful invasion by the North. But the Democratic People's Republic has every right to defend itself against the imperialist aggressors and their puppets."

Janson said nothing.

"Unfortunately," Jang said, motioning to members of the Guard's Command, "the three of you will not be around to witness the triumph of a unified socialist Korea."

Several of the Guard's Command lined up directly behind Janson, Jeon, and General Han.

In a booming voice that echoed off the vaulted ceilings and green marble walls, Jang announced: "Having been found guilty of espionage against the Democratic People's Republic of Korea, the three of you are sentenced to be executed by firing squad immediately." He removed a small device from his ear and motioned to the men standing behind the convicted. "Guard's Command, take them away."

"You can't get away with this," Janson said calmly as one of the guards gripped him by the arms.

Jang smiled. "What a wonderful way to conclude this meeting, with one of your awful Hollywood clichés."

Little did Jang know that Janson had already initiated Plan B. In fact, he'd stolen a page from Gregory Wyckoff's playbook: *If North Korea won't heed your warning, warn China.*

The double doors behind the general suddenly swung open.

Janson watched as a member of the Guard's Command scurried forward, calling General Jang's name.

The general turned, and the guard spoke to him urgently in Korean.

Janson pulled away from the soldier who was holding him by the arms. The soldier, who was listening, did not attempt to regain control of his prisoner.

The double doors slowly began to close.

Jina started to say something, but Janson held up a hand. "No translation necessary."

With his other hand he reached into his waistband and raised Han Yong Chol's smartphone. He aimed the phone's video camera into the next room just in time to capture the image of a surprised young man standing awkwardly before a group of military commanders. Dressed in a black tunic, the young man was short and heavy, with a round face creased deeply with concern.

Janson muttered, "Say 'cheese.'"

Just before the heavy doors swung closed.

FIFTY-NINE

In his office in Washington, DC, Edward Clarke watched the live stream of CNN's coverage on his desktop in silent disbelief. For the past ten minutes Clarke had been focused on Wolf Blitzer's qualification: "We remind you that we at CNN have yet to verify the authenticity of this recording, which is apparently coming to us via a feed from the former Soviet republic of Estonia."

Thus far, there had only been audio.

But then all of a sudden an image appeared on the screen. The image was of an opulent room with vaulted ceilings and green marble walls. The camera then zoomed in on another luxurious room located behind two slowly closing steel doors. Standing in that room were a group of military commanders and a young man in a black tunic.

Christ, it can't be.

On-screen Janson muttered, *"Say 'cheese.'"*

And then the doors finally closed.

* * *

NAM SEI-HOON STARED UP at the beautiful young woman holding the gun. Sweat had started pouring down his face but he didn't dare reach for a hankie or attempt any other furtive movements.

"Please," he said in Korean, "I beg you to reconsider."

The woman, still smiling, shook her head.

"There are people out there," Nam said as he tried to catch his breath. He was beginning to feel faint. "You will be arrested before you leave this office. You will spend the rest of your own life in prison. Are you certain you want to live behind bars?" A white glaze suddenly framed his vision. "Are you sure you want to do this?"

The smile finally melted from the young woman's face.

Nam Sei-hoon thought he might have broken through.

But then in clear English the young woman said, "Sure. As. Shit."

And squeezed the trigger.

* * *

GENERAL JANG SNATCHED Han's phone from Janson's hand and squashed it underfoot.

"*Kill* them," he shouted.

One of the Guard's Command immediately grabbed Janson from behind and wrapped his arm around his throat. With his right hand Janson gripped the guard's fingers and bent them backward until they broke. With his left elbow Janson delivered a vicious blow to the guard's solar plexus.

Another guard approached. Janson slammed his forehead into the guard's chest, then whipped his head back up, cracking the guard's jaw.

With the heel of his palm, Janson drove another guard's nose upward, knocking him out cold. Then he threw an elbow into another guard's throat.

From behind, he snatched by the ears one of the two men grappling with Jina Jeon and hurled him across the green marble floor.

He then ran toward Han, delivering a sliding kick to the knee of the man who had the general in a headlock. Another guard turned toward him, and Janson thrust his boot up into his groin.

When he got to his feet, Janson found that most of the men left standing were running as quickly as they could toward the exit.

General Jang and the officials had fled into the next room behind the closed steel doors.

"Let's get the hell out of here," he shouted to Han and Jina Jeon.

They ran out the door they'd entered and retraced their steps toward the stairs.

At the bottom of the stairs they found Han's men holding their weapons on the runaway members of the Guard's Command.

Janson led the group out of the palace and jumped into the rear of the waiting troop transport. He turned and extended his arm to Jina Jeon, pulling her up onto the tailgate.

The other soldiers piled in after them.

General Han hurried toward the front passenger side, opened the door, and climbed in.

A moment later the troop transport was off, speeding down the empty streets of Pyongyang.

* * *

IN EDWARD CLARKE'S OFFICE, his private line began ringing. He sat motionless, in the dark, as a second line rang, then a third. His cell phone lit up and vibrated across the smooth surface of his desk, until finally falling over the edge and landing on the carpet. How did a man who already lived in the shadows disappear?

Paul Janson's true audience was Beijing, not Washington. Beijing, because China was essential to the North's strategy. Without China, Pyongyang would fall within weeks, if not days. But China could no more enter a war openly started by the North than the United States could enter a war openly started by the South.

Sure, Beijing was Janson's target audience. But Washington was where Janson's conversation with the leadership in Pyongyang would resonate loudest. Albright and Hildreth and Ella Quon would bitch and complain at their next conference at the Meridian, but in the end they'd have no choice but to cover their own asses.

The same was true of Nam Sei-hoon and Ambassador Young in Seoul. Everyone now needed to focus their efforts on damage control. Even Javers, Hastings, and Paltrow. They didn't have jobs to lose, but they had reputations. Even the filthy rich had asses that could be sent to federal prison, Wall Street bankers notwithstanding.

There would be inquiries, to be sure. The press would initially latch on like a dog to a bone, but only until a squirrel scampered into their peripheral vision and drew their attention away. This entire fuckup went down in Korea, not Kansas City. The American public would lose interest in no time. Hell, half the public couldn't find Korea on a map. There was a reason the first Korean conflict was known as the Forgotten War.

So a few soldiers died in the Korean Demilitarized Zone; so what? If no one paid attention to Iraq and Afghanistan, who the hell was going to give a damn about this? Not Congress. Not with elections around the corner. They'd fling some shit at each other across the aisle, and maybe five years from now some obscure

House committee looking to score political points would hold a hearing that no one would attend.

Clarke's phones continued ringing but he hardly heard them anymore.

Paul Janson. He was the son of a bitch Clarke would have to worry about going forward. But then, Janson didn't believe in revenge. It wasn't in his blood. By live-streaming his conversation at the palace in the North Korean capital, he'd effectively defused Diophantus. Shut it down for good. Made it so that Pyongyang couldn't retaliate, couldn't escalate. Not after Beijing had heard their plans. Now Seoul and Washington would simply deny everything, and some poor schmuck who got killed in the shoot-out in the DMZ would be blamed for discharging his weapon into North Korea.

Janson got what he wanted. No one he cared about died. And he'd completed his mission the moment that chickenshit Hammond drank the poison meant for the Wyckoff kid.

The phones continued ringing.

Clarke finally pulled the jack out of the wall and reveled in the resulting silence. Leaning back in his chair, his thoughts slowly drifted from Korea to the Russian Federation. Vladimir Putin was hell-bent on rebuilding the Soviet Union. Pyongyang didn't pose half the threat Moscow did. Clarke rose and stepped out from behind his desk. It was time to move on. The hell with a second Korean War. There was a second *Cold War* coming. And US intelligence needed to prepare.

* * *

KINCAID FIRST SPOTTED them through her field glasses. They were now on foot, scrambling toward her through the Joint Security

Area. She lowered the glasses, lifted her weapon, and charged forward, providing suppressive fire against North Korean soldiers as Janson and Jina Jeon pushed south.

Kincaid ran along the tree line, motioning Janson and Jeon into the forest.

Once they were clear of gunfire, she dropped her weapon and wrapped her arms around Janson and held him close. There were so many times over the past few days when she thought she'd never be held by him again.

Gripping her just as tightly, Janson glanced around. He first nodded to Jina, then looked Kincaid in the eyes with an exhausted expression.

"Sin Bae?" he said.

Kincaid frowned. "Last I saw him, he was walking up the dirt path, heading north, mumbling something about a girl named Su-ra."

EPILOGUE

Wailea Beach
Hawaiian Island of Maui

Janson set the paperback down on his lap and gazed at the horizon through his Wayfarer sunglasses. Jessie stood in the shallows with one hand held over her brow to soften the glare of the sun off the water. She'd spotted a pair of humpback whales the day they'd touched down on Maui; she'd been searching the azure Pacific for more ever since.

Leaning over the side of his lounge chair, Janson dug into his duffel and fished out his phone. He'd been meaning to make this call since arriving in Hawaii, but it kept slipping his mind. He scrolled through his list of contacts and hit "Send."

"Tell me why I shouldn't hang up."

"No reason that I can think of anymore," Janson said. "I'm just calling to tell you that your services are no longer needed. I have someone else."

Janson hung up before Morton could reply.

"You didn't need to do that, you know," Jessie said as she dropped into the lounge chair next to him. "You could have just stopped calling him."

Janson laid a hand on her tanned wrist and dragged his fingers lightly up her forearm to the crook of her elbow. "Sometimes it's OK to do things just because they feel good."

"You'll get no argument from me," she said.

"Besides, after what Kang Jung—excuse me, *Lord Wicked*—pulled off with a borrowed laptop and General Han's cell phone, I don't think we'll need anyone else with her particular set of skills, ever."

He smiled at the thought of the girl going straight at thirteen, with a legitimate role in CatsPaw. Now there *was* something out there for her. Not just a job but friends she could always count on. Friends who loved her. Friends who would give their lives for her.

A few minutes later Jessie picked up her new cell phone and dialed for her messages. When she hung up, she said, "Park Kwan called. He's getting major props from the department for his role in solving Lynell Yi's murder."

"Good for him. Any further word about Mi-sook?"

"She's still in jail; the judge didn't grant bail. But Park Kwan said the lawyer you hired for her is the best in South Korea. Kwan thinks that given Nam Sei-hoon's involvement, the prosecutor will want to deal."

"If she goes to trial," Janson said, "I'll be first in line to testify."

"How's Mi-sook's infant daughter?"

"Jina says she's doing great. Her mother's helping to take care of the baby and Jina's going through the necessary channels to facilitate an adoption. It should be no problem. Mi-sook consents and Jina and her mom have a luxurious brand-new home in one of the most prestigious areas of Seoul."

Jessie smiled. "How much did that run you?"

Janson smiled back. "Don't ask. Next house I blow to pieces, I'm going to make sure the owner has adequate insurance first."

"Who knows, maybe you won't have to blow up any more houses in the future."

"Let's be realistic, Jessie, shall we?"

Jessie lifted a bottle of FIJI to her lips. "We know the usual suspects in government were behind this. But who do you think was financing Diophantus?"

Janson shook his head. "I don't know, and I'm not going to dig. If our client Jeremy Beck was involved, I don't want to know about it."

"Shall I grab a shovel so you can bury your head in the sand?"

Janson sighed. "I know. I'm a bad man, Jessie."

"The hell you are, Paul Janson. You are the kindest, most loving, most generous man I've ever met. You need to realize that sooner or later."

Janson heard Heath Manningham's words in his head.

"Walked away, did you? Tell me. How many have you done since you 'walked away'?"

Janson would always regret what happened in Daeseong-dong. Although Phoenix had no set place, the foundation was Janson's home; its graduates were his family. Yet he was ultimately responsible for Heath Manningham's death. Even though he'd intended for Manningham to survive the fall, he felt as though he'd killed one of his own.

But Janson knew damn well that the things he'd done couldn't be undone.

He closed his eyes, thinking how much he would have liked for

Phoenix to help Sin Bae. But the assassin had vanished into the mist in the DMZ. Had he really, after all this time, gone back to Yodok to find his sister?

Su-ra.

Sadly, Janson was sure that as long as Kim Jong-un was in power, all Sin Bae was likely to find in North Korea was suffering and death.

Janson opened his eyes and glanced at his watch. "It's almost happy hour, Jessie. You still want to go dancing tonight?"

She bit down on her lower lip. "If only my dance partner hadn't stayed behind in Seoul."

"I'd be happy to send the Embraer to pick him up if you'd like."

She turned to him. "What about you, then? Who are you going to dance with, Paul?"

He shrugged. "I don't know. Maybe I'll have to give Kayla a whirl."

Jessie smiled. "You *can* be a monster at times, Paul Janson."

He smiled back at her. "So I've been told."

Acknowledgments

To Henry Morrison and the estate of Robert Ludlum;

To Mitch Hoffman, Lindsey Rose, and everyone at Grand Central Publishing;

To Robin Rue, Beth Miller, and the entire team at Writers House;

To my readers, my wife and children, and my friends;

Thank you.

About the Authors

ROBERT LUDLUM was the author of twenty-seven novels, each one a *New York Times* bestseller. There are more than 210 million of his books in print, and they have been translated into thirty-two languages. He is the author of *The Scarlatti Inheritance*, *The Chancellor Manuscript*, and the Jason Bourne series—*The Bourne Identity*, *The Bourne Supremacy*, and *The Bourne Ultimatum*—among others. Mr. Ludlum passed away in March 2001. To learn more, you can visit Robert-Ludlum.com.

DOUGLAS CORLEONE is the author of the acclaimed Simon Fisk series of international thrillers, including *Good as Gone* and *Payoff*. His debut novel, *One Man's Paradise*, was a finalist for the Shamus Award for Best First Novel and won the 2009 Minotaur Books/Mystery Writers of America First Crime Novel Award. A former New York City criminal defense attorney, Douglas Corleone now lives in Hawaii with his wife and three children. You can visit him online at DouglasCorleone.com.